ANNALEE

Victoria Collingwood

Thank you to my proof readers; Courtney Knowles and Philip Prouse.

To Barnabas Rigden Green and Susan Twigg, for sharing your medical knowledge, enabling my work to remain factual.

To finish, no amount of words could accurately portray my gratitude to David Collingwood and Lydia Watson. In essence, during the past two years, 'Annalee' has been a huge part of your lives too. I could not have done this without you.

Prologue

From: r.arnold@cet.familylaw.net

To: h.pallister@legaltees.net

Harry,

Further to our telephone conversation yesterday, I'd like to thank you again for agreeing to defend my client, and to give you some new details regarding the case.

I met with him again this morning, and I have to say that you have a difficult task ahead of you. I appreciate that you're aware of the charges against him, but now an eye-witness has come forward. The witness, who was out walking his dog, states to have seen him crouching over the victim, then running to his car, with his hands 'dripping' with blood.

Harry, you and I have known each other since university, and there is something about this which just doesn't feel right. I've had dealings with the client and his family for many years. When I spoke to him, he was no longer the confident, mild mannered intellectual with a promising future, but a broken man. Given all that he has been through, it appears he has given up. He's resigned himself to his fate, despite the assumed rationale behind his actions.

I do believe you can help him, and should you need more information on his, or his family's history, don't hesitate to contact me.

Regards, Reginald.

Chapter 1

Twenty Months Earlier.
March 26, 2016 Saturday Morning.
Anna:

For my first house party, last night's wasn't exactly a disaster, but it's the morning after now and I'm beginning to regret not taking Tommy's advice. He's my older brother, and he was so sure that I'd hate it, that he said I should tell Becca that I wasn't going and stay at his instead. I didn't, now my head feels like it's been crushed and I daren't move in case I'm sick. To make matters worse, Becca keeps digging her elbows in my back. I can't recall when, but at some point through the night, we must have crashed on the smallest sofa, the spare one in her dining room.

I blink a few times as I try to see through the doorway, into the lounge. I can't see anyone, I don't even know what time it is, and Becca's pushing me closer and closer to the edge. This is ridiculous, so I move my foot back and give her a nudge. Weirdly, she doesn't say anything. Instead she slides her hand over my hips, and into my knickers.

"Becca! What are you doing?!"

I jolt my head back, and my heart leaps into my throat. It's not Becca.

"Alex! What the hell!" Frantic, I slap his hand away and throw myself to the floor. "Where's Becca?"
He doesn't answer, just shoots me a sly grin.

I'm confused, but it doesn't take me long to figure it out. I'm sore down there and I'm sat here in only my T-shirt and damp knickers. I can't believe this is happening. Oh no, I've lost it to Alex Murray, the most immature boy in our school. Catching my breath I scramble over the carpet looking for my things. Alex won't stop staring, his eyes are piercing, and I hate the fact that he won't even speak. As I slide my jeans on he continually shifts between looking at me and looking at his groin. He's so smug, with his sickly, awful grin, and he keeps running his hands through his ratty hair. I think I'm going to throw up, but I manage to hold it down as I scurry away into the lounge for my bag.

Becca's mum will be furious when she sees this. Amongst the mess and empty glasses, pools of vomit seep into the carpet. I need to get out of here, so I grab my bag and head back through the dining room, to the kitchen.

To my relief Alex has gone, but as I turn the handle on the back door, Becca creeps up behind me.

"Where're you going?" She asks.

"Home, Bec. I'm sorry, but something's happened. I need…I." What am I doing? I can't even look at her. She's so perfect, Becca and her matt chocolate skin, against me, a sweaty hungover mess. I rattle the handle, but she grabs my arm.

"Whoa, calm down, what's wrong?"

"I have to go home! I said I'd go straight to Tommy's, but I can't let him see me like this, I'm a mess."

"But what's wrong?" She asks again.

"I had sex ok!"

"Shut up, Anna! You had sex?" She stares at me in disbelief, flicking her long, glossy hair over her shoulder. "And with who?"

"Alex."

"But you hate him!"

"I know but it's true, my knickers were damp, I'm sore and…I just know, ok?"

"Well you can't just go," she says, "besides, you have to tell me everything, and you promised to help me clean."

"Alright." I can't leave her to do all this by herself, even if I do smell funky and feel like I'm dying.

Many bin bags and cans of air freshener later, I stress that I really have to leave.

8

"Go." She says. "Mam will be home in a minute anyway, then that's me bollocked. I'll text ya tomorrow if I'm still alive."

We both half laugh, and I give her one last hug before I leave.

Outside the blinding sun makes me dizzy, so a few metres along I stop and lean against a garden hedge. From the house a shadow of a man hovers in an upstairs window, ushering me along. I move, but due to the motion and the swimming in my head, I vomit over the pavement. I'm mortified. He's scowling and shaking his head, I can't believe I did that, this isn't me. So, I mouth a sorry to him before moving along as fast as I can, without looking back.

After drudging a few hundred metres I reach my stop, but the bus isn't due for another ten minutes, so I sit on the floor and wait.

When my bus eventually arrives, I pay my fare and keep my head down. I cannot be sick again, not here. There're a few close calls as the driver flings the bus around corners, but luckily I manage to hold it in.

It's only a short walk from my stop, and the sooner I can get home the better. I press on. Third from the end, our house is a large detached with gardens front and rear, and a long double driveway to its left. I didn't want Tommy to see me like this, but I am relieved to see his rusty blue Corsa on the drive.

I hurry past it and stumble through the back door, into the kitchen.

"Tommy?" I call, but he doesn't answer, so I look in the dining room, pass Dad's study and through into the lounge on the right.

I find him perched on the edge of the sofa, hanging his head.

"Tom? You alright?" I can't see his face for his curly, black hair. "I would've gone straight to yours, but I had to help Becca clean up…"

He lifts his head and I freeze. He's been crying, and I mean messy crying. His whole face, all the way down to his stubbly beard is soaked with tears. I don't have a clue what to say now. I haven't seen him cry since we were kids.

"Annie," he says, clearing his throat, "it's Mum and Dad, you best sit down."

Mum and Dad are on holiday in France, right now. They go somewhere near Monaco every year. I lower myself to the floor, between his feet.

"I've…had a phone call," he says, pressing his fingers over his eyes, "from the French police…"

"Are they in trouble?" I ask.

He shakes his head.

"What then?"

"They hired a boat last week…there was an accident. They found the wreckage but Mum and Dad weren't there."

"Where are they?"

"Don't know…gone."

Everything falls silent, I'm numb. My brother's lips move but I can't hear him. All I can feel is the burn of tears rolling down my cheeks.

"This isn't happening." I say, struggling to catch my breath, "someone needs to find them, they need to look!"

"They are, but they didn't sound hopeful."

"What do you mean, 'they didn't sound hopeful?' They found the wreckage, so they can't be far. Did the police say anything else?"

"Just that we have to wait," he sighs, staring at the floor, "that's all we can do. And I have tell Sarah, she needs to know that her sister might be…"

"Tommy, stop!" He can't think like that, he just can't. "It doesn't make sense, I mean did they go on their own?"

"I think so."

"But why? Dad's a surgeon, not a sailor!"

"I don't know, Annie. I just don't know, but you can't stay here. I'm gonna take you home with me." He takes my hands and guiding me onto the sofa, he pulls me in for a

10

hug. I don't know exactly how long we lie there but, as we do, I flit between quiet tears and uncontrollable sobbing.

This is probably the worst time, but I have to tell him. I can't look at him, but I have to.

"Tom, I've done something."

"Right?"

Burying my face in my hands I mumble that I had sex, but he doesn't say anything. So, I open my fingers and peer through, he's just raising his eyebrows.

"First time?"

"Yes! You know that!"

"I had to ask, little Annie." He says tenderly. "I take it you weren't ready?"

"No, I was drunk."

"Hey," he sighs, "these things happen, it's ok. Listen, you go for a shower, it'll make you feel better. Then we'll grab some food on the way back to mine."

"Ok."

4.15pm. Tommy:

Once I've got the food at the drive-thru, I park at the far end of the car park and try to get my head around it all. Why would Dad take Mum sailing on his own? He never takes chances, he always says risks are for fools. Annie's right, it doesn't make sense.

She's hardly spoke since we left the house. She briefly flicked through her phone a minute ago, then laid it on the dash. Now she's just sat, holding a hot chocolate. I can't eat either, it's as though I'm in a trance. I try the coffee, but even that's tasteless. So now we're both just nursing our cups, Annie's looking out of the window while I'm just sat looking at her. She's the smallest sixteen-year-old I know, like a fair elfin tomboy that I could fit in my pocket. A few minutes pass and she nibbles on a fry, but then she starts to sob again.

"I'm scared." She says. "If they have died, what do we do then? What if I'm put into care?"

"Look at me." I say firmly. "There's no way I'd let anyone take you away. Do you understand?"

She nods.

"I'm your brother, Annie. Look, I'm twenty-one, I work, I've got my own house. Please don't worry about that. Listen, I can't eat…"

"Neither can I." She interrupts.

"Should we just get back to mine?"

She nods again, so I bag up the rubbish and take it to the bin. When I return, I find her staring in horror at her phone.

"Why send me that?!" She exclaims.

"Send what?"

"He's sent me his thing!"

"Delete it." I tell her as I set off for home. "Just delete it."

Anna:

I wish we knew where Mum and Dad are, and I wish last night had never happened. My first time should've been with a boyfriend, someone who cares about me, but no, I got drunk and did it with the class idiot. This is all a mess.

I can talk to Tommy about anything apart from sex. It's the only subject that makes him uncomfortable. It's time to be brave though, there're things I need to know.

"Tom? Is it normal to be sore?"

"What?"

"After…you know."

He nods briefly, and I try not to cry but I can't help it.

"Hey," he says, "don't cry."

I can't believe I'm saying this, but I find myself asking about his first time, and cringe as the words fall from my mouth. Then nothing, nothing but awkward silence for probably only a few seconds, but it feels like forever. I think I'll just pretend I never asked.

"It was with Leanne." He says as he turns onto the main road.

I'm not surprised since he was only fifteen when they got together.

"But do you remember it?" I persist.

"Annie, please don't ask me this."

"Sorry." I should drop the subject, but I can't stand silence right now and I can't think about Mum and Dad. I just need him to talk to me. "Tom, if you can't talk about that, tell me why you split up. You were together for ages and weren't you going to marry her?"

"Marry her?!" He laughs, as he stops for a red light. "No, we were barely together two years. We split on Valentines, twenty twelve…"

"She left you on Valentines?"

"No, I left her."

"But why?"

"I'm getting to that, if you'll let me finish."

"Sorry, go on."

"She'd been cheating, An. I found the messages on her phone. When I quizzed her on it she admitted sleeping with him. She said some crap about me not committing, even brought you into the argument. That was when I told her to leave. I couldn't believe it, Annie, she was trying to make out that it was my fault."

The light turns green and he drives on. This is terrible. He loved her and she broke his heart.

"That bitch! Is she the reason you haven't had anyone serious since?"

"Yeah, I've no time for that shit any more."

"Do you still talk to her?"

"No. She tried for a while, so I changed my number."

We turn onto Tommy's street, we pass his house and follow the road around to the back, onto the drive. My brother lives in an ex-council, mid-terraced house on the edge of the estate.

I follow him through the garden gate, where he ducks under the low hanging branches of a birch tree. We cross his small garden to a set of patio doors that lead into a modern, open-plan dining kitchen. His house is so cosy, the only interior door downstairs is to the lounge, at the other end of the hallway. Between that and the kitchen are the stairs. I kick my Converse onto the shoe pile between the patio door and his dining table, then head up to my room.

The stairs lead up into the centre of a U-shaped landing. To my left, at the front of the house, are Tommy's room and a tiny box room that he uses for storage. To my right is the bathroom, then a little further towards the back is my room. Tommy decorated this for me when he moved in. It's simple and clean, just like the rest of the house it's shades of black, white and grey. Tommy doesn't do colours. The bed's just a single, but I don't care. I've always loved staying here, it's like the one place I can go and just be me. And like the flick of a switch, as soon as I lie on the bed my tears erupt. I'm powerless to stop them. Tommy brings me a drink, but I don't want it. All I can think about was the last thing I said to Mum. How I drove her away, I hate myself for it. I try to come clean to Tommy, but he just lays down next to me, strokes my head and tells me that it's going to be ok. It's not going to be ok, how can it be?

Chapter 2

Everyone's given up; the search for Mum and Dad has been called off. So, in a month our parents have gone from being on holiday, to missing and now presumed dead. Well I say presumed, everyone's acting like they're officially dead. Tommy's been going through everything with the French officials and Dad's solicitor. He's organised a memorial service, and we're at their house now, clearing it all out so we can put it up for rent.

I don't want to accept it. My head's full of fog, and navigating my way through my churned up feelings is impossible. It's in doing things like this, sifting through their belongings that make it real. We've been back and forth a few times in the past couple of days, sorting things out, but Tommy wants to finish it today. Neither of us want to be here, so I can see why he wants to get it done, but it's not easy. Even as we pulled up outside, I imagined Mum boiling the kettle, filling the house with the smell of her green tea. I imagined Dad sat in his study, only coming out to either tell me off for something, or to whinge at Tommy for not getting a haircut. Personally, I love Tommy's hair. I mean it's not that long, if it's down it sits nicely on his shoulders or if he wants to look tidy, then he ties it back. And he lets me play with it, so I'd cry if he ever cut it short.

Tommy's friend Rich is helping us, I say friend but he's actually more like family. He's downstairs right now, clearing all the crockery and things out of the kitchen. It's funny, when Becca first met him she was so nervous. I guess he can look scary if you don't know him, to me he's just a big power-lifting teddy bear, with a bald head and piercings.

Becca's on her way over too, or at least she said she was, but that was two hours ago, so whether or not she turns up is anyone's guess. For now, I'm just going to continue working through Mum and Dad's room. I've been in here all morning, and if I'm honest it's the last room I wanted to do, but Tommy needs my help and I'm not about to let him down. Opening the door was the hardest part, I actually stood for a good five minutes contemplating whether or not I should knock. We always had to knock, Mum was private and that's how she kept her room. I did pluck up the courage, and it was the smell that struck me first, as soon as I stepped in I was pelted by her perfume and stale air.

I still haven't got very far. I've sorted some rubbish, bagged up spare curtains and bed-linen for charity, then spent at least ten minutes getting side-tracked by some old pictures that me and Tommy had drawn for her. Mine was a scruffy picture of her holding my hand, not that that ever happened. I don't even know why she kept it, so I threw that straight in the rubbish bag. I've kept the rest.

Now I'm sorting out Dad's shoes. They're really expensive so it feels like a waste to just send them to charity, but keeping them would be a waste too. They're all size ten's whereas Tommy's an eight, not that they're his style anyway. I still set some aside. That's when I accidentally knock the lid from another box. Only it's not shoes inside, but an abundance of handwritten letters. This is so old fashioned, even for Mum and Dad. I know it's wrong because they're private, but it's too tempting not to have a little look.

Amongst many 'I miss you' letters, I find a disturbingly detailed account from one of their weekends away. I can't bring myself to read it all, the first two lines are illustrative enough. Now, I really must get on but, before I do I open just one more. A short one.

"Austin,

Having this baby was a mistake. You were right, and now every time I look at her I see that. This isn't what I wanted. I want my life back, our life when it was just you, me and Thomas, I doubt I've felt true happiness since then. Plus, all this baby does is cry, I'm sure she hates me.

Earlier today I needed a break so, while Thomas was watching cartoons, I laid her next to him, all he did was stroke her face and the little cow fell asleep! I'm sorry to say this in a letter. Darling, please come home.

Ellen."

A mistake? They thought I was a mistake? As I read it and re-read it, I sink lower into the floor and all their belongings seem to rise around me. All I want to do is run home, but I can't. I have to stay here, where I can touch their things and feel them, breathe in and smell them. I have to pack away every trace of them.

As I dry my eyes, the stairs creak with the sound of footsteps. I slide the letter into my pocket, just as Becca pops her head around the door.

"Hey," she chirps, "I brought doughnuts, they're in the kitchen. You'd better get one quick, Rich's had two already."

"Thanks."

"So," she says, looking around at the mountain of everything, "what d'ya want me to do?"

"Um, could you lay their clothes on the bed? I'll sort them out in a minute."

"Move then," she says, "you look a mess, and I need a coffee."

"What?"

"I'll do this while you make a cuppa."

"Oh…thanks, Bec."

"Don't mention it."

In the kitchen Rich is already boiling the kettle, so I ask if he'll make us a drink too.

"Yeah," he shrugs, "what's your friend want?"

"Coffee, two sugars like Tommy, but not as strong."

He takes a couple of mugs from one of the boxes.

"Rinse them will ya." He says. I nod and give them a quick wash. "Listen," he adds as I hand them back, "I'm here for you too, not just for Tommy, you know that right?"

"I do, thank you." I force a smile then turn back around to switch the tap off, and glance out of the window, which overlooks the driveway. My brother's car's gone.

"Where's Tommy?" I ask, leaning over the sink.

"Relax," he says, pressing his hand on my shoulder, "he's just popped home, he won't be long."

It was stupid of me to think he wouldn't have to leave. How else would he clear everything? Releasing a sigh, I knock my head against Rich's arm then take our drinks upstairs.

When I step back in their room, I hear Mum's voice as if she's reading that letter aloud. I can't stand it. I set the drinks down on the bedside table, then tear off another bin bag from the roll and frantically throw all of her things inside. All her jeans, shoes, tops, everything. I don't want to look at them ever again. After a few minutes, Becca grabs my arm, I try not to look at her, but she gives me no choice.

"Anna! Calm the fuck down. These are like ridiculously expensive. You need to keep some of them, they're gorgeous and…and she's your Mam!"

She doesn't understand, I knew she wouldn't. I'm rattled and I hate being here.

"I want to go home!" I shout and slump on the bed, "I… I've kept some things."

"Doesn't Tommy want some of your dad's stuff?"

"I guess so," I shrug, "but him and Dad are so different that I wouldn't have a clue what."

"Well aren't you gonna ask him?"

I nod and check the time. Rich did say that Tommy wouldn't be long, so I tell Becca to wait here while I hurry back down to check.

Becca:

Anna's been gone ages, and I don't know what she expects me to do. It doesn't feel right throwing everything in a charity bag. I get that she's sad and all, but she can't just throw her mam away. If it was my mam I'd keep every last thing, even her hairbrush. Well I have to do something, so I put Ellen's jewellery box and accessories to the 'keep' pile and move the rubbish bags out of the way.

When Anna comes back with Tommy, I try to look busy. He just kills me. It's unreal how sexy he is. She can't ever know that I'm in love with him. I mean those deep dark 'take me to bed' eyes, sexy firm body and that arse. I need to cool it, this isn't the time to fantasise about your best friend's brother. He is lovely though, not like my brother the bossy prick. It's funny, when I first met Tommy, I thought he was the same age as my brother. He looks a lot older than he is, and he's super protective of Anna. Anyway, I fold up some of Ellen's scarves and pretend I'm not watching as they move closer. Tommy's rubbing her shoulders and they're whispering. I wish I knew what they're saying. Aww, she's crying again. This is awful, I never knew my dad, all I know is he's the reason why I'm literally the black sheep of the family. He was Jamaican and that's all Mam's ever said about him, but I love my mam to bits, and I'd die if I ever lost her.

Anna gives Tommy a note and scratches her wrists. I know I'm a nosy cow, but I have to know what's on it, because he just shoves it in his pocket and pulls her in for a cuddle. I can't see much now because her little blonde head is lost behind those biceps.

They're always cuddling, it's weird. My brother doesn't cuddle me, not that I'd want him to. I hate our James, the lecture he gave me after my party was worse than Mam's. He went on and on, he thinks he's so high and mighty because he's nine years older than me. Dick.

They let go of each other and start carrying some bags downstairs. Do I help? I don't know, so I check my phone before grabbing a bag. When I step onto the landing, I hear them talking from the bottom of the stairs.

"Sorry, Annie," Tommy says, "I shouldn't have asked you to do their room."

"It's ok," she says quietly, "you can't do everything, and I was ok until I read that."

Now I really want to know what was in that note. They've gone quiet, so I creep a little closer. She's crying.

"Shh, come here it's ok," he says, "listen I'm almost finished in the study, you two bag up the stuff to keep. Me and Rich'll take some now, then when I get back, we'll go home."

"But there's still loads to do." She says, hardly catching her breath.

"I'll do it tomorrow. You don't have to come back here again."

There's no way I can go down there now, so I drag the bag into her mam's room and wait. When Anna comes back, we spend the next hour or two filling as many bags as we can, before Tommy calls us down.

3.30pm. Anna:

Before Tommy and Rich left with the last car loads, Tommy popped next door to ask Elaine if Becca and I could wait there until he gets back. Elaine's been Mum's friend forever so, there was no way that she'd say no. She practically ordered us into the kitchen, where every work surface is filled with trays of lemon cakes, cooling on wire racks.

This dear old lady can't even look at me. She fumbles through her pockets for a handkerchief, dabs her eyes and offers us a drink.

"I'll make it if you like?" I say as she takes two tea plates from the cupboard and cuts into one of the cakes.

"Yes." She nods. "Here, girls. A warm drink's too wet without some cake." She ushers us to the dining table. There's not much room because it's cluttered with baking tins and clean dishes waiting to be put away. We sit close together.

"You know, love," Elaine says as she sips her tea, "if you or Thomas need anything…I mean it, don't hesitate." Her wrinkly jaw quivers and she excuses herself, before hurrying upstairs.

"Is she ok?" Becca whispers.

"I don't know." Leaving my tea on the table, I go to the hallway and call, "are you ok, Elaine?" she doesn't answer so I call again.

"Yes, pet, I'm ok…I won't be long."

In the kitchen Becca's scrolling through her phone, "Have you seen your Facebook lately?" She asks.

"I haven't been on...not since it happened."

"You need to have a look, An. It's gone crazy since Mr. Rodney told everyone what happened."

I take a look. It's true, my news feed is crammed with messages from people at school. I'm shocked, most of these never even speak to me. I've got a text too, from an unsaved number.

"An, I am so sorry. I'm the worst friend,
Mr. Rodney's just told us all what happened.
I should've called but,
I didn't know what to say.
I still don't, but if
you want to talk, then I'm here.
I mean it x."

"Who is this?"

"It's me,
Dan x."

21

Dan Armstrong. He's been one of my best friends since we were in primary school. To be honest, it kills me that it's been a month and he's only just contacting me now.

"I didn't think you were talking to me, I've called and called and sent so many texts. Where've you been? Honestly, Dan, these past few weeks have been awful."

"I only got back from Spain on Wednesday. On the first day there, the sister dropped my phone off the balcony. I had to wait till we got home to get a new one. I'd lost all my numbers, so I had to get yours from Becca. Please, An. I'm so sorry x."

"It's ok, I guess. I so need to talk, I've missed you. Can I call tonight? X."

"Sure. You can call me anytime, day or night xx."

"Thank you x."

Elaine scurries back in, so I slide my phone into my pocket.

"It's probably a bit early," she says, lighting a cigarette and standing on the doorstep, "but can you ask Thomas to let me know when he's organised a funeral?"

"He's already arranged a memorial service, and we're having a buffet afterwards, at the Tigerlily."

That's where Tommy works, it's a pub in Normanby, the village near his house.

Elaine flicks her cigarette onto the garden path, "I'll just find a pen and paper." She blows out a lungful of smoke and closes the door, before hurrying to another room. While she's gone, I ask Becca how things have been with her mum since the party.

"She's fuming." She huffs, flicking back her hair. "Oh yeah, and you'll never guess the latest, if she goes away again, I have to stay with our James!"

This is bad, Becca can't stand her brother.

"I'm so sorry, Bec…"

"Shut up, Anna!" She snaps. "It's hardly your fault."

I want to say something, but Elaine comes scurrying back into the kitchen.

"Here, love," she says handing me a notepad and pen, "you jot the details down, and I'll wrap you up some cake."

Once I've finished, we hear the tired rumble of my brother's car. Elaine places the foil wrapped cake in a plastic bag, which I exchange for the memorial details. She gives me a hug goodbye, and we both try not to cry.

"I'm going to miss you, Elaine."

"Now go on, pet, or you'll set me off."

Outside, I open the car door and slide the front seat forward, so Becca can climb into the back.

"What's in the bag?" Tommy asks as I reach back to fasten my seat belt.

"Lemon cake."

"Lovely." He smiles.

On the way to Becca's he drums his fingers on the wheel. "Annie, Tracey called earlier, she wants me back at work on Friday."

"No, I'm not ready." Being alone for a few hours at a time isn't too bad, but a shift at the pub means he won't be back till after midnight.

"An, I've been off a month. I'm sorry but I have to."

"I'll stay if you want?" Becca pipes from the back seat. We often have sleepovers, but she's never stayed at Tommy's before.

"Thanks, Bec, but I've only got a single bed, so there won't be much room."

"Look," Tommy says, "why don't you two have my room, and I'll take the single?"

"You sure?" I ask.

"Course."

"Thank you."

6.30pm. Anna:

When we get home, Tommy boils the kettle, and I sit down in the lounge. It's so cosy in here, the walls behind the door and under the window, are covered by a massive corner sofa. On the far wall is a huge, black glass entertainment unit with a fifty inch, flat screen TV. It's so different from Mum and Dad's, Mum loved ornaments and old-fashioned paintings. Tommy's minimalistic, I mean he likes his comfort and soft furnishings, but they're mainly grey or black. He doesn't have a single ornament, but he does like his art. On the wall facing the window, is a large framed charcoal drawing of a semi-naked woman. It's tasteful because you can only see her back and the top of her bum, which is loosely covered with a silky drape.

Today's been a disaster. All Tommy wanted was to get the house cleared, and I know he said that I didn't have to go back, but I want to help him. Just one more trip, the last trip for both of us, then he can hand the keys over to the estate agent, and everything will be fine.

It actually feels like this morning was days ago. Before we left for Mum and Dad's, I sat out in the garden, while Tommy talked and talked to Dad's solicitor. His phone hadn't stopped ringing all morning and, because we left in such a hurry, he hasn't explained much to me yet.

Tommy stands the drinks and cake on the TV unit, then lies back on the huge, fluffy floor cushion.

"Right, Annie. I need to tell you about Dad's will."

"Ok?"

"Everything's ours. The house, car, his flat in London, everything."

24

"Wow, so what're you going to do?"

"We'll sell the flat, it's too far away to maintain."

For as long as I can remember, Dad's worked in a hospital in London. Mum wanted him to get a job up here in Teesside, but he wouldn't. He had a good reputation down there. I guess being a successful vascular surgeon in the centre of London was good for his image.

"And if you're up to it," he adds, "we'll fly over to France at half term..."

"Why?!"

"To get the car, they always drove out remember?"

"Yeah, I remember. So, what will you do with your car?"

"Scrap it." He shrugs. "Can you do me a favour too?" He asks, folding his arms behind his head.

"Yeah?"

"I've got a list of all Dad's contacts; I want you to email everyone with the memorial details."

"Sure, what about Mum's friends?"

"Sarah said she's sorting it."

Mum and Sarah practically lived at the gym. Some of their friends have told me that I'm Mum's double, but she never left the house without her 'face on,' and she was always pristine. I think I embarrassed her because I'm the opposite, I never wear make-up, and I live in leggings or skinny jeans, with little tops. In her eyes I guess I was scruffy.

"No wonder she didn't want me." I find myself mumbling as I stand to pick up my tea.

"What's that?"

"I was just thinking about that letter Mum wrote."

"Hey, come here. Sit down, Annie…I really don't think she meant all that."

I do sit beside him, but I don't think he believes what he's saying any more than I do.

"How do you know?" I snap. "For years, I've been made to feel like a fussy madam because I only settled with you. You read it yourself, she didn't want me."

"I'm not defending her, An. I just want you to know that somewhere, amongst the crap, she did love you."

"Yeah, Tom…amongst the crap."

May 09, 2016 Monday 8.40am. School.
Anna:

My first day back here, and our deputy head, Mr. Garrison is taking today's assembly. It's not that I don't like him, it's just his booming voice makes me nervous, and I haven't exactly had the best morning so far. First, I slept through my alarm and had to wake Tommy for a lift. Then at registration, Miss. Beren pretended she was annoyed that I was late, only to change when everyone else had left for the assembly. She closed her laptop and told me that if I ever need to talk, then her door's always open. I've never liked her, I can't trust her. Not her squinty fake smile, or feigned compassion. I don't know how she can seriously expect me to trust her with feelings this raw.

Mr. Garrison begins by addressing the ever-growing problem of litter in the hallways, and that it's our duty to place rubbish in the correct recycling bins. I don't know if I'm ill or if it's his voice making me dizzy, but heat crawls over my skin like a wave of pins and needles. I take in a deep breath, close my eyes for a few seconds and try to focus. When they open, I see that the hems of Mr. Garrison's trousers are completely sodden. At first, I'm shocked and assume that he's had an embarrassing accident. However, as I look around it seems like no-one's noticed. I look back to our teacher, it appears that he is stood in a shallow pool of water, that's gradually being drawn up his inside leg. This makes no sense, so I press my face into my hands and count to ten. After a slow exhale I look up, and Mr. Garrison's appearance has returned to normal. That was weird, but I can't have been the only one to have seen that.

10.30am. Becca:

We've got a supply teacher today, Mrs. Rivers. She's covered this class loads, so she thinks she's something special because she knows us. Anyway, she's boring me to death, babbling about Macbeth and some witches. I guess she thinks if she's all enthusiastic, then we will be too. Wrong.

Anna's not listening, she can't take her eyes off the tree outside. Everyone's noticed, and Mrs. Rivers keeps doing that pissed off stare, over her glasses.

"Anna?" She says, but Anna doesn't move. "Anna?" She says again, and again and again. This isn't good, I've seen Anna drift off like this before, she kind of goes deaf.

"Miss. Anderson!" Mrs. Rivers snaps. She slams her book on the desk, and everyone gasps. "Can you share with the rest of us, who are actually paying attention, your opinion on the scene?"

Anna can't speak, she looks lost. I have to do something and fast. If I don't, she'll cry, then I'll cry and there is no way I'm letting everyone see that.

"Miss, please," I raise my hand, "I need to talk to you outside. It's super important."

"This better not be something silly."

"It isn't, Miss."

"Ok, Rebecca," she huffs, as we leave the room, "what's so important that it couldn't wait?"

"Don't you know what's wrong with Anna?"

She folds her arms and shakes her head. Shit, how do I say this? I'm useless at explaining things so I just spit it out.

"Her mam and dad died..."

"Oh no!" She gasps. "Ok, you best go back inside."

When I sit down, Anna's staring at the tree again, and everyone's whispering but they soon zip their lips when Mrs. Rivers follows me in.

"Ok, class I'd like you to silently read through act five again, scenes one to eleven."

No one's actually reading, they're watching us. Mrs. Rivers walks over to Anna, lays her hand on her shoulder and whispers, "I'm so sorry, I didn't know."

Anna just nods.

Lunchtime. Anna:

Room thirty-five; we always have our lunch in here. To get in you need a pass, and you earn that with good behaviour. It's a large L-shaped room on the top floor, divided by movable partitions. There are pool tables and games consoles at the far end, table-top board games in the centre, by the entrance, and coffee tables with cosy chairs to the right.

As usual, me and Becca sit at a coffee table by the window. It's not long until we're joined by two of Becca's friends; Chloe and Sophie. A loud and bitchy pair who taint the atmosphere of any room they enter. To your face they'll act like your best friend, then talk behind your back. They don't like me but they're Becca's friends. So for her, I tolerate them.

"So, Anna," Sophie smirks, as they perch on the seats which face us, "where were you this morning? I figured now you're living with Tommy, we'd be getting the bus together."

I'd forgotten about Sophie living so close to us. "I slept in," I tell her, "so Tommy gave me a lift."

"Bit of a cheeky cow, aren't ya?" Chloe sniggers. "Making your brother drive you to school."

Anything I could say would be pointless, so I just shrug, take out my phone and send Tommy a text saying 'Hi.' He replies straight away,

"Are you ok?"

"Yeah.
I'm sorry for waking you earlier xx"

*"Don't be daft.
Sorry, I can't talk.
I'm at the theatre, but
I'll be done by 2
so, I'll pick you up."*

"Thank you x."

Aside from his shifts at the pub, Tommy works on an 'as and when' basis, at a theatre in Darlington. That's his real passion, he's a make-up artist. He says that bar work is just 'a means to an end.'

I wish I could talk to him right now. I don't know what I'd say though, maybe just tell him that I want to go home. I hate sitting here while Becca gossips with Chloe and Sophie. I can't actually hear what they're saying, not that they're speaking quietly, it's just that my ears feel clogged with the incessant buzz of bitching. So, I stare out of the window and pretend I'm not here.

As soon as I picture my escape, Chloe clicks her fingers, drawing my attention to the one person that I really don't want to see; Alex. He sits at a table by the entrance.

"He wants to talk to you." Sophie laughs.

I shake my head. I know it's been a month but I'm not ready, I can't deal with him today.

"Go on," Chloe demands, kicking my shin, "don't be a bitch!"

I look to Becca to get me out of this, but she doesn't. She just looks away, eating her sandwiches as if I'm not even here. Becca changes when they're around, but I thought she could've at least had my back on this.

As soon as I sit at Alex's table, he hooks his foot around my chair. He pulls me towards him and leans in so close, that I can smell what flavour crisps he's just eaten.

"It's shit, what happened to your parents," he grins, laying his sweaty palm over mine, "but we shouldn't let that come between us."

I quickly pull my hand away, but he just smirks.

"Don't pretend that you don't wanna do it again."

He cannot be serious. My first day back at school, and he goes straight in with this? That's low even for Alex, my skin is actually crawling right now.

"No!" I shudder and scratch my wrists. "I don't want to."

"Alright," he shrugs, "friends?"

I nod, then some of his mates burst through the door, and I hurry back to Becca.

1.30pm. Anna:

We've been running for half an hour, and Becca's lagging behind. She hates PE, especially when it's outside. But I love it. I love the fresh air and the grass springing beneath my feet. It helps to clear my head. I don't really think Becca gets that, but I cover a few more metres then slow down while she catches up.

"I can't breathe." She pants. "What's up with you? Why'd you run off? You still pissed that you had to talk to Alex?"

"No. I didn't want to talk to him, but I guess it's out of the way now…do you think Chloe's right? Do I expect too much from Tommy?"

"Nah," she laughs, "he loves you to bits, anyone with eyes can see that!" She's probably right. As we jog along, I remember back to when I was younger.

I was only eleven, Mum was away and she'd left a huge pile of ironing for Tommy to do. His girlfriend, Leanne was staying over and I was bored, so I decided to tackle it. I didn't really know what I was doing but I tried, and it was all going well until I accidentally pressed the iron against the base of my thumb. It was agony, I knew I had to tell Tommy. I didn't want to, I felt like an idiot but I had no choice. When I knocked on his bedroom door, Leanne shouted a breathless 'fuck off,' so I scurried along to my room and laid on the bed. A few minutes later Tommy burst in wanting to know what was wrong. All I'd wanted to do was save him a job and I'd messed up. I cried that I was sorry. I told him to go back to Leanne, but he just sat on the bed beside me, refusing to leave until I told him what I'd done.

2pm. Anna:

I've been looking forward to this lesson all day. Ceramics, it's my favourite, I love taking a lump of clay and twisting and moulding it into something unique. It's also my only lesson with Dan. It's strange to think of it now, because at the time I tried not to, but not having him around after my parents accident was awful. That's in the past though. I did call him when we got back from the house, on Saturday. Since then, we've talked and talked. It's awesome, I feel like I've got my friend back.

The classroom's on the top floor and, to avoid the crowds on the staircase, I always go in a few minutes late. Mr. Coley never seems to mind.

Inside, the tables are set out in a large U-shape with chairs around the outside, facing an amply stocked equipment unit in the centre. Dan and I always sit together at the far side. As I walk over to him, he smiles and pulls out my chair.

"Hey," I say, as I slip into my seat, "I missed you at lunch, why weren't you in room thirty-five?"

"I've had my pass confiscated."

"Why?" I'm confused. Dan never gets into trouble, ever.

"Doesn't matter." He gives me a sad smile and shakes his head. "It's nothing…so are you having a funeral?" He asks quietly, running his fingers over his tidy blonde hair.

"Yeah, a memorial. We're having a buffet too, will you come?"

Mr. Coley then moves to address the class, so Dan leans close and whispers.

"I'll come to the memorial, but the buffet's for your family, and I don't want to impose."

31

He wouldn't be imposing. Mum really liked Dan, she'd even tease him sometimes because he doesn't like butter on his sandwiches. I want to tell him to come, but I can't because Mr. Coley's waiting for everyone to stop talking.

"Good afternoon," he says, "today's theme is transport. Old or modern, it's up to you. Right then, you may all take turns to collect your clay and equipment." Mr. Coley's my favourite teacher. He rarely sits at his desk; he says he'll sit when he grows too old to stand. Preferring to stroll between the equipment unit and the tables, he speaks to each of us individually.

"It's good to see you back, Anna," he says, kneeling down to rest his forearms on the table. "How're you doing?"

I want to say 'ok' but my throat tightens, and I take a deep breath.

"I am sorry," he says. "So, what are you making?"

"A steam train, Sir."

"Do you need any help?"

"I'm ok."

"Well shout up if you do." He then strokes his clean-shaven face, taps the table, stands and moves along to Dan.

As I warm the clay in my hands I begin to reflect. Aside from an awkward lunch break, my first day back hasn't been too bad. Although, I am confused by the image or vision, or whatever it was that I saw in assembly. Logic suggests that water lapping up my teacher's legs is impossible, but it was more than a thought, it was there.

Once the clay is pliable, I form the body of a train and block out the classroom noise. Just focus on what you're doing, I tell myself, as the rest of the class whisper and snigger amongst themselves. Most of the girls in here hate me because I'm friends with Dan. He's the tallest in our year, his features are perfectly chiselled, and he has a sprinkling of freckles over his nose. All that, coupled with the effort he puts into his appearance, it's no surprise he attracts a lot of attention. To me he's just Dan, my friend.

I can't have fully closed the door when I came in, because once Mr. Coley's done talking to Dan, a gust of wind blows it open. Soon there's a strong smell of the ocean, and water seeps inside, soaking the floor. No-one else has noticed but I can't look away. I'm drawn to it, and I don't fully understand why, but I find myself laying my hand on Dan's shoulder to push myself up.

"An?" He asks, as I move slowly to the end of the row, "are you alright?"

I can't answer him. Shrivelled bony fingers wrap around the edge of the door. I need to know who's hiding there and why they haven't come in. I creep forward for a closer look, but stop dead in my tracks and let out an ear-piercing scream. My mum and dad stagger towards me. They're saturated and grey, their faces are like transparent water balloons, filled to bursting. Mum's lifeless yet driven, intent on reaching me. With each step they dump strands of seaweed on the floor. I freeze until they almost reach me, Mum's withered fingers slither within millimetres of my face. I scream for her to leave me alone, but she doesn't. She digs her nails into my skin, dragging them down my cheek. I'd run but my legs are planted to the ground, so in a feeble attempt to protect myself, I raise my arms over my face. Then I hear it. The deafening roar of the sea, and Dad telling me to go with them.

"Leave me alone!" I scream, but he just calls louder and louder. I beg again but now they're closing in, and I can't escape. A chill sweeps around my neck. I can't breathe.

"Anna!" Dad demands. "Come to me."

In that exact moment he wraps his deathly hand around my wrist. The saltwater stings, and every inch of my body is now so gripped with fear that I can't even scream. I force air from my lungs but nothing. Everything's turned black.

When I eventually come to, there's no sign of what just happened. My parents are gone. I'm in my classroom, clinging to a table leg between Dan and Mr. Coley. They're both just staring at me, horrified. I can't speak. My eyes are

33

now wide open and I quickly realise that, besides us three, the room's empty.

"Can you stand?" asks Mr. Coley, "we need to get you cleaned up."

I feel drunk. I'm dizzy and my entire front is caked in vomit. Dan hands me a wad of paper towels.

"I'm so sorry," I cry, "I wan…want to go home."

Our teacher nods and makes a call to the office.

"Where is everyone?" I ask Dan.

"He sent them home. D'ya want to get up?"

I nod and, taking his hands, I crawl out from under the table and lift myself onto a chair. As I begin scraping the sick from my chest, he hands me a drink of water.

"What happened?" He asks.

I wish I could tell him, but I don't even think I want to know what's happening to me.

"Dan," I sob, "I need Tommy, my head hurts."

He doesn't ask any more, just holds my hand.

"Sir," he says as Mr. Coley ends the call, "she can't go to the office like this."

"No, you're right, Daniel. Would you recognise her brother?"

"Yes, Sir. I know him."

"Good. They're calling him now. I want you to keep watch, when you see him go and bring him up."

Dan nods and waits by the window.

My throat is raw and my stomach's in knots. I know I should keep sipping the water, but it's making me feel worse, so I stand the cup on the table and gather the dirty paper towels. After a while, Dan taps the windowsill. "He's here, An." He says before hurrying out.

"I'm sorry, Sir." I say.

"Anna, there's nothing to be sorry for."

A few minutes later, Dan bursts in with my brother. Tommy's jaw hits the floor, the moment he sees me, but he completely ignores the fact that I reek of sick. He just stands me up and hugs me.

May 13, 2016 Friday 3.30pm. Home.
Anna:

I've lost Becca to her phone. So, while she lies on the sofa, I head out to the kitchen, where Tommy's cooking fajitas.

"Hey," he says, as he browns strips of spicy chicken, "slice some peppers, would you?"

"Sure." After washing my hands, I take the peppers from the fridge and he hands me a knife and a chopping board.

"How was school?"

"Ok…well they all think I'm crazy…" Since Monday's ceramics lesson everyone wants to know what happened, and Dan's been circled by the gossip vultures, but I trust him. My problem is that he wasn't the only one there, and word gets around.

"You're not crazy," he insists, "listen, I hope you don't mind but I've told Rich."

"I don't mind." I had a feeling he would tell him. I can't imagine what was going through Tommy's head when he walked into that classroom. All I know is that I needed him, and he was there.

"Good," he nods, "because you know how worried I am?"

"Yeah," I sigh, "I am sorry."

"Don't be sorry, but I don't really want you to be on your own yet. So, Rich said he'll bring you a pizza when I go to work tomorrow."

"Thanks. There's something else too. Tom? Am I a burden? It's just Chloe said something. Well, she's actually said a few things."

"No." He says firmly. "Don't ask that again."

I don't know what to say now, so I just keep slicing.

"Sorry, that was harsh," he says kindly, "just promise, you won't pay any more attention to the kids from school."

"I promise."

Later, while we eat, Becca sucks a blob of guacamole from her fingers, and Tommy rests his elbows on the table. He stares at me for a good few minutes.

"What?" I ask.

"A social worker's coming to see us after school, on Monday."

I've suddenly lost my appetite.

"What for?" I ask.

"There's nothing to worry about," he says softly, "for the most part she'll be talking to me, but she will ask you some questions."

"But why?" I persist. "Can't I stay with you any more? You promised me…"

"Annie," he smiles, "don't be a daft arse, I'm going to be your guardian."

"Ha!" Becca laughs, "he'll be your dad!"

Tommy glares at her. I'm grateful to have never been on the receiving end of that look. Anger masked by methodical calm, he doesn't move a muscle, just glares up through his brow.

"Sorry, um…" She quickly gulps down her drink and rushes up to the bathroom. In an instant his whole demeanour softens.

"Annie, I'm sorry," he says, as he stands to clear the dishes, "I should've told you when she wasn't here. Please don't think I'll act like Dad." He lays the plates on the side, and I follow him. Touching his arm, I turn him to face me.

"You're nothing like Dad. Besides, you don't know what this means to me."

"I did it," he nods, his brow weighing heavy, "so, you wouldn't worry about us being separated. But, Annie, I don't know what you need from me."

"I just need you, not anything special, and…please don't turn me away."

"Never."

Becca:

Fifteen minutes. I've locked myself in here for fifteen minutes. I'm such an idiot, their dad's just died and I go and say something like that. I have to apologise, but I daren't go back after the way he looked at me. He scared me and turned me on at the same time. Shit, Becca, you stupid girl. I can't exactly hide in the fucking bathroom all night. So, opening the door slightly, I wait until I hear Tommy going to his room, then rush back to the kitchen. Anna's not there, so I try the lounge. She's sat on the sofa, flicking through the TV channels.

"I'm so sorry, An. I didn't think."

"It's ok. That's yours," she says, pointing to a mug of coffee, on the TV stand. "What movie d'ya want to watch?"

"Dunno."

We trawl through the menu for ages, eventually agreeing on Thor. We've seen it a thousand times, but he's sexy, so what's a girl to do? As the movie starts, we sip our drinks, and Tommy comes in to say bye to Anna. I still love him, especially when he's dressed for work. Sexy, tight black jeans and shirt. He smells gorgeous too.

"Right, Annie," he says, "I have to go now, are you alright?"

She nods, but I'm just dreaming about later, when I'll get to sleep in his bed. Shame he won't be in it.

"I'll be back around midnight," he says, kissing Anna's head and tucking her hair behind her ear, "but call if you need me."

It's a bit gross, but that doesn't stop me feeling jealous. I wish I could tell Anna, but she'd never speak to me again if she knew. So, once he's gone, I tell a white lie and say that my friend Sophie likes him instead.

"He's a grown man!" She says. "He'd never touch anyone our age."

"Well that's a fucking shame." I mutter under my breath.

Anna:

Becca's engrossed in the movie, but I can't concentrate. I'm chewed, Sophie's mistaken if she thinks she stands a chance with my brother. The selfish cow only wants him for his looks, she'd most likely parade him as a trophy and drop him when she's bored. I can't stand either of them, her or Chloe. They prance around school like they own the place. That's it. I'm super annoyed now.

"Besides," I say bitterly, pausing the movie. "Sophie couldn't handle someone with Tommy's experience!"

"And, what would you know about his experience!?" She gasps.

"Well, obviously I don't know the details, but I've heard him doing it, before he moved out of Mum and Dad's. And he tries to hide it, but I've passed girls leaving here, when I've let myself in."

"So, what's he gonna do now you're living here?" She laughs.

I shrug off her remark, and after an awkward pause she changes the subject.

"You remember Monday?" She asks. "Why won't you tell me what happened?"

"I'm still trying to figure it out, Bec."

"You told Dan!"

"No, I haven't."

"Shut up, Anna. So, he saw the whole thing and didn't even ask what was going on?"

"He asked at the time, but I couldn't say it…he hasn't asked since. He just said he's there for me."

"I bet you've told Tommy!"

"Obviously."

"What did he say?"

I plump up a cushion and lie down. Becca shuffles along to the corner and stretches out her legs.

"He said I'm not crazy." I sigh.

She doesn't answer, only flashes a smile and scrolls through her phone.

"I'm not crazy." I insist.

"No, no, course you're not."

May 14, 2016 Saturday 11am.
Anna:

A week from now, I'll be getting ready for Mum and Dad's memorial. I'm trying to ignore it, but today I can't. I have nothing to wear, not unless I turn up in a pair of leggings, my comfy shoes and a little T-Shirt. So, Becca and I are in Normanby village, waiting to take the bus into town. She absolutely loves shopping. I hate it, but with any luck I'll find something quickly.

"How much are ya spending?" Becca asks, as we step on the bus. I think she's assigned herself the title of 'wardrobe planner.'

"I'm not sure," I shrug, as we pay and find a seat, "Tommy's just handed me two hundred, he said to get something nice."

"Wow, An. We'll easily find you the perfect dress."

I honestly didn't know what to say earlier. I almost choked when Tommy placed that roll of notes in my hand. I know it's Dad's money but still, it's unnerving, carrying so much cash around.

"Can I stay at yours at half term?" She asks. "I know I'm a cheeky cow, but Mam's going away. Please say yes, or I'll have to stay with James."

"I won't be here, we're going to France."

"Why would you wanna go there?! After what happened?"

"We need to bring Dad's car back, and Tommy wants to see where they sailed from. It's how he deals with things, you know, figures it all out."

She nods, and we say no more of it. In fact, she doesn't say anything else until we reach our stop.

I don't know if Becca's in a mood or something but, as we get off, she pushes past a girl who's struggling with a crying baby. I let the girl pass, then jump off and catch up with her.

"That girl's way too young to be a mother," she sniggers, "should have been more careful!"

"That's a bit harsh, Bec…and besides," I whisper, "after what I found on my knickers, I don't think Alex was careful."

"Whoa, Anna! You mean he didn't use a condom?"

"I don't know, ok?"

"What do you mean, you don't know?" She says, "how can you not know? And why won't you talk to me about it?"

"I mean I can't remember; I was drunk…"

"You can't have been so drunk that you don't remember."

"I was…" I sigh, "listen, I'm sorry that I can't say any more, I just don't think he used anything, because his stuff was all in my knickers."

"Then you'll need to do a test," she says, "if you've had unprotected sex, then you might be pregnant!"

I plead with her to leave it alone, but she refuses.

"When're you due on?"

"I don't know." I say hastily.

"Well work it out, when were you last on?"

I can't remember that either, so I check the calendar on my phone.

"I think I've missed one," I tell her, as I scroll back, "either that, or I forgot to mark it down. It'll be ok, I've missed them before when I've been stressed, and I haven't exactly had it easy lately."

There's just no convincing her, shaking her head, she holds out her hand. "Money, Anna. I'm buying you a test."

If only to end this, I pull a twenty from my hoody pocket.

"Wait here!" She snatches it and scurries off towards a chemist.

Marvellous, she knows how anxious I get in crowds, and I now feel even worse. So, I shrink back against a shop window and wait.

She rushes back around ten minutes later, and opens her bag to show me the test inside.

"When're you doing it?" She asks.

"Not now, let's buy this dress first…I'll do it when we go for lunch."

This seems to satisfy, so she joyfully drags me into one of her favourite shops.

"Right," she says, ushering me into the changing room, "you stay here, and I'll bring you a load to try on."

I know she's trying to help, but I'm totally overwhelmed. I don't feel like I have a voice, but I strip down to my underwear anyway, and she tirelessly brings me dress after dress. Many changes later, she thrusts at me a knee length, sage green strapless dress with ruffles over the chest. I hate it, but she insists that I try it on.

"I don't know, Bec. Do they have it in a twelve?"

"Why? You're a six."

"It's not me, but since you love it…"

"Really?" She squeaks, "you'll buy me it?"

"Yes, so long as I don't have to try on any more dresses. This one will do." I hold up the first dress I'd tried. It's black, slim fitting, soft cotton with a plunge neckline and long sleeves. I'm not adventurous, but Becca's half Jamaican, so she looks good in any colour. With the dresses, I buy myself a pair of simple, flat leather pumps, then we head to my favourite coffee shop for lunch.

Inside we buy our toasted sandwiches and hot chocolates before finding a table. As I sit down, Becca reaches into her bag.

"Go on, An." She grins, "do it now."

"Seriously? Let me have this first."

"Alright," she groans, "but you're not getting out of it."

We both smile, as I roll my eyes and bite into my panini.

"Thanks for the dress," she says, "it's gorgeous."

"No problem."

Later, as soon as I finish the last of my drink, Becca reaches under the table, discretely laying the test on my lap. This girl isn't about to let up.

"Ok, I'm going." Hiding the test under my hoody, I stomp off to the bathroom. Ok, so the instructions say to hold the absorbent strip under flow for ten seconds. "Replace cap…" I read aloud, then skip to the important part; how I'll know if I am or not. "Wait for three minutes. Two lines for pregnant and one for not." Ok, I'm beginning to feel a little bit nervous. An hour ago, I hadn't given the possibility a thought, now I'm peeing on a stick. "Come on, Anna, you can do this." Keeping my stream flowing over the end, whilst squatting isn't the easiest of tasks, but I manage. Now to wait.

Three anxious minutes later, and my heart sinks. Two bold lines.

"This isn't happening." I read through the instructions again and again to be sure, but there's no mistake. I suddenly feel sick, and as the harsh reality sinks in, I burst into tears.

For a moment, I hold up the test and will the lines to disappear, but it's no use.

How do I tell Tommy, after everything he's done for me? I'm scared to tell him, but at the same time, I'm desperate to. I need him to tell me that it's ok. What am I thinking? It's not ok, it's far from ok. I don't know what to do, but I know I can't stay here. So, I shove the test into the bin, splash cold water over my blotchy face and hurry back to Becca.

She doesn't say a word. She doesn't need to as the answer's written all over my face. For a while, I stare into the bottom of my empty mug and flit between whimpers and silent tears. Eventually she asks if I'm ok.

"No." I say, as I open my phone.

"Are you texting Tommy? You're not gonna tell him now?"

"I don't know what I'm doing…I'm sorry, but I have to go home."

"Sure. I'm sorry, An. For what it's worth, I didn't actually think you were."

"Neither did I."

One Week Later.
May 22, 2016 Sunday Mid-Morning. Home.
Memorial Day.
Anna:

I don't know how I'm going to get through today, it's Mum and Dad's memorial, and morning sickness is a bitch. "Please, no more." I whimper, as my belly cramps, and I grip the toilet seat, bracing myself for another bout. When it passes, I slump against the wall and call for Tommy, but I've got no energy and my voice is raw. So, crawling to the sink, I pull myself up to take a mouthful of water.

"Tommy?" I call again, then lie down on the cold bathroom floor.

A few minutes later, the door creaks open behind me.

"I'm not very well." I groan.

"I can see that," he says, squatting beside me, "what do you need?"

"This to stop, so I can get through today."

"I can't fix that," he says kindly, holding out his hand, "but I can make you a tea. Will you come down?"

"I want to, but I'm afraid to leave the bathroom."

"Come on," he says, lifting me up, "if you need to be sick again, I'll get you a bucket."

He helps me to the kitchen, and while he boils the kettle, I sit down and lay my head on the table.

I don't know where I'd be without Tommy, how I'd deal with this. It's strange, but last week, when I sat with Becca in that coffee shop, I almost told him over text. That would've been a huge mistake, because when I got home and told him face to face, he absolutely lost it. I've seen him angry before but this was something else. He was scared, I was scared. He yelled, and I screamed and cried that I was

43

sorry, but it was like he couldn't hear me. He was just balling and balling questions at me, I could take that. I could even take it when he punched the wall. What I couldn't take, was when he got right in my face. He was shouting about how, only the day before, he'd told me how unsure he was, how he didn't know what I needed from him. I wanted to curl up and die. That was when I ran. I ran to my room, pulled the drawers behind the door, and curled up on the floor and cried. All the knowing in my heart that he'd never hurt me temporarily vanished.

"Don't run away!" He shouted from behind the door. I didn't know what to do, so I just laid there with my fingers in my ears, praying he would calm down. He did calm down, it took a long time, but he did, and I eventually let him in. We sat there on the floor, I sobbed, and he just watched me. Then he said it.

"I'm sorry, Annie."

I didn't know how to respond, so I just shook my head.

"No, I shouldn't have shouted at you like that. I wouldn't have hurt you, you know that, right?"

"I'm scared." I whispered, choking on my tears. Then he did nothing more than hold me. He held me for ages. I could've stayed there all night, but he had to get ready for work.

"I'll never hurt you, ever." He said. "Know that I love you, and everything'll be ok."

He's been looking after me ever since. Now, he's insisting that I try and eat something, but I daren't.

"There's no point," I moan, "it'll only come back up."

"Not necessarily, if I make you some porridge will you at least try a bit?"

"Alright."

He hands me the bowl and sits beside me, watching as I force myself to eat. I hate this, last week I was normal. Now, after seeing those two lines on that test, I'm automatically throwing up every day. It's like I've told my brain I'm pregnant, and like the flick of a switch it's started. I wish I didn't know. Actually, I just wish I wasn't pregnant.

"You need to take little and often," he says, "it's the only way to get your strength back."

"I'm so sorry, Tom. For all of this."

"Shh." He softly runs his knuckle over the back of my hand. "It's ok."

"Thank you…I've never been to a funeral, I don't know what I'm expected to do."

"You don't have to do anything, just stay with me. Listen, the vicar will use your full name when he makes his address."

"Why? You know I hate that name, even my teachers don't use it."

"Sarah wanted to be involved, and she made a huge deal about how it's what Mum would've wanted. I'm sorry. If it's any consolation, he'll be using my full name too."

"Ok."

My brother's under enough pressure today, so if it keeps Sarah sweet then, I guess I'll deal.

"It will be ok," he says, "funerals are mostly people telling you how sorry they are."

"And what do I say?"

Before he can answer, we're interrupted by a knock from the front door. From my seat I can see along the hallway, it's Becca.

"She's early!" he says, "what time did you tell her to come?"

"Half twelve."

"Oh well," he sighs, pushing himself to his feet. "I'd best let her in."

Along with a little black shrug, she's wearing the green dress that I bought her.

"Sorry I'm early," she chimes, kicking off her shoes. "Our James is over, and I just had to get outta there."

Tommy shakes his head and locks the door, as she rushes over and paws at my face.

"Anna, you look awful."

"Give her some space." Tommy snaps, before handing me a bucket from the cupboard, under the sink. "There you are, I'm going for a shower."

Becca smiles at him and runs her fingers through her poker straight hair.

"Sorry, An." She says, once he's gone. "I wasn't being funny, but you've gotta pull yourself together."

"I'm trying."

"Clearly." She then pulls out a chair and stares at my belly. "You didn't tell me what Tommy said when you told him?"

"He wasn't exactly happy, but he said it'll be ok. You know Tommy, what else would he say?"

"Aww, he's so nice. So, when are you telling Alex?"

I shake my head.

"You have to tell him, he's got a right to know."

"Leave me alone, Bec."

1.40pm. Anna:

Considering the amount of people lingering outside the church, it's eerily quiet. Our every move is being watched, and I can't bring myself to look anyone in the eye. So, as Rich and Becca follow close behind, I hide in my brother's shadow. The vicar greets Tommy under the stone archway, at the entrance. Then he leads us inside, into a small annex and through into the church. It's so cold and overwhelmingly high. I reach forward and briefly touch my brother's arm, so he lifts his hand to the small of his back, and takes hold of my fingers, while we walk down the aisle, to the front row. He guides me to my seat. Rich takes the seat by the isle, Tommy sits between us, and Becca sits on the end.

"What's that?" I ask, as Tommy unfolds a piece of paper.

"My speech." He whispers. "Let's hope I don't mess it up."

"You won't."

Soon, we feel Mum's sister, Sarah, and her husband, John, shuffle along the row behind us. He presses firmly on mine and Tommy's shoulders, pushing me hard into the wooden seat.

"Good turnout," he says deeply, "your dad would be pleased." He doesn't mean to be oppressive, but I imagine it's hard to be anything else when you're six foot by six foot with a voice that can shake the earth. He sits behind Rich, and Tommy stands to give Sarah a hug. I just awkwardly stand too and smile at Olivia, my cousin. She's only twelve. She huffs 'hi' and folds her arms. Then her older brother, Ethan steps onto our row and gives me a massive hug.

"Hiya," he says, "you look lovely."

"Thanks." I step back for Tommy to hug him too, but the vicar moves to the front, so Ethan slips into his seat behind Becca.

"Welcome, everyone." The vicar says. "I'm Reverend Callaghan. We are gathered here today, to mark the tragic and untimely loss of Ellen and Austin Anderson, beloved parents of Thomas Henry and Annalee Elizabeth. A tragedy such as this grieves all, especially Ellen's dear sister Sarah."

Especially Sarah? Um, ok. Tommy must be thinking the same, because he discretely knocks his leg against mine and raises his eyebrows.

"But there's peace to be found in our Lord and Saviour." The vicar continues. "For it is written, 'blessed are those who mourn, for they shall be comforted.' In a moment we'll hear from Thomas, then a Bible reading by Ellen's brother in law, John. First, may I ask that you all be upstanding for the singing of our first hymn, 'All Things Bright and Beautiful.'"

When we stand, my legs quiver and I feel weak. I'm beginning to think Tommy was right, I should have eaten more.

"You alright?" He asks as I take his arm.

"I don't feel good, I'm hungry and the floor's shaking."

"I've got you," he says, "it's ok."

47

When the hymn ends Tommy moves to the front. Sympathetic whispers echo around the church as he thanks everyone for coming and unfolds his notes. A few minutes of him stuttering over the words pass, and he eventually finds his nerve. I breathe a sigh of relief for him, but then the floor begins to pivot, drawing with it a foaming lap of seawater. I quickly tuck my legs under and grip the seat as the ripples reach my feet. In the seconds that pass, I feel the church fall silent and I soon realise that Tommy's stopped talking. His eyes are locked on me, while everyone else's are locked on him. He quickly continues with his speech, and I plead with my brain not to do this now. Before I know it, Rich lays his arm around me and holds me steady until Tommy returns and the service continues.

4pm. The Tigerlily.
Becca:

I don't even know why I'm here. As soon as we got to the pub Anna was pulled away by her mam's friends. Same thing happened at the church, only then it was Daniel Armstrong. I can't stand him, he's so up his own arse it's unreal.

Anyway, I guess I should get some food. No-one's said that we can't start yet and I'm starving. So while everyone stands around talking, I fill a plate from the buffet table, at the far end of the room.

"Can we start?" Asks Olivia, appearing beside me.

"Dunno, but I am."

She fills a plate too, then we sit at a table along the back wall. It's funny how different she is from Anna. Personality-wise, I mean because they both look like mice. That sounds awful, I mean they have mouse-like features and they could be twins. Well, apart from Liv having brown hair, and Anna's is blonde. Oh, and Liv's only twelve.

"I don't get it." She says, tucking into her pizza.

"Get what?"

"Look around! At the church, these were all crying their eyes out, and now they're laughing and joking. People are weird."

I have to admit, the kid has a point.

"Look at my dad," she shouts. "He's probably telling some cringe old story. See, Tommy's doing that smirky smile he does when he's embarrassed."

Rich is there too, but him and Tommy don't exactly look like they're joking. I mean they're just stood sipping their pints.

"Where's Anna?" I ask.

"She's over there." She nods, pointing to a table near the door, "with my mum."

Anna:

"I'd like to say that I'm surprised you're not crying," Sarah bites as she refills her wine glass, "but I'm not."

"I have cried. I'm just numb today."

"Anna, I know you and Ellen didn't always see eye to eye, but what you said when she left was low, even for you."

Mum told her? This is bad, this is really bad.

"Yes." She snaps as I lower my head. "Words hurt."

I'm hurt too, I scream inside. I want to defend myself but I daren't, plus Sarah always has an answer, and by the time I've thought of one it's too late.

"I didn't mean it," I whisper, but she doesn't answer me. We just sit here in painful silence.

"I know you didn't." She says eventually. "But she loved you, and what you said broke her heart."

I wish it was true, I wish Mum loved me, but I can't forget that letter. She regretted ever having me.

"How do you know that?!" I snap, regretting the words the instant I've said them.

"Because she's my sister!" She snarls. "And let's not forget that you weren't the easiest child. You were awful, needy, absolutely exhausting. Ellen was just grateful that

Thomas was there to share the load. All she'd wanted was a nice little girl, who'd do as she was told, but no. She got you, a silly, boyish day dreamer with her head in the clouds. Just look at the state of you." She says, pulling at my sleeve. "Scratching yourself to the point of bleeding, isn't exactly normal is it? No wonder your mum needed so much R and R."

I want the ground to swallow me whole. Tommy was right, I should've stayed with him today. Sarah never goes this far when he's there.

She downs another glass and tells me not to worry about it. How do I not worry about it? I replay Mum's letter in my head, only to find it chewing me up again. My throat's closing, I take a few deep breaths but it doesn't help, so I leave Sarah and hurry outside, just in time to bring up what little food I've eaten.

Becca:

Being first at the food means we're first at the puddings. That's when Ethan comes over. He's just as sexy as Tommy, but totally different. They're both ripped but Ethan's tall and blonde, his hair's gorgeous. Tidy short sides and a silky long top, I just love the way he always has a few strands falling over his eyes. I was only thirteen when he left our school. It's stupid, but I used to write my name as Becca Naylor instead of Becca Clark, and pretend we were married. He only stays long enough to steal some of Olivia's cake, before their dad's calling him away.

"Should we go with?" Olivia says, stuffing her face.

"Sure." I cram the last of my cake in my mouth, then we hover with the rest of them.

"Ethan!" John shouts, "listen to this, our Tom's Anna's legal guardian!"

"Well, I'm going to be," Tommy adds, "it takes a while."

Ethan nods at Tommy, and his dad grabs his shoulder.

"I'd like to see you look after our Liv if 'owt happened to us. Ha, fat bloody chance!" His laugh is so loud that he can't hear Ethan trying to defend himself.

"You be careful son." He says to Tommy. "Young girls are hard work y'know…"

"Dad?!" Olivia protests.

"Quiet, love. You know it's true." He tells Tommy that no matter how well he thinks he knows Anna, she'll keep her secrets. Tommy's reaction doesn't surprise me, he just shakes his head and swills his pint, saying.

"Not from me, she doesn't."

"Where is she anyhow?" John laughs.

We all just stand there, looking at each other blankly, waiting for someone to say something. That's when Sarah, who's sat at a table to our left, props herself up.

"She ran off ages ago," she huffs, "moody cow."

Tommy glares at her, then he and Rich leave their pints on the bar, and storm outside.

Tommy:

"Annie!" I call, as I run down the drive, to the main road. "Annie!"

There's no sign of her at the front of the pub, so I hurry along the path towards Normanby. I bet Sarah's let her mouth run again. I know she's said something because Annie wouldn't have run off, not without a reason. Shit, she probably ran straight past me and I didn't even notice.

"Tommy!"

I turn around to see Rich rushing after me.

"I've found her! She's back there," he calls, pointing his thumb over his shoulder, "in the car park."

"Thanks, man."

We jog back to the pub and see her in the distance. She's sat at the edge of the tarmac, resting her head on her knees. "Catch you in a bit." Rich nods, patting my shoulder before heading back inside. Annie looks tiny today, smaller than usual.

"May I join you?"

She nods, and as I sit beside her, she lays her head on my arm.

"I've been sick again," she says, "and Sarah knows what I said to Mum. She hates me for it."

"Their accident wasn't your fault, I've told you that. It was an accident, you can't blame yourself because of something you said in an argument."

"I guess," she sighs, sliding her hand into mine. "I've been thinking..."

"Right?"

"I don't want to be pregnant any more, I don't want it."

I gently let go of her hand, stand and kick the stones where the tarmac meets the grass.

"Don't make a decision like that today."

She looks at me, defeated. But once it's done, it's done. It's no secret that I'd rather not have a baby in the house, but that's the situation we're in.

"Tom?" She pleads, "won't you help me? Do I have to go on my own?" She turns away from me, and digs her nails into her wrists.

"Look at me." Kneeling down, I take her hand. "Of course I'll help you. When have I ever not? But trust me on this."

She wipes away a few escaping tears and shakes her head.

"Please, Annie, I know what you're feeling."

"How can you?" She jumps in. "I'm sorry, I didn't mean that."

"I do though...I know exactly how scared you are."

She stares blankly at me.

"No-one knows this," I tell her, "not even Rich, but when I was your age, I got Leanne pregnant. I was petrified so I asked her to get rid of it. I pictured what would be be like telling Dad and I panicked, I knew I'd get the belt. But she

52

wanted to keep it. She sat on my bed in tears, begging me to think about it."

"Why would she want to keep it?" She asks.

"Because it was mine and she loved me."

"You loved her too, right?"

"I thought I did, but I didn't even hug her. How can you love someone and not hold them when they're breaking down? I should've supported her, but I didn't. She had an abortion. After, things were never the same. You see, An, this is your baby. You have got to be one-hundred percent sure of what you want. I can help you raise it, or get rid, but it's your decision. So, I think you should wait and think it through, because there's no going back."

"Ok," she nods, "sorry, can I go home?…I'm tired."

"Course," I stand and help her up, "I'll walk with you, but I'm expected back."

"Tom?" She stops me as I turn to start walking. "You're a good person. You were just scared, I get that."

"Thanks, sweetheart. Come on, let's get you home."

8pm. Becca:

It's been ages since Rich found Anna. I knew her and Tommy would be talking, but this is taking the piss. There's no food left, Ethan's taken Olivia home, and I'm bored. When I text Anna to ask how much longer she's going to be, she calls me straight back.

"Hiya, Bec. I'm sorry I didn't come back in, I just couldn't face it, so Tommy walked me home."

"You've gone home? Fine! Nice of you to tell me. I guess I should just go home too."

"No, stay there. Tommy's on his way back now, he'll get you a taxi. Please, just wait."

"Fine I'll wait, I don't want to stress you out in your condition."

"Yeah, about that…I don't think I'm keeping it."

53

"No! An, you can't. You know how I feel about abortions."

"You don't understand!" She cries, "I'm too young for this, and do you really think Alex is mature enough to be a dad?"

"Well no, but Tommy'll look after ya."

"Yeah, but he shouldn't have to…listen, Bec, we're going to France next week, so I can't do anything yet anyway."

I can't deal with this. Abortions are evil. Murdering a baby? I don't know how anyone can think that's ok.

"Ok, An, will you just promise you'll think about it?"

"Sure, I promise."

Chapter 3

May 24, 2016 Tuesday 8.30pm. Monaco, Impound. Tommy:

When we arrived here, Annie and I stood deathly still. The impound was filled with rows of sports cars, so Dad's stuck out like a tank in a playground. Sixteen plate, black Audi Q7. His voice played in my head. 'You'd better not damage it, boy.' And I won't. Collecting it was fairly straight forward, I signed some papers and answered a few questions, and that was that. I suppose Dad was right about one thing, it pays to know the language.

When I'd planned this trip, my idea was to drive along to the marina for a look around. I don't need to do that, because after chatting to some of Dad's colleagues at the memorial, I managed to get the contact details of Dad's friend. The same friend who him and Mum were holidaying with, and who loaned them the yacht. Gerald Moss. I've never met him, but he owns a villa not far from where our parents were staying, and he's agreed to meet us there tonight. That's where we're headed now. From the impound, the sat-nav estimated that we'd arrive in two hours. That was an hour ago, and we haven't got very far. Annie's sick, so we had to keep stopping. She's asleep now, and I'm pleased about that, but I can see she's struggling. When we landed, I asked her if she wanted to cancel. Yes, I would've been disappointed to come all this way, get the car and go, but I had to give her that choice. She agreed to visit Mr. Moss, so long as I don't make her do any talking, a fair compromise in my opinion.

I have to know if this Gerald knew Dad wasn't a sailor, and what possessed him to let them go alone? I can't go straight in with that question though, this man's agreed to meet me, so I can't exactly turn up on his doorstep and start an inquisition. No, I need to tread carefully. Obviously my sister's on my mind too. I don't know much about pregnancy, but I don't think it should be wiping her out this much. I've made sure that she's had plenty to drink, but I just wish she'd eat something. She did try when we stopped off at a cafe, but she could only stomach a few bites.

I need something other than the sound of the road, so I fiddle with the radio and accidentally end up starting one of Dad's playlists. 'Hotel California.' This was his 'good mood' song, but I can't even listen past the first verse without feeling tight. I think I'll stick with road noise until I've synced up my phone.

Later, I bounce the car along a narrow dirt road, in the middle of nowhere. I feel like I've taken a wrong turn, but when I slow down to check the sat-nav, it says we're ten minutes away. I drive on, and eventually, the road leads to a lengthy gravel drive.

"Wake up, An." I say. "We're here."

Once the CCTV cameras have scanned the car, the gates open, and I roll the car onto the drive. Soon the villa door opens too, then out step a couple seemingly in their late fifties.

"This is it." I say to myself as I grab the handle to get out, but Annie doesn't move.

"Come on," I say softly, "I'm here."

She nods and opens the door.

"Good evening," I say, as they move to greet us, "I'm Tom and this is my sister, Anna…"

"Yes, yes." Mr. Moss interrupts, giving me a firm handshake. "Call me Gerald, and this is my wife, Christine."

After the pleasantries they show us inside. Annie's shoes squeak against the marble floor, as we follow Dad's friend along a corridor and into a large kitchen. His wife's eyes linger over my sister.

"You look awfully tired," she says, pulling out a heavy dining chair, "come on, you must sit down."

"Thank you." Annie smiles, and Christine moves to make some tea.

"Look," Gerald sighs, taking the seat opposite me, "Tom…Anna. We can't imagine what you must be going through."

My sister and I nod gratefully, then Christine brings over the tea and a large selection of deli meats, bread rolls and fruit.

"Don't be shy." She says, handing us all a plate. Annie nibbles on a bread roll, but I'm starving. So, I tuck in and thank them again for meeting us.

"The thing is," I add, "we don't actually know much about what happened."

"Well," he says, layering a piece of bread with mozzarella, salami and chargrilled peppers. "Austin and I go way back, we often played squash when he worked in Teesside. You know, he operated on our son after his motorbike accident? He saved our boys leg, amazing surgeon he was." He pauses for a moment and shakes his head, "so, your parent's accident…yes well, that day we'd all visited the Prince's Palace of Monaco, and it was there that I mentioned our new yacht. Austin told me that he was a keen sailor, although he'd not been to sea for some time. When we got back, we all took a drive to the marina. I showed him around. You see, he seemed so familiar with everything, naturally I let him and your mum take her out for the evening. We waved them off, and that was the last anyone saw of them."

Annie and I just stare at each other, neither of us can believe what we're hearing.

"Since," Gerald continues, "we've been questioned and questioned by the authorities…I am deeply sorry," he sighs, "we should've gone with them. I should have."

"Gerald." I say boldly. "This isn't your fault. If Dad wanted something badly enough, he'd do everything in his power to get it, isn't that right, An?"

57

My sister nods, as Christine points out that she's hardly eaten.

Annie apologises, "I um, I don't feel too well."

"Oh, maybe we shouldn't talk so much about what happened?"

"It's ok." Annie shakes her head. "I'm ok."

11pm. Anna:

Christine wasn't going to let us, but Tommy insisted that we helped to clear the dishes. We left shortly after, and have been on the road for just over an hour.

"Do you want some music on?" I ask, but Tommy just bites his lip and shakes his head.

"That selfish prick!" He snarls, slamming his fist against the wheel. "He fancied himself a sailor, took their yacht and got himself killed, and the worst part, Annie! The worst fucking part," he shouts, as bitter tears roll down his face, "he killed Mum too!"

I don't like this. I don't know what to do, so I gingerly lay my hand on his shoulder.

"I'm ok, Annie," he moves my hand away, but gives it a reassuring squeeze, "I'm ok."

It's probably not a good time to tell him, that my insides feel like they're wrapped in barbed wire, and it's tightening.

"Tom?" I ask, "um…how far's Calais?"

"About nine hours, but we'll stop in two. I've booked us a hotel, and there'll be plenty of time, as the last ferry doesn't leave until quarter-to-ten tomorrow night."

"And after that?"

"We should reach Dover around midnight, then we'll find a hotel on the M20. On Thursday, I'll drive straight home."

"Ok." I tell him, as I lay my head back and close my eyes.

Two Hours Later.
May 25, 2016 Wednesday 1.30am.
Tommy:

When we step into our hotel room, Annie rushes to the bathroom. I kick off my shoes and fall back along one of the beds. As I stare up to the ceiling, I replay everything that Gerald said. I wish I knew what Mum thought when Dad told him that he could sail. She certainly wouldn't have challenged him in public, that's for sure. Although, I can't understand why she would step onto that boat…unless she went under the pretence that they were all going. Now I'll never know.

20 Minutes Later.
Anna:

"Annie?" Tommy calls from outside the bathroom door, "are you alright?"

I want to say yes, but I'm not. I've been throwing up since we arrived. It's just bile now, but it's relentless and the pain's unbearable.

"I'm sorry, Tom." I sob into the toilet, "I'm sorry for everything."

"Can I come in?" He asks.

"Yeah."

"Oh, Annie." He kneels down beside me and rubs my back. It's nice, everything else hurts but that bit of warmth is soothing. "Let me run you a bath, it might help?"

I nod and he turns on the taps. I want to tell him that I can't be bothered with a bath. My energy level's hit rock bottom and, I know he's looking after me, but I just want to go to bed.

"Ok, An." He says, drying his hands. "That's on, I'll just be out there, ok?"

"Thanks."

The moment I lie back in the tub, tiredness hits me with a thud. The warmth of the water is helping with the pain, but I can't keep my eyes open, no matter how hard I try. It's no use. I have to sit up, but as I pull myself forward, all the muscles in my belly and lower back clamp down hard. A cloud of blood flushes from between my legs. At first, I don't register what's happening, then with another movement comes another gush. I'm now petrified.

"Tommy!" I yell from the pit of my stomach, as it happens again and again, "help!"

He bursts in, sees the sheer amount of blood in the bath, and all the colour drains from his face.

"Please don't be sick, Tom."

Swallowing hard he grabs a towel, lifts me from the tub and wraps it around me.

"I'm sorry! I'm so sorry." I cry. Fresh blood drips to the floor, as I stagger to the toilet.

"It's ok." He coughs. Grabbing more towels, he kneels in front of me and scrubs me dry. "I'm taking you to a hospital."

"No! I'm losing the baby, I don't need a hospital, I just want to go home."

"Look at yourself! You can't eat, you can barely drink, you're in agony and now you're bleeding! You have to."

All I can do is sob, while he takes my pyjamas from my bag and proceeds to dress me like he did when we were kids. I plead and beg him again to just take me home, but he refuses.

"I can't go to a foreign hospital, what if they don't let you stay? And what if they keep me there for days? This isn't happening...Please!" I grasp the collar of his T-shirt with both hands. "Don't make me go here. Take me to our hospital, at home."

"No!"

"Tommy...Tom, please!"

"Oh, alright!" He snaps. "But I'm not happy about this."

60

I throw myself forward to hug him, then feel a searing pain, as I pass a clot the size of a golf ball. We stare at each other. He's horrified, and we're both frightened, but he pulls me close. For the longest time, I cling tightly to him, hiding my face in his hair.

Tommy:

"Come on," I tell her, "you can't stay on the toilet."

Annie reluctantly loosens her arms from around my neck, and looks down to her blood stained thighs.

"There's sanitary stuff there," she says, pointing to her travel bag, "I always keep it in there…can you pass it?"

"Sure." I hand it over, then go back in the room while she cleans herself up. My head's flooded. As soon as she told me that she'd had sex, I should've taken her to a clinic. Why the hell didn't I? Instead I took her for a bloody drive-through. I could've easily got her some emergency contraception, and none of this mess would've ever happened.

"Tom?" She says softly, as she shuffles from the bathroom. She's shivering, but we're in the south of France, at the end of May. It's far from cold. I help her into bed, but I need to know she's ok, before I even think of going to sleep, so I sit on the floor beside her.

"I'm here," I say. "Listen, when we get to Dover, I'll take you straight to our hospital. I'm not gonna stop for the night."

"When will you sleep?"

"On the ferry. And I'll sleep now, then we'll set off around ten-thirty in the morning. We're not due at Calais till nine-ish tomorrow night, and we should arrive at Dover by midnight. Then I'll tank myself up with coffee and put my foot down. All being well, we'll get there in around five hours."

11.40pm. Approaching Dover.
Anna:

Tommy woke me a few minutes ago. I've been sleeping for well over an hour, but it doesn't feel like two minutes since we boarded the ferry.

"Come on." He says softly, as my eyes adjust to the glare of the lounge lights. "We're almost there."

In the night, at the hotel, I couldn't get comfortable. In agony, I twisted and tangled myself in the duvet until I eventually fell asleep, but not for long. Something felt wrong, warm at first then cold. The sheets were sticky, so I kicked them away and knocked the bedside light on. My bed looked like the scene of a murder, I had to wake Tommy. I felt so guilty, because I knew he had a seven hour drive ahead, but I had no choice.

"Did you get some sleep?" I ask.

"A bit," he nods, holding out his hand, "can you sit up?"

I lean forward and feel another rush of blood fill my pad. I whisper that I need the toilet again, so he lets me hold his arm, while helping me to the ladies.

This is what today has been, an agonising blur of sickness and toilet stops. The bleeding's so heavy that at one stop he helped me to the toilets, then had to run to the shop, to buy me more leggings and pants.

It's hard to even stand, has been since we reached Calais. The dull ache, gripping my belly and lower back is bad enough, but I remember trying to get out of the car, and feeling it spread to my thighs. What's most unnerving is this new burning sensation, like I'm being skewered from my vagina through to my bottom.

"When you're done in there," he says as I reach the toilets, "call the hospital. Tell them everything."

"What? Even these new pains?"

"Yes, Annie. Everything."

Six and a Half Hours Later.
May 26, 2016 Thursday 6am.
James Cook University Hospital.
Tommy:

"Damn it, Annie!" I lift her arm around my neck as we stumble over the car park, and through to the entrance. "I should've just taken you to hospital in France!"

I help her along a corridor, towards the women and children's department. She's getting worse. I don't know if it's the pain, or because she's so weak, but she can hardly weight bear now.

It was optimistic to think I could get her here in five hours, what with all the toilet stops and speed cameras. Thankfully, once we were further north there weren't as many. So, I put my foot down. I'm sure the dial hit one-hundred for a while, but the road was wet and dicey. I had to pull it back. That was when the tiredness hit. As soon as I slowed down, my eyes were closing, and a few times I drifted into the other lane. The only way to stay awake was to open all the windows, not my best driving, but I got her here.

Inside, I give my sisters details to a nurse, who picks up some papers and leads us into an examination room.

"I'm Karen." She says, as I lie Annie down.

"I'm her brother, Tom."

"Can you just confirm again, this is Annalee Anderson? Date of birth, fifth of February, two thousand?"

"Yes!" I snap, "I've just told you that."

She ignores me and continues to scribble on the form.

"I'm sorry," I sigh, as I hold Annie's hand. "Please! My sister's not well, I need you to help her."

"I will, but first I need some details."

I relay our address, Annie's medical history and a whole host of seemingly irrelevant information.

"Thank you," she says, "as she's only sixteen, I'll need to speak to a parent."

"I'm her guardian…look! We're pretty sure she's having a miscarriage, and she was doing ok, but now she can hardly keep her eyes open. Will you just help her? Give her something for the pain?"

"I'm sorry, to confirm a miscarriage I must scan her, but I'll need her consent."

Anna:

Everything's blurry, but I can feel my brother beside me.
"Where am I?" I ask.

"In the hospital," he says, sweeping my hair aside. "This is Karen, she wants to scan you."

"Is that ok, Annalee?" She asks, looking down to me.
I nod.

"Anna," Tommy says, "call her Anna."

"Anna?" She smiles, "I need you to lower your leggings a touch."

I nod, but as I slide them down, I feel the familiar sensation of a pool gathering in my knickers. Instinctively, I touch them. They're thick with blood, and I'm helpless. I'm at the mercy of this woman, who's now pressing the cold scanner so hard, that it takes my breath.

"You're definitely miscarrying," she says, after a few painful minutes, "but it's difficult to get a clear image, I'm afraid I need to…" She mutters something, but I keep slipping. I'm in free fall, only jolted back by my brother's anxious voice.

"And what exactly does that involve?" He nudges me, so I force myself awake, then stare in horror at the precariously long instrument in the nurse's hand.

"Anna, I need to place this in your vagina. It will show me what's happening at the neck of your womb."

I'm petrified.

She lays the instrument back on the scanning unit, and hands me a blanket.

"If you could take everything off from the waist down," she says, "and I'll wait outside."

Tommy follows her to the door, but I can't do this myself. The pain's excruciating now, and I can't even lean forward.

"Tom wait! Please I…help."

He rushes back and kneels beside me, grabbing my hand. "It's ok," he whispers, pressing his forehead to mine, "you're ok." I can't tell if he's convincing himself or me, but he helps me. We lay the blanket over me, and reaching underneath, he holds my clothes at my hips.

"Don't look will you?" I sob.

"Of course I won't." He closes his eyes, as he shimmies them down to my ankles, then kneels back on the floor by my head.

"She's ready." He calls, then the nurse hurries back in and puts on a fresh pair of gloves. I close my eyes.

"Now, lovely." She sings. "Bend your knees and let your legs fall apart."

I squeeze Tommy's hand, as she pushes it deep inside. She tells me to relax but she's piercing my insides. For so long, I silently beg her to stop.

"Well done." She says, eventually pulling that thing out of me. "That's much clearer, yes the miscarriage is proceeding normally, and it shouldn't cause any problems." Then she whispers something to Tommy, and I fall back asleep.

Tommy:

"I appreciate that you're worried," Karen says, as she washes her hands. "But that amount of blood is normal."

"Normal?"

"Yes." She dries her hands and opens the door. "Right, I'll just grab an ob's trolley."

"More tests?" I ask.

"Not invasive tests, and I can do them while she rests."

I nod and stroke Annie's head, as she mumbles that she wants to go home.

"I know, sweetheart." I tell her. "Soon."

Not long after, Karen backs a trolley into the room. With my permission, she places a clip on Annie's finger, wraps the BP monitor around her arm, and checks her temperature. After a moment, she checks the results.

"Ok, right," she says, talking into her notes, "Anna's BP and Sat's are low. I think with the amount of sickness, it'll be best if we keep her in. We can give her some IV fluids and make her comfortable. Just give me a minute to call the children's ward, that way you can stay with her."

"Thank you."

"Don't thank me yet, they might not have a bed." And with that, she hurries out.

The next few minutes feel like an hour. As I pace the floor, the sun shines through the blinds in the window. It's almost seven-thirty.

"Good news," Karen says, bursting back in, "they have a bed."

Later, when Annie's been transferred to the ward. Two girls in uniform wash and change her. They make her comfortable, place an oxygen tube under her nose, and fit a cannula into her hand, before hooking her up to a drip.

"Jackie will be in, in a minute." One of them says, as she hands me a plastic bag, filled with Annie's dirty clothes. "She's the nurse who'll be looking after her."

"Ok, thank you."

In less than a minute, a woman of military precision marches into the room.

"I'm Jackie." She says, flicking through Annie's notes. "So, this is Annalee, prefers to be called Anna?"

"Yeah, she hates her full name." I must sound pathetic, or exhausted, but I find myself telling her everything, from Mum and Dad's accident to all that's happened over the past two days.

"I'm sorry," she says, "you must've been awfully worried."

I nod to Annie, who's fallen back asleep. "Yeah, and she was panicking. It was the middle of the night, and I did mention going to a French hospital, but she freaked. I promised to bring her here. I know it was the wrong decision, but I had to calm her down."

"Well, she's here now." She nods. "I'll give her something to stop the sickness and a painkiller." She points behind me, to a folded 'put up' bed and offers me a pillow.

"If you just set that up beside her, I'll pop the lights off, and you can both get some sleep." She then points to a narrow door, by the entrance. "The toilet's just in here, and there's a family room just where you came in, you can make a tea or coffee."

"Thank you." I nod, as she leaves the room.

8.30am. Leanne:

Of all the days I could've been late, it had to be when Jackie's in charge. She's going to give me every shitty job imaginable now, I know it. I skirt through the swarms of invalids, to the stairs and up to the children's ward. And who's waiting for me when I burst through the doors? Jackie.

"Hello!" She scoffs, "nice of you to join us."

I apologise profusely, but she's having none of it.

"Save the excuses, Leanne. This is the third time in as many weeks, you'll not be a student much longer and this won't stand…anyway," she sighs, "there are no new patients, other than the girl in room two. She's miscarrying. Poor girl's had a difficult time, she's extremely lethargic, hypotensive and tachycardic. Her ob's are due, so could you start with her when you do your rounds?"

"Sure. What's her name?"

"Anna Anderson."

I know that name, my ex had a sister called Anna…no it can't be her, can it?

"Leanne?" Jackie clicks her fingers, "is there a problem?"

What am I thinking? It won't be, Anna's a common name and so is Anderson for that matter.

"No." I smile. "No problem at all."

She hurries off towards the nurses' station, but my feet are glued to the spot. I take a few seconds to convince myself that it's not her, then hurry along for an ob's trolley. Luckily my friend, Emma is returning one. We've been friends since starting college, and she always listens to my dramas.

"Em!" I whisper urgently. "What do you know about the girl in room two?"

"Doesn't say much." She shrugs. "Her brother brought her in through the night. Why?"

"Her brother? Not her mum?"

She nods. "I heard him telling Jackie, their parents died, so he's her guardian. Why? What's wrong?"

I want to pretend that I'm fine, that it can't be them. But if it is, and Ellen's dead, then there's no way he'd leave Anna. He'd be here now, for sure.

"Lea?" She says. "What's wrong?"

"Do you know her brother's name?"

"Tom."

I feel a chill creep over me, and shudder as I remember the hate in his voice, when he told me to fuck off.

"Em. You have to do her ob's for me."

"Why? What's going on?"

"I think he's Tommy."

Her jaw drops. "What? THE Tommy?"

"Yes! THE Tommy."

"I'm on it." She takes the trolley and hurries to room two, but intrigue gets the better of me. I haven't seen him in over four years, so I scuttle along behind her and hover in the doorway. Emma's careful not to wake her. She signals to me that he's asleep too, so I tiptoe over. He looks so old.

Around his eyes are red and puffy, he gets like that when he's stressed or tired, I used to find it cute. The beard's new. Well, it's not a long beard, more like stubble that hasn't had a trim in a few days. I shouldn't have cheated, it wasn't worth it. He's beautiful, and we were good together. Yes, I came second to his precious 'little Annie,' but maybe I should've kept his baby, then he'd have loved something more than her. That's stupid thinking, he didn't even want it.

Emma records her readings and, without disturbing them, we both scurry out. I'll be avoiding this room for the rest of the day.

May 30, 2016 Monday 4pm. Home.
Anna:

Sometime on Thursday, I woke up on the ward, to find Tommy sleeping on a put-up bed next to me. I know we'd only arrived in the early hours that morning, but for some irrational reason I was frightened. I had this stupid thought that even if I were to get better, they would keep me there. I was hooked up to a drip, had a pipe blowing oxygen up my nose and a cannula in my hand. I wanted to rip it all out, and run away. A pointless and stupid fear, because they discharged me the very next morning. It turns out, that they just wanted to see me keeping food and drink down.

Since I've been home, I've hardly left my bedroom, it's awful. When I'm in bed I can't get comfortable, and when I walk around, I feel as though my insides could fall out. But it's not just the physical pain, although I do think that would get better if I could push myself a bit more. What's really bothering me, is that I don't feel like me any more. I don't actually know who 'me' is. It's like I'm old and vulnerable, I noticed this when Becca came over yesterday. When she wasn't battering my head with gossip, she was crying because I'd 'lost the baby.' It was exhausting, convincing her that I'm upset too. She thinks I'm not bothered because I'd considered an abortion. She's wrong. I'm lonely, lying

69

here on my own. I know Tommy would sit with me if I asked him, but staying in bed is just making me feel worse. So, holding my belly, I push myself up and shuffle down to the lounge.

Tommy leaps off the sofa the moment I open the door. He takes hold of my hand, and I don't know if it's exhaustion or hormones, but I feel a cry working its way up my throat.

"I didn't hear you come down," he says, "do you need anything?"

"I need a hug."

"That I can do."

He sits down in the corner of the sofa, and I lie along the side under the window, resting my head on his chest. This is nice, but it doesn't last. After a few minutes, we hear a determined knock from the front door.

"Wait here." He says, as he gets up to answer it.

The parting wall, between our lounge and the front door is thin enough for me to hear Tommy say 'Hello.' Whoever's there sounds vaguely familiar. Intrigued, I pull myself up and step into the hallway.

"Alex, not now." I cry, as I find the cause of so much of my recent trauma, stood at my front door, grinning.

"You!" Tommy snarls, as he steps out onto the path, clenching his fists. "You've got some balls, showing up here!"

"I just want to talk." Alex says, but Tommy's not interested.

"Why would she want to talk to you?"

He doesn't answer, just looks past him and straight at me. We're all locked in a stand-off that could end badly. My brother's ready to punch him in the face, but I compose myself and remember that it's not all Alex's fault. He's an idiot, but he doesn't know what I've been through. So, with a deep breath I step forward and touch Tommy's arm.

"It's alright," I say, "I'll talk to him."

"You sure?"

"Yeah."

Tommy nods, then waits in the kitchen, and I ask Alex into the lounge. He follows me inside, but just stands in the centre of the room, with his hands shoved in his pockets.

"You should've told me you're pregnant." He says, as I awkwardly perch on the edge of the sofa. "I have a right to know."

It's an instant blow to the gut, like I've been hit by a speeding train.

"I…I'm not pregnant." I stutter.

"That's not what Becca said. Don't lie, Anna. It's my baby!"

"I'm telling the truth!" I persist. "I've lost the baby! That's why I'm off school." My face burns, and my pulse is racing, but he just stares at me like I'm a freak. Then I see Tommy emerge from the doorway.

"It's time you fucked off!"

Alex doesn't argue. He leaves, but he makes sure that he slams the door behind him.

"It was Becca, Tom. She told him."

"Annie." He says gravely. "Call her. Go on, and I'll make a cuppa." He leaves the room and I just stare at my phone. Becca knew that I didn't want anyone knowing, especially Alex. I don't even know what to say to her, but I call, and she answers straight away.

"Hey, An. How're you feeling?"

"I…"

"You'll never guess what happened today! Chloe got her lunchtime pass confiscated!"

"Becca, please! I don't care about Chloe. I just need to know something."

"Hang on, An. Don't you want to know why?"

"Not really, I need to know something."

"Well," she sings triumphantly, "I'm going to tell you, because you WANT to know!"

"Fine." There's no point in arguing with her, not when she's in this mood.

"Mrs. Clarkson overheard Sophie taking the piss, because you're off again. She told her off but then Chloe started too. Everyone was laughing, An. Everyone."

"What? In room thirty-five?"

"Yes. Keep with the program. Anyway, I'm sorry, but I said you'd been in hospital and she turned all nasty, saying you're in a mental hospital. We had a proper massive argument, it was wild! Anyway, Mrs. Clarkson kicked her out and took her pass for a week. I'm not talking to her now, I did that for you, An."

"Err thanks."

"It's cool, so what do you wanna know?"

"I um…Alex has just been here. He knew, Bec. He knew about the baby."

"I'm so sorry, An. He was on one today. I don't know what you did to him, but you're all he talks about. Anyway, he wouldn't stop asking questions, and I accidentally told him that it was his fault you're in this mess. Don't worry, no-one heard, but he figured it out straight away and ran off. I didn't think he'd show up at your house."

"I…I guess you didn't mean to tell him. But he…he knew where I live."

"Well that wasn't me!" She snaps. "It must've been Sophie, she knows your address."

I hadn't thought of that. Sophie's friends with Alex, and she lives on our estate, it must have been her. I really hope he hasn't told her, or anyone else about the baby.

"Look, I'm sorry, Bec, but I don't feel good. I have to go."

"It wasn't me." She insists.

"I know, I'm just tired."

We say goodbye, then I shuffle through to the kitchen and relay Becca's story to Tommy.

"What do you think?" I ask, as he hands me a tea.

"Sounds plausible, but you know I don't trust her." He then presses his weight against the work surface, letting out a huge sigh.

"What is it?" I ask.

"Nothing."

I don't believe that. He's tense, and no-matter how hard I try, he avoids eye-contact.

"Tommy?" I say, touching his arm.

"Have you told me the whole truth?"

"Whole truth? About what?"

"The party, An. Is there anything that you're not telling me?"

My heart sinks. I don't lie, and especially not to him. This question hurts me, and he knows it.

"No," I whisper, "I'd never lie to you."

He pushes his hands into his hair, pressing hard against his scalp. "I know that. That's what makes this whole thing weird. You told me that you don't remember it?"

"Yeah?"

"Think, An. What's the last thing you do remember?"

"It's hazy, but I was dancing. I'd finished a drink, so someone gave me another."

"And that's the last thing you remember?"

I nod.

"Annie, you must've been wasted! He shouldn't have even touched you. As far as I'm concerned that's practically rape!"

All the air's knocked from my lungs. I've been pelted by that train again, so I stagger back to the lounge and lower myself onto the sofa. Tommy follows and sits at my feet.

"What do I do?" I ask.

"Let me kill him." He's deadly serious but, as I stare at him in disarray, he flashes an unwilling smile. "In truth I don't know. I don't know what to make of this, something's not right…"

"Stop talking, Tom."

He nods and folds his arms over his knees. My mind's firing out questions, but I don't want to answer any of them. I look down to Tommy, who's just staring at me, he wants to talk and figure it all out. I know he does, but I can't. I wish Alex had never come here.

11pm. Tommy:

Maybe rape was too strong a word. After I'd said that, Annie went on shutdown. She played with my hair for a while then took herself to bed. I offered to go up and sit with her, but she just shook her head. She's not been back down since, and I'm restless. The last thing I wanted to do was scare her, but everyone knows, if a girl's that far gone then you just don't.

My head's all over the place, I keep thinking of things from years ago. I know this is a totally different situation, but once I'd turned ten, Mum would lock us in the house and go out for the night. It's funny, she'd only let me take Annie as far as the local park, but thought nothing of leaving us home alone. Those nights I had to be strong, I couldn't let Annie know that I was frightened, because she was scared too. She was only five, and the house was huge. The boiler sounded like a jet engine. Well, it probably wasn't that loud, but for two little kids it was terrifying. We'd hide in my room, she'd curl herself up, and I'd pull the duvet over us and cuddle her in.

I feel like that ten-year-old boy again. I can't rest. So, before going to bed, I check on Annie. She's asleep, so for a minute or two, I sit on the floor beside her. This past week has changed everything, it's time for me to man up and be whatever she needs. The cool big brother isn't enough any more. As the minutes slip by, I feel my eyes closing, but I can't leave her. So, I pull the spare pillow to the edge of the mattress. It's a bit uncomfortable but it's my best chance of getting any sleep tonight.

May 31, 2016 Tuesday 7.30am.
Anna:

We often keep the patio door open, sometimes just a little. But today, the sky's a lovely hazy blue. So, I slide the door wide, throw my hoody on over my pyjamas and take my mug of tea outside. Before we went to France, Tommy bought a new patio set for the garden. It's solid oak and wrought iron, the chair's heavy, and it makes a loud screech as I drag it over the paving stones.

Shielding my screen from the sunlight, I check my phone. There's a missed call from Becca, and a long text from an unsaved number.

"Anna it's Alex
Can we talk?
Away from your psycho brother."

How am I supposed to answer that? Tommy's no psycho, he was quite restrained considering.

I ignore him for now and call Becca.

"Anna," she says, "I thought you weren't talking to me."

"Course I am. Yesterday was just…well Alex turning up and knowing everything, I wasn't prepared."

"I know yeah. So, have you got a dress yet? You need one, it's like three weeks tomorrow!"

"What is?"

"The prom. Tell me you're still going?"

I've been so overrun with the accident and everything, that I'd completely forgot about the prom.

"Yeah," I sigh, "I'm still going, I gave you my word, didn't I?"

"Yes, you did. So, what're you doing today?"

"Tommy's working at the theatre this afternoon. I'll probably go with him."

"You remember last Halloween?" She laughs, "when he made us look like we had a flesh eating disease?"

"Yeah, that was so much fun."

It's strange how my brother can create gruesome effects, but he's sick when faced with actual blood. A sobering thought, considering how he's looked after me. I mean, that bath alone was like a crime scene.

Becca keeps talking, but it's so fast now that I can hardly focus. I just keep dwelling on what Tommy said last night, about Alex.

"Becca," I interrupt. "I don't feel right about what happened at your party. What do you think? Because I can't figure it out."

"There's nothing to figure out," she groans, "if you went to more parties you'd know. Listen! You were pissed, he was pissed, and you had sex. Everyone does it, it's no big deal. You need to get out the house, come and stay at mine tomorrow night?"

"I can't, I um…I'm still bleeding."

"So? You've stayed when you've been on, what's the difference?"

"Bec, I…"

"Anna, you're staying. You can't hide away forever."

I hate this. I wish I could just say no, but as I stutter, I find myself saying ok.

"Great," she chirps, "see ya tomorrow." And just like that, she's gone. Then I hear Tommy rummaging around in the kitchen.

"You eaten yet?" He calls out.

"Not yet, I've just got a drink."

"D'ya want some toast?"

"Yeah, not cremated though."

"I know." He laughs.

My brother likes his toast in a very specific way. He says it's a perfect balance of blackened on the outside and fluffy in the middle. To make it right he uses the grill, and he always lets it go cold before putting any butter on.

A few minutes later, he brings himself a mug of coffee outside. He sets it on the table before going back in for the toast.

"Thanks," I say, as he hands me my plate. "I've just been talking to Becca."

"Oh yeah, and what pearls of wisdom did she give you today?"

"Where do I start?"

He takes a large bite of toast, brushes the ash like crumbs from his lap and says, 'the beginning.'

"Well, it's our prom in three weeks and I've got nothing to wear. Oh, I may have agreed to stay at hers tomorrow night and…"

"And what?"

"You know what you said about the party and…Alex?" I pause for a second, hoping he'll stop me and say he was just being over-protective. He doesn't, he nods and says, 'go on.'

"Becca thinks I need to get over it."

"Annie, you know how I feel about Becca bloody Clark. Now, what exactly have you told her?"

"I didn't use the 'R' word, I just said that it didn't feel right, and I need to figure it all out."

"Ok," he says softly, "please don't tell her any more than that." He then takes a gulp of coffee. "So, tomorrow, what time do you want me to take you over there?"

"I don't want to go."

"Then don't go." He says with an impassive shrug.

"I've agreed now, I have to."

"You don't have to do anything, but it's your choice."

For the next few minutes we're silent; not an uncomfortable silence, quite the opposite. I smile to him as the birds whistle in the trees. I do feel churned though, like the morning after a storm; everything's still but littered with debris.

"Was I crying?" I ask, as I stare at a blob of butter, melting on my toast.

"When?"

"Last night, when you slept in my room."

"No, I just didn't want to leave you."

"Oh…thank you."

"You're welcome."

It was actually the best night's sleep I've had since the accident. I always wake up through the night, and him being there, just made it so much easier to fall back asleep, but it's been years since I've needed him like that.

"So," I say, changing the subject, "what do I do about a prom dress?"

"If you're feeling up to it, we could go to the Metro Centre in the morning."

The Metro Centre's a large shopping mall in Gateshead, about an hour's drive away.

"I'd like that." I know it's ambitious, but I doubt it'll be busy on a Wednesday. And if we're only going to one or two shops, I'm sure I can pace myself.

12.45pm. The Theatre.
Tommy:

The show doesn't start until three, but backstage is buzzing. So, as Stu and I work, Annie sits in the narrow gap between our stations. Stu's a very good friend of mine; he's as camp as Christmas and not always taken seriously, but behind the panache, he's one of the most level-headed people I know.

When we arrived, before setting out a single styling tool, he took my sister's hands and kissed her cheek.

"Hello, little lady," he said, flicking his platinum college-boy hair from his eyes; "I do hope my Tom's looking after you?"

It's funny, her instant answer was that I am, but I can't help but feel like I'm screwing it up.

"Anna's got her prom in a few weeks." I tell him, as I finish with the girl I'm working on.

"Yeah," Annie says, "we're dress shopping tomorrow."

78

"What colour are we going?"

"Black, I guess."

"No, no, no!" He shrieks. "You're so fair, your complexion would be waisted in anything other than pastels." He then takes a step back, tilts his slender hips and hums. "I'm thinking baby pink, or a very soft green. Obviously, you'll have to complement with your make-up."

Annie looks worried and shakes her head. "I can't do make-up; I'll mess it up."

Stu smiles and hangs his arm over my shoulder. "Sweetie! You live with an *artiste!* Utilise him."

"Sure, I'll do it," I smile, "if that's what she wants."

Annie nods, and Stu takes a bow. Bloody drama queen.

Anna:

If I'm going all out on my dress and make-up, then I should probably do something with my hair too. So, I ask for Stu's opinion, and before I know it, he's pulling me to my feet and teasing my bobble free. He runs his hands through my hair, studying every strand as it falls.

"Well I must say, it needs chopping! What you want are layers and lots of them. I'm free tomorrow night, I'll be happy to come over?"

I so want to say yes, but I said I'd go to Becca's. I guess I could have my hair done, and go to Becca's after.

"Is that alright, Tom?" I ask.

"Course it is, daft arse. You don't need my permission."

Over the next hour or so, the room gets busier and busier. This heavy wooden chair, where Tommy's sat me down, is hard and uncomfortable. My belly's cramping. I need to walk around, but I'm stuck amongst a buzzing hive of actors and backstage staff. They're all weaving around in a high paced yet tranquil flow. I'd be in the way, so I figure it's best if I just go to the toilet.

The ladies' is little more than a cupboard. A tiny hand basin sits next to the toilet, with a dirty mirror on the wall above. I change yet another sodden pad, and for a while, I just sit and watch the drops burst into the water like tiny red clouds. I'll need plenty of painkillers, if I'm going to get through tomorrow.

"Gotten yourself into quite a mess, haven't you?" Sneers a distant voice. Sounds like it came from behind the wall, probably a room next door. I guess the actors have to rehearse wherever they can.

"Really, Annalee?" The same voice growls. Ok, now I'm panicking. Heart pounding, I jump up from the toilet, and quickly pull up my pants and jeans. I'm about to reach for the door, when I hear.

"Don't you run away from me, young lady!"

Releasing my fingers from the rough brass door handle, I turn and gaze upon the mirror. My reflection is covered by a layer of condensation. Pulling my sleeve over my hand, I wipe the water away, to reveal the bitter face of my mother.

"You silly girl." She scoffs. "You've done some stupid things but to get yourself pregnant? Did you not think of the pressure this puts on your brother? You, darling…are a selfish, little cow!" She moves from edge to edge, within the confines of the mirror, flitting between sarcasm and sheer disdain. "Do Thomas a favour, let him live his life. Overdose if you must, rid him of the burden that you are!"

"I'm sorry," I shout, "I'm sorry!"

Waves lash against her, reducing her to dust. I have to get out. Pressing down the handle, I push the door with all my might, but it doesn't budge, not even an inch. My pulse races, I sweat with fear, my hand slips from the handle.

"No!" I cry. The walls are closing in. I can't breathe. Over and over I slam my body against the door, then with a terrified roar I pull. The door flies open, and I crash back against the basin. I can't escape quick enough, and throwing myself out of the door, I almost knock a stage-hand off his feet.

"Tommy!" I call, rushing towards him.

He drops his brushes and grabs my arms. "What? What's wrong?"

"Sweetie!" Stu gasps. "You look like you've seen a ghost!"

My eyes dart between them and I beg Tommy for the car keys.

"What's happened?" He repeats.

"I saw something! Please." I try to pull away, but he doesn't let go and I cry, "please!"

"You're ok, Annie." He says, holding me way too tight. "Nothing's gonna hurt you here."

June 01, 2016 Wednesday. Home.
Tommy:

Since we're going out early in the morning, I figured I'd have an early night. It's now 2am and I'm still wide awake, I can't switch off, or stop replaying what happened with Annie at the theatre. She seemed fine, then for some reason it all went wrong. All I could get out of her was that she saw something, but when I asked her what, she just reminded me that she'll never lie, but begged me not to ask. No-matter how many times I punch the air from these pillows, I can't get comfortable. Great, now I need a piss.

Once I've used the bathroom, I see my sister's door is open. A dim light shines from inside and there's movement.

"Are you alright?" I call to her.

"Not really."

"Can I come in?"

"Yeah."

As I step in, she shuffles upright and moves over, so I can sit beside her.

"Can't sleep either?" I ask.

She shakes her head.

"Is it what you saw at the theatre?"

She doesn't answer me. She just lays her head on my shoulder, so I leave it for now and rest my head on hers.

81

"I just don't feel right, Tom. Plus, it doesn't help when I get sent these in the middle of the night."

She hands me her phone; the screen's full of messages from an unsaved number.

"U talkin' to me yet?
You know, I
loved fucking you.
Anna?
Annaaaaaaaaaaaaa?
I'm not going away."

"If you scroll," she says, "there's more from yesterday. I don't know what to do."

"I know what I'd like to do! I'd love to break his face."

"Please, don't…"

I swiftly turn to face her. "Why the hell are you protecting him?"

"I'm protecting you!" She rubs her temples and sighs, "Don't you see? You're twenty-one, he's sixteen. I know you, if you hit him once you won't stop. Then what?"

"Alright, alright, I'm going back to bed." I stand and give her the phone. "Look, just ignore him. Actually, turn your phone off and get some sleep."

"Tommy?" She says, as I move to the door. "Are you ok?"

"Yeah, get some rest."

11am. School.
Becca:

I hate French. I only chose the subject because Anna did, and now she's never here. So, I've started being friends with Isabelle Maltby, she usually sits alone but not any more, now she's got me. We sit on the back row, and Alex plonks himself on the seat in front, twisting around to talk to me.

"You heard from Anna?" He asks.

"Yeah, why?"

Isabelle leans forward to listen, giving him an eyeful. She's got like the biggest tits ever, and doesn't even bother hiding them. If I was that big, I'd wear a fourteen, but she doesn't. Issy insists she's a twelve like me, but her clothes are bursting at the seams, and you can always see her bra through her gaping blouse. Alex can't take his eyes off them, and she loves it. She smiles and flicks her wavy brown hair.

"I just wondered if she's still alive." Alex grins. "She's not answering my texts."

I do feel a bit sorry for him. Anna could at least text him back, even if it's just to tell him how she feels.

"You haven't said that I gave you her number, have you?"

"Nah."

"Good. What have you said to her, like?"

"Not much, I just asked her to talk to me…away from her psycho brother."

"You didn't call Tommy a psycho, did you?"

"Yeah," he laughs, "in a text."

"Oh, you've pissed her off. They're so close. She'll ignore you now, it's what she does…"

"What d'ya mean?" Isabelle interrupts.

"Yeah, Bec," Alex says, "what d'ya mean?"

"Don't say 'owt, but Anna shows him her texts, if she doesn't know what to say. He'll have told her to ignore ya… and she will."

"That's a bit fucked up," he huffs, "don't you think?"

"A bit, but I can't say anything. If I did, she'd take his side. I know it."

Alex flips a joker smile and starts to tell me something, but Mr. Torres claps his hands, ordering everyone to stop talking. Then, as Alex turns around, my phone vibrates. Obviously, I check it, but I'm super discrete. It's a text from Anna.

*"Stu's cutting my hair tonight,
I won't be at yours till 8.
Is that ok?"*

"Oh, is Anna staying at yours tonight?" Isabelle asks.

I was too busy replying to notice her looking over my shoulder. Alex turns and smiles but I'm not answering either of them.

**Lunchtime. Metro Centre.
Tommy:**

Of all the dresses Annie's tried on this morning, this one's the best; knee length, plunge neckline and diamanté waist. It's pastel green satin, under layers of chiffon with gathering to the straps. She holds back the curtain of the changing room, just as the assistant hands me a coffee. I'm speechless. My little sister's beautiful. Awkward but beautiful.

"Yes, Annie." I smile. "That's the one."

"Do you really like it?"

"Yes, I do."

She's never been comfortable in dresses, which is a crying shame as her legs were made for them. "You know, An. You'll need new shoes."

"It's ok, I'll just wear my black pumps, or maybe my white Converse?"

We both laugh as I shake my head. "Annie you *need* heels."

"We do have some beautiful low courts," says the assistant, "if you'd like to try those?"

"Yes, please." Annie says quietly.

"What size are we?"

"Three."

The lady hurries away, and I give Annie a hug. "You'll be fine in heels, trust me."

"I do…I'm just really tired now."

84

"I know, listen you're doing great. Besides, you're out with me and let's face it…I'm awesome."

"Daft arse." She laughs, giving my arm a playful slap.

"Nah." I wink. "You are."

Annie eventually chooses a pair of pale pink suede courts, and once she's changed back into her regular clothes, I take them to the till and pay.

"Slow down." She says, taking hold of my arm, as we head out and back through the mall.

"You alright?"

"I'm sore and, well I just…when we booked the prom, I went dress shopping with Becca and it was a disaster. I couldn't find anything and…"

"Hey, it's ok. You should let me dress you more often…I mean, pick your outfits."

She smiles and we head out towards the escalator.

Being a Wednesday, we both expected it to be quiet here; it's not. People keep bumping into her but she doesn't say anything. Annie isn't confrontational in the slightest, she just lowers her head and, as I step in front, she grabs my hand. She hates crowds, has done since the first time Mum let me take her into town on my own.

Annie had begged Mum to take her to the cinema, and to be honest, I think she only agreed that I could take her so she didn't have to. We were under strict instruction not to tell Dad. The bus journey took us twenty minutes, and I remember tucking her into the seat next to the window. She was so excited. Despite the cinema being ridiculously busy, Annie was fine as we took the escalator up to our screen. She did exactly as I asked and, even though she was nervous to be left alone, she stayed in her seat when I had to use the toilet. After the movie, we waited while the screen emptied, then I took her hand and made for the exit. A crowd of older kids were messing around at the top of the escalator.

"Stay behind me." I told her, as we weaved through, but when I reached the bottom and turned to take her hand again, she was gone. I was petrified and my heart thumped through my chest. I remember desperately pushing my way up the other escalator, screaming her name while some lads laughed as I barged past. I practically flew back down the other side to the ticket desk.

"I've lost my little sister!" I yelled. They were stunned at first, but I just kept screaming till they barred the doors and a lady sat me down. She wanted Annie's description.

"She's only seven." I cried.

"We need a bit more than that." She said.

"Her name's Anna. She's got blonde hair…it's straight." I described her clothes and it seemed to take forever.

"…And she's seven?"

"Yes," I said, "but she doesn't look seven. She's tiny!" Then I broke into tears.

"Come on, let's find her." She stood me up and, along with a team of staff, we searched every screen, the toilets, they even checked behind the 'staff only' doors. Eventually, I saw her, pressing her hands to her ears and her head to her knees, on the floor behind the popcorn stand. Adrenaline took over, and I grabbed her by the shoulders and shook.

"Why did you do that?! Don't ever hide from me again. D'ya hear me!" I remember shouting, as two of the staff prized my fingers from her arms. Only then, as I stepped back, I knew she hadn't been hiding. She cried so hard, I thought she was about to be sick. She wasn't sick but she had wet herself. I felt like the worst brother imaginable, so I stroked her face, and she threw her arms around my neck. I hugged her tight and promised never to lose her again.

We head up towards the car park, but Annie's slowing down. The first floor of the shopping centre is more of a balcony, with a barrier and handrail running all the way around. We stop for a minute, lean against the railing and look down to the ground floor.

"I'm hungry," she says, "can we get some lunch?"

"Sure, what d'ya fancy?"

"Dunno, burgers?"

"Ok," I say, pushing back off the barrier, "come on then."

We head down a thoroughfare into the food court. To our left, the seating is sectioned between the restaurants, so Annie takes the bags and finds a seat, while I order. As our food's being prepared, I grab us both a drink from the dispenser. I take them over, and Annie stares into her phone and sighs.

"You alright?" I ask.

"Yeah, it's just Becca. She wants me over earlier."

"Tough. Stu's doing your hair." I head over to the counter, grab the food and head back. "Honestly, An, she's lucky you're even going."

"I guess." Putting her phone away, she smiles, and we share out the food.

"I feel weird leaving you tonight."

"Don't worry about me, Rich's coming over. He's got a best man speech to write so I'm giving him a hand."

"Whose wedding?" She asks, taking a sip of juice.

"His cousin, Kevin. I've served him in the pub a few times and between me and you, he's a dick."

"So, he's not like Rich then?"

"Not in the slightest."

She smiles and tucks into her burger.

"It's nice to see you enjoying food again."

"It's lovely," she says, catching a couple of escaping shreds of lettuce, "and I was starving."

Later, when we've finished, I bag up the rubbish and shove it in the bin, before heading down a small corridor to the toilet.

On my way back I see her threading her way through the crowd, towards the centre of the mall.

"Annie!" I call, "wait up."

She can't hear me, so I grab the bags and jog after her.

"Excuse me, sorry, excuse me." I say, as I push my way through. The floor dips before reaching the centre, and it's there that I briefly lose sight of her. But a second later, I see her in the distance. She stops abruptly at the barrier, looks out over the drop to the ground floor and screams. Someone close by offers her their hand, but she just grabs the rail and lunges forward.

"SHIT!!" I shout. "SHE'S GOING OVER THE BARRIER!!"

Everyone side steps out of my way, as I cover the last few metres in seconds. I drop the bags and, just as she throws a leg over the top, I grab her and pull her towards me. It all happens so quickly that my feet slip out from under us, and we fall back to the floor. She scrambles back to the barrier, but I throw myself forward, locking my arms around her. I drop us both to the floor and like a wild animal, she kicks and fights against me.

"Calm down, Annie! It's me."

She strikes me hard across the face and shrieks.

"Please help," I beg, as onlookers move to intervene, "I can't let her go, she's not herself." I've no idea what I'm supposed to do, or how to fix this, so blocking out the noise, I press my forehead to hers.

"Look at me, Annie. Look at me." I repeat. "Please!" I don't know what else to do.

Anna:

When we've finished eating our burgers, Tommy bags up the rubbish.

"Right," he says, "I'll just pop to the loo, then we can head home."

I nod and watch the crowds of shoppers bumble past. There's the typical young family; mum stressing over the kids, and dad making matters worse by telling her to calm down. Then there's a couple holding hands, giggling as she tries to take something from her bag, but neither of them want to let go. I smile and turn to see if Tommy's on his way back, but he's not. When I turn back my heart stops. Everyone's staring at me. It's like a scene from a horror movie, the entire shopping centre is silent. Even the music's stopped and every single person is frozen. Their eyes are fixed on me, and I'm suddenly deafened by a tremendous bang from the centre of the mall. Drawn to it, I move gingerly, but some invisible force pulls me hard, and I pass through the human statues.

Another bang. The ground begins to crumble beneath my feet, so I run. I run down the ramp, crashing into the barrier, overlooking the ground floor. Above me, the glass roof creaks. Through it, a darkness appears as though the building has been submerged, plunged to the bottom of the ocean. It only takes a few seconds before the roof starts to yield. Like a fork of lightning, cracks splinter through the glass, and I scream with all my might as the tidal wave breaks through. But there's more, as I protect my head, I look down to the floor below, and see her standing there. Only for a second, then she herself is swept up by another enormous swell, this time rising from the ground. She reaches for me as the watery tornado swirls around my feet.

"Mum!" I scream, but it's too late. She's swept away, and I have to choose. Do I stand here and watch her die again, or save her? I have to save her. I don't know how, but I have to try. I push my body forward, climb onto the barrier and lift one leg over the top.

"I'm coming, Mum, just hold on!"

Something grabs me from behind and pulls me back, it starts crushing my chest to the point where I can't breathe. With every ounce of energy, I fight it off, but my strength wanes, and I see Mum falling further and further into the abyss, until she's gone for good. Everything's silent, silent and black.

As time stands still, I wonder if I'm alive or dead, but there's a gentle voice on the waves and warmth against my face. I rub the water from my eyes, but they're glued shut. Blindly, I concentrate on the voice, until my eyes can eventually open. I'm cradled in my brother's arms, and his forehead is pressed to mine.

Everyone's staring, then some woman, stooping over us, nods to Tommy and asks if he's hurting me.

"Of course I'm not!" He snaps.

I shake my head and hide my face in his chest, until she leaves us alone.

"What was that, Annie?" He asks.

I can't speak, where would I begin? How do I tell him that I'm losing my mind? I whisper 'sorry.' That's all I can say.

"Alright, sweetheart." He hugs me tight and breathes a sigh of relief. "It's alright."

3.30pm. At a Standstill on the A1.
Tommy:

As soon as Annie could stand, I got her out of that shopping centre and straight into the car. I've only just joined the A1, and the traffic's crawling. She's not stopped clutching her head since, and I'm left wondering what the hell just happened. All I know is that she must've seen some scary shit to try and throw herself over the barrier. For goodness sake, if I'd have been a few moments longer in the gents, I'd have been too late. I'd have got there right as her tiny body crashed onto the ground floor.

"Stop." She says, signalling that I've been drumming my fingers against the wheel. "My head hurts."

"Sorry."

The traffic creeps along a metre or two, and I fight the urge to tap by squeezing my fingers until the ends turn white.

"Hey," I say, gently nudging her arm, "talk to me."

A few seconds of silence pass as she keeps her face towards the window. But it's what she says next, that makes me realise that the problem is far bigger than I'd imagined. In little more than a gruff breath she says, 'you should have let me fall.'

"What the hell, An! Don't say shit like that!"

Burying her face in her hands, she bursts into tears. "It was Mum…Mum, Tommy!"

"You saw Mum again?"

"Yes!" She cries. "Yesterday, at the theatre. She told me that you'd be better off without me, that I should kill myself."

I can't believe what I'm hearing. I just sit there staring at her, mouth open like a dumb fish.

"She said you need to be free of me. Then back there, that was my opportunity…you should've let me fall!"

"Shut the fuck up!"

The traffic's not going anywhere, so I let go of the wheel and pull her to face me.

"I don't know what's going on inside your head, but that was not Mum! Yes, she was shit, but she knew what you mean to me! Answer me this, who have you always gone to after nightmares?"

"You."

"Yes, me. And only last week, when you were in hospital, did I leave your side? Have I ever not been there for you?"

"No."

"I just can't see how you'd think like that! I mean, I've never once pushed you away, have I?"

"No."

"Annie, you know what it was like, when we were kids. Yes, Mum was around, but it was me that made all your food, me that showed you how to dress yourself, me that held you when you were scared through the night. Me that practically brought you up. Me! Why? Because I fucking love you!"

"I love you too." She sobs. "Please help me."

"Have you forgotten?" I ask, giving her my hand. "How I asked if I could take you with me, when I bought the house? Would I have done that if I wanted to be free of you?"

"No, but why were you so desperate to move out? You were only eighteen."

"Precisely. Dad wanted me to stand on my own two feet." I drive a little further as the traffic begins to move. "You know, he laughed in my face? He said I could barely look after myself, let alone a thirteen-year-old girl. And don't you remember what I said to you?"

"I remember," she nods, "I am sorry."

"I know, Annie. I know."

She brings her feet up on the seat and presses her forehead to her knees.

"My head hurts, can you ask Stu to re-arrange?"

"Sure." I tell the car to call him and it only rings a few times before we hear his voice through the speakers.

"Mr. Anderson. To what do I owe this pleasure?"

"Hiya, mate. Sorry to mess you about but Anna's not well, any chance we could re-arrange?"

"I am sorry, Stu." Annie says softly.

"No problem. If you're still wanting it doing though, I'm free Saturday afternoon?"

"Thanks," I say, "that's great."

"Thank you." Annie adds.

"It's fine," he sings, "anyway, lovelies, got to go, I'm on my way out."

"See ya, mate. Thanks again."

Anna:

I've never hurt Tommy like that before, and the guilt's crushing me. After the next junction, the congestion's eased, and in silence he puts his foot down and weaves through the traffic. I want to talk to him, I have a ton of things to say but they're all tangled up like weeds in my head.

When we get home, I follow him into the kitchen, where he puts the bags on the table and kicks off his shoes. For more than a second, I look him in the eyes. I almost cry, I can feel it crawling up my throat, but I resist and swallow it back down. He strokes my cheek then goes into the lounge, I want to follow him but I just stand here, in the kitchen.

I do remember what he said, what he told me on the day before he moved into this house. I hated the thought of him leaving me. It was just going to be Mum and me, rattling

92

around that big house, and all talk of him moving out made me feel empty. He knew I was struggling, so he picked me up from school and drove us here. When he parked outside, I just sat and stared blankly at the front door. Until then I'd refused to go. Mainly because Mum or Dad were there, and I'd drown in the busyness of it all. But he'd made time to take me there alone. He led me along the hall into the cold, empty kitchen and gave me a keyring. It was a picture of us from a few years earlier. We'd been messing around in a passport booth; he was laughing, while I pulled a goofy face. Attached to it were two silver keys.

"These are yours." He said.

I didn't know what to say, my heart was breaking. Then he took me upstairs and across the landing, to the back bedroom.

"This isn't a spare room." He said. "It's your room, only yours. Annie, I want you to see this house as a second home. Let yourself in whenever you want."

I cried, then hugged him as hard as I could.

Now, holding the same keyring, I creep to the lounge and just look at him. He's lying along the sofa, eyes closed, ankles crossed and hands behind his head. He must have sensed that I'm there because he narrowly opens his eyes.

"I think I might be going crazy, Tom. I didn't mean what I…"

"Come here." He uncrosses his feet and opens his arms. So, I crawl over him and cuddle in.

"You're not crazy, little Annie," he says wrapping his arms around me, "you're just grieving."

I really hope he's right.

9.15pm. Becca's House.
Anna:

"You're late!" Becca bites as she opens the front door.

"I know, I'm so sorry. I was asleep, I only woke up at half past, and Tommy brought me straight over."

"Howay in then." She says, dragging a towel over her freshly washed hair. I follow her inside and straight up to her room.

I didn't mean to be late, and I honestly didn't feel like I'd been asleep that long. Neither did Tommy. We hugged on the sofa and, in what felt like a blink later, we both woke with a start. Rich was banging on the front door. By then it was almost half past eight.

Now, Becca's sat on her bed with her legs crossed, looking at me through pissed off eyes. I can't stand it when she's upset with me, sometimes I think it would be easier if she'd just shout and get it off her chest. She doesn't, she sulks. I don't actually think I could cope with her shouting at me right now anyway. So, I hover by the window and run my fingers over her new, silver curtains.

"Your room's nice, Bec."

"Thanks."

She's just had it decorated and it's lovely. The old pink and white wallpaper has been replaced with a shade somewhere between white and grey. The carpet is a bluey grey with hints of silver which when the light hits, look like specs of glitter.

For a few seconds, she stares at my hair and sucks the inside of her cheek. "Thought you were getting that cut?" She snarls, "that's why you weren't supposed to get here till eight!"

I don't know what to say. Tommy didn't want me to stay out tonight, and when we woke up so late, he said there was no point even going. He was right, but I haven't stayed for ages, and I didn't want to let her down. I felt so ill when I woke up, sickly and with that awful groggy taste that you get at the start of a cold. Even so, I had to come. Now I'm here, and she's waiting for an excuse. That's what it feels like anyway, and as the seconds tick by I flinch, my wrist burns. I've scratched too hard and broken the skin again.

"I'm sorry, Bec. I wasn't well so we re-arranged…then I only meant to lie down for a minute. Before I knew it, it was half past. Please?" I say again, lowering myself to the floor, "I'm sorry."

"So, what's going on?" She asks, unsympathetically, "is it your belly?"

"It still hurts but no, it wasn't that."

"What was it, then?"

How can I tell her? It feels like I'm about to pull open a wound, just for her to prod it. I wish I could lie, then I'd have just said that I was tired. That would be believable, after all I have just lost a baby, and today was my first 'big' outing since. I've backed myself into a corner now. So, I close my eyes, rest my head on my knees and just say it. I tell her what happened at the shopping centre. That's all I say though. Only Tommy can know about the suicidal thoughts.

"It was awful, Bec. I didn't know that it was Tommy pulling me down."

"What did he do?"

"He just held me."

A few awkward seconds pass, and I slide my head forward, to rest my chin on my knees. She's not even looking at me, she's picking away old nail varnish from her toes. Really, Becca? Really? I scream inside, not actually saying a word. This is what she'd do whenever I'd rant about Mum. How can she just sit there?

Eventually, she opens her mouth to speak but stops when we hear the doorbell ring. Instead of ignoring it, she leaps off her bed and hurries downstairs, closing her bedroom door behind her. I shouldn't have told her. Maybe this is a thing now, maybe my brain wants me to pretend that Mum and Dad are still here. But what if Becca tells someone that my 'one off' incident in school isn't actually a one off? I need to talk to Tommy, so I send him a text, a simple, 'love you.' He replies instantly.

"Are you ok?"

"I guess, are you busy?"

He doesn't reply again, instead calls me straight back.

"What's wrong?" He asks, the moment I answer.

"I should've stayed with you. You were right, why are you always right?"

"Aww, Annie," he says kindly, "I assure you I'm not."

"Yeah well, you were tonight."

"Do you want to come home?" He asks, "Should I call you a taxi? I'd come myself but I've had a drink."

A taxi home sounds so appealing right now, but if I did leave, then I just know Becca would fall out with me.

"I don't know what to do." I sigh.

"Just come home."

"No, I can't I…could you just talk to me a while?"

"What would you like me to talk about?" He asks tenderly.

"Anything."

"Listen, Annie. I am troubled and we do need to discuss things, but not over the phone…"

"I didn't mean *that*," I interrupt, "I want you to take my mind off *that*."

He makes a brief 'oh' sound, as though I've wounded him.

"I will talk about it," I promise him, "if you want me to."

"Tomorrow, Annie, we'll talk tomorrow. But for now, try to relax, imagine we're out walking on the hills. Do you remember what you always say to me, when we reach the top?"

"That I don't feel so small."

"I promise you'll feel like that again…soon."

We talk a little more, until I hear Becca's footsteps on the stairs.

"I have to go." I say anxiously.

"Don't take any shit."

96

I tell him that I won't, as Becca's door opens.

Becca:

I wanted to stay mad, just once. I know that sounds bitchy, but she always pisses me off, then has a problem so huge that mine doesn't matter. Now she nearly fucking kills herself. Great. I should probably say sorry, but I wouldn't mean it. Obviously, I'm sorry that she's out of her fucking mind, and it would kill me if she died. I hate myself for thinking like this, I do love her, I do. Right that's it, I don't know what to say, so I'm just going to hug her. But I can't even do that, because there's someone at the door. I know who it'll be, so I close my bedroom door behind me, and rush down to answer it.

"Hey," he says, poking his head inside, "she here?"

"Yes, but you can't come in."

He just grins and tries to nudge me back into the hallway.

"Alex, I said no!" We both laugh, but mine's more nerves as I push him back onto the doorstep.

"Oh, come on, Bec. You said I could talk to her. You agreed, she owes me that."

"I know, but trust me. You don't want to talk to her right now."

"Why not?"

"She's fucked up pretty bad, I can't let you in."

"Please, you never know, I might cheer her up." He laughs, with eyes all wide and excited.

"Al, no! Honestly the state she's in, if I let you in now, she'd never speak to me again."

"And that's a bad thing?"

"Yes!" I shove him back harder, this time he trips and stumbles onto the garden. I can't wait around for him to speak. I slam the door and turn the key. After a second he knocks again, so I open the letter box.

"I am sorry, Al. Can I just talk to you tomorrow?"

"Sure." He laughs. "You know, you're actually quite sexy when you're serious."

June 02, 2016 Thursday 8.15am.
Tommy:

After everything that happened yesterday, I was sure to pick Annie up early.

"Did Rich get his speech sorted?" She asks, as I pull onto the main road.

"Ha. Not exactly, he wrote a few lines, tore it up, wrote a few more, tore it up. In the end he flung the pen across the kitchen then drank half of my whiskey!"

"Oh dear." She smiles.

"So, how're you feeling?"

"Not now, Tom." Her smile fades, and she stares out of the window.

"I meant how was Becca's after I called."

She shakes her head.

"Annie! Why won't you talk to me? You used to tell me everything."

I only asked how the rest of her night was, but if she can't even tell me that, then what hope do I have of getting to the bottom of these visions?

"I thought you meant what Mum told me to do…"

"*That* wasn't Mum." I interrupt.

"Yeah, you've said that already…Could you stop the car?"

"Yeah why? D'ya need to get out?"

"No," she sighs, "but I guess we should talk."

Finally. I find a safe place to pull over and turn off the engine.

"Like I said last night," she says, "I should have stayed at home. After you called, Becca stormed back, growled something, then slammed her face into the pillows. I asked if she was ok, and who was at the door, but she just bit my head off. And I'm starving. You know I've had nothing since we stopped for lunch! I'd have asked her for some toast or something, but with the mood she was in, I didn't dare."

"So, you haven't eaten?!"

"No. Anyway, she said she was tired, so we went to bed. I laid there and cried, I didn't want to but I couldn't help it, then she told me she was glad I didn't die…"

"You told her?"

"Only what I saw and that you saved me." Her voice shakes, so I take her hand. "You saved me." She sobs.

"Go on, Annie. It's ok."

"When she went to sleep, I just laid there looking at the ceiling. Then, when I heard Ruth come home, I got up and went downstairs. All she did was ask how I was, and I burst into tears. She hugged me. No-one besides you has hugged me like that…I'm sorry, I told her everything."

"Everything?"

"Yeah, I'm sorry. I told her about what I heard Mum say…then I had to explain about what happened at the party, and with the baby and everything."

"Annie…"

"It just all came out. She promised it would stay between us."

"Do you believe her?"

"Yeah. She promised she wouldn't tell Becca what's going on in my head…I don't think she wants her knowing shit like that anyway."

I can't say I'm comfortable with this, and for the next few minutes I silently mull it over. Annie's still holding my hand, grazing her fingers over mine.

"What did you see, little Annie?" I ask gently.

"Mum was drowning, and I climbed the barrier to save her." Tears roll down her face, as she looks me square in the eyes, "I only wanted to save her."

I have no words. This is agony, but I can't think about Mum right now. If I dwell on that, it'll cloud my real priority; Annie's safety.

"There's something else," she mumbles, "but I don't know how to say it."

"Try."

Turning away, she lets out a huge sigh and scratches her wrist.

"Do you remember when we were kids? And you'd let me…"

I move her hand from her wrist and nod.

"Tom. I know I'm too old but…" Leaking fresh tears she shakes her head. "It doesn't matter, I'm ok. Can we go home now?"

"When you've told me everything."

"Please just leave it, I said it doesn't matter."

"Yes, it does! For goodness sake, Annie. Talk to me!"

Throwing herself forward, she tears out her bobble and begins yanking her hair at the scalp.

"Hey, stop that now."

"I can't sleep without you ok! There, I said it!" She flings herself upright, and screams in my face. "I knew it when you stayed with me after Alex turned up. I knew, because that was the only night since the accident that I haven't laid awake watching shadows…first time I've felt safe!"

"You are never too old to need me." I say softly.

"But do you know what I'm asking?"

"Of course I do. And yes, you can sleep in with me."

"Thank you," she cries, leaning in for a hug, "thank you."

Her hair clings to my stubble and, as I kiss her head, I notice a distinct musty smell. This isn't like her, but I doubt she's washed it in days.

"Annie, when we get back, why don't you have a nice shower while I clean up? Then I'll take you out for lunch, anywhere you like."

"I'll help you clean the house first, then I'll have a shower."

I nod and start the car. "Just to pre-warn you, when I left earlier Rich was still passed out on the sofa."

"So, he's going to need bacon?" She laughs, drying her cheeks.

"Yeah," I add, "and coffee."

Anna:

I didn't want to ask him. Well, that's not strictly true. I did *want* to, I just didn't want to *have* to. I'm scared that things could go back to how they were when we were kids. We were always close, but it was different then, he used to do everything for me that Mum or Dad should've done. He was my constant. It was his door, not Mum's, that I knocked on in the dead of night, when tree branches battered against my bedroom window, or when monsters peered out from the door of my cupboard which never fully closed. I was a child. Tommy's still my hero, he's my best friend, but I'm not a child now. I'm just Anna, a girl falling apart.

As he turns onto our road, a flash of morning sun bounces from the wing-mirror. There're hardly any clouds today, and the sky's a clear blue. Perfect for a drive over the moors to Whitby; a seaside town, with almost two hundred stone steps which scale the cliff to the old Abbey. Me and Tommy sometimes race to the top, I never win but that doesn't matter.

At home, I follow him into the kitchen, where the air reeks of leftovers and alcohol. Every surface is littered with dirty containers, dishes and empty whiskey glasses and lager bottles. I kick off my shoes then begin clearing the dining table.

"Leave them, An." He says as he walks towards the lounge door. "I'm just gonna wake Rich up…" He turns around and stops mid-sentence, then looks down at me as though I'm ten-years-old. I don't know what to do with myself, so I just stand there, holding their dirty plates. I hate feeling like this.

"Tommy, don't look at me like that."

"Like what?"

"Like that!" I turn and dump the plates in the sink. "Like you pity me…like I'm a child."

"Hey," he says, following me back into the kitchen, "there's no pity. Is this because of what you asked me in the car?"

"I guess…I'm not a child, Tom. And if this makes you look at me like that, then it doesn't matter. I'll sleep on my own."

"Listen to me." He tenderly rubs my shoulders. "I know you're not, and there's no need to feel funny about needing me. It doesn't change anything; all it means is that we'll both sleep better. You'll feel safe, and I won't lie awake worrying."

"You lie awake worrying?"

"I have done recently, yeah."

Maybe I'm overthinking this. I mean, I do need him, but here's the test. "Can we go to Whitby for lunch?"

"What'cha say?" He laughs, "Did you just ask to go to Whitby?"

I nod.

"Is that wise?"

"I know you're worried that the sea might trigger something, but it was Mum's favourite place and…please?"

"If that's what you want, but I'm not leaving your side, ok?"

"Ok."

We both then hear a thud and a groan, which I can only presume is Rich rolling off the sofa.

"Do you wanna make some drinks?" Tommy smiles "I'll get the bacon on."

"Sure."

10.30am. Tommy:

Rich left straight after breakfast, and Annie didn't want to wait. As I saw him out of the front door, she gulped down the last of her tea and set straight to the cleaning. For a

102

moment, I just stood and watched as she buzzed around the kitchen, mopping up splatters of curry sauce and scraping dirty dishes. She didn't complain, but she did catch my eye. In that split second she looked like a tiny version of Mum. It's funny, but I don't think I've ever snapped into action so fast. Together we cleaned the house in just shy of an hour.

Now, while she's in the shower, I head up to my room and lie back on the bed. Whitby's the last place I thought she'd pick, but I can't reassure her that she's not a child in one breath, then in the next say, 'no you're not going.' I had no choice.

"Ah well," I sigh, as I change into some clean black jeans, and T-shirt. Shit, this room's a mess. I gather up my sweaty clothes and throw them into the wash basket, in the spare room. "I'll just have to keep my wits about me today."

"You talking to yourself?"

Shit she's quiet. She must've crept across the landing.

"Ha, yeah." I pull the door closed behind me, as Annie rubs her hair with a towel. "You got dressed quick." I say. "Not drying your hair?"

"I was kinda hoping you'd put it in a French braid for me." Smiling sweetly, she hands me a comb and a bobble.

"Turn around then."

"You sure you wanna go to Whitby?" I ask, while sectioning her hair to tease out the knots.

"Yeah," she says, "I want a race to the Abbey. I'm gonna beat you this time."

"Um, do you really think that's a good idea? And what about your belly?"

"I knew you'd say that. I'm not going to see Mum you know, and yes, I'm still sore, but I've ran up those steps a million times…I need to do it, to prove I'm ok."

"Fine," I sigh, "you don't need to prove anything, but ok."

11.45am. Whitby.
Anna:

There are so many people here today. Parents navigate pushchairs over the uneven cobbles, between rows of rugged shops. I feel sorry for the babies, being bounced around as their wheels catch between the stones.

"So?" Tommy smiles as the pathway narrows towards the bottom of the infamous steps. "You sure you're up to this? We can just take a walk up for today?"

"No, I want a race." I don't sound it, but he's probably guessed that I'm nervous. I mean, the narrow pathway forces everyone tackling the steps, into a bottleneck. It's made worse by all the mum's waiting with pushchairs at the bottom, but I wanted to come here. I look up and watch the sun lighting up the Abbey, so bright and yellow. It's time to be brave.

Me and Tommy wait for a break in the crowd, then as I position myself for a race, he casually starts walking up the steps. He must've thought I wasn't serious, either that or he plans to race from the halfway point. Well, I am serious. I'm doing this.

I leap over the first two steps and run until I'm almost right behind him. I should stop now and tell him he was right. That initial leap was agony, but Tommy glances over his shoulder, sees me gaining on him and speeds off up the steps. Looks like the race is on. There's no way I can win, but I have to at least keep up. With each stride my belly tugs but I push through and, as I get closer, I try to grab him. I can't quite reach, and my insides are burning. My heart's pounding but everyone's cheering us on, so I push myself harder, yelling 'Come on!' In the distance I see him slowing, surely he's not getting tired...but he is. This is it, summoning one last burst of energy, I dig deep and my feet spring from each step, bouncing as I stride two at a time. I ignore the sudden gush filling my pad, and clear more and

104

more until I ascend on the Gothic graveyard. We're side by side as we reach the top and with one last step to go, my foot touches the ground a fraction before his.

"I did it!" I shriek, falling into his arms.

"Well done, little Annie."

That hurt so bad, but I don't care. I did it.

He stands behind me, giving me a massive bear hug, and laughing as the breeze blows my loose strands of hair against his face. I take our picture, and it's instantly my favourite. I upload it immediately with the caption.

Tommy #bigbrother#bestfriend#hero#lovehim

Tommy:

We find a patch of grass away from the cliff's edge. I stretch out my legs and lie back against a surprisingly comfortable rock. Annie sits beside me, fiddling with her phone.

"Thanks for your help earlier."

"It's fine," she says, "I enjoyed it."

"Ya what! You enjoyed cleaning?"

She doesn't answer, only shrugs.

"You were just happy to be home, weren't you?"

Nodding, she puts down her phone and fidgets with my leather wristbands.

"Did you let me win?" She asks.

"Annie, you won."

With each glance she looks right through me. She wants to believe it, and why shouldn't she? She did push herself harder than she ever has, and I think that if she wasn't still in pain, then she probably would've won.

"I did, didn't I?…Tom, do you remember when Dad separated the garden?"

"Yeah."

Mum was a perfectionist. She loved her flowers, ha, they were even colour co-ordinated. So, when we were kids, Dad sectioned us off a messy play area at the far end.

105

"I remember burying you up to your neck."

"Well," she laughs, "I remember you screaming like a girl, when I dropped a massive spider down your back."

"It tickled!"

She lifts my arm, so she can lie down and cuddle in.

"They were good days," she says, "weren't they?"

"Yeah, Annie. They were."

3pm. Leaving School.
Becca:

I've been irritated by everything and everyone today. Anna's going through some serious shit, and last night I practically told her to get over it. I'm not that bad though, I did fall out with Chloe and Sophie when they were running their mouths off about her. I didn't get much thanks for that.

"Becca!" Alex shouts as I cross the car park, "wait up."

I turn, just as he practically runs into me, pushing his phone in my face.

"I thought you said she was in a state!" He says.

"Ya what?"

"Look."

Anna's posted a picture of her and Tommy on Instagram, they're both all smiley and happy.

"It's nice." I shrug.

"Nice? Bec, look at it, he's all over her!"

"He's just hugging her. I know it looks weird but that's just them."

He looks at it again, laughs, then slides the phone into his pocket.

"What's funny?" I ask as we cross the road.

"Nah, nothing."

"What?"

"You don't think he's knobbin' her, d'ya?"

"Shut up! He's her brother! You're sick you are…and I thought Anna had issues!" I instantly speed up. I can't even look at him right now. It's bad enough that everyone thinks Anna's crazy, I'm not letting him start something like that.

"Ok, ok," he says, "maybe that's a bit much, but look at the hashtags…Hero? Love him? Best friend? Just saying that Anna Anderson's fucked up."

"Why are you so desperate to talk to her, then?"

At last, the boy with all the answers has nothing to say. What could he say though? I don't even think he knows why. Ever since the party, he's just had this strange obsession with her.

"They're just close, Al. And don't forget, he's practically her dad now."

But he just sniggers, 'whatever,' and runs off. He's gone through the old park, it's a short-cut that goes right past the back of my street.

I slow down a bit, then wander down the cut, between a load of overgrown trees, into the park. Alex must've ran because he's not here, actually there's hardly ever anyone here. That's why I come here, I mean, who'd bring their kids to a park with nothing in it? Well there's an old rocket climbing frame, a few benches and a broken swing. I sit down for a minute and take another look at Anna's picture. It's funny; she only ever smiles like that when she's with him. Well, since the accident anyway.

His eyes are darker than mine, and I just love those cute little creases when he smiles. If he held me like that, I'd rub my cheek against his stubble and slide his hand down into my bra. He wouldn't be rough, but he would squeeze. I want him so bad; I love imagining him kissing my neck. I can't help it, I need him. So, I lean back and slide my hand under my skirt, and into my knickers. At first, I hope no one catches me but it feels so nice, and after a while I stop caring. But I'm interrupted by a bunch of lads, bursting through the cut. I quickly stop what I'm doing, grab my things and leg it out of the park. Only when they're out of sight, I smile with excited satisfaction and head home.

Mam's stirring a pan of Bolognese, when I walk through the back door, into the kitchen.

"Hiya." I say dropping my bag and books on the table.

"You can move them!" She snaps.

Clearly, she's in a mood. I've learned that when she's on one, it's best to get out of there, pronto. So, not saying another word I take them up to my room.

"Why are you so late anyway?" She shouts, but I don't answer. "Oh, just wash your hands then, tea's nearly ready."

I'm upstairs for all of two seconds, before she's calling me again.

"Becca! Come on will you, I'm dishing up."

I give my hands a quick rinse in the bathroom and hurry back down. Mam dumps scoops of spaghetti onto my plate, grunting as if she's answering a voice inside her head.

"Mam? You ok?"

"Love," she sighs, "that girl's broken."

I guess she means Anna. I heard them talking last night, but I couldn't make out what they were saying, and Anna was super secretive this morning.

"I'm worried about you, Bec." She says, as we carry our plates to the table. "You're in your last year of school, got your GCSEs coming up and I think you need to be careful. Anna's dealing with things way too big for you."

What does she mean by that!? I'm Anna's best friend. I know what she's going through. As soon as I think that, I remember the hashtags on that picture. I'm not her best friend at all. He is.

"I know, Mam, but she's not on her own. She's got Tommy and he'll look after her…he's lovely, unlike my excuse for a brother!"

"Rebecca, that's not fair, James is a good man." She screws up her face as if I've just spat in her dinner. "You were five when your father walked out, and your 'excuse of a brother,' at only fourteen-years-old, did everything he could to help me. He's no Tommy, not full of cuddles and 'I love you's,' but if the shit hit the fan, he'd be there. For goodness sake, he's about to become a father himself!"

Something tells me she didn't mean to say that.

"Mam?"

"Yes, love," she sighs, "he told me yesterday, Emma's going for a scan soon. I'm going to be a Nana, I'm too bloody young to be a Nana."

James and Emma have lived together for years, but I never thought they'd have a baby. This is so exciting.

3pm. Travelling Home.
Anna:

There's a tractor chugging along, about a mile ahead of us, but we're unfazed; we don't care about the traffic. We're both relaxed, and I'm so happy that I wasn't scared when I heard the waves. I didn't see Mum's or Dad's faces in the water. It was like old times, and after my victory on the steps, we just sat, enjoying the cool sea-breeze as we soaked up the sun.

Tommy's singing his head off now, and one thing I've learned from today is, that it's ok to need him, that he actually wants me to. So, there's no better time to tell him exactly what's going on. I just hope it won't spoil the day.

"Tommy?" I say, turning the music down, "can we talk?"

"Sure, what's wrong?"

"It's um, about my head."

"Tell me." He says, and turns the music off completely.

Two minutes ago, I had all this planned out, but now I have his undivided attention, I can feel it all jumbling up again.

"Ok, you said I could tell you anything. Well, please don't freak out, because I don't know how this is going to sound."

"It's alright, Annie. Just relax."

"Right, you know what I saw at school, and then at the theatre, and yesterday?"

He suddenly has that look about him, where he's almost frightened of what he's going to hear. What was I thinking? I can't put this on him.

"I'm sorry. You don't need this right now, I'll be ok."

"No, please tell me." He pleads. Grabbing my hand, he rubs his thumb over my knuckles. "I want to know."

"Ok. This is going to sound crazy, but I feel like I can't control my brain, it's not just the things I've seen, I'm having nightmare's too."

"Nightmares? What happens in those?" He asks.

"Mainly it's different variations of the accident…or what I imagine of it. The last one was bad. You were on the boat too, and I was stranded on the rocks when it crashed. I could see the whole thing. I called down to you, then Mum and Dad were gone. You got pulled under! I screamed but I couldn't move, then more rocks collapsed above me, and I was crushed."

"Shit, Annie. But from now on, I'll be with you through the night. I want you to wake me if you see anything like that, ok?"

"From now on? Are you sure?"

"Yes." He says. "About the hallucinations?"

"Don't call them that." I interrupt. "It makes me sound crazy, and…and it's not like that, they're like dreams but, I'm awake.

"You're not crazy, sweetheart, but that's what an hallucination is. Listen, I need to know if there's any other connection? A trigger maybe, like something that happens each time?"

"I see the ground pivot or crumble; kind of like quicksand. Sometimes it happens slowly, other times it's instant. When it's all over I get the worst headache, it burns like metal rods are being pushed through my head. Can you see why I didn't want to tell you?"

"Yeah, but I need to know all this. What happens when the ground crumbles?"

"I feel dizzy."

"Ok," he says, "I think you should tell me if that happens, and then I'll know to talk you through it. You said yesterday that you heard me?"

"Yeah, it was very faint though."

"No matter, the key is that you heard me. If I'm there when it happens great. If not, then call me. I mean it, if anything seems weird just call me, ok?"

I want to say yes, I want this to be the answer, but there's so much to think about. What if I'm in the middle of a lesson? I can't just pull my phone out and give him a call. Or what if he's at work?

"I'll help you." He insists. "But you have to let me. I need you to be open with me, promise you won't keep this shit to yourself, no secrets?"

"I promise but, Tommy…it scares me."

"It scares me too." He says, giving my hand a reassuring squeeze. "We'll get through it, I won't abandon you."

5pm. Home.
Anna:

A nap on the sofa, with the sun shining through the blinds. That's the perfect end to a perfect day. Tommy commandeers one side of the sofa, and I take the other. Before closing my eyes, I have a quick look through some of the pictures I took today, and see a text from Becca.

"Hey, An.
You'll never guess what.
You know Emma?
James's girlfriend? She's pregnant!!
I'm gonna be an Aunty!"

I'm gutted. Has she forgotten why I'm off school? I get that Becca loves babies, but I've just lost one. She probably still thinks I'm happy about it, but it's not like that. I couldn't explain it to her because she wouldn't understand.

111

She wouldn't understand the constant tug-of-war between relief and loss. The knowing that I'm in no way ready, but convincing myself that, with Tommy's help, I could've tried. Then the physical pain, it's not so bad now but at its worst I couldn't even walk.

"Tom, are you awake?" I ask, reading her text again.

His eyes are closed, but he only laid down a few minutes ago, so I'd be surprised if he's asleep already.

"Yeah," he groans, opening one eye, "what's up?"

I slide my phone across the carpet. "What do you make of that?"

Astonished, he asks 'is she for real?' Then, shaking his head, he places the phone to his ear.

"What are you doing?" I gasp.

"Trust me."

This is bad, this is really bad. I can't watch so, while he waits for her to answer, I hide my face in a cushion.

"Hello, Becca." He says firmly.

I peer over the top, he's rubbing his fingers over his eyes.

"She's very upset, if I'm honest." He says. "Do you know why?"

My heart's racing, and I start making a mental list of excuses for why I let him call.

"I understand you're excited," he says, "and I…ok, ok, will you please calm down and let me finish. Thank you. I just feel that with everything Anna's dealing with, a text like that's a bit insensitive…alright, alright," he says, "yes, I'll tell her. Bye." He then slides the phone back to me and closes his eyes.

"Sorted, Annie. She said she's sorry."

June 03, 2016 Friday 11.50pm. Home.
Anna:

My brother never fully closes his bedroom blinds. There's a yellow street-light on the road outside, behind the trees. When it shines through, the branches look like they're in a kind of rugged sword fight. It's hypnotising. I rest my head back against the headboard and watch.

Dan came over after school and only left an hour ago. It's funny, but no matter what's going on, he just seems to breeze through it. Well, I say breeze through, what I mean is he talks through. I could listen to him for hours, it's not always anything in particular, just talking. He's refreshing, being around him is like a pocket of calm. Which, when your head's as noisy as mine, can only be a good thing. He did say something that made me sad, he said he misses me. I miss him too. I wanted to spit it all out; Mum, Dad, Alex, the miscarriage, everything. I couldn't. Dan hates Alex, and after Tommy, Dan's my best friend. What would he think if he knew what I'd done? I wanted to talk about the things I've seen too; not to ask for help, because I doubt he'd be able to. Just to tell him. After all, he was with me when I saw Mum and Dad at school, and it hasn't changed anything. He doesn't look at me like I'm crazy, or bombard me with questions. And he'd have a right to ask, he watched me scream to the point of vomiting.

I couldn't tell him. There were times I tried, but the words wouldn't come out. So instead, he talked. Then we sat and laughed our way through episode after episode of 'Red Dwarf. My eyes are heavy, they fall closed but spring open at the last second. I hate not being able to sleep without Tommy. It's exhausting, so I check my phone while I wait. There're more messages from Alex. I wish he'd leave me alone.

"Hello, my girl.
I came to see you at Becca's,
but she wouldn't let me in."

So that's who was at the door. She must have told him that I was staying, but why? Why would she do that? As I stare at the screen, more messages appear.

"Anna?
Annaaaaa?
Talk to me, if you
don't, I'm gonna call."

In less than thirty seconds, my phone rings, but I'm not going to answer it, I'm not. I swipe my thumb to cancel, but it slips, I accidentally press 'answer,' and drop the phone. It bounces, landing face up on the mattress. 'Shit!' What do I do now? He knows I'm here. I pick up the phone, but just sit there, looking at the screen.

"Anna," he says again, "don't you want to talk to me?"

I have to act natural, I have to speak to him. "Hello?"

"There she is!" He says. "That wasn't so difficult, was it?"

"What do you want?"

"I want to know when you're coming back, I miss you." I can hear a laugh trying its hardest to break through, but he doesn't quite let it.

"Monday," I say plainly, "I'm back on Monday."

"No, you're not, teacher training on Monday. School's closed."

"Well Tuesday, then. Look, Alex. What do you really want?"

"Oh, what do I really want? I don't know if you can handle what I really want."

I hate this. All I can think of is Tommy saying, 'he shouldn't have even touched you.'

"I remember the party now." My voice is shaking so bad. I wish I could lie, but I'm a total giveaway. Silence. Just for a second there's silence, then he laughs.

"And what's that then?"

I wish I could remember. Which drink was the 'one too many?'

"You don't remember anything, do you, Anna? Ha. You know it's not healthy to get that wasted!"

"I wish it'd never happened."

114

"Well it did, and I'd do it again in a heartbeat. You were so tight, like sticking my cock in a vice."

Don't cry, I tell myself. Don't give him that satisfaction, just don't. "Leave me alone." I beg, pressing my head to my knees. "Please."

"No," he sniggers, "I want you, Anna, again and…"

"Please, Alex! I've lost my Mum, Dad and my baby! Just leave me alone."

He mutters something, then ends the call. As the phone slips from my grasp, I'm left staring at my shaking hands. The light from the landing dims, so I look up to see my brother, leaning against the door frame, staring at his feet.

"Tom, that was Alex."

"Yeah, I figured."

He sits down beside me, as I press my face into the duvet and sob.

"Come here," he says, pulling me close. "Why'd you answer it?"

"I didn't mean to…it was him, at Becca's. He knew I'd be there!"

He doesn't answer, he's distracted. He's just glaring at his chest of drawers, like he's overseeing an imaginary battle.

"You asked him to leave you alone," he says, "what did he say?"

"He said no. He said he wants to do it again…I don't think he's gonna give in, Tom!"

"Lift up," he says, tapping my shoulder, "I need to move." He tears off his socks and jeans, flinging them onto the landing. "I've had enough of this shit, who the fuck does he think he is? Getting all creepy after one drunk shag!" Furious, he rips off his shirt. Throwing that too, he rages downstairs, punching the door as he goes.

Tommy:

Twice! Twice she begged to be left alone. Pouring a large whiskey, I imagine what happened at that party. Was she willing? Or did she say no? Did she beg him to stop? Did she freeze? She told me that she was sore after. I should have paid more attention at the time, but I was so damn preoccupied with Mum and Dad, I just wasn't ready for my little sister to be doing that. She tried to talk to me, but I wasn't listening.

I throw the drink down my neck and pour a second. After downing that, I pour a third and a fourth. Clenching my fists, I press down hard upon the work-surface. I want to hurt him but he's a sixteen-year-old kid. A fucking sixteen-year-old kid. Downing four whiskeys on an empty stomach isn't a good idea, but I pour a fifth regardless. I can't stand this. A quiet girl has too much to drink, and he thinks it gives him a right-of-passage.

"No, it fucking doesn't!" I snarl and throw the glass across the room. The sound of it smashing on the slate floor is undeniably satisfying. So, from the cupboard, I throw another and another, but I can't stop there. I pull out a stack of plates and launch them to the floor. They don't all break, and with my adrenaline pumping, I grab them, hurling them one by one. I will make sure that they do. If I could just get my hands on him, I'd…I'd…

The room's spinning, but I grab the neck of the bottle and down what's left. Then raise it high above my head. I'm ready to hurl that too, but something makes me turn. In a split second, I freeze, the haze of rage falls, my poise is locked, and Annie's staring at me. She's horrified.

Deathly quiet, she surveys the floor. I drop the bottle, and as it bounces, her eyes dart to me. She doesn't say a word. She just tiptoes to the patio door, slips on her shoes, takes the sweeping brush and begins clearing the shards. She shouldn't even be down here.

"Annie, give me the brush, I'll do it."

She shakes her head and continues sweeping. I have to fix this so, I move towards her, but the floor's wet. My heel slips, and my left side goes down as I skid over the tiles. It all happens so fast, and as I stretch out my hand to break the fall, I feel a searing pain through my palm.

"Annie!" I gasp. But she just continues sweeping the mess into a pile.

"Help me!" I retch, as I pull the glass from my palm.

She turns, drops the brush, falls to her knees, and pulls my hand towards her. Blood pumps from the gash, through my fingers, over her hands, and drips onto her pyjama shorts.

"I'm so sorry."

"Shh," she says softly, "I can't tell how deep it is without cleaning it, you'll have to stand."

Easier said than done. I'm dizzy as hell, and I don't like blood at the best of times, especially my own. She brings me a chair over from the dining table and places it by the sink. Once I've pulled myself up, she holds my hand under the cold tap.

"I think you need to go to hospital," she says, "it's really deep."

"No." I press my head against her hip and close my eyes. I can't go to the hospital; one smell of my breath and they'll assume I'm just another stupid drunk. "Get the first aid kit from the leccy cupboard," I tell her, "and strap it up…I'll be fine."

"I can't, it's pouring."

"Just do your best."

At least five minutes pass, and my arm is still stretched over the sink.

"It's slowing, but you've lost a lot of blood. Tom, please get it looked at."

"Don't worry, sweetheart. I'm ok."

Truthfully, I feel like shit. My head's swimming, I'm nauseous and the only reason I can't feel my hand, is because it's gone numb. My sister fills a cup from the draining board. "Drink some water." She says.

"Thanks."

After a few more minutes, she lifts my hand and, taking a wad of kitchen paper, lays it on my lap while she fetches the first aid kit.

"I am sorry." I tell her, as she kneels at my feet and dresses my hand.

"It's not your fault, it's mine. If I'd have just ignored the phone, he wouldn't have said those things, then none of this would've happened."

"What? No, Annie. I lost control…I…I didn't mean to frighten you."

"Ok." She nods, and we sit in silence while she tapes down the bandage. Then hands me some pain killers. "You should go to bed," she says, "I'll just clean this."

"Please, An. I'm sorry, you know I'd never hurt…"

"I know," she interrupts, "go to bed. I'll be up in a minute."

1.30am. Anna:

Once I've scrubbed the kitchen and changed into some clean pyjamas, I plod back to Tommy's room. He's still awake, propped up on the right side of his bed, with his bedside light on.

"Are you ok?" I ask, as I crawl in beside him.

"It fucking hurts."

"Let me call a taxi, you need it looking at."

He clutches his arm, keeping his hand to his chest. "I said no, An."

"What would you say if it was me? You'd tell me to go."

"And you wouldn't listen!"

Swallowing hard, I nod and look away.

"Look I'm sorry," he sighs, "I shouldn't have said that."

I hate seeing him like this. It's not us, he's the strong one not me. "How can I make you better?" I whisper.

"I'm alright. Just let me sleep."

He turns off the light, and I roll over, pulling the duvet over my head. I feel as though I'm in a living nightmare. It's agony, he's in agony, and I don't know what we're going to do. Crying's not going to help but I can't stop. It's swelling up from my gut, and no matter how hard I grip my belly, or tuck up my knees, I just can't hold it in.

"Don't cry," he says, flicking the light back on, "I didn't mean to snap. Come on, if we swap sides then you can still cuddle in."

"I want to but, Tom? You need help."

"Annie, I'm tired." He pushes himself up and nods for me to swap sides. So, I move over. "Just let me sleep," he says, lying back down, "that's all I need, everything'll be ok."

I nod and cuddle in, but it isn't ok. I don't know how he expects me to just go to sleep. I can't deal with this. I feel sick, and I just end up lying here in some kind of emotional limbo, wishing that I'd never answered my phone.

June 04, 2016 Saturday 11.45am Home.
Anna:

Either Tommy's lost his appetite, or my attempt at cremating his toast has failed. He took a few small bites and the rest just sits on the plate, while he sips his coffee.

"I guess you'll have to take a couple of nights off?" I say, holding my mug.

"Yeah, a one-handed bartender's a bit useless."

"You're not useless."

He gives me a half smile and sighs.

"You were my rock last night. I won't do anything like that again."

"Ok. I guess we'll have to buy some more dinner plates. Or eat off tea plates?"

"I'll order some, and some more glasses."

I don't really care about the plates. I just want to know why he won't go to hospital. He needs to. Fresh blood is seeping through the bandage, he tries to hide it but it's obvious, and his fingers are puffy. I need to convince him to

119

get it checked out. I stare at him, waiting for the opportune moment, when the postman shoves a bunch of letters through the door.

"Get them, will you?" He says.

"Sure." I drop the post on the table, sit back down and sort it into piles. "You, junk, you, you, junk, me and lastly you."

Tommy doesn't even look at his. He's moved his injured hand to his lap, tucked it safely under the table, while he lays his head on his other arm. "What's yours?" He groans.

"My counselling appointment."

It feels like so long ago now, but when Tommy applied to be my guardian, our social worker suggested counselling. It was the kind of thing that I just agreed to, because I didn't know what would happen if I didn't. I mean, would that stop Tommy from being my guardian? Who knows? I guess I'll have to see it through now.

"When is it?" He asks, keeping his eyes closed.

"This Wednesday at two. It's in our doctors building, I didn't know they held counselling sessions?"

"Yeah, they do."

"Will you still be able to take me? I don't mind walking if you can't drive."

"It'll be fine, the car's an automatic." He moans, then suddenly thrusts himself upright, squeezing his wrist till his knuckles turn white. He sucks the air through his teeth and beads of sweat collect on his brow.

"Tommy! What is it?"

"My hand! It's killing! There's something in it!" He gasps, "you have to have a look!"

I really don't want to. That gash runs the entire width of his palm, but what if there's still some glass in there? There can't be, I'm sure I got it all out last night. As I argue with myself, he pleads again.

"Ok," I say, standing up to get the first aid box. "Just let me get some fresh dressings."

Tommy looks ill. So, as I grab the first aid box, I push the patio door wide open. I just hope the cool breeze will prevent him from being sick. He keeps his forehead pressed to his arm, and I begin peeling away the dirty bandage. It's a bit sticky, but it comes away easily enough. The real struggle is changing the dressing, it's stuck to the wound. I carefully lift the edge but as I tease it, Tommy winces and frantically taps the table.

"Two minutes." I tell him as I stand to get some water and kitchen paper. "I need to soak it off. If I just pull, I'll rip it open."

It takes a few minutes of gentle dabbing for the dressing to yield, and the gash looks awful. It's impossible to see anything past the mass of fresh and congealing blood. I take a long close look, and I'm not sure if cleaning it's the best thing. While I figure out what I'm doing, I dab away the excess blood from around the wound. As I concentrate, I feel someone behind me. By the time I've realised that it's just Stu, it's too late. I've already leaped out of my skin, and knocked Tommy's hand, re-opening the wound.

"Shit! Sorry, I'm sorry."

Tommy groans, and Stu rushes to his side.

"Oh my goodness!" Stu drops his styling equipment on the table and stares in horror at my brother's hand. "What on Earth have you done?"

"I'm fine." Tommy moans.

"You're not fine, you silly boy!"

There're a thousand thoughts swirling around my head, and I'm just sat here holding my brother's dripping hand, with no clue what to do.

"Hey, little lady." Stu clicks his fingers. "Get your shoes on, I'm taking you both to A and E."

"Tom?" I whisper, lifting his hair from his face, "will you go…please?"

He responds with a nod the size of a blink.

"I'll leave my things here." Stu says as I re-dress Tommy's hand. "We'll do your hair when we get back."

"You're staying with us?"

"I'm in no hurry, sweetie."

I nod and help Tommy to put on his shoes.

2.30pm. A&E Waiting Room. James Cook University Hospital.
Anna:

The waiting room's packed; there's a block of chairs in the centre facing a reception desk, and another row running along under the windows, to the left. This is where Tommy's sat now. It's so busy that for the past ninety minutes I've sat on the floor between his feet, while Stu's sat on the end seat of the row nearest us.

"Are you sure you don't want to sit here?" He asks me. "You'll get a numb bum down there."

"I'm ok." I rest my head against my brother's knee and close my eyes. I can't help but feel like everyone's staring at us. I guess this is why he didn't want to come here. There's a little boy sat next to Tommy. When his mum takes him through to the doctor, I jump up to his seat and Stu moves beside me.

"He'll be alright, you know," he says.

"I hope so."

Tommy's guarding his hand, holding it close to his chest.

"Please be ok." I whisper, laying my hand on his arm.

"I'm ok," he says quietly, "I'm ok."

"Do you want me to go in with you?"

"Please."

Just as I begin to relax, a man storms from his seat to the reception desk. He's hurling abuse at the receptionist, slamming his hands against the screen that separates them. I turn to Stu in disbelief. He demands to be seen now, because he thinks he's got a broken arm. I'm no doctor, but in my opinion that's highly unlikely.

"Somebody's got a temper." Stu mutters under his breath.

I nod, and watch the others who are waiting and wishing they were somewhere else. An old man in a wheelchair has been parked by the wall, opposite. I'm guessing he lives in a care home, he has a carer by his side, generic hospital blanket over his knees and tatty slippers. His face is worn with memories and sadness, like he's craving one more day with his soulmate. I wonder what she was like, did she treat him like a king? Did he hold her steady while she reached up to place the star on the Christmas tree?

I'm snapped out from my daydream, when a nurse calls Tommy's name.

"Is there anywhere I can get a beverage?" Stu asks, as Tommy and I stand.

"There's a Costa around the other side," I say, handing him a twenty-pound-note, "Tom'll need a coffee with ten sugars after this."

"And you?"

"Hot chocolate."

We then follow the nurse through a narrow doorway and into a cubicle. There's not much here, just a trolley-type bed and an ob's machine.

"Thomas Anderson?" He asks as Tommy sits on the bed.

"Yeah."

"So," he says, scanning over his notes, "you have a nasty cut on your left hand. Can you tell me how it happened?"

"I was washing up when I dropped a glass, then I slipped and landed on it."

I bite my nails, as the nurse raises his eyebrows and stretches his hands into a pair of vinyl gloves.

"Well, I think I should take a look."

Tommy closes his eyes.

"Hmm! Yes, it's quite deep," he says, inspecting the wound. "Have you experienced any numbness? Tingling sensations in your fingers?"

"I can't feel my fingers."

"You can't feel your fingers?"

"I can, well I don't know…it just hurts."

"Ok," the nurse says kindly, "you may have disturbed some nerves, but until the pain settles and the wound heals, it's difficult to tell. Can you just wait here a moment, while I ask the doctor to take a look?" He's already leaving the cubicle and drawing the curtain before we have a chance to answer.

"Are you ok?" I ask. A stupid question considering he's been left staring into an ugly, gaping gash. He nods.

A few minutes later, the nurse returns with the doctor, she introduces herself before examining Tommy's hand. She asks him the exact same questions that the nurse did, and my brother mumbles the exact same answers.

"Ok, Mr. Anderson," she hums as she inspects his hand, "I'm afraid you need stitches, but we'll numb the area first. Is that alright?"

His brow glistens, and his already pasty face turns grey.

"He's going to be sick!" I yell.

The nurse rushes out and brings back a bowl with only seconds to spare. I pull the spare bobble from my wrist and tie back his hair. I want to help him, but I don't know what else to do. So, while he heaves, I just stand there stroking his head, trying not to inhale. The doctor signals to the nurse and they move out of the cubicle, I can see their silhouettes through the curtain.

"I'm sorry, Annie."

I move the bowl aside, as he wipes his mouth with his sleeve. There's no need for him to keep saying it. I know he's sorry, I can see it in his face. So, I just gently hug his head, and he takes hold of my hand. When the nurse returns, I step back, but he squeezes my fingers for me to stay put.

Stu:

Every door I try in this place seems to be staff only. Fancy that, a building of this size and they expect everyone to walk the long way around, outside. According to Anna, the coffee shop is through the other entrance. But there are actually two other entrances, on opposite sides of the hospital. It's a good job I'm not above asking for directions.

There must be something about me, because whenever I do ask for directions, I always wind up chatting away for at least five minutes. That's precisely what happened when I asked this lovely old couple, Doris and Albert. Apparently, they've been here every day visiting Doris's elder sister, Elsie. She had a fall two weeks ago fracturing her hip. God bless her.

"Anyway, Dot," Albert says nudging her arm, "We best get home, your tablets are due."

"I'm coming." She says, turning to me. "Make sure your friend gets fixed up proper."

"Oh, I will. Bye now."

I dance my way towards the revolving door at the south entrance, when my phone rings.

"Hello, Tom," I say, "are you finished already?"

"Stu it's Anna." She says urgently. "We're gonna be ages, Tommy's having an X-ray now then they're going to stitch it! I don't know what you want to do?"

"Don't worry, honestly, I don't mind waiting. I'll just chill with a drink and when you're nearly done, drop me a text and I'll get yours to go."

"Are you sure?"

"Of course, now stop your fretting."

"Sorry, I just don't like seeing him like this."

"Chin up, little lady. You can't help him if you get yourself in a flap."

"I know…thanks. I'll text you when we're done then."

"Okey dokey."

When I join the queue at the coffee shop, I clap my eyes on the most beautiful treat-to-the-peepers barista. My goodness, he's tall, tanned and toned. Oh, what fun could be had with a man like that.

"Hi, there," he smiles, making sure I see the streak of naughtiness in his eyes, "what can I get for you today?"

You naked, under my satin sheets and smothered in baby oil. In that split second, I manage to convince myself that he heard what I was thinking.

"Yes, I'll have a medium skinny, soya latte with two shots of sugar free caramel please. To sit in."

When I hand him the money, I make a special point of touching his fingers, then he winks and says.

"Would you like to take a seat, and I'll bring it over?"

Oh, my temperature's rising today.

6pm. Home.
Anna:

While Tommy rests in the lounge, Stu lays his styling tools out on the dining table, and I head up to wash my hair. My head's buzzing, so much has happened today. When they'd finished stitching Tommy's hand, they dressed it and wrapped it in a bandage. I was given spare dressings and a leaflet on spotting signs of infection, I think he's going to be ok. I just hope he doesn't knock it and pull the stitches. To be honest we are both relieved that they'll dissolve, then we can put all this behind us.

It doesn't take me long to wash my hair. I don't ever bother with conditioner, just a decent moisturising shampoo and I'm good to go. When I'm finished, I throw a towel around my head and rush back down.

"There you go." Stu says, pulling me out a dining chair.

"Thanks, and thanks for waiting for us."

"No problem." He combs my hair through and clips up sections. "Anna," he sighs, "forgive me for prying, but how did he hurt his hand so badly? If he was working at that pub, he can get compensation, you know."

I don't know what to say. Tommy's ashamed of his temper, it doesn't surface very often, but once he's crossed that line, he loses control. Only me and Rich know how bad it can be. I can't tell Stu. Even if I did, I couldn't say why Tommy lost his shit in the first place, he'd think I was a slut.

"Anna?"

Shit, I forgot there was a question in there. "He wasn't working, he just…slipped on a glass."

He's not convinced, just squeaks an accepting 'ah ha,' and in silence, I watch strands of my hair fall to the floor.

"So, sweetie?" He asks, "did we buy a prom dress?"

"Yeah, it's knee length, soft green with twinkly bits. I think you'd like it."

"Sounds like you'll be the belle of the ball."

I can't help but giggle when he talks like that.

"Don't laugh, I'm serious."

"I'm not sure about that, but thank you. So anyway," I say, changing the subject, "Tommy said you're practically full time at the theatre now?"

"Not exactly, I do every house show, but it can be a feast or a famine. To be honest I'd love to open my own salon."

"You should do it."

"One day," he sighs, "small matter of funds, I'm afraid."

I don't know much about finances, but Tommy would help him if he asked, I know he would. I want to ask him more about it, but I don't want him to think I'm being cheeky, so instead I close my eyes while he snips away.

"You're almost done," he says, competing with the whirr of the hairdryer. "You should have a lot more bounce, I've put you plenty of layers in."

Once he's finished, he kneels in front of me, to check it's right.

"Right then," he says, moving back, "take a look."

I skip onto the second from bottom stair and look into the mirror. I love it, I don't know if it's because he took the weight out of it, but the colour appears lighter. My parting's just off centre, and the length is only an inch or two past my shoulders.

"Here?" Stu takes my hand and, as I move down, he gathers my hair back. "You see, when you tie it back these shorter strands at the front will fall, giving you a softer, natural look."

I throw my arms around him and give him a massive hug.

"I love it, Stu. Thank you so much."

"Aww it's ok. I'm going to head off now and give you two some peace."

As he packs away his things I tap his arm.

"I know I've already said this but, thanks for everything, you've really helped us today."

"It was worth it," he grins and pulls a napkin from his pocket. It has a phone number with the name Dylan and a heart written on it. "Always on the pull, Anna. I'm always on the pull. Bye, sweetie," he kisses my cheek and opens the patio door. "You look after that brother of yours."

Once he's gone, I quickly clean up and head into the lounge.

"Hey you." Tommy yawns, as I sit on the floor beside him.

"How're you feeling?"

"Been better." He says, running his good hand through my hair. "But you look beautiful."

Chapter 4

June 08, 2016 Wednesday Lunchtime. School. Anna:

I don't know what's going on with Becca today. She didn't want to eat her lunch in room thirty-five, or outside. I'd happily sit out on the field, but she wasn't having it, and there's nowhere else to go. In the end she did agree on room thirty-five, so long as we could sit around the back, behind the partition. It's empty. There're only a couple of pool tables here and some hard chairs, so we tuck ourselves in the corner.

She was acting strange in our last lesson too. It was French, and at the start, Mr. Torres and Mr. Garrison were trying their best to have a heated argument through whispers. Becca wanted to listen in because Mr. Torres is usually so calm, not today. He was that mad, the veins in his neck were bulging. Becca made us move to the front row. I hate the front row. We always sit at the back, so I can see the exit, and so I don't have anyone breathing down my neck. Anyway, I know now that this was a huge mistake, because Alex was sat two rows behind. I know that Tommy told me not to discuss it with Becca any more, but it's been on my mind. I had to tell her that it shouldn't have happened, Alex shouldn't have touched me. I tried to explain that I remember not feeling right, that's when she said it, but she didn't just say it.

"What?" She proclaimed, for the whole class to hear. "I thought you couldn't remember doing it with him!!"

I wanted to sprint from that desk, down the stairs and out of the building.

Now we're here. Facing each other, tucked behind a partition, balancing sandwiches on our laps, away from anyone.

"Are you alright?" I ask.

"An, why won't you talk to Alex? That's all he wants. I mean, you were pregnant…"

"I'm not pregnant any more." I interrupt and take a bite of my lunch.

"He does have a right though. It was his baby too."

I don't know what she expects me to say, so I just shrug. She shrugs too, and I slowly pick at the rest of my food.

Then I hear Alex and Chloe talking, they must be right behind this partition. I don't think Becca's noticed. She's just sat, sucking the juice from an apple, while flicking through her phone.

"Babe," Alex says, "is there any way that she could know?"

He sounds tense, and he's calling Chloe babe? That's weird.

"Who?" She asks, "and don't call me babe, not here anyway."

"Howay, don't play dumb."

They're lowering their voices, so I press my ear to the felt cover, on the partition.

"Oh right…course not." She says. "Why would you think that?"

"She called me on Friday, she said she knows. I didn't believe her. You know she's bat shit crazy, but in last lesson she said something to Becca, and if her reaction's anything to go by, then she fucking knows!"

The lying prick. He called me. And I knew something was wrong. I knew it. Taking a deep breath, I keep on listening.

"You said all I had to do was stay with her, and she'd assume we'd just spent the night together."

"Don't worry, Al. She was out cold; I gave her enough to be sure of that."

I feel as though I'm falling into an abyss. I need to focus, so I tap Becca's leg and motion for her to listen too.

"Chlo. Will you fucking listen…Anna knows something's up!"

I look up to Becca, she's confused.

"Babe, relax." Chloe says. "She was gone."

What did she give me? Drugs? It must have been, what else is there? I feel like I'm riding the waltzers and they're getting faster and faster and faster. My pulse thunders in my ears, I can't breathe.

Becca:

While Anna has a mini meltdown, I lean back and watch Alex and Chloe walk away.

"They're gone, An." I tell her, but she's a mess. "An! Sit up. Ok, so you were more pissed than you thought, but you need to calm down."

"Didn't you hear?" She snaps. "They drugged me!"

"What the fuck?"

"I need Tommy." She says, but her hands are shaking, so bad that she can hardly hold her phone.

"Give it here, An. I'll do it." I find his number, hand it back and lean in close to listen. Her knees bounce, and she squeezes her hand into a fist, while she waits for him to answer. It takes ages, then eventually goes to voicemail, but he calls her straight back.

"Hey, Annie," he says, "sorry, I left my phone on charge."

As soon as she hears his voice, she bursts into tears.

"An? What's wrong?"

She tries to talk, but she can't stop crying.

"Hey," he says, "what is it?"

"You were right." She pants. Then spews everything out. I can't believe it, I mean Alex is daft, but he wouldn't do that, would he? Anyway, Anna's not making any sense. I doubt Tommy will figure it out because she just keeps saying, 'I heard them,' over and over.

"I'll fucking kill him!" He yells.

131

Ok, I was wrong; he totally got the picture. Tommy's raging, and Anna's wheezing like she's having a panic attack. I know about that shit because my mam's had loads.

"Help me." Anna begs. "The floor's crumbling! I can't have another one, not here help me, please!"

She's frantic. She's out of her fucking mind. Never mind Tommy, she needs a doctor. I'm just about to go and get a teacher, but he quits shouting, sighs and says her name so softly.

"I'm here, sweetheart." He says. "Nothing's going to happen, because I'm with you. Can you still hear me?"

She squeaks a 'yes.'

"Ok, concentrate on my voice and imagine me right there. Keep looking at me. Can you see me?"

"I see you." She sobs.

"I've got you, you're ok."

"Tom, I'm sinking…"

"No, you're not. I promised to look after you and I will."

It feels wrong to keep listening, so I sit back and watch. She just keeps nodding and saying ok. My mam was right, she is broken.

Anna:

"Listen." Tommy says urgently. "He cannot know what you just heard. Do you understand?" He sounds like one of Dad's old cassettes, that's been played so much that the tape is warped. I can't focus. I just want to get out of here, skip my counselling appointment and run away.

"I want to come home, Tom."

"I know." He says. "Believe me, I want to come for you now. Listen it's almost one, what time do I need to pick you up?"

"My appointment's at two, so one-forty."

"Right, I'll get there about half past. Can you keep your head down for half an hour?"

"Yeah, he's not in my next lesson. But, Tommy? Becca heard too, and she walks home with him."

"Well she might want to get the bus and, Annie, tell her to keep her mouth shut."

"Ok." I say as Becca takes our rubbish to the bin. We say goodbye then I join her at the door. We make our way out, and I relay Tommy's instructions.

"But what was that?" She says. "And what do you mean drugs?"

"I heard Chloe, Bec. She drugged me, she said I was out cold."

"Shit, An. Really? Are you sure?…And what was all that talk of sinking? What you just said to Tommy."

"I wish I could explain it, Bec. He just helped me, that's all."

She just stares at me like I'm speaking a foreign language. Since the accident I've been so swept up with visions, a miscarriage and just trying to survive. I've left Becca behind. I didn't mean to, I just don't want to drag her down with me.

"I get it you know." She nods. "He's your best friend, but I'm your friend too."

"I know you are, and I'm yours."

I give her a hug goodbye, then head up to ceramics.

When I go in, I hurry over to Mr. Coley's desk, where he rummages through piles of books on ancient artwork.

"Sir, can I speak to you?"

"Yes of course." He says, flicking his hair out of his eyes.

"I'm sorry but, I'll need to leave early." I lower my head and whisper, "I'm starting bereavement counselling."

"No problem," he whispers back, "I'm pleased you're getting help."

"Thank you, Sir."

It's weird, but I wish he was my therapist. I trust him. He's the one teacher who I genuinely believe gives a shit. All the others say the same old spiel, 'my door's always open.' Mr. Coley doesn't. He asks how I'm sleeping, if I'm eating enough, if I need help with my work, do I need a break. He doesn't make a big deal when I don't get what he's talking about, because my head just zones out. He seems to understand.

Then there's Dan; he's watching me now, waiting for me to sit with him. If only I could've told him what happened at that party, I hate keeping it all a secret from him, it tears me up.

"Hey." I say, slipping into my seat.

"You've had your hair cut?" He smiles, leaning back in his seat.

"Yeah."

"Can I have a proper look?"

I tease my bobble free and shake the strands into place. He moves to touch it, but stops and lowers his hand. Dan's never shy with me, and him pulling away now, just makes me feel worthless. I don't want to cry. My heart's so raw today, and I can feel my stomach knotting, but with a quick deep breath and a brave smile, I manage to stop it.

"It's nice," he says, "you look pretty."

"Thank you."

"Good afternoon." Mr. Coley says, as he paces around the equipment unit, in the centre of the class. "As you're all aware, it's exam time soon, so we'll use the lesson to practice. This year's theme is felines and the range is fairly broad. You'll need to incorporate basic cat-like features such as ears, eyes, claws etcetera."

Once everyone has their clay and equipment, Mr. Coley makes his usual rounds. After a few minutes, of warming the clay in my hands and listening to Dan telling me all about a new thriller he's reading, our teacher kneels in front of me.

"Right, Anna," he says, "you're always good with ideas, any thoughts on your exam piece?"

Usually that would be true, but not today. I can't get past what I heard Chloe say at lunchtime.

"Sorry, Sir." I say. "I…my head's a mess."

134

"I know you've had a difficult time," he says kindly. "I'm not going to put you under any more stress, so here's what I suggest. Use this time to practice different modelling techniques, just make anything. Then later," he adds, "when your head's less messy, maybe try Googling some ideas."

"I will, thank you, Sir."

He then taps the table and moves along to Dan.

How am I going to concentrate for my GCSE's, when I can't even figure out what type of cat I'm going to make? I need a miracle. I need to get Alex out of my head, I need to fill that space with something else. It can't be Dan, I know he's right beside me but, if I think about him I'll end up dwelling on the secrets I've kept. It has to be Tommy, he's the only one that can keep me focussed. I squeeze the clay between my fingers and close my eyes.

When we were kids, he'd sit on a massive bean bag and play video games. I would beg and beg for a turn. Sometimes he'd let me and fall about laughing at how useless I was. Other times, I'd just stand behind him and play with his hair.

"Hey." Dan gives me a nudge, and I stare down to my hands, buried in a sloppy mound of clay. "What were you smiling at?"

"Um, ha I was just remembering something from years ago…oh no." I say, noticing the time. "I'm leaving in a minute."

"Where're you going?"

"Bereavement counselling." I whisper.

"Here," he says, and begins scooping up the mess, "I've got this."

"Oh, Dan. Thank you."

I quickly wash my hands and gather my things, Mr. Coley nods as I leave the room. Outside, Tommy jumps out of the car and rushes towards me. The moment we meet, I plant my forehead in the centre of his chest. He hugs me, and for a minute or so we just stand there. I so wish we could go straight home.

1.50pm. Medical Centre.
Anna:

Our medical centre is a two-story building, with the GP surgeries upstairs. The ground floor is a large square, open-plan reception area, with a small pharmacy and a few other rooms around the outside. For such a large building it's eerily quiet. My shoes squeak against the polished floor, as me and Tommy cross the square to the reception desk, at the far end.

"Hello, I'm…" before I give the lady my name she, without even looking at me, raises one finger and continues tapping the keys of her keyboard. Looking at her, I'm surprised she can type anything with those ridiculously long false nails. Tommy raises his eyebrows and folds his arms, clearly biting his tongue. After a few awkward minutes, she finishes her tasks, takes my name then sends us to the waiting area.

I feel sick. I'm so nervous, and Tommy keeps looking at me. He's desperate to know exactly what Alex and Chloe had said earlier. I know he is, but he won't ask me now, not here, but he will ask me later. I hate being like this, I wish I could've stayed calm and told him everything earlier but my stupid head started spinning, and I was a blubbering mess.

"Don't do that," he says, moving my hand off my wrist, "they won't heal."

"I know, sorry." There's nothing even medically wrong with my skin, they just itch when I'm anxious. I have to scratch, I can't help it.

In only a few minutes, I hear my name. I turn to see a smart looking lady by the reception desk. I really hope this isn't my therapist. She looks like a lawyer, platinum blonde, skin-tight blouse and pencil skirt, full face of make-up and four inch high stilettos.

"Annalee Anderson?" She says again. I so want to go home.

Tommy assures me that he'll wait in the car until I'm done, but I don't want him to go. I wish he could just sit in and listen. He gives me a quick hug, and I have to stand there and watch as he heads outside. Then I scurry after her and follow her into a small room.

This is strange. I feel like I've just stepped into an alternate reality. Outside everything's clinical, but in here, I could be standing in somebody's living room. To my right there's a panelled window spanning floor to ceiling, looking out onto a pretty stone courtyard. There are two sofas facing each other in the centre of the room, with a small coffee table in between. Ok, maybe this isn't so bad.

"Annalee," she chirps, "would you like a drink?"

"I'm ok, but can you call me Anna, please?"

Squeezing her knees together, she nods and daintily bends beside a small table, filling herself a disposable cup of boiling water from a dispenser. She stirs in a spoonful of coffee. That's when I notice the old-fashioned painting to my left; a sad little girl leaning against a wall, ignoring a beautiful sheepdog who just wants to play. Mum had the exact same painting, at the top of our stairs. She always said that girl was me, moody.

"Do you like the picture?" She asks.

"No, I mean yeah, I…my mum had that painting." I move over to the drinks table, look at the options and make myself a tea. I can feel her watching me while I squeeze the teabag. "Where should I sit?" I ask as I add the milk.

"Anywhere you like."

There's no way I'll be able to stay focussed with that painting looming over me. So, I choose the sofa which faces the courtyard.

"Right then." She says, making herself comfortable on the opposite sofa. "My name's Julie, and I want you to know that whatever you tell me is confidential, unless there's a child protection issue. So, if that's ok, why don't you begin by telling me about yourself?"

Suddenly the room is silent, and I don't know what to say. She's so prim and perfect, what if she wants something specific? Like how I miss my parents. Should I be crying for them? How can I when Mum didn't want me, and Dad couldn't care less? He'd just throw money at us and that was that. But, I do miss them. I don't want to, but I do. This silence is too heavy, so I just start babbling.

"I'm Anna…sorry, you already know that. I'm sixteen and…I don't know what else to say. My parents had an accident nearly two months ago. Do you want me to talk about that?"

"If you'd like, but might I suggest you start small. Tell me your interests, what you like to do with your friends."

"Ok." I press my feet together and take a sip of tea. "I like to run…and I love going to the woods."

"Do you go there alone?" She asks.

"No, I go with Tommy, he's my brother. We go climbing too, you know with harnesses and stuff, but we haven't done that for a while." I want her to say something, but she just nods. So, I scour my brain for something else and laugh nervously. "He took me to Chillingham Castle a few months ago, that was good."

What do I say now? I ask myself. I could tell her about Dan, but that's tricky when I'm keeping so much from him. Then there's Becca, I don't know what's going on with us lately. Today was the closest I've felt to her in a while, but talking about that would lead me onto Alex, I can't go there. I feel like I'm navigating my way through a minefield, every time I avoid him, I end up where I started. I need her to say something. As I perch on the edge of the sofa, anxiously rubbing my thighs, she leans forward.

"It's ok." She says. "Just say what's on your mind, anything at all."

That's the thing, the party's on my mind. I can't escape it.

"I didn't want to go." I say, swallowing hard. "My friend, Becca said I had to. I need you to know that I don't do parties, but Becca's a really good friend, and it was hers. I'd been at her house all day, and I was ok until people started turning up. Nearly half of our year were there, in the house, garden, everywhere. Becca got embarrassed because I panicked, I'm claustrophobic you see, so she poured me a Malibu. It was so strong, I nearly choked but she said to just down it, so I did. She kept giving me more till I relaxed."

Remembering us all crammed into her little house, makes me shudder. Julie just smiles and waits for me to continue, but I can't. I have to stop there, or I'll end up back at Alex. Avoiding him, I skip forward to when I staggered home. I'm struck hard, by the image of my brother; how broken he looked as he sat on that sofa. I can't shake it away and I begin to sob.

"I hadn't seen him cry since we were kids."

"Sorry," she says, "but you'd not seen who cry?"

"Tommy!" I yell, "I'm talking about Tommy." My legs bounce as I rub tears off my face.

"Oh, was he at this party too?"

I shake my head. "This was when I got home."

"And it was the first time you'd seen him cry?"

"First time in a long time." I pause to take a deep breath. "He lets me see him cry now, but before then, the last time was years ago. I was supposed to be in bed, but I heard him and Dad arguing. So, I sat on the stairs, wishing that they'd stop. It was awful, Dad shouted louder and louder, then Tommy cried out. I tiptoed downstairs and pressed my face against the lounge door. Neither of them noticed me, when it creaked open. Tommy was holding his cheek. He was so angry, and he screamed, 'Why are you even here? You've never loved any of us!' Dad was raging. He ripped off his belt, grabbed the collar of Tommy's pyjamas and hit him over and over. He wouldn't stop. I was hysterical, I burst into the lounge, screaming. It was like he didn't even know I was there. In the struggle, Tommy's top lifted and his back was covered with bright red streaks. I didn't know what to do, so I locked my arms around Dad's, even lifted my feet off the floor but it didn't work, I was too small. All I did was make it worse. Dad couldn't stand me hanging on him, he flung me off and I crashed into the TV stand. Then he stormed out, and I flung my arms around Tommy's neck…I didn't dare let go."

I don't know what I expect her to say. I guess she'd want to know where Mum was. She doesn't, she only asks how old I was.

"Eight…I was eight."

Raising her eyebrows, she whispers that age back to herself. I have to stop now; I've said way too much.

2.50pm. School.
Becca:

That stupid party was Chloe's idea. As soon as she heard that my mam was going away, it was all arranged, and everybody knew. I shouldn't have made Anna go, she never wanted to. Now her life's ruined and it's all my fault.

I'm in no mood for school. I want to talk to Alex, but Tommy said I can't say anything. Who does he think he is, bossing me about? And telling me to get the bus? There's nothing stopping Alex from following me, then what would he expect me to do? It's all fucked up. I can't believe I'm doing this, but hiding my phone under the table, I text our James to ask for a lift home. He'll probably say 'no,' he'll want to know what's wrong with my legs.

Here we go, I think as my phone buzzes, he's replied.

"No probs,
I'm leaving Mam's now."

Who's this, and what's he done with James? I don't know who gave him the happy pills, but I'm not about to complain.

When the bell rings, I grab my stuff and leg it. I fight my way down the stairs and through the car park, that's when I hear Alex, shouting for me to wait.

"Sorry." I huff, right before throwing myself into James's car.

"Everything ok?" He asks.

"I'm fine."

Alex walks slowly past the front of the car. He holds out his hands, like he's asking me 'why?' James watches him walk away, then turns and glares at me.

"Becca, why did you ask me to pick you up?"

"I'm fine, James! Will you just fucking drive!"

He folds his arms. "Not until you tell me what's up. I'm not daft ya know, I can tell when something's wrong." He's not joking either, he's so stubborn. He'd sit here for an hour if he wanted to.

"Fine! If I tell you will you just go?"

"Ah ha."

"Well, go then."

He nods and pulls out of the car park, onto the main road. "Let's have it." He says.

"Promise me, you won't breathe a word of this to anyone?"

"That depends on how much trouble you're in."

"I'm not in trouble!"

"Then you've got my word."

"Ok." I sigh. "It's not me…but now I know, I'm kinda involved."

"Involved in what?"

"Alright, you know I had that party?

"Yeah, your dumbest moment." He glares. "I know you're young, but you're meant to go to parties, not host them… everyone knows that."

"Shut up about that, ok? I'm trying to tell you. Anyway, that night Anna was like, super pissed and she had sex…"

"Ya what? Shy Anna?"

"Yes!"

"Seriously?"

"She did, honestly. The thing is, the boy…he's my friend. Anna heard him talking to someone today, and they said that

141

they gave her something…to knock her out! I just thought she couldn't remember because of the drink, or she didn't want to, or maybe because of her parents. But now it all makes sense. She was out cold!"

"She needs to go to the police!"

"She can't! She's a mess, you should have seen the state of her. She couldn't even work her phone. I had to call Tommy for her, and he said not to let on that we know."

He flings the car into a lay-by and yanks at the handbrake.

"Hold up! Was that him, back there at school?"

"No!"

"Ok, but did you just say you're friends with this lad?"

"Yeah."

"Not any more, you're not."

"Well, I can't be now anyway. Tommy said I can't let him know that we know. How can I talk to him and keep quiet? And, what gives Tommy the right to tell me what to do?"

"He's right." He says, knocking his knuckle against the wheel.

"Right? Why are you agreeing? You don't even like Tommy! Anyway? I can talk to who I want, if anyone can get the truth, it's me."

"Becca wake up. You think you know this lad but, if he's capable of doing that, then you don't. True, Tommy's soft as shite, but he's just protecting his sister…as am I. So keep your gob shut, clear?"

"Perfectly."

9pm. Home.
Tommy:

Of all the things that Annie could've told her therapist, I never expected that. I'll never forget the way she clamped her arms tight around my neck. She was still holding on when Dad came back. He tried to prise her off me, but she just squeezed her eyes closed and clung tighter. They both

142

changed that night, before then her and Dad had been close. Annie would make him carry her everywhere, but after that night, she pushed him away. He tried for a while but soon gave up, he'd say to Mum, 'if she wants me, she knows where I am, but I'm not fighting for her.'

That's not a night I want to re-live. There's something much more pressing, that needs dealing with. I need to know exactly, what Annie heard at lunchtime. But since she's now taking a bath, I'll have to wait…I can't wait. She's been in there ages, and this is important. I head upstairs, but she opens the bathroom door, just as I'm about to knock.

"Are you alright?" She asks, and for a split second, I just stand there while she dabs away the water, tracing over her shoulders.

"I…I wanna talk, is that ok?"

"Sure, just let me put some pyjamas on."

I hover on the landing, until she opens the door.

"What do you want to talk about?"

"Come on, An. You know." I say, as I lie down along her bed.

She sits on the edge and looks right through me. "Alex?"

I nod and offer her my hand. She plays with my bandage but doesn't speak, just concentrates on running her fingertips over the ridges in the fabric.

"Tom…I don't want to say it, but I do want you to know. Would you understand me, if I said that I wish you could just look inside my head?"

"Of course, but I can't see in your head. I only know what you tell me." I shift myself back and tap the duvet. "Lie down, I've got you. Listen, you don't have to go over it all, I just need to know if you heard him say that he gave you drugs?"

"Pretty much, but it wasn't him. Chloe said that she'd given me enough to knock me out cold. It's been driving me crazy all afternoon…I keep going over it. Anyone could've been there, if I was 'out cold,' then who else saw? And, what would've happened if I'd woken up? What would he have done then?"

I hold her close to soothe her but, my mind's like a scene from Reservoir Dogs. If I got my hands on him now, I'd destroy him. The reality is we can't do anything. It's sickening, but she can't go to the police. It would be her word against his, and we can't rely on Becca to back her up. Then there's these visions, they can come at any time, it's not a thing we can easily hide. Those, coupled with the time that's passed between that party and now, I'd worry that she wouldn't be taken seriously. They'd practically interrogate her. I can't put her through that.

"Annie, you can't let him, or that bitch know what you've heard."

She presses her forehead to my chest and sighs. "I know. Why do you keep saying that?"

"Because if it got out, he'd be scared, then he might hurt you and I'm not taking that risk. Please, sweetheart…look, I want to rip out his windpipe, but I can't. Not till you leave school anyway."

"Tommy, no!" She sits bolt upright. "You can't touch him! You'll get arrested and…"

"I know, I know." What the hell am I doing? Telling her to keep her head down while I'm dreaming of breaking his fucking face. I need to keep it together. I need to calm down. She moves out of the way, as I sit up and fling my legs off the bed.

"An, I promised you that I won't do anything, and I won't…listen, I'm gonna make a cuppa, d'ya want one?"

Anna:

I don't want a drink. I want him to stay with me, but instead of saying that, I end up saying, 'please.' Then I'm left alone with my thoughts.

"What would Alex do to me?" Despite getting into a few fights at school, I've never known him to hit a girl. Though

144

until today, I never thought he'd drug someone for sex. How am I supposed to face him now? How can I hide the fact that I know? I would never be so stupid as to confront him, but I know me. I know that as soon as I look at him, I'll start imagining. I'd picture him holding me down, and then what? Shit, not again. I can't breathe, the room begins to spin. I tell myself to calm down, but it speeds faster and faster until my bed starts sinking, it's pulling me further down. Drawn into the floor, I grab the duvet, and that's when I see the carpet disappear beneath me, sucked into an abyss. In an instant, the foot of my bed drops, and I'm thrown into water.

"Tommy!" I yell, but all that leaves my mouth is air. I look up for a way out, and find Alex's devilled face, hovering over me. Unable to let go, I plummet into darkness with a thunderous crash.

I'm naked, lost and cold. I can't even feel my bed any more, there's nothing around me, only darkness. The ground is icy stone. I have to get back, but I can't see clearly. All I can hear are waves, crashing around me. I grab hold of, what feels like rock, and wait until my vision improves. Then I see it. I'm suspended on the narrow ledge of a cliff; like an arrowhead, it pierces the sea below me. Back against the wet stone, vertigo kicks in. As I force myself not to look down, my vision blurs again, now with flashbacks of a dream. It's not clear at all, but the sound is; it's a baby, my baby and it's crying. I know it's mine, because as I move towards it I can see its umbilical cord, which is still hanging from my vagina, and my legs are thick with blood.

"Help." I sob, slumping to the floor. The crying stops, my baby's dead. Left alone in the crevice of the cliff. It's staring at me but there's no life in its eyes. I scream from the pit of my stomach, but I'm too late. Tears of blood blind me, and I claw at my eyes, desperate to find a way home. When I eventually manage to open them I see Mum and Dad from deep within a gigantic wave, rising high above me.

"Dad!" I scream. He's holding Mum by her neck, squeezing tighter and tighter until the raging saltwater disintegrates her face. I try to run, but I can't move. The baby has been washed away, and the cord's pulling me down, tripping me up. I need it gone, but pulling against it is pointless.

"Come on!" I growl. It's excruciating, it burns with every strain, but it doesn't budge. It's part of me, I could no more remove it than I could pull off my own arm. I'm wasting time, that wave's getting higher, and if I don't move soon I'll be pulled under. I'll be swept away with Mum, Dad and my baby.

"Ok." I say, coiling the cord around my arm. I scramble up the rock face, but there's a voice on the wind. I can't wait around to listen. I have to get away. Leaping over a gap, I throw myself forward, smashing my face against the rock, as the swell of ocean falls and crashes behind me. It burns, and for a second everything's still, but there's that voice again.

"Leave me alone." I cry.

With each passing second, it gets louder until it eventually becomes clear.

"Look at me." It says again. I press my fingers hard over my eyes. It's like I'm rubbing the darkness away, and I begin to see a blurry, but familiar face.

"Tom? Is that you?"

"It's me," he says pressing his forehead to mine, "it's me."

June 09, 2016 Thursday 3pm. School Changing Room.
Anna:

My head's somewhere else today. I've tried to act normal, so has Becca. She lifts her PE top over her head, freshens up with a quick spray of deodorant and slips back into her blouse. I'm relieved today is almost over. We smile to each other but, on top of what we heard yesterday, I can't forget what I saw last night, that was terrifying. That vision was the worst yet. Tommy laid next to me, but I couldn't speak. He just held my hand and waited. At least an hour had past, before I plucked up the courage to tell him what I'd seen. He was great. It's like he's not freaked out any more or, if he is, he doesn't show it. We talked all night, going over everything from the accident, my miscarriage, exams, everything. We didn't make it back into his room and, when I got up for school, he was fast asleep beside me, still wearing yesterday's clothes. I couldn't bring myself to wake him, and I didn't want to catch the bus, so I crept out early, slung my bag across my body and walked to school.

"How was your therapy thing?" Becca asks.

"Yeah, it was ok. Were you alright? Did Alex see you get the bus?"

She shakes her head. "I couldn't do it, An, I hate buses. I got our James to pick me up. He was in a good mood ya know," she adds cheerily, "he even asked me what was wrong…"

"What? Becca, tell me that you didn't tell him?"

"No, Anna, n-no," she stutters. "I just told him that I was pissed at Chloe, you know because of that fight we had. That's all, I swear."

I don't believe her. I want to, but I don't. Becca always stutters when she's lying.

"So, how many therapy things are ya gonna have?"

I'm not in the mood for this, so I just shrug and quickly get changed.

She has to be lying. If I hadn't have stopped her, she would have told me. It doesn't make sense, she never tells James anything, he's not interested in her drama's. So, if she didn't tell him what actually happened, then she'd have no reason to tell him anything at all. And if she is telling the truth, then why would she feel the need to mention it to me? No, I know Becca's lying. I grab my things and make for the door.

"Anna! Will you just wait?!" She shrieks, as I dart past the teacher outside.

I'm livid. I wish I was still out on the track. I'd push myself to the absolute limit, I'd churn up the grass with every stride and get away from here. But I'm not, I'm in the corridor, and Becca soon catches up.

"You have to believe me," she pants, grabbing my arm, "I didn't breathe a word of what Alex said." She looks desperate, and I don't know what to think. So, I just sigh and tell her 'ok,' but I don't feel right.

Outside, we see that Tommy's parked the car near the gates.

"Ask him to take me home." She says anxiously.

"Sorry I can't, we've got a meeting with Mr. Rodney."

"Why?"

"Tommy's worried, he wants to talk to him about…you know…the things I've been seeing."

"Really!? So, you've had more?"

I nod, as Tommy steps from the car. "I um, had a bad one last night."

Alex crosses the car park. He's a few metres ahead, but he hasn't seen us. I'm guessing that he hasn't noticed Tommy either, because he almost passes him. But my brother steps in his path, folds his arms and stands fast in Alex's way.

"Whoa!" Becca gasps, "your Tommy's fuming!"

I don't have time to answer her, I need to stop him before he does something. I rush over, grab Tom's arm, and Alex scurries away.

"Tommy! What're you doing?"

"I just wanted to scare him."

"But you said…"

"I know," he sighs, "I just saw him and…I'm sorry. You ready?"

"Yeah, I think so." I nod as Becca catches up.

She's usually all smiles around him, but today she can't look him in the eye. She keeps glancing over her shoulder, like she's waiting for something to happen. Then in a second, she seems to just snap out of it. She flicks her hair back and hugs me goodbye. We always hug to say goodbye, but this is different. It feels forced, as though she daren't hug me properly in case she gives something away. I'm fairly sure what that something is, she did tell James.

Becca leaves, then we walk back down towards the main entrance. We pass reception and head up a split-level staircase to a balcony, overlooking the main hall. There're two offices here, first is Mr. Rodney's office then a little further along is Mr. Garrison's. Tommy knocks on the first door, then we lean against the railing and wait.

"I was forever sent up here." He laughs.

"Really? I know you were a bit cheeky, but you weren't that bad, were you?"

"Kind of," he says with a reminiscent chuckle, "I got into a lot of fights, but mainly because me and Rich were being daft."

"What did you do?"

"Just silly stuff, ha, and we always turned the pens into pea shooters."

"How?"

"Just take the ends off and pull out the middle, then chew up bits of paper and pick your victim."

"As if you were naughty, weren't you scared of getting into trouble?"

"Nah," he shrugs, "I didn't care…that's probably why I failed, but you won't. You're too bright." He turns and looks me in the eyes, "I mean it, Annie. You're far cleverer than I ever was."

I shake my head. Fair enough, he didn't take school seriously, but he certainly isn't slow.

"Don't be daft, Tom. You can speak fluent French, I can't."

"Tu pourrais si tu essayais."

Maybe I could. I wish I'd tried harder when Dad taught us. He was fluent, and Mum too, but I was lazy and only learnt enough to get by.

Mr. Rodney opens his door, and I nudge Tommy to walk in first.

"Afternoon, Thomas." Mr. Rodney gestures for us to sit down, then steps behind his desk. He straightens his tie before taking his seat.

"Afternoon." Tommy says. "Thanks for meeting with us."

A hazy stream of sunlight beams through the window, making Mr. Rodney squint. He raises his palm over his brow, and I glance around the room. I don't know how he can concentrate in here; his desk is a mess, it's covered in papers, post-it notes and decorated rocks. He must really love his family, because there are photographs of them everywhere; on the desk, shelves and filing cabinets. This room's like a messier version of Dad's study. There's a picture on his desk of a lady, maybe thirty-something. She's wearing one of those dresses that you throw on over a bikini, and she has her arms around two little girls. It's a perfect family, having a perfect holiday, on a perfect beach. I imagine the kind of day they're having, and if the kids like to explore. They've probably been collecting seashells, and Mum will carry their finds while they all go out to eat.

Tommy nudges me, and I quickly realise that I've missed half of the conversation. Embarrassed, I stare blankly into his eyes.

"I was just informing your brother, that you've missed two exams," Mr. Rodney says, "and study leave begins on Monday."

Two exams? Shit. They must have been while I was off sick. I daren't look at him now. I whisper, 'I'm sorry,' to Tommy, but he just smiles and turns back to Mr. Rodney.

"Is there anything you can do?" He asks, "could she still sit those exams?"

Mr. Rodney watches me for a moment. Each second feels like an hour, while I wait for his verdict. He takes off his glasses, rubs his eyes then with a huge sigh, he pushes himself to his feet.

"Yes," he says, opening his filing cabinet. He pulls out a sheet of paper and lays it on his desk. It's an exam timetable. "Right, Anna you should have already been given one of these, but never mind. He highlights my upcoming exams and adds in the ones I've missed. As he hands it to me, Tommy raises the main reason why we're here, and I suddenly feel sick. I want to run away, but I can't. I have to sit here while all my issues are laid bare. Shuffling my seat back, I hide my face behind my brother's shoulder.

"As you can imagine," Tommy adds, "these visions are frightening."

"Yes. Mr. Coley informed me of her episode in his class."

"Well," Tommy nods, "recently, I've been able to talk her through them and bring her round. You see, I'd feel a lot better if I knew she could contact me, if she feels one coming on."

Silence, for an agonising second there's silence, and I turn back as Mr. Rodney hums and drums his fingers on the desk.

"I understand that you're both dealing with a lot at the moment, and if things are as severe as you're making out, then I strongly recommend that you seek professional help."

"We have." Tommy interrupts.

"Good. Anna, you may use your phone in class to call your brother. Only your brother, and only if you are feeling a genuine episode coming on. It must be kept on silent and otherwise remain in your pocket, are we clear?"

"Yes, Sir."

"I can't allow this during your exams, but I can arrange for you to sit them in the quiet room, with an invigilator. Would that help?"

"It would, Sir. Thank you."

My brother thanks him too, and as we stand, Mr. Rodney shakes his hand, then moves to hold the door open for us.

Outside, Tommy puts his arm around me and smiles. "That wasn't so bad, now was it?"

"No, Tom…not so bad."

June 13, 2016 Monday 9.15am. Home.
Tommy:

"Damn it! I've missed her."

I'd planned on taking Annie into school, for her first exam, but she must've crept out quietly, because I didn't hear her getting out of bed. Now, as I throw back the duvet, I see a text from ten minutes ago, saying that she was going in. Sitting here, wondering whether she's ok or not, isn't going to do anyone any good. So, I tuck in the loose edge of my bandage at the wrist, and head to the bathroom.

A buzz over my face with the clipper is long over-due. With that, and not being able to tie my hair back, I'm beginning to look like I belong on the streets. After I tidy up the facial hair, I have a quick wash and scrub of my face, then take Dad's Rolex off the windowsill and slip it on my wrist.

This was his Christmas present from Mum, last year. Dad hated it, he always liked 'a timeless piece,' whereas this is chunky and black. Mum told me, that it was her way of giving him a gentle nudge towards something modern. In my opinion, twenty-something grand is one hell of a gentle nudge. That Christmas morning was awkward. Dad opened the box, glared through his brow and asked who she was thinking of when she bought it.

Anyway, after I've cleaned up in the bathroom, I throw on some clothes and head to the kitchen. First things first; kettle on, next up, I call Rich.

"Young Thomas?" He groans.

"Hey, man. You sound rough."

152

"Messy night," he coughs, "I'm good." I hear him turn on a tap and take a drink. "You alright?"

"Yeah not bad," I say, "listen are you busy?"

"Nothin' planned why? You at a loose end?"

"Could say that. I'm worried about Anna, it's her first exam today."

"Say no more, I'll be round in fifteen." He says, "just tell me you've got coffee in…and bacon, I need bacon."

"What kind of house do you think this is? Of course I have."

I spend the next twenty or so minutes going over everything. It's in these quiet moments, that things you'd forgotten spring back into your head. I should've paid more attention when Annie staggered home, reeking of booze after the party. Of course there was something wrong. She didn't know how bad it actually was, but I should have clicked. She was crying for fucks sake, and not just about Mum and Dad. She had no memory of doing anything with him, and that fucking dick-pic he sent her. I shouldn't have said to delete it, I could have reported him for that at least.

When Rich arrives, he slumps at the dining table and nurses his head.

"That good a night eh?" I say, as I make him a large mug of sweet coffee.

"Ha. Now, Tommy, you know I can drink." He twists his body around, propping the wall up with the back of his head. "It was our Kev's stag do. They're all squaddies ya know, have you ever been out with squaddies?"

I refill my mug and join him at the table. "Can't say I have."

"They're lethal, I'm telling ya…we crashed some bird's hen party. Two of the lads ended up giving her a strip tease, and I had me a bit of fun with one of her friends. Fuck me, Tom! Her mouth knew its way around a cock."

"Ha." I laugh, taking a swig of coffee. "You know it's a good night when you get a decent bj."

"Fact…you getting that bacon on, man? I'm starving."

153

"Yeah, I'm on it."

After turning on the hob, I arrange the rashers in the pan, but Annie calls as it begins to sizzle.

"Keep an eye on that pan, Rich," I say, wiping my hands, "I'll be two minutes."

He gives me a thumbs up and grunts, as I take my phone to the lounge.

"Hey you," I say, closing the door behind me, "you ok?"

"Yeah, I'm ok," she says wearily, "that's one down, I'm on a five minute break before the next…I wanted to know if you were ok." She sounds so tired, but she doesn't go to sleep until I get in from work, so it's no surprise.

"Don't worry about me, An. Listen I wanted to take you in today, something must've gone wrong with my alarm."

"It was me, I turned it off. I'm sorry, it's just you were so stressed last night, and I didn't want to wake you."

"Don't be sorry. That stupid bitch pissed me off, not you."

Last night at the pub, I had to split up a fight, and wound up getting a full pint of cider thrown at my face.

"I know," she says quietly, "I would've washed your hair, you know. You didn't have to struggle one handed."

"I know you would've," I sigh, "but you know how I feel. I hate needing help, it's like a constant reminder of how stupid I was…"

"You weren't stupid." She interrupts. "You were angry, there's a difference."

"Alright, sweetheart, ok." I say, as I lie back along the sofa "So, how do you think your first exam went?"

"Well, I kept my head together," she says optimistically, "I'm ok at maths. Oh, and the lady who's watching me is so nice, she's old and doddery. The thing is," she sighs, "my next one's worrying me. I'm tired now, my head's aching, and I feel like my mind wants to be anywhere but here."

"You're ok, just take a deep breath and try to stay calm. You're doing great."

"I'll try," she whispers, "will you pick me up later?"

"I was planning on it, daft arse."

"Thanks. I have to go back now…Tom I, I love you."

"I love you too. Come on, focus now. You're ok."

"I know. See ya later."

"Bye, little Annie. Call me at lunch."

This is why I wanted to take her; I could've helped her to clear her head, before going in there. I don't know if she'll get a chance to check it, but I send her a quick text, then head back to the kitchen.

"Are you wanting any?" Rich asks, as he assembles his sandwich. I shake my head, slide the patio door open and lean back against the frame.

"Talk to me, Tommy." He says, as he sits at the table. "I know Anna saw something weird at school, but why are you all chewed up over her exams? Hell, you hardly gave a shit about your own."

"She's just delicate at the moment, mate." I say, as I stare at the tree at the bottom of the garden. It's not the best-looking tree, shabby and overgrown, but Annie loves it.

Rich washes down a mouthful with a swig of coffee and chuckles. "As if your sister's finishing school, I remember me and you teaching her to walk."

"Yeah, she's not a kid anymore."

I still remember the day Mum brought her home. It's funny, I was only five but that memory's vivid. I must've been staying at John and Sarah's, because when John took me home, I saw Dad in the kitchen. He nodded towards the dining room, so I crept through and into the lounge. Mum didn't look like Mum; she looked tired, pale and for the first time ever, she hadn't done her hair.

"Where's the baby?" I asked.

Mum held her belly and nodded to a frilly white basket, on a stand against the wall, behind me. When I peered over the edge, I saw her perfect little face. She squirmed, and when I laid my hand against her cheek, she squeaked. It was strange, I remember feeling happy and I couldn't stop grinning, but I had this feeling in my chest that made me cry. The instant she gripped my finger, she became my favourite person.

"What's her name?" I asked.

"We're not sure," Mum said, "I like Elizabeth and Daddy likes Annalee."

"Can we call her Annalee?"

"Why?"

"If she's Annalee," I grinned, "she can be little Annie."

Mum smiled, "Would you like to hold her?"

I shook my head. I was scared, she was so tiny, and I couldn't stand still. I honestly thought I'd break her.

"Come on, Thomas." She tapped the sofa. "You sit here, pop a cushion under your arm and one on your lap."

My legs jittered as Mum pushed herself up. She carefully lifted my kitten-like sister from the basket and laid her on my lap. I cuddled her close, kissed her soft, fluffy head and whispered. "Hi, little Annie, I'm Tommy."

I'm snapped back to the present, as Rich coughs and beats his chest.

"Come on, mate," he says, pushing his back against the wall, "There's something else, what is it?"

I kick myself off the doorframe and clear my throat.

"It's a number of things." Lowering myself to the floor, I sit back against the fridge. "Mainly that little bastard."

"You'll have to give me more than that, Tom. What bastard?"

"The twat who got her pregnant."

"Right," he nods, "what's he done now?"

"He fucking drugged her, man! There was a reason she couldn't remember sleeping with him…she was unconscious!"

Rich balls his hand into a fist, but he doesn't move. "You want him dealt with?"

"Anna won't let me touch him. She knows me too well."

"I don't mean you, Tommy."

"No, man it's ok. This isn't your fight, but thanks anyway."

We both sit in silence for a minute, as Rich takes it all in.

"Are you sure, dude?" He says. "You see, what I have are a particular set of skills. Skills I've acquired over a very long career…I will find him and I will kill him."

"You can quote Liam Neeson all you like, mate. But I doubt killing him's gonna help."

"You know what I mean."

"That I do."

11.55am. School.
Anna:

As soon as my invigilator tells me to go for lunch, I gather my things and hurry up to meet Becca in room thirty-five. When I get there, I see she's all cosy and Isabelle Maltby is in my favourite seat, by the window. Becca has her feet up on the seat opposite. Noticing me, she slides them to the floor, so I can sit down.

They're watching a video or something on Isabelle's phone, I say 'hi' and Becca flashes a smile, then from behind the phone, Isabelle smirks and they both giggle. I suddenly feel both unseen and exposed, so I reach into my pocket for my phone and call Tommy.

"Hey you," he says, "how did it go?"

"Ok, well I hope it did. Especially if I'm going to start college without re-sitting."

"I take it you're still wanting to go into nursing?"

"Yeah."

Most people go into nursing with a sense of duty, to 'care for others', or 'make a difference.' It's different for me, it's not that I don't feel that way, but nursing is familiar. Growing up with a Dad who was a surgeon, it was all around us. There were always huge textbooks, lying around the house. If I was bored, I'd sit and read them, but if I'm honest, I don't really know what else to do.

"You'll make a great nurse," he says, "you're certainly better at dealing with blood than I am."

"That's not exactly difficult, Tom."

I hear him laugh, and Becca taps her foot against my leg. She points to the phone and makes the action of a steering wheel.

"Becca wants a lift home," I tell him, "would you mind?"

"I suppose so. Rich is here too, so we'll drop her off then us three can go out for tea, if ya like?"

"Sure, I fancy a curry." I tell him, while nodding to Becca.

"Fair enough." He then clears his throat. "I've been thinking, It's been a shit few months and I need a break…"

This was the wrong time to bite into my sandwich.

"What?" I gulp, as I force it down. "Is it because of me?" In this moment, I'm actually grateful that Becca and Isabelle aren't paying me any attention. But I still turn aside and hide my face.

"Of course not!" He says firmly. "Don't be daft. I want to take you away," he adds, softening his tone, "just me and you."

"Where?"

"I was thinking, we could go to that campsite, near Hamsterley forest. What do you think?"

"Yes! I'd really like that."

"Great, I'll get it booked…and, Annie?"

"Yeah?"

"You're not what I need a break from. I'm not about to abandon you…I promised, didn't I?"

"You did."

We talk some more, then as I hang up, Becca asks what I'm grinning at. I explain, and Isabelle sucks in her cheeks as though she's chewing the inside of her face.

"That's not my idea of fun." She laughs.

"It is for her," Becca says, "she'd live outside if she could, Anna likes nothing better than a run up a hill. Aint that right, An?"

"I guess." For a second, I consider justifying myself. How I love fresh air, nature, building campfires and just

158

going 'off grid,' but I already know that Becca doesn't understand, so I doubt Isabelle would either. Instead I change the subject.

"Anyway," I say, "are you ready for this afternoon's French exam?"

"I guess." Becca nods, taking a swig of juice. "We've been revising, haven't we, Issy?"

"Yeah."

"Are you ready?" Becca asks me.

"Yeah, Tommy's been helping me over the weekend. All of Saturday, he only spoke to me in French, and if I replied in English he wouldn't answer, he'd just say, 'tu sais.'"

"What's that mean?" Becca asks.

"It means 'you know.'"

"When did he learn to speak French?"

"Years ago."

"Must be nice," Isabelle says, "having a big brother who helps you and takes you places."

"There're not all like Tommy," Becca huffs, "mine's a dick."

Earlier That Day.
10.10am. School.
Alex:

We've been together ages, but Chloe still wants to keep us a secret. It's getting a bit boring, but she's good in bed, so I'm not about to complain. Once we're past the school gates and out of sight, I wrap my arms tight around her waist, pulling her into me while she tickles the back of my neck.

"So, what ya doing now?" I ask.

"Waiting for Soph, we're going into town. You see, some of us only have one exam today." She leans in for a kiss, but nibbles my bottom lip instead.

"You're lucky, ya know that! I have to be back at one for French."

"Shame, you could've come with us."

"It's alright, our Jake's just texted asking me to look at something, so I'm gonna go home and check it out."

"If it's your Jake, it'll be porn."

"Hopefully."

She kisses me, but pulls away when she sees Sophie, dragging her fat arse past the gate.

"See ya, babe." She says, patting my face.

When I get home, I slam the front door behind me and run up to my room. My curtains are still closed from earlier, so I drop my pants, fall back on the bed and open Jake's video. I skip the first few minutes till the action starts; one dude pushes a girl so she's bent over a bed, and slams her from behind. Then, all of a sudden another guy comes in, and starts fucking her throat. Boring. It's not even getting me hard, once you've seen one spit-roast, you seen them all. Fucks sake, I've got myself worked up for a wank now, so I squeeze my balls, close my eyes and think about that night, with Anna. Just remembering the sight of her, slumped on the sofa with her legs spread, makes me throb.

I'd watched Anna all night. She was wasted, thanks to Becca for continually refilling her glass. That's when I knew it'd be easy and, when Anna was drunk enough to let me dance with her, I nodded to Chloe. She asked Becca what Anna was drinking, she poured her another, this time with a little something extra. We didn't have to wait long before Anna was ready. I held her up, while Chloe kicked a couple of girls out of the dining room. Once they'd gone, we dumped her on the sofa. She was gone, but I had to be sure, otherwise all the planning would have been for nothing. I stood behind the sofa, slid my hand into her bra and squeezed her tiny tit. She didn't respond. This was it. Chloe locked the double doors and stuck a wedge under the door, into the kitchen, while I peeled off Anna's jeans.

"You're gonna give it to her good." She said, with a sexy smile.

I didn't say anything, I just pulled my jeans down and stared at Anna's skinny thighs. Then, taking a deep breath, I ran my hand from her knee up to the sweet spot, moved her knickers over and slid a finger inside, but Anna moved. So, I stopped and pulled back.

"Chill." Chloe snapped, giving Anna a slap across the face. "She's not gonna wake up, see? Get on with it, we ain't got all night!"

"Ok, ok." I kicked off my pants and hooked my hands behind Anna's knees, then rocked her arse to the edge of the sofa. Chloe held her knickers to the side, so I could push my end in. But she was so dry and tight, I couldn't get up her. It was so frustrating, and I was about to quit when Chloe leaned over and drooled spit onto Anna's pussy, she rubbed it in and I tried again. My cock slid in easily, right to the base. I knew I wasn't going to last, she was tighter than anyone I'd fucked before, and it felt like she was pushing me out with every thrust. But I just gripped her legs tighter and forced myself in. It was awesome. The whole time I was fucking Anna, Chloe rubbed my arse and even tugged on my balls, it was everything we'd fantasised. The pressure was immense, and without a second thought, I emptied my load deep inside her. We'd done it. Chloe threw my underpants at me as I sat watching my jizz soak into Anna's knickers.

Remembering that night seems to be the only thing I can wank over lately. Chloe's hot but she wants it just as much as me, so there's no danger. I'd love to fuck Anna again, I mean sure she'd put up a fight at first, but in the end…I think as I cum and almost shoot myself in the face, she'd love it.

There was only one part of that night I'd change; when I pulled my jeans back on, Chloe kissed me and said that I had to stay with Anna. I thought she was winding me up, but she wasn't. She said that I had to cuddle up with her, so when she woke up in the morning, she'd just think I was a drunken mistake.

"If you stay," she shrugged, "then you've got nothing to hide, right?"

This wasn't part of the plan, but she had a point.

161

"Come straight to mine in the morning," she said, "I'll make it up to you." And she really did.

June 15, 2016 Wednesday 3.20pm. Medical Centre Waiting Room.
Anna:

We haven't been waiting long but Tommy's irritated. He keeps prodding at the dressing on his palm. He doesn't need a bandage any more, just a dressing. The last time I changed that, his wound was healing well.

"What's wrong?" I ask.

He takes my hand and rubs my fingertip over the edge of the dressing, closest to his thumb. "You feel that?"

"Yeah." There's a bump the size of a pea, where they tied off his stitches. "Does it hurt?"

"A bit. Will you take a look when we get back?"

"Sure, but you should get it checked in case it's infected."

He swallows and shakes his head. "You just take a look, ok?"

"Yeah, ok."

"Thanks. Anyway," he says, nodding across the square to my therapy room, "how are you feeling?"

"My belly's in knots, she hardly speaks you know. She just sits there waiting for me to trip up…and I'm sure she puts truth serum in the tea!"

"Don't drink the tea then." He laughs.

"I'm serious, Tom. How else does she manipulate me into revealing my secrets…our secrets."

"She's not manipulating you, daft arse." He says. "She's trying to help you."

He's probably right, so I nod and rest my head on his shoulder. My issue is that I don't know her and she doesn't know me. What happens if I see something weird? What do I do then? After that bad one at school, Dan said he'd been talking to me the whole time, but I never knew, and he's one

162

of my best friends. If I couldn't hear him, how could I hear her?

"Look at me." Tommy says softly. "Don't worry about what you told her, about us and Dad. I've been thinking about it, and if it helps you, then I don't have a problem if you share anything that involves me. All I ask," he adds, raising his left hand, "is that you don't tell her how I did this."

"I wouldn't."

Julie is the last person who I'd want to know about Tommy's temper. Even if I assured her that he'd never hurt me, she'd most likely flag me as 'in danger', then I'd kiss goodbye to him being my guardian.

"What do I do if I have another…you know?"

"Hallucination?" He asks, itching his stubble.

I nod.

"You could tell her about them."

I sit upright and look him straight in the eyes.

"Explain them," he repeats, "get it out of the way when you first go in."

"Are you mad!?"

The eyes of the woman on reception suddenly dart at me. My cheeks are burning, so hiding my face I whisper, 'are you mad?'

"Hear me out. I know what's worrying you, and I promise she won't think you're crazy. Mr. Rodney didn't when I explained it to him, did he?"

I shake my head.

"Just tell her what happens and how we deal with them. Then, if anything goes wrong, she can send for me. I told you, I'll always be in the car park."

"How *do* we deal with them?"

He looks puzzled.

"How do you bring me back?"

For a few seconds he looks at me as though he doesn't want to answer, then he says tenderly. "I hold you, stroke your face and I tell you to look at me."

"And, what do I do? When it's happening?"

Shaking his head, he looks away.

"Tom?"

"You're not yourself." He whispers, staring off into the distance. I lay my hand over his, and he turns back to me. "You fight, Annie…and you look like you're in pain."

"Do I hit you?"

"Sometimes, yeah."

I feel like Jekyll and Hyde, like these attacks bring out a monster that I can't control. I open my mouth to say I'm sorry, when I see Julie trotting over to us. As I stand to follow her, Tommy takes my hand.

"As soon as you go in," he says, "tell her as soon as you go in."

I nod.

Inside the room, I plonk myself in the centre of the sofa, facing the courtyard; avoiding both the dog picture and the refreshments table. I know the idea of her lacing the tea with truth serum is outrageous, but I'm not taking any chances. My palms are sweaty so I rub them over my school trousers. If only I knew where to start, I can't even remember how Tommy told Mr. Rodney, I was too busy looking at his photographs.

"Are you not wanting a drink, Anna?" She asks.

"No, I um, I, there's something I need to tell you."

She perches on the sofa facing me, holding an empty cup that she was about to fill with coffee.

"What is it?" She asks, "what's on your mind?"

How do I explain that my mind's on my mind? But I try. I'm not sure if she's understanding, because she just tilts her head and nods, while I navigate my way through it all. I'm kind of listening to myself as an onlooker, and I'm actually surprised by how concise I sound. I think I'm doing well at disguising that my heart's beating so hard, it could break through my chest. I do need a drink after all.

"If I feel one starting," I say, as I stand to make myself a tea, "will you get Tommy for me? He'll only be in the car park."

She narrows her eyes and smiles in the most patronising way I've ever seen.

"I don't think that'll be necessary," she says, "I've dealt with this kind of thing for many years. You're safe here, don't worry"

Hold on a minute. How can she be so arrogant? She's heard one painful memory of mine, and now she thinks she understands me. I don't trust her. I beg her to change her mind and dig my nails into my wrists, until they burn.

"Please!" I cry, "I can't come back for anyone else!"

No-one has ever kept me from him before. I don't know what I'm going to do, I can't open up to her now, that's for sure.

"Anna, come and sit down." She says, suddenly changing her tone.

I place the cup on the coffee table and hug my body tight. She's going to think I did that on purpose; had a tantrum because I can't get my own way, but it's not like that. I just need Tommy.

"If anything happens," she says, "then yes, I'll send for your brother, but I'll need you to describe his car."

"Black Audi Q7," I sniff, wiping my face, "it was Dad's." I give her the registration too, and she jots it down while I squeeze my fingertips, it's the only way to stop my hands from shaking. Julie's eyes dance over me.

"I'm sorry." I say. "I…"

She dismisses my apology with a wave of her hand.

"Right," she says after a long, uncomfortable silence, "last session you spoke of your brother. Today why not tell me who else is important to you. For example, your friend from school, what was her name?"

"You mean Becca?"

She nods and squeaks a sort of high pitched hum. What on earth is going on? Have I missed something? Has she

165

missed something? I didn't mean to freak out, but I panicked, and she doesn't even want to address it. Why? She's messing with my head. She has to be, it's the only explanation. Perfect Julie, sitting there all prim and proper. She's pressing all the right buttons, so she can sit back and watch me crack. I'm so tempted to leap from this sofa and make my escape. She'd never be able to catch me, I could be out of here and in the car, before she even had chance to kick off her heels and cross the square.

"Are you ok?" She asks. I don't know what she expects me to say, or how talking about Becca is going to help me. Then I remember what Tommy said, yesterday. I told him that I was anxious about coming here again. He said that, even if it doesn't make sense, I should just go with it. So that's what I'll do.

"Yeah, Becca." I say, sitting myself up straight. "We've been friends since we were eleven, when our year went on an outward bound trip."

She looks semi interested, so I continue.

"We weren't exactly friends before then. I mean we spoke, but my only real friend at school was Dan. I've never really been friends with girls. And I couldn't exactly share a bunk with him, as the boys and girls had separate dorms. I was put with Becca. Neither of us were happy, I had to bunk up with the pretty, stuck up girl, and she was lumbered with the freak who loved PE, but hardly ever spoke. She hated the outdoor stuff, complained constantly, cried that she was cold, and when we were orienteering she got bored. She couldn't even be bothered looking for clues, me and Dan were so annoyed, we left the rest of our team and finished the activity on our own."

"What changed?" Julie asks.

"One day the instructor planned a hike, and because it was going to be tricky, I couldn't pair with Dan."

"Why not?"

"Because we knew what we were doing. If you knew what you were doing, you had to pair with those who didn't. I was put with Becca.

She'd been whinging since we set off, but after a couple of hours it turned colder. Then it started snowing, you know that wet snow that melts as soon as it touches the ground? Obviously the trail was slippery, and we were lagging behind. I could've caught up with the others, but our teacher had made a massive deal about staying with our partners. We walked along a narrow ledge, a mud path with trees that almost touched the sky on one side, and a rugged bank that dropped to a stream on the other. Becca was behind me. She kept tripping on roots that poked up from the ground, and she went on and on about getting a shower and a hot chocolate. Suddenly she slipped and fell, her head jerked back, and she went sliding down the bank. I shouted the instructor, then carefully followed her down. You see, I knew how to get down safely, because those types of walks are what me and Tommy do for fun.

Anyway when I reached her, her foot was caught on a raised tree root. She freaked out, and I found myself talking about anything and everything. I had to take her mind off it, until the instructor came and helped her back up. I know it doesn't sound like much, but in those few minutes I saw a different Becca, she was just scared and wanted her mum. We've been friends ever since."

I lean forward to take a drink, and she tells me that I'm doing really well, but I don't see how. I didn't come here to talk about how I became friends with Becca Clark. I came to learn how to deal with these ugly feelings. I came to put some order into my head, to figure out why it hurts so much to miss a mum that I was a burden to, and a dad who was so distant, that he just became a figure who was sometimes there and sometimes not. This is not how I imagined therapy.

For the next forty minutes or so, I answer Julie's irrelevant questions on how I felt that day. I give her more and more generic answers, gradually shutting myself down. It's strange, I can't help but feel like one of those electronic toys, and Julie's the child who's played with me for too long. My batteries are fading.

When the session ends, I gather my things and calmly walk out to the car. Tommy rubs his eyes as I open the door.

"How was it?" He yawns, "did you tell her?"

"Yeah, I told her. It wasn't easy convincing her, but she agreed to bring you in if I need you."

"Wasn't easy?" He asks.

I shake my head. "She said she'd dealt with things like that forever…that it's not necessary to get you!" I remember the self-sure smile on Julie's face. It makes me angry. "I did what you said, Tom. I was clear and calm."

"I'm sorry," he says, "I honestly didn't expect that."

"You weren't to know."

Tommy:

I think everyone has some kind of preconceived idea of therapy; mine was that a warm, patient woman would ask Annie about Mum and Dad. She'd reassure her that she's normal, and try to make my sister aware of her qualities. She'd help her to focus on the good memories. It's stupid, but I'd hoped she'd unearth some proof that they did love her.

"I'm not sure if counselling is right for me." Annie sighs, as she stares out of the window. I slow down for a red light, and almost say that she doesn't have to go any more, but I can't. She's only had two sessions, and I need her to get well.

"I know how you feel, An, but she did agree in the end… if anything goes wrong, I'll be there." What do I sound like?

"I know you will." She lowers her head, she's tracing lines over the scars on her arms. She curls her fingertips ready to scratch, but stops when she catches me watching. I don't need to mention it, I just need to get her home.

When we get back, Annie kicks off her shoes. She washes her hands and fills a jug with cold, boiled water, that's been sitting in the kettle. I watch her as she flutters around the kitchen, gathering bits and pieces from the first aid box. She lays them on the dining table, with the water and a roll of towelling.

"Are you alright?" I ask.

"I'm going to look at your hand. You asked me to, remember?"

"I did." I say, laying my hand on her shoulder. "Annie you've hardly spoken to me."

"Can I just see your hand?"

I nod, and we sit at the table. She carefully teases away the dressing and sets it aside. Then shields my palm with her left hand, crumples a square of kitchen paper with her right, and dips the edge into the water.

"It might sting." She says, gently dabbing it over my palm.

"It's ok."

"Your stitches have dissolved," she says, "but not where they tied them off." She offers to show me, but I shake my head. Fair enough, there's no blood but I don't feel like looking at that scar just yet. "Do you want me to pull the knot out?" She asks.

I nod.

"I'll need tweezers?"

"Bathroom cabinet."

She rushes off upstairs, clatters around the bathroom and hurries back.

"Ok, Tom. I'll be super quick ok?"

I nod again.

She presses the cold metal against my skin, squeezes and gently teases the knot free.

"Much blood?" I ask, as she cleans the area.

"Not really, have a look. It's pretty much healed, see." She moves my hand towards me, slowly pulling hers away. I

169

stare at the pink flaky scar. The end under my thumb's weeping, but it's not bad.

"Are you ok?" She asks expectantly.

"I am. Thanks."

My sister begins clearing the table, but she's not right, and I can tell she's not herself. She's keeping busy, waiting for me to look away so she can dig her nails into her arms. After last weeks therapy session she told me everything, and it wasn't easy for her. She ran back to the car and spat it all out. Everything she'd told her therapist, she told me. Not today. I keep trying to make eye contact, but when I do, she looks away.

"Leave that for a minute." I lean back in my seat, and rest my head against the wall. "Will you talk to me?"

"Fine." She throws on her hoody, slides her hand up her sleeve and slumps back in her seat. "What do you want to know?" She seems defeated. It feels wrong to ask her now, I want her to tell me because she wants to, not because she has to.

"It's ok, An." I sigh, and stand to fill the kettle, "you want tea?"

"Sure."

She still has her back to me. Her feet bounce under the chair, as she slides her hands over her head, and presses firm on the back of her neck. "I need something, but I don't know what."

I stand the mug of tea beside her. "An early night?" I ask. "I'll stay with you."

She shrugs and blows ripples in her drink. "I didn't talk about you today, or Mum and Dad."

"Ok?"

"Julie wanted to know about Becca." She takes a sip. "Don't ask me why, because I don't know…she wanted to know how we became friends. I was confused, but then I remembered what you'd said, so I told her. I told her everything about that trip. I deliberately kept mentioning Dan, and how we've been friends for longer. I thought if I

170

could steer the subject away from Becca, then it would be easier. If I'm honest I didn't want to talk about Dan either."

"What did you want to talk about?"

"Mum." Her bottom lip quivers, she grips the handle of her mug, and looks right through me. "Tell me the truth, Tom. Did she love me?"

"Totally. You're the kindest person I know. You're honest, loving, quirky, complex."

"That's how you see me," she sighs, "I know you love me…but did she?"

"Yes. I believe in her own way, she did."

My sister sobs, slowly at first then harder. It's painful to watch her tiny body hunching over the table.

"I miss her." She cries.

"I know." I sigh, resting my head by hers on the table. "Me too."

June 18, 2016 Saturday 11am. Middlesbrough Town Centre.
Anna:

Tommy has a mischievous look in his eye. He winks at me as he speeds up the ramp, to the top of the multi-story car park. I know what he's planning, because he's parking as far from the stairs as possible. A race. I zip my phone into my hoody pocket and clasp my fingers tight around the door handle, I'm poised and ready.

He counts down, and I fly from the car, but he rockets past me. I've beaten him before and I know I can do it again. So I push hard, sprinting over the tarmac and squealing with laughter as I almost catch on his heels.

"Too slow, little Annie. Too slow." He jumps through the open door, to the stairwell. If I stand any chance of beating him, then this is where it's at. My heart's pounding. He darts down the first flight, I run a few steps then jump the rest. Overtaking's impossible, because on the next flight he blocks my way. So, I leap onto his back, and he stumbles to the bottom, where we crash through the double doors, and into the busy shopping centre. Despite a sea of disapproving glares, neither of us can breathe for laughing, but after a moment or two, the crowds continue on.

As we compose ourselves, we're both surprised to see our aunt and uncle, just a few metres away. John's just staring at us in disbelief, while Sarah scowls and shakes her head. Can't be seen having fun in public, no, that just wouldn't do.

They greet us with awkward hugs.

"You two look happy!" John booms, "ya pair of silly sods."

Sarah tuts.

"So what're you doing in town?" John asks.

"It's Anna's prom in a few days, so we're make-up shopping."

"You gonna try and show her how to use it?" John laughs.

"Nah, I'm going to do it for her."

"Never mind proms." Sarah interrupts. "What're you doing for your birthday?"

Tommy's birthday is only ten days away, and he doesn't want to face it. I get that, it's the first 'occasion' since the accident.

"Honestly," Tom says, "I don't want any fuss, I was planning on a few drinks and a takeaway at home... probably ask Rich and Stu over."

"Well we'll be there," Sarah insists, taking hold of John's arm, "won't we, love?"

"Sure, we will."

Tommy doesn't argue, it's not worth the hassle.

"Of course, being midweek," Sarah adds, "you cant expect Ethan to leave university, for just one day. You'll have to catch up with him when he's next home."

"We speak regularly," Tommy says, "don't worry about it."

"Well, just you make sure that he lets me know, if he's planning on coming home. I've been using his room to do my nails. Poor John can't stand the smell, and if Ethan wants somewhere to sleep, I'll need time to clear out my things… or the bugger will have to take the sofa."

Tommy runs his knuckle over his brow and nods. "I'll pass on the message."

Then an awkward silence, but it doesn't last. Sarah starts quizzing him on what present he'd like. Saying things like 'I need an idea, or I'll end up picking anything and you probably won't like it,' and 'now no glum faces, Ellen would still want you to celebrate.' As usual Tommy's unfazed, he just brushes it off with a smile. He tells her that he's sure whatever she buys, will be fine. She's not speaking to me today, and to be honest, I don't care.

John catches my eye and gives me a kind of fatherly smile, it's nice. He manoeuvres me a step or two aside.

"Are you ok? I only ask," he says, "because our Liv said you've missed a lot of school."

"I'm ok. I was sick for a while, but I'm on study leave now, so I only have to go in for exams. That'll be why she hasn't seen me."

"Fair enough, pet."

That's it, one question and one lousy answer and his job is done. He lays his hand in the small of Sarah's back, and just like that, we're saying goodbye.

"So much for no fuss." I sigh, as we watch them walk away.

"Ha. Now I know why Ethan didn't want her knowing that he's coming up, next weekend."

"Is he?"

"Yeah, a week today. He's gonna kip at ours."

"But, where will I sleep? Will I have to go back to my room?" I'd love to see my cousin, but…

"You're with me." He shrugs. "He'll sleep on the sofa, so just keep your bedroom door closed. To be honest, even if he did find out, I think under the circumstances, he'd understand."

He's probably right. Ethan's not like the rest of our family, they all know that I'd sleep in with Tommy, when we were kids, and he's the only one who's never teased us about it. I take my brother's arm, and he weaves us through the crowds into Debenhams. I follow him towards the make-up department. There're so many different brands, all with their own displays. We stop at the Benefit stand, and Tommy grabs a basket.

"Here," he says, picking up a few different products, "these'll suit you."

I have no clue what will suit me or not, so I just nod and smile. While he fills the basket with brushes, powders, lotions and potions, a lady behind the counter catches my eye. She's stunning and her entire face glows. Her hair looks like it's woven and pinned up to the side, like a flower, with soft fallen strands, brushing against the cheeks of her perfectly painted face. She's smiling, as she draws lines of lipstick over the back of a girls hand. I wish I was like her. I turn suddenly when Tommy, from behind me, leans close and says, "What'cha looking at?"

"Can you make me look like that lady?" I nod towards her.

"Nah…I'll make you look better."

I can't help but laugh. My brother's talented, but he's not a miracle worker.

"And the hair?" I ask, "can you do that too?"

"I'll have to see." He hands me the basket and strolls to the counter, lingering close behind the girl who's choosing a lipstick. He's blatantly staring at the pretty lady's hair. I just stand back and watch. I expect the girl to ask him to step back, but she doesn't. They both just look at him and blush. Tommy says something to them, and the lady turns her head to show him her hair. Never mind her confidence, I want some of his.

"I'm not sure," he says, as he steps back to me, "I can do simple braids, but that's actually quite intricate. Stu could though, d'ya want me to ask him?"

"Yeah, but only if he doesn't mind, I don't want to put him out."

I love Stu to bits, but I still feel cheeky asking him for favours.

"Here," he says, giving me his bank card, "you pay for those, while I drop him a text."

At the till, a lady wraps each item individually, and places them into a pink and black glossy bag.

"That's one-hundred and fifty-six pounds, eighty, please."

I almost choke on thin air and quickly flick Tommy, with the back of my hand.

"It's like, a hundred and fifty odd quid!"

He just nods, so I pay, and the lady hands me the bag.

As we leave the store, Tommy shows me his phone; Stu's replied.

"Oh, prom hair!
She can count on me."

"This is super exciting! Tell him thank you."

"Will do," he smiles, as we head outside, "you fancy a hot chocolate?"

"I sure do."

Tommy:

In the coffee shop, Annie finds us a table with a sofa, tucked away in the corner, while I buy the drinks and cake. As I set the tray down, she looks into the bag and smiles.

"You know?" She says, "I don't have a clue how to use any of these."

"That's what you've got me for."

I hand her the cakes, a knife and two tea plates. She slices them both in half.

175

"True. So, when are we going camping?" She asks, handing me mine.

"Day after my birthday, I've booked it from the twenty-ninth till the third. You see, I'm at the pub next Thursday and Friday, then the theatre on Sunday and Monday."

"Can I go to the theatre too?"

"Too right," I laugh, "Stu wouldn't forgive me if I left you at home."

She smiles and takes a sip of hot chocolate, when her phone vibrates from on her lap.

"It's him again." She sighs.

"Show me."

She hands me the phone.

"Had a wank last night,
guess what I was thinking of?
So, are u giving me a dance
on prom night?
Annaaaaa talk to me."

Fucking bastard. She won't reply, I know that much but she will re-read them. They'll gnaw at her, every time she picks up her phone. I delete the lot and lay the phone on the table. As she picks it up, fresh specks of blood on her wrist, poke out from under her sleeve. She catches me looking.

"I'm sorry," she says, covering her hands.

"I wish you wouldn't do that." I tear open the sachets of sugar for my coffee, and as I pour them, I hand her a napkin. "It must be really sore."

"I don't feel it till afterwards…I don't want to do it, you know that?"

"I know."

Annie nibbles her half of the lemon cake, while I throw mine in whole. I hate that bastard for what he did to her, and for what he's still doing.

"An, how long have you got left on your contract?"

"You mean my phone?"

176

"Yeah."

"Ages," she shrugs, "Dad bought it for my birthday, and it's a two year contract, why?"

I take a swig of coffee and suggest that we change her number. "We can buy you out of this contract and get you added onto mine, then we can put an end to that twat getting in your head."

"I can't expect you to do that," she says, as she stirs the cream into her drink, "you've already spent a fortune on me today."

She doesn't get it, so I tease back her sleeve, move the napkin and run the back of my fingers over her scars. She flinches, but doesn't pull away. Her eyes fill. "Will I ever stop owing you?"

"That money," I say softly, keeping my hand on her arm, "was Dad's, and he left it to both of us."

She slides her arm away.

"Look at me." I lower my head to hers. "You don't owe me anything, you'll never owe me anything."

She nods and breaks off a small lump of chocolate cake.

"Tommy?" She whispers, "how did Dad have so much money? I know he had a good job, but to have two clear mortgages and nothing owing on the car…it doesn't add up."

"He inherited most of it. You know it was just him and Granddad, when he was growing up?"

"Yeah?"

"Well Granddad had a decent job too, but he hated spending. So, when he died, Dad got the lot. It'll have easily covered both mortgages, oh, that reminds me, we've had an offer on the London flat…four hundred grand, An. Four hundred grand!"

She looks at me, stunned. "What are you going to do with it?"

"Well, after we've paid all the fees and things, we'll split it. I'll use part of my half to clear my mortgage."

"How much is that?" She asks, as she stares into her mug. "You don't have to tell me," she adds, "not if you don't want to."

"No, no it's fine. Dad put a forty percent deposit down, when we bought it. So, around fifty grand."

"I want you to pay that off, then we'll split the rest."

I shake my head and down the rest of my coffee. "Don't be daft."

"Tom, please, will you just listen to me?"

"I am listening to you, but what you're saying is daft. There's no reason for you to give up twenty-five grand of your share. I said you don't owe me anything."

"It's not daft, I want to."

She grabs my arm, forcing me to look at her. She's deadly serious.

"Why?" I ask.

"It's your mortgage, but it's my home. And I…I just want to."

Just then, her phone vibrates again.

"Is it him?" I ask.

She shakes her head.

"It's Becca. She's sent me an essay, hold on." When she's finished reading, she sighs. "Firstly," she says, "she wants to know where I am, she said her and Isabelle have been to ours, and she wants to know why I'm not in."

"Who's Isabelle?"

"A girl from school. Becca's been hanging with her while I was off. Anyway, then she goes on and on about the prom. She's got us moved onto Isabelle's table for the meal. That's good actually, we were going to sit with Chloe and Sophie."

"What else is she saying?"

"Loads. She wants to know how we're getting there… now she's sending links for limo companies! I don't want to turn up in a limo, can you imagine how tacky that would look?"

"Yeah." I laugh.

"Oh hang on, she's just sent another, saying that I have to stay at hers on Friday night." Setting the phone down, she presses her face into her palms. "I can't even sleep in my own room, let alone there…where it happened."

"Just say no."

Becca annoys me. She knows how to put the pressure on, exactly what buttons to press. She knows what Annie's dealing with, and I hate that all Becca has to say is, 'you have to,' and my sister caves.

Annie bites her knuckles and stares at the screen.

"Did you say that you're working Friday night?" She asks.

"Yeah?"

"If I go, will you pick me up when you finish? That way, I'll see her but still sleep at home…with you."

"Sure, no problem. Tell her I'll take you both to your prom too."

"Really? Thank you."

June 22, 2016 Wednesday 8am. Home.
Prom Day.
Anna:

I've hardly slept. When my eyes close I feel sick, nauseous, like I'm on a boat and waves are rising around me. And when I open them, I feel Alex pinning me down, or see Julie screwing up her face. She watches me, waiting for details of some distant trauma. She wants to fix me, wants me to hurt, so she can be the one who makes everything right. I have to tell her that Mum wasn't evil, she was just… distant.

Tommy's still sleeping, so I shuffle over and curl up behind him. When I press my forehead against his back, he reaches for my hand and pulls my arm over his waist.

"Busy day today, little Annie." He mumbles from somewhere between asleep and awake.

"Yeah, I guess." I want to sound excited and I am, but I can't think about tonight, not until I've survived today's therapy session.

He rolls over to face me. Staying close, he lays his arm over me and rubs my back, while I play with the strap of his vest.

"Are you alright?" He asks.

"Yeah, I'm just tired."

"Been a bad night again?"

I don't exactly answer, I just sigh.

"Annie, how many times? If you need me, wake me."

"I would, but you're tired too."

"Hey, I promised I'd get you through this, but I can't if I'm asleep."

He's got a point, but I don't like waking him. Even as a kid, I'd mostly just sneak in and snuggle up behind him, but on the times where I did have to wake him, he was never annoyed. So, I don't really know why I feel this way.

9.55am. Medical Centre.
Julie:

I find it peculiar, that Anna believes her only way out of her 'episodes' is through her brother. From what she has described, I suspect she's experiencing a sort of panic attack. Although, panic attacks are not usually linked with hallucinations. I'm concerned that there may be more than one mental health issue. I don't suspect immediate danger, however I am watching her closely, and should this 'condition' worsen then I'll make the relevant recommendations.

I slide away last weeks notes, as it's time to bring her in. In the waiting room, Anna looks adoringly at her brother, while he tells her an elaborate tale. It is nice to see her smile. However, that smile slips away the moment her eyes meet mine.

My usual clients are younger; often grieving the loss of a beloved pet, a grandparent, and in some rare cases, a sibling. Never have I dealt with a child who's lost both parents, and in such a sudden and tragic way. Plus, teenagers are notoriously difficult when it comes to gaining their trust, so far every angle I take with Anna feels like a gamble. So today, I'm handing over control of the session. We can spend this next hour in silence if she wishes, what matters is that she learns to trust me.

Once she's made herself a drink and taken her seat, I sit down on the opposite sofa.

"Today, Anna, you're free to discuss anything you'd like. The session is yours, and if you'd prefer not to speak at all, that's absolutely fine."

Her body stiffens as she takes a sip of her drink. She says nothing, testing my resolve, she remains silent for at least five minutes. This is good, her silence shows me that she's confident to exact her will.

When she does open her mouth to speak, the words fall dead on her lips. I lift a plate from the coffee table and offer her a biscuit.

"I…" she says quietly, refusing the biscuit, "I've finished school now. My last exam was ceramics. It didn't feel like an exam because we had it in our normal classroom." She stands her cup on the table and rubs her hands together. "Our usual teacher was invigilating and he even let us talk quietly. My piece had the body of a dragon, but it's head was like one of those cats that the ancient Egyptians worshipped." Using her hands, she mimes the design. "On the second day, after everyone's work had been fired, I painted mine jet black. Oh, I forgot to say, I'd carved the whole surface so the scales looked furry. I'd modelled it's mouth open, with a tongue of flames, as though it was hissing, then painted the eyes green."

This girl is incredibly creative. I want to hear more, so I smile and gesture for her to continue.

"Our old house was only a five minute walk from school, so at lunchtime, me and Dan visited my old neighbour. She's called Elaine, she makes gorgeous cakes. I asked her if she'd make one for Tommy's birthday, he's twenty-two next week. It's going to be lovely, a lemon drizzle with butter-cream."

Anna hunches over her cup and takes a drink, then shudders suddenly, followed by a sharp inhale.

"It's ok," I tell her, "this is good, you're doing really well."

"Can I walk around please?" She asks.

"By all means."

She pushes up the sleeves of her hoody, and I notice her wrists. Usually, her arms are covered by her school uniform. As she walks past me to the window, overlooking the courtyard, I see clearly, a mix of new and old scars. The grazing and irregularity suggest that they may be self inflicted. Anna's silent again, but she smiles at some finches on the bird feeder outside.

For the next few minutes, she appears to zone out. Her face fills with sadness, then in a surprising turn of events, she brings up a subject that I didn't expect for quite some time; the day her parents went away.

"Mum loved France," she says, "every year they'd drive out, and me and Tommy would fly over in the school holidays. This year they had to go earlier to fit in with Dad's work. Dad loaded the car and was ready to go, but Mum couldn't find her vanity bag. I heard her frantically running around the house, searching for it. All the while, calling for me to come and help. Dad just wanted to go, he didn't want to miss the ferry. If I'd have just helped instead of hiding in my room, it would have been ok…everything would have been ok!"

Anna turns around, stares at a picture on the wall and begins to sob. She slides down the window, to the floor and presses her head against her knees.

"Mum wanted me to find her bag, but I didn't care. I was just hoping they'd go so I could get ready, because I was staying at Dan's that night. It's stupid, it was just a bag, I could've helped but I didn't. I stayed in my room. Then Mum stormed in, she was stressing like she'd never stressed before, and when Dad burst in demanding that she hurry up, she growled at me. She said I was lazy, useless and selfish. Dad didn't even look at me, he just said 'come on, Ellen. We have to go.' Then he stomped downstairs, and I said it. I shouldn't have. Now, just talking about why I said it sounds stupid, but it happened so quickly…I said 'go on, fuck off on holiday.' My heart was thumping out of my chest. I never say that word, I hate it, but I did, and to my own mother! Mum turned and slapped me hard across my cheek, then told me she'd deal with me when she gets home. I…"

Anna lifts her head and cries, "I told her that I hope they never come home. I didn't mean it." She weeps, dragging her nails over her wrists. "I want her to come back, I want to tell them I'm sorry…I need them to know."

"You mustn't blame yourself for your parent's accident, it was precisely that; a tragic accident."

Anna nods, but continues to scratch. I gently point out that it looks sore, and she quickly slides her hands under her thighs and apologises.

"I know I didn't cause the accident." She says, "I wasn't even there, but she died thinking that's what I wanted…I texted to say I was sorry, but she didn't reply. They'd been gone a week, and she hadn't even let me know that they were there safe."

Anna tells me more, and it sounds to me that her relationship with her mother was strained. From what I can gather, she sounds like many other teenage girls; dealing with the pressures of exams and her peers. I believe Anna's also suffering from anxiety and, due to this trauma, she's trapped herself within a cycle of self rebuke.

"You've been extremely brave," I tell her, "sharing what you just did. Anna, it's healthy to be accountable for our own mistakes, but it's not healthy to continually punish yourself. Of course you didn't wish harm upon your parents.

Yes, they may well have been angry with you, I doubt they believed you actually meant it."

"Aren't you going to tell me off?" She asks, "don't you think I'm a bitch for saying that?"

"No. Why would you think that?"

"Mum's sister, Sarah…she hates me for it. She was drunk at their memorial, and she told me that she knew. I felt like my dirty secret was out, and everyone was going to hear."

I probably shouldn't ask this but I'm intrigued.

"Does your brother know?"

Anna nods and sobs some more.

"He looked wounded, but he said they were just words, and it wasn't my fault. He doesn't want me blaming myself."

Interesting.

"Your brother's right. Those words clearly hurt your mum, because she felt the need to share it with her sister and, as I've said, a certain amount of regret is healthy. I'd like to explain if that's ok?"

Anna nods.

"In this particular case, I feel you're dealing with what we call unproductive regret; this is a critical way of thinking or feeling, where you blame yourself entirely. It's dangerous, as it can create chronic stress, leading to further health problems. Constant re-thinking can increase anxiety and leave you feeling defeated or hopeless. Given what you shared last week, this concerns me. Now, the past cannot be changed, but what you can work on is the future. I suggest you make a list, write down your regrets, along with any questions that you regularly ask yourself. Go through them daily, until you've changed them from 'why didn't I?' to 'what can I do now?' Teach yourself not to make the old mistakes within your other relationships. Most importantly, forgive yourself for the things you cannot change."

Anna's clearly more receptive. She listens intently, and for the last portion of the session, we expand on the process of self forgiveness.

11.30am. Home.
Tommy:

We were both starving after Annie's therapy session. So, on the way home I swung by the shop, for some chocolate.

"What time's Stu getting here?" She asks, as she drops her wrapper in the bin.

"About one ish, he's having lunch with us."

"So I've got time for a nap then?"

"Yeah."

"Will you sit with me?"

I nod, throw the last of my chocolate in my mouth and follow her to the lounge. She lies down along the sofa.

"I can't believe I'm so tired from just talking." She says, as I drag over the floor cushion. Her hair's falling over her face, so as I lean against the sofa, I brush it from her eyes.

"I can believe it, you've dealt with a lot today…it's good."

"Do you think? I didn't want to tell her all of that, but it just came out. I told you…" she smiles, "truth serum in the tea!"

"Give over, daft arse."

She closes her eyes, and I keep stroking her head until she eventually falls asleep. Her fine golden strands fall through my fingers, and I just look at her. She's perfect. From her flawless, milky skin to that dainty nose. Even the way she breathes is beautiful. Her mouth opens ever so slightly, and when she whimpers, I can't help myself. I lean in and place two soft kisses on her lips, the moment I taste her cherry lip balm I pull back. What the hell am I doing? She's my little sister. I back away and scramble to my feet, but when I turn, I catch my reflection in the TV.

"It was just a kiss." I mutter under my breath. I was just loving her, that's all. Shit, I need a coffee, a strong coffee. Before leaving the room, I cover her over with a blanket from the back of the sofa.

"I'm sorry, sweetheart," I whisper, closing the door behind me, "I'm so sorry."

After filling the kettle, I stare blankly out of the kitchen window. It's genuinely frightening how natural that felt, almost as natural as her cuddling into me every night. What if she'd been awake? Would she have freaked out, or smiled and kissed me back? What the fuck, Tommy? You can't be thinking like this, she's your sister. Sort your shit out. For the next few minutes, I splash my face with cold water then growl into a tea towel.

"Are you alright, Tom Tom?" Stu sings, poking his head through the half open patio door. He's early.

"Yeah I'm fine, just tired." I take a couple of mugs from the cupboard and point to the kettle, "d'ya wanna tea?"

"You don't, per chance have any green tea? I'm reducing my caffeine."

Here we go, he's about to give me the benefits of this weeks fad.

"It's just loaded with antioxidants and it improves brain function, who can say no to a little extra in that department?"

"Absolutely." I say, whilst rummaging to the back of the cupboard. "I should still have a box somewhere, I always kept them in for Mum." Behind all the regular tea and coffee, I find an unopened box of apple flavour green teabags. "I've got these." I tell him, but as I glance over my shoulder, I catch him gawping at my arse. "Hey! You can pack that in."

"Oh, how I would love to." He winks, then pivots to check his hair in the mirror, at the bottom of the stairs. "Those will be fine, sweetie. So, where's the little lady?"

"She's asleep in the lounge, so keep your voice down."

He nods and mimes a zip, closing over his lips.

Anna:

I heard Stu arrive some time ago, but I haven't moved. I've just been lying here, listening to him and Tommy talking in the kitchen. I can't make out what they're saying, but that doesn't matter. It's just nice to know that they're there. As I stretch and contemplate getting up, my phone vibrates with a text from Becca.

> *"I'm like, sooo excited for tonight.*
> *Issy's getting ready at mine.*
> *Can Tommy take her too?*
> *Pleeeeeeease."*

I want to say no. I only agreed to go tonight because Becca wanted me to, and if the way her and Isabelle act at school is anything to go by, I'll be pushed out.

"Tom?" I call.

After a few seconds, he pops his head around the door, and I shuffle myself upright.

"Look." I say, handing him my phone. "I don't want to be awful to her but…"

He nudges my feet aside, so he can sit down.

"Annie, we can't really say no, but tell Becca that her friend will have to find her own way home."

"Alright, but this was meant to be our night…I don't want to sound selfish, but Becca changes when Isabelle's around."

"How so?"

"They're sly, you know? Whispering, as if they've got some private joke. It might be nothing, but it's not nice when you're just sat there. She's started lying to me too. You remember when Alex turned up at her house, when I stayed over? I asked her about it, and she denied it, she said he was lying. And she's told her brother about what happened to me."

"What?!"

187

"Yeah. She almost admitted it, then realised what she was saying, so fed me a bullshit story instead. And another thing, when Isabelle's there she makes fun of how close me and you are...like it's weird. I always thought she understood?"

He hands me back my phone and pulls the spare bobble from my wrist. "I don't think she ever understood," he says, tying his hair back, "how could she? She hasn't had our life. She doesn't know what it's like to have a mum who you couldn't even hug. Or to lie in bed, pushing your fingers in your ears, to block out the sound of your parents screaming at each other...and I bet she didn't spend nights hiding under her brothers duvet, because she didn't know where her mum was!"

"You're right." I sigh, as I send her a reply.

"Why don't you hang with Dan tonight?" Tommy says.

"I don't even know if he's going, he hasn't mentioned it."

"You'll be alright, and if you're not, you can always call me, and I'll come and get you. Anyway, you getting up? I've just made a load of sarnies and the kettle's on."

"Yeah, I'm starving." I rub my eyes and follow Tommy back into the kitchen.

"Afternoon, sleepy head." Stu says.

"Hiya." I sit opposite him, on the seat that faces the garden. A huge plate of ham sandwiches is ready and waiting in the middle of the table, and Tommy brings over three steaming mugs.

"Help yourself." He says, but as he hands Stu his drink, a familiar smell wafts past my face. It jolts me back to our old kitchen. I close my eyes and picture her, taking a drink as she gossips on the phone. I blink again and see the lipstick mark on her cup. I don't want to cry, I've cried enough today, so I just hide my face.

Tommy touches my foot with his. "You alright?"

"Mum's tea." I whisper.

"Are you ok?" Stu says kindly. He must have good hearing.

"Yeah, I'm ok...it just took me back, that's all."

188

"You guys are so strong," Stu says, "I'm so sorry about not making their funeral."

Tommy shakes his head dismissively. "Couldn't be helped, mate. You were away."

I don't want to risk an awkward silence, so I take a huge gulp of tea and change the subject.

"So, Stu, did you call that number?"

"What number?" Tommy asks, taking a bite of his lunch.

"Well, Thomas, while you were having your hand stitched, I happened to obtain the number of a deliciously sexy man named Dylan. And yes, sweetie," he adds, winking at me as I tuck in, "I did call him. We've been on so many dates, practically see each other every day. He's just wonderful. I know what you're thinking, Tom. You're thinking that I should take it easy, as it's only been a couple of weeks, but I say why? When we're so comfortable with each other?"

"Nah, mate," Tommy says, "sounds like you really like him."

"I do, he's beautiful; tall, dark hair, green eyes, he's got muscles like yours, and he wears the most adorable little earring…and he's an amazing kisser, not to mention his other talents. Well, Dylan the Dyson is all I'm going to say."

My brother almost chokes. "Stuart! Not in front of Anna!"

"Chill, Tom," I giggle. "He's not likely to do that in front of me." Tears of laughter roll down my cheeks. I try to compose myself, but when I look at Stu, he hides his face and his whole body shakes. I can't hold it in. Tommy just smiles, and shakes his head at the two giggling idiots beside him.

"Well, time's getting on," I say, still chuckling. "I should probably go for a shower." I finish my drink, then make my way upstairs.

Stu:

If we're going to work our magic, we best get a wriggle on. After finishing what's left of the lunch, I help Tom to clear the table. He then sits down to peel away the cellophane from Anna's cosmetics, while I lay out my styling tools.

"You didn't buy all new did you?" I ask.

"Yeah, I wanted her to have her own." He says, gathering the pile of plastic for the re-cycle bin.

Just then Anna calls from the top of the stairs.

"Stu? Do you want me to blow dry my hair?"

"No, sweetie I'll do it. But you'll need to put on a loose fitting top, a blouse or something."

Tom scoots past me, to the bottom of the stairs. "Wear one of my shirts." He calls up.

"Your sister reminds me of a flower." I tell him, as he steps back to the table. "She's just too precious."

"Tell me about it."

"Is everything alright?" I ask, as he neatens his brushes.

"As well as it can be. I just worry about her, that's all."

"Worry how?"

"I don't know," he says dismissively, "she'll be starting college in September…"

"Don't fret, Tom, I doubt the little lady would fall in with the wrong crowd."

"No, no, I know."

"You can't protect her from everything."

"I can try."

These two break my heart. He's bearing the weight of the world on his shoulders, he can hardly look at me. His eyes are fixed to the table, as he picks up each brush and bottle and lays them straight back down.

"She'll be ok, you know."

"Yeah," he nods, "thanks."

In the next second, my heart jumps to my mouth, as Anna launches herself down the stairs. She must have skipped half the bloody staircase. Clearly, she finds my near coronary hilarious.

"Don't do that! You'll do yourself a mischief!"

"Sorry." She giggles and sits down between us.

It takes me a moment to catch my breath.

"Right, sweetie," I say, "let's get those locks dry."

Once I've finished with the hairdryer, Tom tenderly smooths primer over her face. He's not that gentle when he's working on other girls, that's for certain.

Anna's hair is so beautifully soft and shiny that it's almost a shame to backcomb, but she has her heart set on a style that requires volume, so for that, it must be done. After smoothing the surface, I begin the braid, weaving through a fine wire, adorned with petite crystals. Tom leans in to begin work on her eyes. They're his speciality, he's like a wizard. I love Anna's eyes, they're a perfect bright jade green. To make them pop, he tidies and fills in her brows, applies varying shades of gold eyeshadow, then frames them with a fine black liner, and little more than a hint of mascara. As I tease the braid to look like petals, he contours; blending seamlessly with her foundation, finishing with delicate highlights and a soft pink, lip and cheek tint.

"Will it look like a rose?" She asks me.

"That's what you asked for, was it not?"

"It was."

"Yes, you'll have a beautiful blooming rose." I say, pinning it up behind her left ear and curling some of her loose strands. "And if I say so myself, it's looking gorgeous."

Tom shields her face while I cover her do with hairspray. This baby won't fall out, even if she dances all night. Oh, to be sixteen again.

Anna:

When I saw how my brother and Stu had made me look, I could've cried. That would've ruined my face, so I held it in. It wasn't easy, but I held it in.

Now, standing in my room, I peel off my leggings and unbutton the shirt I borrowed. There's no way I can wear a bra tonight. I remember thinking that when I first tried the dress on, the back's just too low. So I reach behind me and un-clip the clasp. As my bra falls to the floor, I stand and stare at myself in the mirror. I'm just a plain girl, all dolled up to look pretty, and if it wasn't for my wrists I'd be believable. I hate myself for scratching, I shouldn't even need to as there's nothing medically wrong with my skin.

Mum's and Sarah's voices play in my head. I imagine them stooping over me, saying 'you've spoiled yourself.' Perhaps I have, I think as I massage in some antiseptic cream. Perhaps I have.

I open my dress's protective cover, revealing layers of soft sheer fabric. It is beautiful, but it's not me. Every detail is perfect and delicate, from each tiny fold to the sparkly jewels, scattered over the waist. I take it from the hanger, undo the zip and step into it. After sliding the straps over my shoulders, I reach to the back to pull up the zip, but it catches. Now it won't budge, great. If I tug then it's going to rip, so I open my door and call Tommy.

Moments later, I hear him hurry up the stairs, he taps on my door before coming in.

"Help." I huff, turning to show him my predicament. "I'd hardly moved it an inch before it jammed."

He tries to loosen it, but what am I going to do if he can't?

"Stand still," he says, "I can't do it while you're fidgeting."

"Sorry, I'm just nervous."

"I know." He says. A few seconds later and it's free. He carefully slides the zip to the top. I turn around, and he takes a step back. In silence, his eyes dance over me and I suddenly feel naked.

I hug my middle tight. "Say something, Tom."

"Y-you're stunning." He takes my hand and leads me over the landing, to his room. "Close your eyes." He says, sitting me on the edge of the bed.

By the sounds, I guess he's rummaging through his chest of drawers. After a moment, I feel him kneel down in front of me, and fasten something around my neck.

"Now open your eyes." He moves aside, so I can see myself in the mirrored door of his wardrobe. I'm speechless.

"I wanted to give you this for your sixteenth, but Mum thought I should save it for tonight. I need you to be careful though, it's a real sapphire and platinum, so it wasn't cheap."

For my sixteenth? I just stand and stare at him. He smiles, that kind of smile that confirms what I'm thinking. He bought this with his own money, not Dad's.

"Tom? It's beautiful but how did you afford it?"

"I saved," he whispers, gently taking hold of the pendant. "I wanted to give you something special, so I saved."

So that's why Mum warned me not to be upset that he hadn't bought me much for my birthday. Not that I would've been, I didn't care. All I wanted on my birthday, was to stay here, and I did.

"How do you expect me not to cry now? Thank you. Do you even know how much I love you?"

"I have a fair idea." He moves his hand from my necklace, and brushes his thumb to my cheek. For a moment we just look at each other. Maybe we are different to other siblings, and what does it matter if people don't understand?

"There's something else." He says. Reaching under the bed, he pulls out one of Mum's jewellery boxes. I shake my head. I can't wear anything of hers, not yet. "Please?" He asks, carefully lifting a diamond solitaire ring from its box. "I get why you're reluctant, but she wanted to see you in the necklace, and I thought…" he sighs, "I just thought that since she's not here, you could take something of hers with you. I'm sorry, you don't have to."

"No, no, it's fine." I give him my right hand, "you'll have to put it on my middle finger, Mum wasn't as skinny as me, so it'll probably slide off the other one."

The thing is, I'm not the only one who's lost them. Tommy's hurting too, so of course I'll wear her ring…I just hope I don't lose it.

"Come on," he says, hugging me tight, "let's go downstairs. Stu wants photos of your hair."

4.30pm. Becca's House.
Becca:

My dress has definitely shrunk since I bought it. It's still gorgeous though, and the extra stretch to it has definitely helped to show off my arse. I stand in front of the mirror and squeeze my tits, got to love a halter-neck, now they're nearly as impressive as Issy's. Her dress is nice too, but I don't think going strapless was a good idea, if anyone steps on the front, they'll be blinded. She's brushing her hair for the fiftieth time, so I sit back and check my phone. Anna's posted some pictures.

"What'cha looking at?" She asks, leaning over my shoulder. "Oh! Who is that?"

"That's Stu and that's Anna's brother, Tommy."

"That's who's taking us tonight?"

"Sure is."

"I can't get in a car with him…I'll die."

She's flapping. She gathers up her dress, rushes to the mirror and spreads on even more highlighter.

"I thought you couldn't stand him, Bec." She rubs some more blusher into her cheeks. "You didn't say he was lush."

"He pisses me off sometimes, yeah, but I don't hate him. I'd let him fuck me."

"So would I! Are you on his page?"

"Nah, I'm on Anna's. His is boring, just full of theatre stuff."

"Shame," she sighs, "I wanna see more."

"Go on Anna's."

"I'm not following Anna." She snaps.

"Well you'll have to change that," I laugh, "if you wanna see more of Tommy."

We adjust our hair and make-up a bit more, then head downstairs to show the family our dresses. Everyone's here today; James, Emma and Mam's twin sister, Shelley. I know she's only here to say that I look fat. In the lounge, Issy sits on the puffy and I just hover, because that lot have taken all the seats. I can forgive Emma though, she is pregnant after all.

"You look gorgeous, Bec." Emma says. "You're so lucky, having dark skin, I'd be like Casper in that."

"Yes." Shelley butts in, "but she'd better not eat, or she'll bust a seam!"

"Shut up, Shell. You're only jealous." I'm not in the mood for her today. "Where are they?" I grumble, as I stomp to the window.

"Is Anna late, love?" Mam asks.

"No, not yet, but she probably will be, she's been useless lately. And I don't see why she can't just stay all night… she's supposed to be my best friend, and she won't even stay over."

Everyone just stares at me. Shit, I don't even know where that came from, but I've started so I'll finish.

"I want her to stay on Friday, when you go out, so I don't have to stay with him," I say, flapping my hand at James. "But she'll only stay till Tommy finishes work, at midnight. What's the point of even coming, if she's gonna go home in the middle of the fucking night!"

"Watch your language, young lady!" Mam snaps.

I want to answer, but before I know it, James stands up and orders me into the kitchen.

"What did you tell me, when I picked you up from school?" He growls.

"Leave it, James. That has nothing to do with it."

"It has everything to do with it. Put yourself in her shoes and switch your brain on." He keeps flicking my forehead, I fucking hate it when he does that.

"Leave me alone." I say, knocking his hand away.

He folds his arms and sighs.

"I'm trying to help you. Now, tell me what I do for a living."

Oh here we go, another self righteous speech about how he deals with damaged kids on a daily basis.

"You help children and young people, from difficult circumstances to integrate into society, through a non-threatening medium of team building exercises."

James is the only person I know, who recites their job description so often that even I can memorise it. It's basically a posh way of saying he plays footie with kids.

"Listen to me, Becca. The fact she's agreed to come at all says a lot. Think about it, where was she when she was raped?"

"Shh! Keep your voice down will ya. And I don't think it was rape."

Alex is my friend, he's daft and does some stupid things but to call him a rapist…

"Of course it was, you idiot! She was 'out cold,' she gave no consent, had no choice and it happened here. Every time she comes in this house, she'll wonder how it happened, and who knows what she'll think of. So, quit your whining and be a friend." He gives me a high and mighty glare, then strolls back to the front room. He must think I'm a bitch, but I'm not. I just didn't think.

5.20pm. Anna:

Tommy rolls the car onto Becca's drive, and I'm faced with her entire family. Even James and his pregnant

196

girlfriend. They're all laughing and taking pictures of Becca and Isabelle. Seeing them all here, makes me realise how big tonight is. This is the last time that all of our year will be together, in one place.

"I wish Mum was here." I whisper. As Tommy turns off the engine. I imagine that the accident had never happened. How he'd have done my make-up at the big house. I hold my necklace and wish that Mum would've smiled when he gave it to me. I'm snapped from my thoughts, when he runs his knuckle along my arm.

"I've been thinking," he says, "I might change the car."

"Why?"

"It's not me. I want something less showy, this has Dad written all over it. Big and brash…it's completely ostentatious."

I can't help but smile. "Yeah it is a bit. So what would you get?"

"I've been looking at the A5 Quattro. It should be a straight swap, give or take."

"An A5 is less showy? Are you serious?"

"Hey, little miss. There's a huge difference between a big brash 4×4, and a sleek, smart coupé!"

"Ok," I laugh, "if you say so."

"Here," he says, showing me a picture on his phone, "you've got to admit that's nice."

"You're right, it is…does it come in red?"

"Ah ha."

"Would you get it in red?"

"Sure."

Just then, Becca hoists up her dress and scurries to the car. She hugs me so hard as I step out, that she almost knocks me over.

"Sorry," she giggles, grabbing my hand, "come on. I need a pic of me and you."

I turn to Tommy and smile, maybe I'm not losing her after all.

6.30pm. Spencer Hall Hotel.
Becca:

No-one said anything about our prom being in a mansion, it's like something from Harry Potter. I can't wait to see what's lurking behind those big, old Gothic windows. I've got chills already and Tommy hasn't even parked up yet, I'm so excited.

"It's really busy, Tom," Anna says quietly, "how will I find you?"

"I'll text when I get here, then meet you in the lounge."

There's a kind of gravel roundabout near the entrance, Tommy pulls in there to drop us off. Issy gets out first. As usual Anna kisses his cheek, then we get out too. The atmosphere's proper tense between Anna and Issy. My fault I guess, I shouldn't have sprung her on Anna tonight. I'm not totally to blame, all the way here, Issy kept trying to flash Tommy her tits in the rear view mirror. She made it totally obvious that she's on heat for him. Awkward.

Everyone's waiting outside. I've got to say, I didn't expect to see so many teachers here, there's like six or seven at least. Poor Anna's struggling in those heels, they're not even high but she hobbles on in front. Issy grabs my arm and rolls her eyes in Anna's direction, then stops dead, when Dan ducks under a rose arch and puts his arm around Anna.

"Hiya! I didn't think you were coming."

"I didn't think you were!" She smiles and hugs him.

He grabs her hand, and they move to the side. Seeing them, as they sit down on a little marble bench, Issy turns away and breaks into a complete emotional meltdown.

"Calm down, Issy. Everyone's looking!"

"That's him! I've loved him since year seven, and he doesn't even know I'm alive!"

I want to like, calm her down or something. But she's that pissed, that I could say anything and she'd probably slap me one.

"I should have known he'd be with her! Look at them, Bec. He's touching her fucking hair. Bitch! I mean just look at her, and look at me; she's little, pretty and blonde. I'm just fat! Even her make-up's perfect, I wear it every day and can't make it look like that."

"Anna's not with him. And she didn't do her own make-up, that's for sure. Tommy did it, that's what he does."

"Serious?"

"Yes." I look over her shoulder, to see Anna coming back. "Ask her yourself. An, tell Issy who did your face."

"Tommy, why?" She takes one look at the mess of Issy's eyes and lays her hand on her arm, but Issy's having none of it.

"I want the truth, Anna!" She snaps, knocking her hand away, "are you with Daniel Armstrong?"

"Dan?" Anna laughs, "we're just good friends. Why? Do you like him?"

Issy blanks her.

"It's a bit more than 'likes' An," I say, "she loves him."

"Have you told him?"

"No!" Issy growls and stamps her feet, "and you two looked pretty cosy, if you're not together why was he touching your hair?"

Anna looks well shocked, and I half expect her to start crying but she doesn't. "He's my friend, Isabelle! I don't have to justify that to you."

"Look! She's not with him ok?" I don't mean to shout, but I'm not in the mood for this, not tonight.

Anna:

Isabelle's friends have called her over, but Becca stays with me, near the entrance to the lounge. For a while, she rants to me about her mum, her aunt and James, completely ignoring what just happened. I feel like I should apologise, after all Isabelle was clearly upset, but when I try she changes the subject. And after a while, Mr. Rodney calls for everyone to make their way to the gold room. A few people listen, but most just carry on their conversations.

Me and Becca head inside. We weave through many wing back chairs and coffee tables, pass a grand staircase, leading to a bar. On the left, is a room signed The Gold room, and our seating plan is listed on the door.

Inside, the room is huge; crisp white walls, elaborate golden coving and chintzy curtains with swags and tails. The far left wall is full of tall windows, looking out onto the gardens. I feel tiny. To my relief, our table is by those windows, in the far left corner. From here I can see the entire room, and I make a mental note of the exits, I can relax. When Isabelle and her friends join us, I sit back and watch the room fill up. Some tables are circular, some are square and there must be around twelve in total, all randomly placed around the room. I'm glad to see Mr. Coley, he's sat between Mr. Garrison and Miss. Beren, noticing me, he nods and smiles.

After five or ten minutes of people-watching, I send Tommy a text.

*"Hiya, so far everything's ok,
apart from an altercation
with Isabelle,
it's ok though."*

"Altercation?"

*"Just a strop,
she didn't like me talking to Dan,
apparently she's in love with him."*

*"What's with this girl?
I'm happy Dan's there."*

*"I don't know, Tom,
can't read her.*

200

*I'm happy too,
it was a good surprise."*

*"Well don't take any crap,
she's just a silly girl.
BTW my phone's playing up,
signal's rubbish.
I'm going to Rich's now."*

*"Ok,
tell him I'm gonna
need his help."*

"May I ask?"

*"No.
Birthday related,
love you."*

*"Alrighty then,
I'll let him know.
Enjoy your night, sweetheart x."*

I look around our table. Besides me and Becca, everyone's talking, but no-one appears to be listening. They're all so loud, continually interrupting one another, in a bid to see who can get their point across the quickest. I couldn't keep up even if I wanted to.

Becca turns to me, "Can I ask you something?"

I nod.

"I wanna know why you won't stay all night…on Friday. If it's Alex you're worried about, then you know I wouldn't let him in, right?"

I get why she's upset, before the accident I'd often stay over. I have to explain.

I can't risk anyone overhearing, so we shuffle our chairs back a little.

201

"Bec, have you ever had that feeling where something evil's coming after you…and no matter how hard you scream, nothing comes out?"

"A nightmare? Like you're running but you can't move?"

"Yeah, well since the accident and after I heard…you know."

"Alex?"

"Yeah. I've had nightmare's, like nearly every night. It's awful, sometimes I don't know if I'm awake or not."

"I get it, you know," she says, "whenever anything bad happens, you get nightmares, you always have. I don't see why you'd let it stop you staying."

"Ok listen, there's something you don't know. Me and Mum used to argue…"

"I know that!" She interrupts, "I've witnessed it."

"What you don't know, is that she wasn't like your mum. Do you know what happened when I had my first period?"

"What?"

"She left tampons and pads on my bed, and told me to read the instructions. No hugs, no explanations, nothing. I didn't know what was going on."

"Cold. So didn't you talk to anyone?"

"I tried calling Dan, I wanted to talk to his mum, but there was no answer. Tommy found me crying, so I told him instead."

"What did he do?"

"He answered my questions and fixed me a hot water bottle."

She looks like half of her pities me, and the other half is still trying to figure out what all this has to do with Friday night.

"You see, Bec, I need him. When I had nightmares as a kid, I'd get in with him, and now… well these ones are bad."

"Do you sleep with him!" She whispers.

"Don't say it like that. But yeah, since the accident, I cant sleep without him."

"Aww, I didn't think things were that bad." She leans in and gives me a hug.

"Please don't tell anyone," I say quietly in her ear, "even Isabelle."

"Don't worry. You can trust me."

Soon the starters arrive, and I dip half of my bread roll into a dish of spicy vegetable soup, it's delicious and velvety smooth. Savouring each mouthful, I could forget that I'm in a crowded room, but then I look up and suddenly lose my appetite. It's Alex, standing against the far wall. All the tables between us seem to fade away, he's locked onto me, like he's holding me by some invisible tether. He leans back and rubs his groin. I anxiously spin mums ring around and around, and nudge Becca's arm.

"Bec, it's…it's Alex."

As soon as she looks up he just laughs and turns away.

"Chill," she says, "he's not about to do anything here."

No, I don't think he would. That's not his way. His way is to get under my skin and he's succeeding.

8.30pm. Anna:

Once we'd finished the meal, Mr. Rodney ushered everyone out, so the hotel staff could clear the tables from the dance-floor. This time, Becca waits with Isabelle in the lounge, and I head outside for some fresh air. My shoes are gorgeous, but the back rubs against my ankle, so I hobble to a bench in the courtyard and slide them off.

It's beautiful here; huge trees frame the crimson sky, and the whole building is surrounded by a luscious, sweeping blanket of green.

"Lovely isn't it?" Dan says, poking his head from under the rose arch.

"It sure is." I nod to the sky, as he sits down beside me. "I wonder if my mum and dad are up there, and what they'd think of me."

"They'd be proud."

We give each other a half laugh.

"I'd like to think so, but you knew my mum…I do miss her though."

"Course you do, she was still your mum."

I nock my head against his shoulder and let out a sigh. This isn't the time or place for grief. I need to change the subject.

"What're you doing over the summer?" I ask.

He cracks his knuckles, "I don't know yet, I um…I might be moving away."

My heart sinks. Dan's been my friend forever, he can't leave.

"Why?" I ask, trying not to let it show.

"Mum's getting married and moving to London. She said I can choose to go with, or move into Dad's, but that's in Stockton. I don't know what to do. I know it's only two buses away, but I don't know Stockton. It's going to be a new start no matter what I do…and then there's Eva, she wants me to go with Mum."

Eva's Dan's little sister, she's only eleven and I can empathise, I remember breaking my heart when my brother moved only a thirty minute walk away. But I can see both sides, yes they bicker more than Tommy and me, but Dan does care about her.

Dan's a creature of habit and he likes what he knows, so no wonder he's torn.

"Only you can decide," I say, "but if you do stay and go to Stockton college, you'll know someone."

"Who?"

"Me. I'm doing health and social care."

"Well," he smiles, "that's one good reason to stay."

Just then, we hear the ting of my messenger tone, it's my cousin, Ethan.

"Anna, where are you!
call me."

204

"Sorry, I just need to call our Ethan."

"Sure," he says, raising his thumb back towards the entrance, "should I…?"

"No, no, stay."

My cousin answers immediately.

"Ethan it's me. What's wrong?"

"Thank fuck you're ok. I've tried to call you for over an hour, and Tommy's phone too, but that goes straight to voicemail."

"Oh sorry. Tommy's got no signal, and I've changed my number. I meant to text you…"

"Yeah you should have." He interrupts, "You always have your phone on, you're the only one who always answers! An, I thought something had happened, and I'd be the last to know…again."

"Ethan, I am so, so sorry, are you ok?"

"Yeah, I'm just kind of out-of-it, down here…anyway all I originally called for, was to ask what Tommy wants for his birthday, any ideas?"

"He has mentioned the new 'Gears of War?'"

"That's not out till October."

"I'm not sure then, he'd never say no to a bottle of JD. I'm getting him a coffee machine, but I don't know what else to suggest. He hasn't asked for anything, he doesn't even want to celebrate it, to be honest."

"It's alright, I'll come up with something. See you Saturday."

"You sure you're ok?"

"Yeah, An. Sorry."

I don't want to just say goodbye when he's feeling chewed. But he ends the call, and I look up to Dan. He most likely heard all of that, at times Ethan's voice can be as loud as his dad's.

"Are you alright?" He asks.

"Yeah, I just didn't think. When I got my new number, I texted you and Becca, I didn't even think about Ethan. I should've, he's my cousin!"

"Don't beat yourself up, he's got it now."

"Yeah, you're right." I rest my head on his shoulder, and we just sit here. That accident has affected all of us, changed everything. I didn't want to think about Mum tonight, but no matter how hard I try, I cant seem to escape her.

"The pain's different now, Dan."

"Different?"

This is weird. I haven't troubled Dan with any of this, all he knows is what he witnessed all those weeks ago, in our ceramics class. He doesn't know that I heard her tell me to die, or how angry she was with me. I've wanted to tell him everything, but didn't know where to begin. Since talking with Julie this morning, I'm remembering the nicer moments. Little smiles when I'd make her an apple tea, or years ago, when she'd stand at the window and watch us play in the garden. Thing's I'd never noticed before.

"An?" He says, "how different do you mean?"

"I want to bring her back, Dan. Just for like an hour, I wouldn't argue or anything. I just want to hear her voice again."

"I'm so sorry," he says softly, "do you want a hug?"

I nod, and as he shuffles closer, awkwardly wrapping his arms around me, I slide mine around his waist. He's careful not to knock my hair, as he lets his cheek rest against my head.

"Anna, I…" we hear music from inside, and he stops, "I guess the disco's starting," he says, "should we go in?"

I slide my feet back into my shoes. "Yeah, I should probably check in with Becca."

"I'll catch my mates then."

We head back inside, where the atmosphere's dense. Low lighting fills the narrow gaps on the dance-floor.

"Can you see her?" I shout, competing with the music.

When you're only four foot eleven, an advantage of having a best friend who's almost six foot, is that he can see above everyone.

"She's over there." He says, pointing to the DJ desk.

"Thanks." I practically hold my breath, as I weave my way through to her. She has her back to me, and it's only when I reach her, that I see Isabelle's crying, and Becca's livid.

"What were you two talking about?" Becca snaps, "we went out and…"

"You were cuddling!" Isabelle cries, "I bet you told him didn't you! Had a proper good laugh about it."

Have I missed something? Only an hour ago, I poured my heart out to Becca, and now she's like a different person.

"Well then?" Isabelle demands.

I look up to them and feel tiny, but I'm not taking this any more. With a deep breath I shout.

"We talked about my mum! Is that ok!"

I hate this, Becca never fusses over anyone like this. Isabelle's got her wrapped around her little finger, and it's pissing me off. She moves to try and hug me but I can't, to let Becca hug me would be saying it's ok. I'm so angry that I turn around and push my way into the crowd. I don't care if they follow me or not, but when I reach the centre of the dance-floor., I stop. I hastily look around, voices around me blend with the music, I'm on the brink; I could succumb to the fear, or use it as fuel. Leaning towards the latter, I begin to dance by myself, but as bodies push and shove around me, their laughter intensifies. I clutch tightly onto my phone, wince at the stinging from my shoes and briefly close my eyes. I can feel myself edging further in, so I open them and see that I'm within reaching distance of Alex and Chloe. They don't say a word to me, but being this close is enough to knock me off my stride. All I can do is back away, but I'm not watching where I'm going. I can't take my eyes off him, as he pulls Chloe in close, grinning to me, while he kisses her ear. Suddenly, two lads crash into my back, I don't know what they were doing, but they hit me with such force, they send me crashing forward, right into the chest of Mr. Coley.

"Sorry, Sir. I'm so sorry."

He says something, but it's so loud that I can't make it out. What am I doing? I shouldn't be here. I look up to see that I'm wedged between him and Miss. Beren.

"Sir I…"

"Are you ok?" He asks, leaning closer.

The room and bodies close in around me. I want to be strong, but panic takes over.

"I can't breathe." In only a moment, I feel someone grab my hand. Thankfully it's Dan.

"It's ok, Sir," he says, "I've got her." They exchange a few words, then he pulls me to the edge of the dance-floor.

"Thank you." I gasp, holding onto my necklace.

"It was nothing," he laughs, "it could've been worse, you could've fallen on your arse." I'd laugh too, but all I can think of is the look of disdain on Miss. Beren's face. A moment passes, and Dan lays his hand on my shoulder. Until now, I hadn't noticed that I'd been staring blankly into the crowd, still clutching my necklace.

"Anna?" He asks kindly, "are you alright?"

"Yes. Um yeah I…it's just really warm in here."

"Should we go outside?"

There's nothing I'd like more, than to escape this stifling room, but a swarm of dancing bodies stand between us and the exit. As I stare at them, Dan steps in front of me and grins.

"Do you trust me?"

I shake my head.

"Come on, trust me." And with that, he squats and, keeping my dress in place, wraps his arms around my thighs and lifts me up. Holding onto his neck, I break into nervous laughter. He carries me towards the exit and, as he ducks under the doorway, I catch Isabelle shooting me eyes of pure hate. Part of me must be getting stronger, because as Dan carries me above the cheering crowd, I realise that tonight, I truly don't care.

Outside, he carefully puts me down.

"I cant believe you did that!"

"Well," he says, " I could see you planning your exit, I just gave you a helping hand…that's ok, right?"

"Course it is." I take his arm, and we start to walk. "I'm used to Tommy picking me up, I didn't expect it from you. It's cool though, and kind of fun."

"Only kind of?"

I just smile. We stroll through a maze of gardens, to a beautiful stone staircase, leading to a green that has a pretty fountain in the centre.

"You know," I say, as we walk down the steps, "I'd love to run over that field. To just kick off my shoes and fly so no-one could catch me."

"Let's do it."

"Are you serious?"

"Are you? You said you wanted to run, so let's run."

This is crazy. I'd love to, but we're not exactly dressed for a sprint.

"But what about my shoes?" I ask. "I can't run in these."

"Here." He buttons his phone into his back pocket. "You hold your phone, and I'll hold your shoes."

I agree, and yet again, they nip as I wiggle my feet free. I hold my phone in my left hand, and straighten up Mum's ring on my right.

"Ok." Dan points, holding my shoes by the heels, "once around the fountain and first back here's the winner."

I'm ready, I'm in position. 'Come on, girl,' I tell myself as he begins the countdown.

"…and three, two, one, go!"

We leap onto the grass, and despite Dan's restrictive smart trousers, he speeds ahead. The cool grass springs beneath my feet, I love it. My dress fly's up in the wind, but I don't care, I imagine the fresh air lifting me high off the ground, I'm free. Dan reaches the fountain only seconds before me. I circle it clockwise, and he anticlockwise, doing a goofy dance as we pass. I can't stop laughing, clearly a tactical move, because he sticks out his tongue then jets across the field.

"I'll get you, Dan Armstrong!" I shout, scampering after him.

"You'll have to catch me first."

Gold Room.
Becca:

Issy's been torturing herself for like twenty minutes; she's sat with her face glued to the window, watching Anna and Dan outside.

"They're not together," I tell her, "I know what it looks like, but they're not."

"They look pretty together to me."

I can see her point, they do. If I didn't know Anna then I'd think the same, but she's just running. That's Anna, she forgets her problems when she runs, most normal people get pissed, Anna runs.

"Issy. I promise they're not. They've been friends forever. Can't see what all the fuss is about, he's a dick anyway."

Issy shoots me a glare. Oops, I should know better, I can't be insulting the love of her life.

"Whatever, Bec." She stands, pulling her dress up to stop her tits falling out. "I'm going to the loo, you coming?"

"Sure."

10pm. Anna:

I'd love to stay out here all night, but it's getting chilly, so we decide to head back inside. As we walk through the lounge, we hear the intro to one of Dan's favourite tunes, coming from the gold room.

"Come on," he grins, grabbing my hand, "we have to dance."

I'm apprehensive, but I have no time to let it show before he's leading me through the crowd, and into the centre of the dance-floor. This is it, I'm conquering my fears, but that doesn't stop me from squeezing his hand so tight, that his fingers probably turn white.

"You can let go," he calls in my ear, "I won't leave you."

We both smile, and the bright lights flash as he performs his intricate trademark steps. Then he holds out his hands as loaded guns. We dance for ages, alternating moves, each time bettering the last. I'm swept up with adrenalin and I love it. The song ends and another begins. We dance to so many, that I almost forget the bodies around us. My shoes are killing me, but I don't care. The tempo increases and I spin, screaming with joy at every turn. Dan laughs at first, but soon joins in. Faster and faster and faster, I'm dizzy but not frightened, I feel sick, but I'm laughing, and as the song comes to an abrupt end, I crash into his chest.

"Easy," he laughs, holding me tight, "I've got ya."

For a second I look up to him, like we're in the eye of a hurricane. Colours of blue, red and yellow shine on his smooth, fair face. I'm grinning like an idiot, like a kid at Christmas, then the music starts again. I don't want to stop, I'm having the best night of my life, but I need a drink. Taking his hand, I lead him to some chairs by the wall, and ease off my shoes. He winces at the sight of my raw ankles.

"Yeah," I nod, "it's not going to stop me though. I'll just have to dance barefoot, but could you just grab us a drink?"

"Yeah, course." He rushes off to the bar, and I slot my shoes neatly under the chair. For a moment, I scroll through my phone, spinning Mum's ring around while I wait. Then in the corner of my eye, I see his shadow.

"Wow that was fast!" I laugh, turning to face him. Then every hair on my body stands on end. It's not Dan, it's Alex.

"Hello, my girl. You owe me a dance."

I'm frozen, but he grabs me by the wrist and squeezes.

"Let go, you're hurting!" I try to pull away, but he just laughs and drags me onto the crowded dance-floor.

"Come on, Anna," he goads, "I've had my eye on you. You weren't so shy with Dan."

I yank my hand away. I've got to get out of here. I scan for a break in the crowd and take my chance, but he grabs my wrist again and pulls me back. This time digging his nails hard into my scars.

"Get off me! I don't want a dance, I…"

"Yes, you do," he shouts in my ear, as he runs his hand over the jewels on my waist, "why else would you wear such a pretty dress?"

I need Dan back now. Everyone around us is dancing like nothing's going on, they've no idea how desperate I am.

"Leave me alone!" I manage to shuffle a few steps back, but he closes in so I shout again, "I hate you, Alex…I hate you!"

"Hate?" He laughs. As he throws back his head, I seize the opportunity to get away. But, again, he doesn't let me. He grips my arm hard above my elbow, jerking me towards him, and breathes down my neck. My skin crawls.

"I remember, you said we could be friends," he says, "that was the day your dead parents paid you a visit, and you threw up all over the art room floor."

I stagger, unable to catch my breath. Those around us take a step back, but he's laughing so hard he almost cries.

"Anna, you're a mess, bat shit crazy. Even your best friend's given up on you, now she's hanging with the best pair of tits in school." He goes on and on; insulting me, goading me. He wants me to cry…no, he wants to trigger an hallucination, he wants to witness one for himself. It's not happening, I tell myself It's not happening.

He locks one arm tight around my back, and with his other hand, gathers my dress up and pushes his fingers into my knickers. I instantly freeze, I have to get him off me, but I can't move. Lights and faces flash before my eyes, adding to the deafening hum of music and noise. Before I know it, my right arm swings. Fuelled by fear, anger and hate, I strike my palm hard across his face. He staggers, drops to one knee and holds his cheek. He looks like a wounded dog. The crowd, now paying attention, all look towards him, watching as he lowers his hand. His cheek and palm are both streaked with blood.

"You fucking little bitch!" He lunges towards me, I back away, but not quick enough. He grabs me by my hair. Pulling my head down, he raises his hand to strike. As I instinctively close my eyes, his momentum shifts and we fall to the floor. I land hard on my back, and when I look over, I see Dan has Alex pinned to the floor.

"Get the fuck off me!" Alex yells.

I scurry to my feet. All of the crowd are chanting 'fight, fight, fight,' and then some commotion, as the teachers push their way through. The music stops and the lights are raised.

"Quick, Dan," I say, "get up, get off him!"

This isn't his fault, I cant risk him being thrown out. He jumps up and pulls me close, as Mr. Garrison and Mr. Coley emerge.

"That bitch cut my face." Alex shouts bitterly.

"Sir, I…it was my ring. I didn't mean to…"

I didn't want any of this. I just wanted to get away. Luckily, Mr. Coley knows me, and he knows Alex. He walks with me and Dan to the chairs, where I'd left my shoes, while Mr. Garrison escorts Alex out.

"I'm so sorry, An." Dan says, sitting beside me," I didn't mean for you to fall, I saw him go to hit you and I…"

"It's ok, I…I'm ok."

"Are you sure?" Asks Mr. Coley.

"Yes, Sir. Thank you."

He asks again to be sure, before leaving to settle the crowd.

"I did it, Dan." I laugh, not a nonchalant laugh, but a relief. "I finally stood up to him. You know, I honestly expected him to punch me in the face…he would have done too, if it wasn't for you."

"Anna, I'd do…" He stops, as Becca pushes her way over to us.

"What's happened?" She calls, as a not so enthusiastic Isabelle follows. "I just saw Alex being taken outside."

"Nothing, I'm alright." I tell her, as I turn and take hold of Dan's hand. "Thanks to you."

"There's no way I'd have let him hit you." He says.

"Hit you?" She exclaims.

I nod, and at the same time my phone vibrates in my hand. It's a text from Tommy.

"Hey,
finally got a signal.
I'm in the lounge."

"Tommy's here. Bec, I can explain in the car?"

"She's not going with you now," Isabelle snaps, "she's coming with me."

"Oh right, ok." I reach under the seat for my shoes, and Dan nods for us to leave. Clearly Becca's made up her mind, so there's nothing else for me to say. I stand with Dan, and he loosely lays his arm over my shoulders.

"I'm sorry," Becca says, "tell me, you're still coming on Friday?"

"Yeah, I said I would."

"You alright?" Dan asks, as we head out to the lounge.

"Yeah. I'll talk to Becca later. Right now," I grin, "I'm just gonna enjoy our victory."

We both smile, and in the corner of my eye, I see Tommy at the far end. I'm super excited, so much so that as we rush over, I practically bounce into him.

"Hey," Tommy says, as I hand him my shoes, "how was it? And what happened to your hair?"

Alex has pretty much destroyed my flower braid, not that I care.

"It was awesome. I did it, I finally did it!"

Tommy's cautious eyes dance between the pair of us. "Did what?"

"You should've seen her." Dan jumps in. "I mean, Alex was being an absolute tit, but that slap she gave him…" he stops to give me a celebratory hug. "Then I got there just in time."

Tommy does not look pleased.

"What's wrong?" I ask, "aren't you proud of me?"

"Annie I…there's blood on your dress!"

"It's not mine…I'm fine, really I'm better than fine."

He stares at me for a second, then something seems to click, and he glares at Dan. "In time for what, exactly?"

"He was gonna hit her, but she stood her ground, and don't worry, I stopped him. I wouldn't let him hurt her, I promise."

"I know you wouldn't, Dan. But, Annie, please be careful."

I feel deflated and chastised. So, I look away and nod.

"Listen," Tommy gestures to the door, "We should get going. I'll just be outside, so you two can have a minute. Night, Dan and thank you."

"See ya, Tommy."

Tommy wanders around the courtyard with his hands in his pockets. Once he's a few metres away, I turn and hold onto Dan's waist.

"I still had the best night." I tell him. "Will you let me know if you decide to stay?"

He leans down, smiles and kisses my cheek. "Yes. Anna, there's something I want to tell you…I um, I…I had the best night too."

I giggle, as he gives me a massive hug, "Night, An."

"Goodnight."

As he heads back inside, I hurry over to Tommy.

"It's a fair walk." He says. "You should put your shoes on."

"I can't. They've scuffed my ankles." He crouches down to take a closer look, and I beg him not to touch them.

"Relax, daft arse. I won't. They do look sore though. Sorry, I should've said to break them in, around the house. Ah well," he stands up, offering me his back, "jump on, I'll carry you."

Tommy:

"So what happened?" I ask, as I carry Annie to the car park. I don't want to destroy her good mood, but it begs questions when she leaves her prom, with blood on her dress and talk of that bastard.

"I'm fine, Tom. Honestly."

"Annie, I need to know."

"I'll tell you in the car. I want you to know the good bits first."

I give in, as she hugs me and kisses my cheek.

"I had so much fun." She says. "You know, Dan practically threw me over his shoulder, then we raced across the green. It was awesome."

"So, when are you two going to just admit it?"

"Admit what?"

"Come on, Annie, he likes you and I think you like him."

"Shut up. We've been friends forever, if he liked me he would've said already."

A man can tell when a boy likes a girl. It was written all over him, but she's got no clue. It's kind of sweet that she's this naïve. I'd be happy for her to be with Dan. He clearly cares about her, and she'd be safe with him too.

"Trust me, Annie. If I'd have been a bit further away, he would've kissed you properly, not just your cheek."

I stop for a second, as she taps my shoulder. "Put me down a minute." She holds my arm and tiptoes over the gravel, as we weave through a few rows of parked cars. "I do like Dan." She admits, after a few minutes. "He's lovely, but I don't think he likes me like that. Anyway, how was your night?"

I can take a hint. I drop the subject, stop and stretch out my neck.

"Alright yeah, we…" in the distance, I see something odd on the car. Could be a trick of the light, but it's hard to tell. "D'ya want to jump back on?" I ask her, "it's just over there."

216

"I'm alright."

We walk a little further, and I see that it was no trick of the light. "What is that?" I mutter.

"What's what?"

"The car. Come on." I run on ahead to check it out. "What the fuck!"

A deep, rough scratch snakes from the fuel cap, right along to the wing mirror. Fucking typical, as soon as I decide to sell it, some prick does this. Marvellous.

Annie scurries up beside me. Her jaw drops, and she reaches onto the bonnet.

"Tommy," she says, lifting up a rock, "it was him, I know it."

She's right. Intent on finding the bastard, I frantically start to search around the surrounding cars. Obviously he'll be long gone by now. Lucky for him, because if I got my hands on him, I'd break his neck.

"You!" I yell, storming back to the car, "are going to fucking tell me what happened tonight!"

I warned her to keep her head down, I fucking warned her. "This is what happens when you push lads like him." Kicking up the gravel, I slam my fists on the bonnet, but I'm stopped by a sudden thump to my back.

I quickly turn. Annie's enraged.

"You think this is my fault? Really!" She silences me with a blow to the chest, and another then another. "I didn't want to tell you now!" She cries and hits me again. "I stayed with Dan all night, but Alex was watching me."

I stand stunned, while she paces, kicking her bare feet into the gravel.

"He waited till Dan went for a drink. Then he dragged me into the crowd. I couldn't get away, Tommy. I tried, two, three, four times…I don't know but I tried." She clenches her fists and lets out a roar. "He touched me, Tom! Shoved his hand up my dress, into my knickers! What was I supposed to do? Open my legs, so he wouldn't damage your precious car?"

"Don't be stupid! Of course not."

"Tell me then!" She screams. "What should I have done?"

"I…"

"I'm just as angry about this as you, if not more. It was me that he raped! Have you actually thought about that? Because I have! Just picture it, Tommy. I can't get it out of my head, every time I close my eyes, he's on me!"

"Annie, stop."

"No! I won't stop. All I did was defend myself! So, don't you dare make out that this is my fault!"

I've well and truly fucked up. I pull her close, I just want to hug her, but she fights.

"Get off me!"

"Annie, I'm sorry."

I plead with her, but she just shakes her head and shouts, "Don't touch me."

"I didn't mean it, it's not your fault." I try to hold her again, but she uses her knees to break free. "Of course you were right to fight him off. I'm sorry, I am."

Again, she pushes me away. Helpless, I watch her. She doesn't look like my sister; she's furious, and her hair's a mess. Dan said that she stood her ground, I take a second to let that sink in. She would've taken a hit, rather than backing down.

"Little Annie?" I say softly.

This seems to work, she drops her shoulders and sighs.

"You were right." I tell her again. "I'm so proud of you. Will you come here, please?"

She shakes her head and, still facing away, says, "I need this to stop. I need him to leave me alone…I've had enough."

"I know, Annie." I move closer to her, but stop myself. "Please, can I hold you?"

She nods, and I hold her head close to my chest. As I feel her hug me back, I breathe a sigh of relief. I can deal with her shouting at me, hitting me, but I'm useless when she pushes me away.

June 24, 2016 Friday 9.30pm. Becca's House.
Anna:

Becca's been helping her neighbours with their TV, for the past ten minutes. So while she's not here to complain about wasps flying in, I open her bedroom window and lean against the sill. James came over earlier to mow the lawn, and for me, nothing beats the smell of freshly cut grass.

I've tried to talk to Becca about Alex, and what he did at the prom, but it's like she doesn't want to know. In two days he's become taboo. I'd like to think if the tables were turned, and he'd done those things to her, I'd be more caring. At first she was lovely, but now she just expects me to move on. How can I? Sometimes I'm thankful that I was unconscious; that way, I don't know how rough he was, or if he did it as a show for his mates. I guess he didn't, if he had, then someone would have filmed it, and I'd know by now. Shit like that gets about.

I honestly believe Becca's given up on me. My issues are too big, that's why she's friends with Isabelle, her problems are superficial, and Becca can deal with that. Maybe that's what she needs, easy conversations with no real stress.

As I watch the sun set behind the distant trees, I try to focus on the good, reminding myself why we are friends. I form a list in my head, I like lists, strong people have lists, and that's what I am now, strong.

My mental ramblings are broken when my phone rings, it's Rich.

"Hey, kidda," he says, "young Thomas said you needed me?"

"I do. You know it's his birthday on Tuesday? Well, I usually order from his Amazon, but I don't want him to know what I'm buying…"

"Say no more. Just send me the link, and we'll square up next week."

"Thanks, could you do one more thing?"

"Ah ha?"

219

"Elaine's making his cake, could you give me a lift when I collect it?"

"Oh, now you're pushing it," he laughs, "just kidding. I'll just pick it up on my way over."

"Awesome, Rich. Thank you."

"Shut up. It's my best mates birthday, it's fine."

"I know, but thank you."

We end the call when I hear Becca, slamming her front door closed. She potters around downstairs for a while, then brings up two steaming mugs.

"There y'are." She sets them down on the bedside table, before throwing herself on her bed.

"Thanks." I take a sip while it's nice and hot. "Are you looking forward to college?" If she needs to talk trivial then so be it. For a good few seconds she doesn't answer, just stares at her phone.

"Yeah, about that. I don't think I'm going to Stockton college now, I'm going to Redcar... with Issy."

What? Redcar's about the same distance away, but in the opposite direction. Why is this happening? There's some kind of invisible barrier between us. I know that sounds dramatic, but it's how I feel. It hurts. All I've done is take some time. I tried to get better, and Isabelle's pulled her away. A few weeks off school, and now I've lost her. To who? A childish diva, who threw a wobbler because I'm friends with the boy that she daren't even speak to. I want to object, but I've got no right to tell her what to do. Now, more than ever, I really hope Dan decides to stay.

"Aren't you gonna say something?" She asks.

I hadn't realised that I'd just been standing there, clinging to a mug of tea.

"I um, thought we were going together?" I say cautiously, as I perch on the bed. She turns her phone over and, for the first time tonight, she actually looks me in the eyes.

"Anna." She says. "Can you really see me as a nurse? It's not me, you should know that."

"Why didn't you say? Or pick another course?"

220

"I'm doing performing arts, and Issy said Redcar's better for that…you never know," she grins, "I might end up working with your Tommy."

I'm sure he'd love that, I think to myself. I'd better not say that aloud, I doubt my sarcasm would be helpful right now.

"Your choice, I guess."

For the next ten minutes at least, we sit in awkward silence, scrolling through our phones. And I ask myself why I'm even here, then it dawns on me, her mum's out. That's it, if I wasn't here she'd have to stay with James. Maybe that's why he cut the grass today, so he could confirm Becca wasn't alone. She probably asked Isabelle first, but had to settle with me, I don't know. Before I have chance to think myself even further into a downward spiral, Becca breaks the silence.

"Anna, I need to know something. I know your mam was a bit distant, but she wasn't always like that, was she?"

"What do you mean?"

"I just can't see a mam being cold with a little kid, like couldn't you have got in her bed when you were little? Why Tommy's?"

Oh, here we go, I knew I shouldn't have told her. I'll have to explain it, again.

"I only tried once." I say, sliding myself to the floor. "When I was little. I must've had a nightmare, but when I got up and knocked on her door, she shouted, 'Go back to sleep.' I was frightened, and Tommy heard me crying. He stepped onto the landing and told me to get in with him. He let me cuddle in. After that night, I didn't bother trying with Mum, I just went straight to him."

"Don't ya think it's a bit weird?" She squints, and sucks the inside of her cheek.

I'm taken aback. "Can you clarify what part you find weird, exactly?"

"It's just that, my mam would wanna be the one I went to…I guess what I'm saying, is that you still sleep in with him now, so you never grew out of it. Didn't your mam or dad, ever say you were too old?"

Dad never liked it, but I'm not about to tell her that.

"No," I tell her, "I did grow out of it. Before the accident, the last time was the night before starting secondary school. Besides, it wasn't every night."

"It's every night now." She laughs.

Tommy was right, I can't expect her to understand. I'm a fool. I don't have an answer, and although I hate myself for being weak, I find myself scurrying off to the bathroom.

"Let it go." I tell myself, whilst splashing my face with cold water. "Stay strong and let it go." I take a few deep breaths and open the door. I'll change the subject, and this time, I'm keeping it trivial.

"So." I say as I go back to her room, "prom was good?"

"I guess." She says blankly.

This is painful. I just want her to put the phone down for two minutes, and talk to me. I've clearly done something. Usually, I tentatively ease in questions to find out what, but I'm tired of doing that.

"Becca. I'm sick of going through this stupid guessing game. I've clearly upset you again, so tell me, just tell me what I've done."

She jumps to her feet, brushes past me and starts rummaging through her drawers.

"Anna, you're my best friend, but Issy's my friend too. I feel like I'm stuck in the middle, I get that you're different, but I thought you'd try. I thought if we went to the prom together, you'd get along. I do love ya, An, and I know you've had it bad." She says, quickly changing into her pyjamas. "The thing is, Issy really loves Dan. I know you're friends with him, but you just rubbed it in her face. I know she can be extra, but that was pretty bitchy, Anna. I never thought you were like that."

What am I hearing? As I stand here in shock, she unleashes a torrent of pent up bitterness. With each harsh word my cheeks burn.

"How exactly, was I rubbing her face in it? All I did was dance with him...for crying out loud, Bec, he's been my friend since I was six!"

Furious, I leap to my feet. "And do you really believe that she loves him? She doesn't know anything about him, not his interests, things that annoy him, what he likes to watch, read, nothing. What she loves is an idea, a fantasy of how she'd like to be with him, what she'd make him do for her. That's not love. What she needs to do, is buy some clothes that fit, wear a decent bra, wash the crap off her face and talk to him! Even if he doesn't feel the same, he wouldn't be a dick about it. And you should pass on my advice, instead of demonising me for enjoying a night with my oldest friend!"

"Anna. You acted like a proper bitch! You were like 'this is my night, fuck everyone else.'"

"A bitch? That's what you think of me, is it? I'm sorry, Bec, but we're done. I thought you knew me." I push past her and hurry downstairs for my shoes.

"Where're you going?" She shouts. I don't answer.

"You're running to Tommy aren't ya? God help you if he ever gets a girlfriend!"

I throw on my hoody, zip my phone into the pocket and storm to the door. All the while Becca's screaming at me, intertwining insults and apologies. I no longer give a shit. I run out of her house and up the road. She calls for me to go back, but makes no attempt to run after me. It would be pointless, she knows she couldn't keep up.

I speed along streets, over roads and through the cemetery. I know I shouldn't go through here after dark, but I'm too fired up to care. I weave amongst the eerie gravestones, then speed out the other side. I catch a quick breath, before pressing on. I pass my old primary school and go through the estate, to an alleyway. It's straight on from here. Tommy's pub's in the distance, when I get closer, I see him outside, he's crossed the road and is rushing towards me.

"I've been worried sick!" He says, as I crash into him. I try to apologise, but I need a second to catch my breath. "You're ok," he says, as I hold his arms for balance, "I've got you."

"It's that Isabelle, Tommy. I hate her. Now, Becca thinks I'm a bitch, because I danced with Dan."

Tommy just stares, as I get madder and madder, spewing out everything from the past few hours. Then I realise how hard I'm squeezing his arms, and I quickly let go. "Are you upset with me?"

"No, not at all. I didn't know where you'd gone when I got Becca's message, and…and you weren't answering your phone. But you came to me." He puts his arms around me and squeezes tight. "Annie, I'll never be upset with you for doing that."

"Thanks. So, Becca sent you a text?"

Letting go, he takes his phone from his back pocket. "There, it's in Messenger."

"Anna's ran off,
we had a fight,
you need to find her,
she could be anywhere."

"What the actual fuck?
When did she leave?"

"10m ago
I asked if she was going to you,
she said no."

"That's a lie. I didn't say no, I just didn't answer her."
"Give it here, An."
I hand it over and watch him type a reply.

"Anna's with me.
You need to give her some space."

224

"Come on," he says, as we head back to the pub, "I'll get you a lemonade."

**June 28, 2016 Tuesday 11.30am. Medical Centre.
Tommy's birthday.
Anna:**

No matter what I've overcame in my therapy sessions, the start of each one always feels like my first. I've hardly said anything to Julie, since coming in. Only the usual, 'hello,' before making myself a drink. I'd stand by my previous belief, of there being truth serum in the tea. But, I haven't drank any yet, and a thought that I'd rather keep secret, is already on the tip of my tongue. When I've not been trying to push it out of my head, I've been asking myself why. Why did Tommy kiss me? Why did it feel nice? And why did I want to kiss him back. I thought about it this morning, before we got up. He was facing me, still fast asleep. I wanted to try it, to kiss him, and I almost did. My lips were a fraction away from his, and I couldn't do it. 'He's my brother,' I said to myself. Instead, I kissed his forehead, and he smiled. That was when the confusion reared it's ugly head. What if I'd dreamt it? Until now, the nightmares and visions, have been dark and terrifying. Not soft, warm and gentle. Maybe my mind is fighting against me, in a bid to destroy my most positive relationship.

"Anna?" Julie asks kindly, "are you alright?"

"Yeah, I'm ok. Could you just tell me what you want me to say, please?"

Last weeks session was good, and I can't deny that it helped me, but I don't trust myself to lead today's. She sips her coffee and moves to sit beside me.

"You're free to talk about anything." She says.

I nod, and find myself falling out of focus. I feel like I'm aware of her, but not, at the same time. There's a blackbird in the courtyard, he's hopping along the rim of the bird bath, free of troubles. I envy him. Watching him, I mumble that I've read the leaflets that she gave me.

"They were really helpful. I feel stronger now, and I won't be pushed around any more."

She looks puzzled, and I'm not surprised; those leaflets were to help me deal with regret, not improve my confidence. Although, I don't see how having more of that can be a bad thing.

"Do you feel pushed around?"

"No more than usual," I say, as I stare out to the courtyard, "but I'm more aware of it now. I…me and Becca had a fight, we're not speaking." I slide my hands under my thighs to stop myself from scratching. "It wouldn't hurt so much, but I trusted her. She knows my secrets."

"I'm sorry to hear that."

I glance over to her, and she smiles, but today I notice something different. Perhaps it's because she's sitting closer, or maybe I'm paying more attention, but there's a sincerity there that I hadn't seen before.

"Thank you." I lower my head and rub the soles of my shoes together. "It's been a strain since the accident, if I'm honest. She was really nice at first, but she doesn't understand. I've been having nightmares too, is that normal?"

"Yes," she nods, "in your situation that's perfectly normal, you've experienced great trauma. You may also find, that memories of your parents occupy your mind without an apparent trigger. This can be painful, you see the brain reacts to trauma in a very specific way; difficult memories are stored in a different state to regular memories. Are you able to describe these nightmares?"

I look at her for a second and take a deep breath, "I can, but it might not make much sense…it's like I'm in one place, then another without moving. There're always waves; huge, aggressive waves and they're higher than houses. It's the noise that hurts, it wakes me up, but the dream doesn't stop. It just plays on, over and over like it's on a loop. They're like

226

the visions, I had my first one of those at school. My friend, Dan stayed with me the whole time." I glance to Julie before reaching for my drink.

"Did your friend help you?" She asks, as I take a sip.

"He tried. Afterwards, he told me that he'd been talking to me the whole time, but I couldn't hear him. I don't know why, but when it happens I can only hear Tommy, I mean I hear Mum and Dad too, but they aren't really there, are they?"

I want Julie to say something, to re-direct me, but she doesn't, and I find myself admitting that I heard Mum telling me to die. My hands shake, so much that I drop my cup, and a wave of tea splashes onto the carpet.

"I'm sorry, I'm so sorry." I leap up, grab a handful of paper towels, and press them down on the mess. I've said too much, she's going to think I'm a suicide risk. Anna you stupid girl. I need to be careful, or our social worker will get involved. What if they think Tommy can't protect me, they'll take me away, and then what?

"They can't split us up," I whisper over and over, as I scrub the floor. Julie tries to help me, but I shake my head.

"Anna?" She asks worriedly, "can you hear me?"

"Yes. They can't take me away…you can't let them!" What am I saying? My pulse booms as I will myself to calm down.

"Who?" She asks.

"Please, get Tommy."

"Come on," she says, holding out her hand, "leave that, lets sit back down."

I take her hand and begin to relax, but I can't help but feel that my recovery's going nowhere.

"I'm sorry, I didn't mean to freak out. I'm just scared that me and Tommy'll be separated."

"Why would you think that?" She asks, handing me a tissue.

"Because of what I just said."

"No. Anna, it's perfectly natural for you to need your brother. You trust him, and you're in this together."

Did she just miss the whole, 'my dead mum told me to die?' I ask myself, as I stare at her, confused.

"Just relax," she says, "he's a great source of strength to you, which is a good thing."

Ok, if she's not about to take me away from him, maybe I can trust her.

I listen for a while, as she goes on about how trauma can disrupt something in the brain. To be honest, I am trying to listen, but it's almost impossible to take anything in. My head's pulling me in a thousand different directions; Becca, the possibility that Dan could be leaving, Tommy's birthday, and the fact that we'll have to entertain John and Sarah later today. I think Julie can tell that I'm struggling, because she keeps pausing, waiting for me to catch up.

2.30pm. Home.
Anna:

Tommy wakes me from my usual post therapy nap, with a warm drink. We're going camping tomorrow, and he wants everything sorted and packed this afternoon. I promised to help him, but it feels like he's just going through the motions; taking me to therapy, cleaning the house, insisting that we load the car. Aside from when I gave him his card, this morning, he's avoided talk of anything 'birthday related.' I just hope that when Rich gets here, with my present and the cake, he'll let himself smile. After all, coffee and cake are two of Tommy's favourite things.

"Have you read your note yet?" I ask, resting my feet on his lap.

I've always put a note in Tommy's birthday cards. When I was small, I'd draw him a picture, or make up silly rhymes, but this year's different. He shakes his head.

"Could you?" I ask him.

He flashes me a sideways glance, then smiles briefly, as he pulls my note from his pocket. I ask him to read aloud, because I hope that hearing the words might cheer him up.

"Alright," he says, smoothing out the paper.

"Tom,
You are the best brother a girl could ever wish for. I can't imagine anyone else being as understanding, fun or as patient as you. But not only that, you are, and always have been, my rock and best friend. Even when we were kids, and some of your friends would tease you for playing with me, you didn't change. You always made time for me, I'll be forever grateful for that. Which brings me onto my next point, I can't think of a time where you haven't been there when I've needed you; you took me in, you looked after me in France, and above all, you didn't kick me out when I told you I was pregnant. There is absolutely nothing that I would hide from you, and that's why I feel like I'm more than your sister now, I'm your friend, and I'm here for you. (You're still my hero though. You always will be.)
I love you. Happy birthday, your little Annie."

He lays the note on the carpet. "You're so precious," he says, "but it's not strictly true."

"Tom?"

"I haven't always been there, have I?" He sighs, leaning forward to rub his eyes.

"Yes you have."

He shakes his head. "Annie, I know you don't want to talk about this, but I do."

He means what happened after my prom, and no, I don't want to talk about it.

"Leave it." I say, as I stand my mug on the floor. "You were just annoyed about the car, and you didn't know what Alex had done."

"That makes no difference. I knew what he'd done to you at Becca's party, and I know you. You were having a great

229

time, you weren't bothered that he was there. He saw you with Dan, and that got under his skin. That's why he started, I should've figured that out. And while we're on the subject, the day after Becca's party, you tried to talk to me, and I shrugged you off. My head was so full of the accident and I couldn't face the thought that you were having sex…An, you knew something was up. You didn't know what exactly, but you knew, and you tried to talk to me. Hell, you said you were sore, how rough must he have been?"

"Stop!…I don't blame you, ok? I kind of expected worse, you didn't even want me to go to that party, then I come home looking like that. I didn't even want you to see me. Anyway, look at what you have done, you wait outside all my therapy sessions. You give a shit about every little thing about me. We survive together, me and you."

"We do," he says, "listen, I don't want to sound ungrateful. I know you meant what you wrote, and I do love you. I just keep going over it…what he did to you. You must've been terrified."

"It scares me when I think about it. But, remember, I didn't know it was happening. One minute I was dancing, then the next, it was morning, and I woke up to him sliding his hand in my knickers!"

He takes a huge deep breath and grabs my hand, "I should've dealt with this a long time ago…but it's not too late?"

"No, Tom. You can't."

6pm. Anna:

It's a funny thing about get-togethers, everyone hovers in the kitchen. Stu's brought his boyfriend, Dylan. This is the first time I've met him, but he seems nice. Every time Stu speaks he'll touch him, not in a vulgar way, but discreetly, attentively. I don't think I've ever seen Stu look so happy.

Tommy loves my gift, he's using it right now to make John and Sarah a coffee. Olivia's wandered off into the lounge, she told me to go with her, but I don't feel like it. Instead, I just stand by the door and look out to the garden. Today feels strange.

"You alright, kidda?" Rich asks, handing me a drink.

"Yeah, I guess. I've got that money for you." I turn to go upstairs, but he lays his hand on my arm to stop me.

"Get it later. Listen, like I said when we cleared out your mum and dad's, if you ever need anything…"

At this exact moment, I look over to Tommy. He nods, like he knew what Rich just said.

"Yeah," I say, "there might be one thing…"

July 01, 2016 Friday Evening. James Cook University Hospital, A&E.
Alex:

"She said hold on." Jake says, shaking his head as he walks back to me. "She said you're next in."

"I hope so. I can't handle this, it's agony."

One second I was fine, just walking home. Then in the next, I was face down in the mud, in absolute agony. I knew I had to get to the hospital. I couldn't call Dad to bring me, he'd want to know who did it and why. Not that I'd tell him, I mean how could I? But my dad's suspicious, he'd figure something out, then most probably break my other arm just to prove a point. Well, he might not go that far, but I'd definitely be in deep shit. That's why I called my brother, Jake, he's just been talking to the woman on reception, because we've been here over two hours already. I don't think I can take it much longer. It's burning, the pain's shooting down my arm. I can't sit, I can't stand, and I'm freezing, but my body's pouring with sweat.

"You gonna tell me who did this?" Jake asks.

"I, um I…" I don't know what to tell him, but luckily, I don't have to worry about that yet.

"Alexander Murray?" A nurse calls, from a doorway.

"Come on, kid." He hooks my good arm around his neck, and we follow the nurse into the cubicle.

"Can he lie down?" He asks, "he's burning up."

"Yes. Can you confirm his details, before I check him over?"

He helps me onto a trolley. Then she asks him loads of questions, and I try to get comfortable, but it's pointless. Each position I try just adds to the pressure.

"Come on," says the nurse, "I need you to sit up now, so I can see your range of movement."

I nod and try, but every muscle burns and my arm shakes, I can barely move it an inch.

"That's it!" I yelp, "I can't!"

"I'm sorry, I know it hurts. Can you tell me what happened?"

"I…I fell down the stairs!"

"Ok," she nods, turning to my brother, "you'll need to take him to x-ray."

He helps me down, and we stagger into the corridor. "I bet you think I'm a right pussy."

"Nah, mate," he laughs, "I wouldn't be crying so much, mind."

"Fuck off."

In the x-ray department, we wait for another hour, before they call me in. Then another nurse stands me on a cross, marked on the floor.

"Stand as still as you can," she says, then pulls my arm straight by my side. It burns, and I shout out in pain.

"I know it's uncomfortable, but I need you to keep still."

"Please hurry." I say, as she runs behind the screen. I can't stand it. I feel like I'm going to faint.

"Two minutes," she calls, "keep still."

I'm trying, I really am, but I can't breathe.

"Ok, love." She says, after a few minutes. "You're all done. If you could just go back to A and E, so the doctor can see you."

"I have to wait again?"

"Afraid so, but it shouldn't be too long."

I hobble out to Jake, in the waiting room. "I have to go back to A and E."

"Come on then," he says, wrapping my arm over his shoulder, "off we go."

The x-ray woman was right. I've barely sat down two minutes, before I'm called back in. Jake helps me to lie down again, while the doctor checks my results.

"Ok." He says, "you have a subluxation of your right shoulder. Essentially, the joint is partially dislocated from the socket. Not an injury synonymous to a fall down the stairs, but relatively simple to reset. I can do that now, with the permission of a parent or guardian?"

Before I have time to think, Jake says that he's my guardian. Lie.

"Right, Alexander." He says, stepping over to me, "I need you to sit up and move to the edge of the trolley. Now, this will hurt, are you happy for me to continue?"

Truth be told, I'm bricking it. I'm genuinely shitting myself. "Not exactly," I say, "just do it quick."

He nods, cleans his hands and gloves up. Then injects something into my shoulder.

"Try to relax," he says, "keep your muscles loose."

Relax? He's on another planet. He grips my elbow hard, bends it, then says something about traction, before moving one hand to my shoulder. He slowly rotates it till we hear a loud pop.

"Aargh! Ya bastard!"

He nods, as I suck the air through my teeth.

"You should feel better within a few days." He says, as he coolly washes his hands. Then, he tells the nurse to fit me with a sling, before leaving.

"Can he have some painkillers?" Jake asks her.

"Paracetamol and ibuprofen. I'll get you some, two minutes."

She makes the sling as comfortable as possible, then goes to find me some drugs. That's when Jake folds his arms and stares me out.

"You gonna tell me then?"

"Yeah, yeah, I'll tell you in the car."

1 Hour Later. Journey Home.
Alex:

I figured, with the hospital being so busy, they'd want me out quick. They didn't, they spent ages going over everything, telling me what to watch out for. What a fucking day, and I still have to face Dad.

"What you gonna tell him?" I ask Jake, as he stops for a red light.

"Dad?" He shrugs. "Dunno, I don't know anything." The light turns green, but he doesn't move; just sits there staring me out. He doesn't even flinch when the car behind, blasts his horn and over-takes. "I'm not moving, until you tell me what's going on!"

"Nothing, I fell down the stairs."

"Righto." He says, turning off the engine. "We'll stay here all night."

"Alright, I'll tell you. Just drive."

He nods and re-starts the car.

"I think it's got something to do with a girl from school. I mean, I recognised him…I think."

"What're you on about?"

"Someone jumped me, on the way back from Chloe's. Well, he was walking towards me. I knew I'd seen him before, he was a skin-head, with two silver bars on his chin. Anyway, he just walked past, and I was like, 'thank fuck for that.' I was down near the beck. Anyway, I heard a shuffle from the gravel, so I turned and, before I knew it, he had me in a half-nelson. He prodded at this," I say, showing him the scratch on my face. "He said, 'that's nasty, who'd ya piss off?' It was like he already knew. Then I was on the floor, in

234

agony. He knelt down and said, 'that must hurt. Ya wanna get it looked at.'

"And he looked familiar?"

"Yeah."

Jake drums his fingers on the wheel, it gets louder and louder, until I can't stand it.

"Quit tapping!"

"Sorry. You gonna tell me what you've got yourself into?"

"It'll be that bitch and her brother."

"What bitch?"

"Just a girl that I fucked at a party."

"A girl got someone to jump you, because you fucked her?"

"Yeah, she's crazy...I mean, I probably should've left her alone after her parents died, but she's been acting like we raped her! I mean yeah she was wasted..."

"Tell me she was conscious?"

"Yeah, well kinda."

"Hang on," he says, tapping the wheel again, "who's we?"

"Chloe."

"Ya what? Chloe was there? Why were you fucking her, when your girlfriend was there?"

"It was her idea. She wanted to watch, she's kinky like that."

"Ok, ok, just give me a minute." He drives on until he finds a lay by, then parks up and turns off the engine. "So, her brother did this?"

"Nah, he's a psycho. This bloke was calm...too calm. That's it, I know where I've seen him now, it was at the school, he was with her brother."

"You stupid twat!" He snaps. "They think you raped her!"

"I didn't!"

"You sure about that?" He says firmly, knocking his knuckle on the wheel.

"I didn't hold her down, didn't hit her, for fucks sake she was half asleep."

"Half asleep?! Lads have been done for rape, when the lass's just pissed!"

"I didn't rape her! I stayed with her all night! Right till the morning."

"You think that makes it right, ya fool? This was a warning, and you're lucky it wasn't the brother, cos if he's owt like me, you'd be in the ground! Alex, I'm serious, you need to fucking dump Chloe! She's trouble."

"Ok, ok. And what do I tell Dad?"

"Tell him you fell down the stairs."

Chapter 5

Six Months Later.
December 22, 2016 Thursday 2.30pm.
College.
Anna:

Shortly after our prom, Dan and I had a real heart to heart. He told me that he loved me, that he's loved me for so long. It's funny, I mean, I knew that I liked him in that way, but it wasn't until he said those words, that I realised that I had feelings for him too. So, I told him. I felt like I was about to discover a whole new side to him, to get to know him, all over again. It wasn't to be. Dan was holding something back, he said that he loved me, but…then he said it.

"I'm going with Mum. I want to stay with you, Anna, but I have to go with Mum."

I desperately wanted him to stay, but I couldn't ask. I didn't know if it was some kind of test, like he needed me to say it. I didn't actually say anything, I just held his hand and nodded. So, now he's gone. We're still just friends, but we're closer now, and despite the distance, we talk almost every day.

I still had a great summer. Before working things out with Dan, Ethan came up and stayed with us. Tommy was right, he didn't even notice that I was sleeping in with him. I really had nothing to worry about, and it was so nice for us three to catch up. And Tommy took me camping. It was just what we needed, we both switched our phones off and shut the world out, for a few days. When we got back, I expected a few missed calls and texts from Becca, but there were none. I texted her a few times, but she didn't reply. I guess she didn't like the 'Anna' who stands up for herself.

It's funny, but part of me toyed with the idea of changing colleges, to one that I'd at least know someone. I'm glad I didn't, coming here alone was so daunting, but it's made me stronger. If I hadn't, I wouldn't have met Emilia. She's just like me, her friends are mostly boys, she can't stand small talk, and she's little. Yes, another person my own age, who's under five foot tall. We're leaving college early today, because it's Christmas Eve soon, I've finished my first term.

"You doing much tonight?" Emilia asks, as we put on our coats.

"Going for a drive, Tommy's getting his new car today."

"He's waited ages for that?"

"Yeah, he had to. He wanted a manual, for the 'full driving experience.'"

She shoots a sideways smile, and we head downstairs, when my phone beeps. It's a text from Tommy.

"Running late, An,
still at the garage."

"Should I get the bus?"

"No, just wait there.
I won't be long."

He doesn't like me getting the bus, because I have to change in Middlesbrough. I don't mind, although I only need to when he's working at the theatre.

"Everything alright?" Emilia asks.

"Yeah, Tommy's going to be late, that's all. So, what're you doing tonight?"

"Family meal," she groans, flicking her untamed, fiery hair away from her freckled face. "My cousin's just got engaged, and that means one thing…tonight's gonna be the Amy show."

"Oh dear."

"Don't worry," she laughs, "I'll survive."

3.20pm. Car Dealership.
Tommy:

"There you are." The salesman grins, as he hands me the keys. "She's all yours."

"Thanks." I eagerly shake his hand, before dropping into the drivers seat.

A5 Quattro in red, as requested by the sister. That smell, nothing beats the smell of a new car. Nodding to the salesman, I start her up, and roll out of the forecourt. Right, now to get Annie, then I'll be heading straight for the open road. The traffic's moving steadily, so I sit back and cruise along to the college.

The car park's almost empty, so I pull over by the main entrance and send her a text.

"I'm here."

"Coming."

The moment she steps outside, she zips up her coat, pulls up her hood and smiles at me. Then an over excitable boy appears from behind her. I nod back and watch, as he prances around her. It's quite pitiful really, amusing but pitiful.

"See you tomorrow." She tells him, as she opens the car door.

"Hold on," he says, "it's definitely a date?"

"Yes," she laughs, "it's definitely a date."

Anna:

If I wasn't blushing before I got in the car, I certainly am now. Tommy's just sat there, staring at me, itching to tease me.

"Oh, this is nice." I say, running my hand over the fabric on the door. He raises his eyebrows, so I quickly look around for something else. "The lights are pretty, aren't they?"

He says nothing, so I fight back a nervous laugh, grab his phone and flick through his playlist. In the corner of my eye, I see him grinning. Don't look at him, I tell myself. I press play and make myself comfortable, that's when I feel it.

"Oh, Tom, you've put the heated seats on. You're awesome you know, have I ever told you just how awesome you are?" I'm smiling as sweetly as I can, but he just grunts, 'ah ha.'

"So," I say, "how're you liking the gears?"

"Drop the act, daft arse. What was all that about? Is that the lad who keeps getting Emilia to ask you out for him?"

"Yeah that's Eden," I giggle, as I fasten my seat belt, "he asked me himself."

"So you've relented?" He tuts playfully, as he pulls away.

"I needed to be sure he really liked me."

It's not that I don't trust Emilia, but when she kept insisting that the most freakishly beautiful boy at college, is interested in me, I was sceptical. Eden Morris could have any girl he wants, why would he be interested in me?

"So where's he taking you?"

"For a hot chocolate, then the cinema."

"Ok, just be careful and keep your phone on."

"I will."

"So do you actually like him," he asks, joining the dual carriageway, "or have you just agreed because he's been so persistent?"

"No, I like him…he's just kinda out of my league."

"Don't be daft! Listen, I'll drop you off tomorrow, then when you're ready, text me and I'll pick you up."

"I'll be alright you know."

"Please, little Annie, let me look after you."

"Alright." I lay my head on his shoulder and fiddle with the cuff of his jacket. "Could you make me look pretty tomorrow?"

"Course I will."

December 23, 2016 Friday 10.45am. Home.
Anna:

Most girls would wear a dress for their first date, I'm not most girls. Plus, I only own two; the black one from Mum and Dad's funeral, and my prom dress. There's no way that I'll wear the funeral one again, and I'd look ridiculous if I strolled through town, wearing floaty chiffon in December. Instead, I pull some dark blue, skinny jeans from my wardrobe. I'm going to wear them with a new jumper, that Tommy bought me. He's easing my transition from tom-boy to lady. It's pastel pink cashmere, slim fitting with a plunge neckline. It sits just below my hips, and looks perfect with my sapphire necklace. After getting changed, I brush my hair for a third time.

"Right," I say, as I stare into the mirror and play with my necklace, "all I need is my face doing, then I'm ready."

Suddenly, the most eerie feeling sweeps over me. Something's here. I look around the room, only to feel a thump in my chest when I turn back to my mirror. It's her, It's Mum.

"You look lovely." She says.

This isn't real. I know how to make this go away, but I can't. It's my mum, and she's smiling.

"Cat got your tongue?" She says, "where're you going?"

"I…I've got a date. Tommy's going to do my make-up."

"You'll be in good hands."

I have so much to say, so much to ask. For a second, I raise my hand to the mirror, my fingertips feel the cold glass, and she moves back.

"I'm sorry," I say, "I miss you."

"I miss you too, tell your brother that I love you both."

In haste, I fling my bedroom door open. "He's just downstairs!" I turn away and call him, but she shouts for me to stop.

"Anna! Do you actually believe that I'm in your mirror?" Her eyes burn with tears, as waves crash against her. "You

241

know where I am." On her final word, she's pulled under by the current, my reflection returns to normal, and I slump to the floor.

"You alright?" Tommy calls from the landing, but I can barely catch my breath let alone answer him. When he opens the door, I raise one arm up to the mirror.

"I saw Mum."

"Shit!" He drops to the floor behind me. "It wasn't her, Annie." He says, pulling me towards him.

"It was! She said she loves us, but she's trapped…she's trapped in the sea! It's winter, Tommy, she'll be so cold."

"Annie. It wasn't real. You know that."

In this second, I realise how ridiculous I must sound. "I'm not getting better, am I?"

"You are," he says, "but why didn't you do what Julie said? You can stop these now."

I shake my head and wipe away the tears, rolling down my cheeks.

"Oh, sweetheart. Listen, I know how badly you want to square things with her, I do too… but she's gone."

I can't speak, so I lay back against his chest. Then I hear Julie's voice in my head. Using her steps is usually simple, not so when I see what I long for.

1.50pm. Middlesbrough Town Centre.
Outside The Coffee Shop.
Eden:

There's no sign of Anna, so I check my phone again, in case she's cried off. She hasn't, but I'm early. Good plan, get here ten minutes early because that's not desperate at all. I must look like a right muppet, I can't stand still, my palms are sweaty, no girl's ever reduced me to this. I could take a wander, not too far then, after a minute I'll turn around and walk back. Actually, that's a bad idea, I don't know which direction she's coming from, and knowing my luck, I'll end up bumping into her. I'd have to explain why I'm heading

242

away from the meet, when she's walking to it. I'll just wait, besides, it's almost two, and she doesn't know how long I've been here. After a few minutes, I feel a light tap on my arm.

"Hiya." She says.

"Anna? I didn't know if you'd turn up." Great opening line, Eden. She'll know I'm a tool for sure.

"Don't be silly," she smiles, "come on, should we go inside? I'm freezing."

Anna:

I tried to give Eden some money, but he wouldn't take it. While he buys the drinks, I find us a little table tucked away in the corner. As usual, I take the seat with my back to the wall so I can see the exit.

He sets the tray down as I take off my coat. He's stunning, it's actually hard to believe that I'm really here with him. I try not to stare as he unbuttons his smart winter jacket, but I can't help it. Underneath, he's wearing black, skinny jeans and only a thin cotton shirt. He must be freezing. It's bitter today, and not just cold, it was starting to snow when Tommy drove me to town, and even he had the sense to wear a sweater.

His eyes linger over me, and he smiles. I take a sip of my hot chocolate and try my hardest not to get whipped cream on my nose, or blush, but my cheeks betray me. How can I not turn red when I'm out with Eden Morris? He's perfect, Mum would've said he is 'well groomed'. He's not exactly fair, but his skin's pale, and he has one of those pompadour quiffs; it's not excessive, just tidy and nice. I smile back, over the rim of my mug, I'm mesmerized. I've never seen anyone with rich brown hair and eyes so blue.

"So, what made you change your mind?" He asks.

"What do you mean?"

"You know," he says, looking around, "to this."

"Oh, I…well it didn't really count when you got Emilia to ask for you." My cheeks are burning again, "I agreed because you asked me…and because you're nice."

"Oh, I can be very nice."

"Sure you can," I giggle, as I slice my chocolate muffin in half. "Do you want to share?"

"Yeah, do you want some of mine?"

I nod, and he digs a knife in the middle of his caramel shortbread. When the chocolate cracks, the base crumbles and the caramel oozes from the sides.

"Sorry." He whispers, as it sticks to his fingers. "Sorry, I'm making a right mess."

I shouldn't laugh but I can't keep it in, he's clumsy and cute. I hold out my plate and pass him a wad of napkins, as he hands me the messy, crumbling lump. He's embarrassed but still smiles, I'm glad he sees the funny side.

Eden:

Any minute now, she'll get a text and have to leave for some convenient emergency. Story of my life; I take a girl out, and it all goes well, until I say something stupid, or forget what I'm doing and send her drink flying. Luckily, I haven't done that, but destroying the shortbread was just as bad. All I had to do was cut the thing in half, for fuck's sake. Here we go, she's just got a text. I may as well put my coat on.

"Do you need to go?" I ask her.

"No, I'm just telling my brother that I'm good. Well, that you're good, I mean nice." She blushes and hides her face, so I lay my hand over hers. This isn't like me, but when she lifts her face to look me in the eyes, I freeze. It's like she can see my thoughts, she can see every dream I've had about her, It's scary but, I really want to get to know her. Kiss her, Eden, now's your chance, just lean in and kiss her. I do lean closer, but when my fingers slide under the cuff of her jumper, she pulls her arm away.

"Sorry," she says, "I um, so, I don't know much about you."

Ok, I didn't expect that, but she did say that I'm nice. I can hear my stepdad's voice saying, 'take it easy, don't push, if it's meant to be it will be'.

"I like footie." That's it, Eden, keep it cool. "My stepdad got us season tickets. Are you into footie?"

"Not religiously, but I can follow a game…oh, and I know the offside rule."

"Really? Tell me then."

"Alright," she grins, "this saucer's the goal." She takes three sachets of white sugar, one of brown, and arranges them in front of the 'goal'. "Ok, now being a huge football fan, you obviously know this, but I'll explain as if you don't, to prove I do, ok?"

"Fair enough," I smile, "go on."

"Now, he's in an offside position," she says, pointing to the closest white sachet, "if he receives the ball here. You see, he's nearer to the oppositions goal line than the second, last opponent…"

"Ok, ok, you've proved your point." I'd let her go on, but I'm not about to let the whole coffee shop think that I don't know the offside rule. "So what music d'ya like?"

"It depends what mood I'm in," she says, "anything I can sing to really, you?"

"Same. So what else do you like?"

"I love running…mainly cross country. You might not believe it, because I'm little, but I'm actually pretty fast."

"I'll have to race you sometime."

Anna smiles and tackles the mess that was once millionaires shortbread.

"So, have you got any brothers or sisters?" She asks, pinching off bite-sized pieces.

"Two half sisters, they're twins."

"Older? Younger? Do they have names?"

"Sorry, yeah they're fourteen. Neve and Ellie."

Anna coughs and pats her chest. "Sorry," she says, taking a drink.

"Are you ok?"

"Yeah, did you say Neve and Ellen?"

"Ellie, why?"

"Sorry, it's just Ellen was my mum's name."

I do know that Anna lost her parents, but Emilia said not to talk about it. I kind of have to now, or she'll think I'm cold.

"I'm sorry."

"It's ok...Emilia told you?"

"Only that it was recent, and you live with your brother now. She didn't say how they...you know."

"That's because she doesn't know." She dabs her lips with a napkin, and looks away. "They drowned...on holiday."

"I am so sorry."

"Not your fault," she brushes herself off and smiles, "way to put a downer on things. Sorry, I shouldn't have brought that up."

Go on, Eden, this is the perfect time to offer her a hug. No, actually it isn't, if I hug her now she might cry, and yeah I've had some disastrous dates, but I've never made a girl cry.

"So do you and your sisters get along?" She asks.

"Kind of. Ellie's alright, but Neve thinks I'm annoying."

As I say this, Anna watches me repeatedly fold up a napkin, "I don't think you're annoying," she says, slowly running her knuckle over the back of my hand. I want to hold her, but after she pulled away earlier, I don't know if I should.

Anna:

Anna you stupid girl. Who brings up their dead parents on a first date? No wonder he won't hold my hand. I don't want to go to the cinema now. I'm not saying that I want to go home, I just don't want to sit for two hours and not be able to talk. My stomach's in knots.

"Listen, Eden, is there anything you'd rather do, than watch a movie?"

"Um, we could go bowling, but we'd have to get the bus over to Stockton."

"That's ok."

We put our coats on, and I send Tommy a quick text to let him know. Outside, the main walkway between the shops is swarming with people. I want to grab his arm, but that would look pathetic. Instead, I walk closely beside him, as we head down to the Christmas market stalls. Amongst the usual sellers of mobile phone cases and cheap, tacky gifts, I spot a cute little stall full of festive sweets. Without thinking, I grab Eden's hand and pull him closer. They've got mince pies, Christmas cake and every flavour of fudge imaginable. I stand there wide eyed like a ten-year-old, and that's when I spot my favourite. Stollen; bite-sized spiced bread, with fruit and marzipan, all covered in icing sugar. I have to buy some, so I give the lady some money, and she fills me a paper bag.

"Here," I say to Eden, showing him inside, "do you want some?"

"Nah, it's ok. You saw the mess I made with the shortbread, can you imagine the carnage with all that sugar?"

"It's ok," I smile and take out a piece, "go on just try it."

He nods, so I hold it up to his lips, cupping my hand under his chin. "Ok," he says, "that is nice."

"It sure is." I squeeze the bag back in my pocket, and we step aside, but as we do, I hear someone call my name. I look to Eden, just as Becca bounces over to us, with a not so enthusiastic Isabelle in tow. I'm confused, Becca hasn't spoken to me since we fell out, six months ago.

"Hiya." She says, throwing her arms around me. "You're the last person I thought I'd see today. You alright in crowds now?"

I nod, and she stares at Eden, and grins. "So, who's this?"

I have no time to think, I just slide my hand in his and find myself saying, "He's my boyfriend." She stares again, and Eden casually says 'hi.'

"Good for you, An." She says. "He's cute. So anyway, what're ya doing over Christmas?"

"Christmas day, we've got the family over for dinner, then Tommy's working."

"Is he doing a show?"

"No, he's working at the pub."

"I just wanted to see ya, that's all." She says, hugging me again. "You free Tuesday?"

"Sorry I'm not, Dan's coming over."

"Him?" Isabelle growls. "You can tell that Daniel that I'm over him, I'm seeing someone else."

"Issy, shut up!" Becca snaps. "See ya, An, I'll text ya." And with that, they rush away. Then I realise that I still have hold of Eden's hand. He hasn't let go, but he looks confused.

"Anna, were you serious?"

"Yes." I whisper. "I can't believe I'm saying this but, I really like you, and until you asked me yourself…I thought you'd been mocking me."

He moves to face me, and takes hold of my waist. "I wouldn't mock you, I'm not like that."

"So, you want to be my boyfriend?"

"Hell yeah."

He immediately leans in to kiss me. His lips are soft and warm against mine, I love it. I can taste the sweetness from the stollen as he massages my tongue with his. My heart's racing. I know I should close my eyes, but I want to soak in every detail of his face. He's firm and gentle, and I could easily fall if he wasn't holding me so tight. Schools of busy shoppers hurry around us, then the moment slows to a natural end, but I wish that it wouldn't. Neither of us can stop smiling, I run my fingers over his neck, and before I know it, I'm saying,

"Do that again."

Earlier That Day.
9am. Becca:

Marvellous. First lie in of the holidays, and some dick thinks it's funny to call me. I'm not answering it. I push my head under the pillow and try to go back to sleep, but I can't. Each time it rings off, they call again. 'Oh alright!' I heave myself over and grab my phone. Shit, it's Alex.

"Alex, hi. Um, Y'alright?"

"Yeah. Why did you warn Issy against me."

Great. She's told him. I caught them kissing in college yesterday. Getting with him would be a bad idea, I had to tell her.

"I think you know why."

"No, Bec. I don't."

"Does the name Anna ring any bells?"

"And?" He huffs. "What of her?"

"I know what you did."

"Sure, I got carried away at the prom, but you're not even friends anymore. I don't see what it has to do with Issy."

"That's not it, Alex. We know you drugged her at my party."

"What the fuck?!"

"You can't deny it. We both heard you freaking out to Chloe about it."

"Err when?"

"Ages ago, in room thirty-five. Jogging your memory yet?"

"And, what exactly do you think you heard?"

"Alex. Chloe said Anna was out cold. You drugged her and fucked her."

"I gave her vodka, ya silly cow, not drugs! And, I wasn't the only one…I remember you topping up her Malibu, more than a few times. It's not my fault she can't handle it."

He goes on and on about that night, and the more he talks, the fuzzier it all becomes. What did I actually hear? All I remember, was Chloe saying she was out cold, then Anna was a mess. What if she heard it all wrong, and he's telling the truth?

"Becca," he sighs, "she was wasted, and I probably shouldn't have fucked her, but I was wasted too. I didn't mean to hurt her. Listen, Issy knows about the party and, I really like her. Please don't ruin it for me."

I don't know what to think now. I should've asked him about it at the time. I wanted to, but Tommy wouldn't let me.

"Alright," I tell him, "fine, just don't hurt her."

"I won't."

December 24, 2016 Saturday 6pm. Home. Christmas Eve.
Anna:

Mum had a tradition. Every year, she wouldn't wrap a single present until Christmas eve. She'd lay out all the wrapping paper and bows, on the lounge carpet. She'd play Christmas tunes and sip on her Irish cream, while she wrapped them all. Last year, she asked me to help. To think I whinged about it, I'd give anything to sit and wrap presents with her now. This year Tommy's carrying on her tradition, but instead of Irish cream, I've got a cider, and he's drinking whiskey.

I break off pieces of tape, and stick them along the edge of the TV stand. Our lounge is much smaller than Mum's was, and as we lay the gifts on the floor, we soon run out of space. So, he moves against the sofa, and I try not to knock the Christmas tree, as I shuffle back towards the wall. Aside from the family's presents, Tommy always buys a little token gift for the girls at the pub, and something for Stu and

Rich. Dan loves anything retro, so I've bought him another lava lamp to add to his collection. It's Dr. Who themed, like the inside of the T.A.R.D.I.S. He's going to love it. I wasn't planning on buying Eden anything, as we only got together yesterday, but I couldn't not. So Tommy took me out earlier today, and I bought him a little teddy wearing a Middlesbrough strip. It's so cute. Tommy glides the scissors through a sheet of wrapping paper and smirks, as my phone beeps again. It's Eden, we've been texting each other, pretty much all day.

"Hey, beautiful,
Emilia knows about us,
I had to tell her.
Sorry, I should've checked.
Is that ok?"

"Yes!
I was going to tell her anyway.
So, what're you up to?"

"With Mum and Adrian.
Planning my birthday party"

"When is it?"

"New years eve,
please come.
Everyone's dying to meet you."

I instantly feel 'old Anna' coming out. A party? I can't go to a party, can I? I spend the next minute or so, staring at my phone. The last party I went to was Becca's, and I just can't put myself in a position like that again. But Eden's sweet, he's as far away from Alex, as Mercury is from Pluto.

Then there's logistics, Eden lives near the college, that's two buses away. I can't expect Tommy to pick me up, imagine that, 'oh sorry, Tom. Yeah, I'm just gonna leave you on new years eve, but you can't have a drink, because I'll need a lift home.'

"I'd never do that to him." I mutter, as I try to figure out what to reply.

"You alright?" Tommy asks, as he snaps off a piece of sticky tape.

I take a gulp of cider and nod.

"You don't look alright."

"Just read from there to the bottom, don't scroll." I say, sliding my phone over the carpet. "What do you think?"

"What? He's asking you to his birthday."

"It's a party, Tom."

"Yeah but look, he's arranged it with his mum, and I'm guessing Adrian's his stepdad, so I don't think you need to worry. Don't you want to go?"

"I don't know…what about you?"

"It works perfectly for me. I'm working new year now, so if you want to go, I could take you over and pick you up around one. Then I won't worry about you being alone."

Maybe I'm being silly. Eden did tell me that his mum's old fashioned, so I doubt it'll be wild. Yes, I'm going to go and it will surely be wonderful.

"So, why are you working both?" I ask Tommy, while sending Eden a reply. "It's not exactly fair is it?"

Usually, if Tracey asks him to work Christmas, she'll give him new year off.

"It's a compromise," he sighs, "in the next two weeks, I'm working tomorrow, new years eve, new years day and the second of January. That's four nights, rather than my usual six."

"That's not so bad."

"Nope, it's not…listen." He pauses and reaches for a label. "I didn't bring this up yesterday, because I didn't want you upset before your date…and after, well you were all happy and…"

"You wanna talk about me seeing Mum?"

252

He nods.

"What do you want to know?"

"Is that the first time it's been…positive?"

"I think so."

He gives me a questioning look, like he wants me to explain. I can't, this was the only vision I've had that was kind of nice, other than the one where he kissed me. Although, part of me now thinks that could have been real.

"Yeah," I tell him, "you know what they're usually like."

"Do you know what triggered it?"

I shake my head and stick a bow on Eden's teddy bear. "No. That's why I didn't use the steps, it all happened so fast. Can I ask you something?"

"Sure."

"What did you mean, when you said that you wanted to square things too?"

"I don't know, I've just been going over stuff."

"Can you tell me?"

"Don't worry, Annie. I'm alright."

"Come on, Tom. I talk to you."

"Ok," he nods, "it's that night mainly."

"What night?"

"You know, that night when Dad lost it with me. You brought it up in a therapy session."

"You want to square that? That wasn't your fault!"

He pulls out his bobble and sighs. "It was."

He's wrong, it was Dad's fault, it was all Dad's fault. He had a short temper and unrealistic expectations. If only he could see us now, see what my brother's carried me through, and how he's taken care of me.

"Come here." He clears the paper in front of him, and taps the carpet.

"Have you really been beating yourself up over this?" I ask, as I move to face him, "I'm so sorry, I should've never told Julie what happened."

"No, no, you needed to. I wanna know what you remember?"

"Waiting…I remember standing in your doorway, the next morning. I remember crying when I saw the bruises on your back. Then you told me it was ok, and took me down to the kitchen, to make our breakfast. I remember feeling desperate. I couldn't stand it when he was hitting you. I tried to stop him, but I was too small."

"You did stop him. He could've killed you, throwing you like that."

"Don't say that. But anyway, why would you think it was your fault?"

"Because that night I heard them arguing, worse than usual. Mum was crying, and you know Mum didn't cry, she'd give as good as she got. She said she felt trapped. The thing is, Dad wasn't meant to be home that weekend, he only came back because I'd been in trouble at school. Mum got called in because of my 'anger issues', then all of a sudden Dad came home. That has to be why."

"Possibly," I say, "but you didn't deserve that."

"Annie, right before Mum stormed out, Dad said he'd had it with this failure of a family…a failure. He had to mean me. I know I should've left it, but I needed to know why Mum stormed out. He told me to shut up, but I couldn't, he was angry, I was angry, and I said it was all his fault. That's when he slapped me…and you saw the rest."

I can't believe I'm hearing this. He's wrong. I lean forward quickly, and hold his face.

"No, Tom! It doesn't matter how bad you were at school, or how many times he told you to be quiet, he was the one who ripped off his belt, he was the one who wouldn't stop hitting you. He was the one…"

My brother does nothing but close his eyes and press his forehead to mine.

"It wasn't your fault," I repeat, "it's not your fault."

December 25, 2016 Sunday 9.30am. Christmas Day. Anna:

The sheets are cold on Tommy's side of the bed. He's probably downstairs, prepping the dinner for later. I'll get up in a minute and give him a hand, but first, I wriggle over to my side and check my phone. Eden's called me. I sit up quickly and call him straight back, but I can't hear what he's saying, as there's so much commotion in the background.

"What was that?" I ask.

"Neve! Will you just shut up!" He snaps, "Sorry, Anna, um merry Christmas."

"Merry Christmas. What did you just say?"

"I asked if I'd woke you?"

"No, I mean I'm still in bed, but I was awake. Anyway, it's nice to hear your voice."

"Which voice is that then?" He asks, playfully repeating my name in a variety of silly accents."

"Stop it," I giggle, "I was being serious."

"Aww, it's nice to hear your voice too. You know, I had a great time the other day," he says, "and was kinda hoping I could see you tomorrow…if you're not busy?"

"I'm not busy!" I say, grinning like an idiot. "Do you want to come here? Tommy wants to meet you."

"Sure, what bus do I get?"

"You'll need to go to Middlesbrough, then get the sixty three to Normanby."

"Where the hell's Normanby?"

"It's about half an hour from Middlesbrough. Don't worry, I'll text you all the details, and I'll meet you at the bus-stop."

"And you'll definitely be there? You won't leave me standing like a muppet?"

"Course I'll be there."

"Great. Sorry, I've got to go. Mum's on one."

"See you later."

After a huge stretch, I throw on my hoody and head downstairs. In the kitchen, Tommy's moving sausages and bacon around on a skillet, he's not dressed yet either.

"Hey," I say, taking the milk out of the fridge. "D'ya want a coffee?"

"I've got one." He then turns down the heat and gives me a massive bear hug. "Merry Christmas, little Annie. Do you want some breakfast? I've made pancakes too."

"Yeah, that'll be nice."

It's Christmas day. We should be happy, and earlier, when I was talking to Eden, I was.

We sit at the table, both trying to keep things as normal as we can. There's not much conversation, we're just in a strange state of comfortable contemplation. It's like the accident's just happened, and we're raw again. Christmas was Mum's favourite time of year, and the easiest way through it, would be to push her completely out of my head, or to just pretend it's a normal day. Then there's Sarah, this is her first Christmas without her sister, how do I know when a smile will lift the atmosphere, or offend?

"I want to give you your presents before they get here, is that ok?" Tommy asks, mopping up some runny egg yolk.

I nod.

"Eat up then."

After breakfast, I grab his gifts from my room, then meet him back in his. We sit on the bed, and he hands me a rectangular box. Judging by the weight, I'm guessing that it's shoes. I peel back the edges of shiny paper, see the logo and grin. I quickly tear away the rest to open the box, purple Converse. I love them.

"They're awesome!" I say, handing him a small box, "you open one."

"Thanks."

It's a braided leather bracelet, with a brushed titanium plate in the centre.

"Turn it over," I say eagerly, "I've had it engraved."

"Brother and friend," he smiles, as he runs his thumb over the words, "thank you, sweetheart."

"It's ok. It wasn't easy, finding someone who'll engrave onto titanium. Did you know, they use a laser?"

"I did." He nods, as he fastens it to his wrist, before handing me another. Opening it, I find a beautiful, silver bracelet, laden with charms.

"It's lovely." I say, draping it over my fingers. "As if we bought each other bracelets."

He reaches over and gently takes it from me. "There's a purpose behind this," he says, fastening it to my wrist, "most of these charms have movable parts, so when you get anxious, rather than scratching, you can fiddle with these. Hopefully, we can give your wrists a chance to heal."

I don't want to cry, but a few tears still manage to escape. "Thank you." I tell him, as I wipe them away.

"You're welcome."

We spend some time opening the rest, before getting ready for the family coming.

12.30pm. Tommy:

So far, everything's going to plan; turkey's in the oven and the Yorkshire pudding batter's made, and resting in the fridge. Earlier, Annie prepped all of the veg for me, and while she's upstairs getting ready, I set the table. As I fold the last napkin, through the window I see our cousin, Olivia storming over the garden.

"I'm asking her!" She screeches.

Ethan lunges after her and grabs her by the wrist. "No you're not!" He says, but she shakes his hand away and bursts through the patio door. She tries to close it behind her, to lock him out, but he just holds the handle, and it doesn't budge.

"What the hell's going on?!" I ask them. Ethan shakes his head, and Olivia tries to push past me, without success. "I don't know what's going on with you," I tell her, pulling out a chair, "but don't bring it here. Now, sit your arse there and calm down."

"Sorry, Tommy." Ethan says, as he kicks off his shoes. "She doesn't know when to shut up."

"I just want to know if it's true." Olivia says, pulling off her shoes and throwing them onto the pile, by the door.

"If what's true?" I ask.

"If…"

"Nothing." Ethan interrupts, grabbing himself a drink from the fridge. "Like I said, she needs to shut up."

I'm confused, but these days Olivia can turn from sweet, to teenaged angst in seconds, and the last thing I want is conflict, so I nod and fill the kettle. That's when I notice the garden gate's open, but there's no sign of John and Sarah.

"Where's your mum and dad?" I ask.
Ethan shakes his head. "I thought they were right behind us."

"They're in the car," Olivia huffs, "she'll be crying again…she needs to sort herself out."

"Excuse me?" I say.

Ethan turns away.

"I just mean it's not fair." She says. "Mum was getting better, even gone back to work. Now it's Christmas, and she's miserable again."

"Not fair! We've lost our mum and dad…you wanna talk about fair?"

"I didn't mean it like that, and you know I didn't. I just want Mum to go back to normal."
I'm not cut out for an argument with a thirteen-year-old right now, so I wave my hand dismissively and make a cup of tea.

"Here, Liv," I say, handing her the mug, "take that up to Anna, and mind your tongue."

"Sorry, Tommy," Ethan says again, "she just doesn't think."

"What was she on about, knowing if what's true?"

He shrugs. "I don't know if it's anything, but I caught her eaves dropping outside Mum and Dad's room. She heard something, and she's ran with it. The thing is, Mum was pissed, well that's nothing new lately, and she was crying and…"

"Merry Christmas." Sarah sings, as her and John step inside. Looks like that conversation will have to wait.

"Hiya," I say, "do you want tea or coffee?"

"Oh, give us one of those fancy coffees." John bellows. "Sarah?"

"I'll have a glass of wine, love."

Ethan's uneasy, he looks at me first, then asks tentatively. "Why don't you start with a tea, Mum?"

"Thanks for the concern, darling. But, it's Christmas and, I'd like a glass of wine."

One thing I've learned from working at the pub, is not to deny a woman who wants a drink, even if it's clearly not her first. So, I open a bottle of prosecco from the fridge, and stand it on the side with a glass, then make John a coffee.

"Thank you, Thomas," she says, as she begins to pour, "at least one of you is festive."

Nobody acknowledges her remark.

"How's work going?" John asks, as I steam the milk.

"Yeah, alright…"

"Never mind work, you miserable lot," Sarah interrupts, "it's Christmas, let's do presents."

"If that's what my lady wants," John says, "then I'd best get them from the car."

I think we've established how today is going. Once I've finished making John's coffee, Ethan and Sarah take their drinks into the lounge, while I head upstairs.

"Hey," I say, as I pop my head around Annie's door, "Liv, your mum wants to do presents, can you…" before I can ask her to give us a minute, she pushes past me and stomps downstairs.

"You've no idea how grateful I am, that you're not like her." I say, but Annie just smiles and turns away. So I sit beside her, on the bed. "Hey, what is it?"

"She's just asked me if I really told Mum to die."

"What? That's not what you said!"

"No, but that's what she's heard Sarah telling John."

So that's what Ethan was going to tell me. "Wait there, sweetheart, we'll get this sorted."

I rush to the top of the stairs and call Olivia back. After a few seconds, she appears at the bottom, hand on her hip, flicking her hair."What? You just told me to come down."

"Just come here, please." I ask, as calmly as I can.

She doesn't say anything, just follows me back into Annie's room, where I close the door behind her.

"Right, Liv. Anna did not tell our mum to die."

"Mum thinks she did, Ellen told her."

"I didn't," Annie whispers, "I told her not to come home."

"That's not much better!" Olivia laughs.

"Don't you think I know that?" Annie cries. "Don't you think I've tortured myself over this?"

"Liv." I snap. "How many times have you argued with your mum, and said things you regret? What were you thinking, asking her something like that, today of all days?" I'm absolutely raging, but I keep my eyes on Olivia, only to remind myself that she's a kid, and I need to keep my cool. After a moment or so of me staring, she breaks into angry tears.

"What about me?" She cries. "You've got Anna, Anna's got you. Mum's got Dad, Ethan's never here, no-one gives a shit about me."

"That's not true," I tell her, "and you can't just come in here, asking her questions like that."

"I'm sorry ok! I didn't think, I just..." she tries to talk, but all that comes out are splutters and cries. Annie does no more than stand and hug her.

"Alright, Liv," I sigh, laying a hand on her shoulder, "it's alright."

"It's not alright!" She pushes Annie away and steps back from us both. "You don't know what it's like, we can't talk about your Mum and Dad. I can't cry…fuck, whatever we do or say is nothing, because she's feeling it worse. She's lost her sister so no-one else matters. And Dad doesn't help, he just says 'don't upset your mother'…it's fucked up, Tommy." And with that, she pushes past me and locks herself in the bathroom.

Annie touches my arm."What do we do?" She asks softly.

"I don't know, but they're all waiting. We should really go down."

"Ok."

I knock on the bathroom door as I pass, and ask if she's ok.

"Yes! I'll be down in a minute."

"Alright."

"Tom wait," Annie whispers, as I cross the landing, "I don't know if I can do this."

"Hey," I say, taking her hand, "I'm here."

In the lounge, the atmosphere's thick. John and Sarah whisper to each other, as they wait on the sofa. I sit beside Ethan on the other side, behind the door, and Annie sits at my feet.

"Merry Christmas, An." He says quietly.

Annie smiles.

"Nice of you to join us." Sarah huffs. "Where's the moody cow?"

"Liv's in the bathroom," Annie says, "she won't be long."

This is painful. When Olivia does come down, she sits on the floor cushion, and John hands out the presents.

"There you go, Anna." He says, handing my sister hers, "now, if you don't like it, we've kept the receipt." It's a jumper, like the one I bought for her, only this is pale blue rather than pink.

"It's lovely, thank you." She folds it up neatly, and hands them theirs. Finally the tension's lifting and while everyone's getting along, I pop out to baste the turkey. In hindsight, I shouldn't have asked them over. I think under the circumstances, it would've been completely acceptable for Annie and I to want to spend today by ourselves.

When I go back to the lounge, John hands me a huge bottle of bourbon.

"There y'are," he says, "we know how you like a tipple."

"Wow! This'll keep me going."

"We just thought you'd appreciate it," Sarah laughs, "we're not saying you're an alcoholic or anything."

"What?" Olivia sniggers, "like you?"

No-one speaks, but John leaps from his seat, grabs Olivia by the wrist and frog marches her out of the room.

"Well!" Sarah says, downing the rest of her wine, "this is all I bloody need! I'm sorry, Thomas, but if she carries on like this, I'll be putting her up for adoption." Then she storms out too.

"What's become of this fucking family?" Ethan sighs, "I hate coming home, all they do is fight."

"How bad is it?" I ask, as Annie rests back against my leg.

"Pretty bad. Look I'm sorry, you two have it hard enough without our problems."

"It's alright, if you need to get it off your chest?"

"Nah, talk about something else. How's your theatre stuff? You getting many more shows yet?"

"Dribs and drabs. I'm beginning to think it's a waste of time. You see, most travelling theatre groups have their own teams for all that. Take my mate Stu, he's the primary stylist, and even his work isn't regular."

"So, what you gonna do?" He asks, "give it up?"

"Not sure, I might look at moving on."

"What? Move out of Teesside?"

"No, no, I mean move out of theatre work. I wouldn't mind selling the stuff and doing demo's. Anyway, how's things with Kara?"

Kara's Ethan's girlfriend. They met at uni, and got together over the summer.

"She's good, yeah." He's totally smitten, and I'm not surprised. From the pictures I've seen of her, I've got to say, she's hot. He talks and talks about her, and I'm glad of it. I'd much rather listen to that, than the screaming match from the kitchen. "Listen," he says, "I haven't told the family yet, you know what Mum's like, she'd want her to come and stay, and…"

"And you can't deal with that right now?" I ask.

"Nah. Anyway, you know how sometimes people pop into your head, for no apparent reason?"

"Yeah?"

"Well, I was at this party, right? And there was a girl there, who looked just like your old girlfriend."

"Leanne?"

"No, the other one."

"What other one?"

"The one from new year, the bunny boiler."

"Megan? She was not my girlfriend. That was a no strings thing, that went horribly wrong."

"Didn't she used to call you in the night, pissed?"

"Yeah, she bloody stalked me. She'd sit in her car out the front. One time, she saw Anna letting herself in and went mental. She threw mud at the windows, screaming, 'you cheating bastard!'"

"Crazy bitch."

"She was, mate." As we laugh, I lay my hand on Annie's head, but she flinches. "Hey, An," I lean down, to speak in her ear, "are you alright?"

She doesn't answer, so I nudge her again. "Annie?"

It's clear, by the incoherent way she's attempting to name the things around her, that she's fighting an hallucination. This is the grounding technique that Julie gave her, usually it works, but not this time.

"Stop, stop, no." She cries, as her eyes flicker.

"What's up, Tom?" Ethan asks.

263

"She's not well." I shuffle my leg free and drop to the floor, beside her. "Annie, can you hear me?"

"Please, too loud, coffee, I smell coffee, no, don't leave, come back, stop…it…it's dark."
Pressing her forehead to her knees, she mutters desperately.

"Look at me, Annie," I say, but the moment I take hold of her face, she fights. She pushes me away, then clasps her hands over her ears.

"Stop!" She begs, rocking back and forth, "it's too loud."

"Tommy, what's up with her?" He asks worriedly.

"Just give me a minute…Annie, you're ok, look at me."

Aside from the other day, she hasn't had one of these for months, and I'm trying to bring her out of it, but I can't get close enough. Her eyes are tight shut, her arms clamped to her head. I need her to hear me but, there's no breaking through.

"You're ok," I tell her again, "look at me, An, look at me."

At first there's no response, but I keep repeating myself, all the while stroking her head, until it eventually passes. She's disorientated when she opens her eyes, she looks to me, then to Ethan who's now stood over us.

"Back up." I tell him. "She's ok, she's ok."

"Tom!" She cries, "my head."

"I know. Ethan, get some paracetamol?"

He rushes out to the kitchen where, remarkably, it seems that the rest of the family are so consumed in their own argument, that they're completely oblivious to what's gone on here.

"Did he see?" She asks.

I nod, and she slumps forward, planting her forehead on my chest. Ethan hurries back, with the pain killers and a drink.

"Here, An," he says, as he sits on the floor beside us, "are you alright?"

"Not really, I need to lie down. Tell him, Tom." She says, as I help her onto the sofa. "Just tell him."

I sit on the floor, and she presses her forehead against my arm. I try and explain these attacks, or whatever they are.

"Do you want me to stay with her tonight?" He asks. "Till you get back."

"If you wouldn't mind."

5.40pm. Anna:

Today was never going to be easy, but stupid me, hoped it would've been better. It's childish I guess, to expect us all to support each other, and even though Tommy's not naive like me, I think deep down he wanted the same.

John and Sarah didn't stay long after dinner. I haven't eaten any, actually, I couldn't even make it to the table. Sometimes I wonder what's worse, the vision itself or the headache after. I couldn't lift my head off the sofa, and that didn't go down well. Before they left with Olivia, Sarah laid on the guilt about how Tommy had stood and cooked a lovely dinner, and I was too selfish to try it. I've given up trying to defend myself to her, I'm just grateful that my brother's understanding. He's about to go to work, but he sits on the sofa beside me, for the precious few minutes before he leaves.

"Hey," he says, raising his arm, "come, give me a hug."

I flip back my blanket, shuffle over and cuddle into him.

"I've saved you some dinner," he says, "it's in the fridge."

"Thanks. I wish you didn't have to go."

"Me too." He kisses the top of my head, and I stretch my arm over his belly, as Ethan brings in two teas.

"Sorry, Tommy," he says, placing them on the TV stand, "were you wanting one?"

"Nah, I'm going just now."

"Alright, what do I do if she has another?…" He asks, before slumping on the sofa. I sit up and whisper that I'm sorry, but Tommy shakes his head.

"How do you feel now?" He asks.

"Ok, I'm just tired."

He nods and gently pulls me back into his chest. "She should be alright," he tells Ethan, "she's never had more than one in a day…but there's always a first time. If anything does happen, just hold her, don't let her hurt herself, and call me. Put me on speaker, so she can hear me."

"I'm ok." I tell them both again.

"We know, Annie."

"We just want you to stay ok," Ethan adds, "that's all."

I guess it's understandable, watching me go through that must be pretty scary. Part of me wants to ask Tommy to film one, I'm curious, but then, I don't know if I could watch it if he did.

My brother taps my shoulder, 'it's time,' he says. I want to hold him so he can't leave, I want to cling on tight, but instead, I shuffle upright and say 'ok,' then follow him to the kitchen, while he gets ready.

"It's only a few hours," he says, "I'll be back before you know it."

"I know." I hug him again, then lock the door behind him.

As I watch him walk to the gate, I check my phone. Shit, I've got over ten messages from Eden, and at least four missed calls. I must've knocked my phone onto silent. Within seconds of me calling him back, he answers.

"Anna. What's going on? Why haven't you texted back?"

"I am so sorry."

Just then, Ethan steps into the hallway and asks if I'm ok. I nod, showing him that I'm on the phone, so he goes back into the lounge.

"I didn't hear my phone." I tell Eden.

"You didn't hear your phone for an entire afternoon?"

"I didn't, I promise."

"I don't know," he sighs, "do you even want me to come tomorrow?"

I've only just got him, and now I'm going to lose him. I suddenly feel sick, as a cry works it's way up my throat.

"Please, Eden." I squeak. "I wouldn't ignore you, you have to believe me. I've been ill all day…"

His voice quickly softens and he asks what's wrong, but I feel awkward now.

"I've had the worst headache, all afternoon. I couldn't even eat any dinner. Eden, I'd never ignore you!"

"Are you ok now?" He asks tenderly.

"Yeah, I'm a bit dizzy and tired, but I'm ok. Will you come tomorrow?"

"Anna, I didn't mean to go off like that. It's my sister's fault, she got in my head."

"What do you mean?"

"Neve. She can be a right bitch." The line then goes quiet for a few seconds. "Anna, she grabbed my phone at dinner, I'd just texted you and I hadn't locked it. She read them before I could get it back…she told everyone what I'd said. Then, they all said I sounded desperate, she somehow convinced me that you were ignoring me, because I was clingy."

"Why would she be so spiteful? She doesn't even know me."

"That's just her. Anyway, I was worried. I thought I'd said something wrong, or that you were upset about your… you know."

"Mum and Dad?"

"Yeah, and I wanted you to talk to me. Then…anyway I'm sorry, I'm a dick."

"You're not a dick. I mean you've got one, but you're not one." Shit, Anna, you stupid girl, what are you saying?

"And how do you know? For your information, I could've been Alexander the Greats chief eunuch!"

"No way! That's from Red Dwarf! I love that."

"Me too!" he teases in a particularly girlie manner.

I just give him an uneasy half laugh. After a moment, I take a deep breath and ask softly, "Eden?"

"Yeah?"

"Please come tomorrow?"

"Babe, of course I'm coming."

11.30pm. Anna:

The heating turned itself off an hour ago. It's freezing, so I cocoon myself in a blanket and shuffle along the sofa, next to Ethan.

"You alright?" He asks.

"I'm cold."

"It's not that cold." He laughs, as he piles the cushions against me, then pulls the other blanket from the back of the sofa, and throws it over my head. "There you go, still cold? Or should I get you my coat?"

"You're a tool," I laugh, kicking them all away, "you know that?"

"Yeah, I've been told."

He's funny, my cousin. After a few silly shoulder barges, he grabs me and starts a tickle fight.

"Get off." I squeal, I'm totally helpless. He knows the exact part of my waist that renders me paralysed, and in the kerfuffle, I slide back and fall to the floor.

"Shit, Anna," he chuckles, "you alright?"

"Yes!" I leap up on top of him, my knee in his belly, knocking him back, "But you won't be."

Just then, his phone rings, so he plonks me down on the sofa. "Shh, it's Kara," he places his finger to his lips, and answers it. "Hey, baby…"

Giving him some privacy, I head to the kitchen, fill the kettle and I check my phone. Aside from the ongoing conversation I'm having with Eden, there's a new and lengthy text from Dan.

"Hiya, been wanting to call,
but I didn't know what to say.
The irony, the boy who doesn't shut up,

*not knowing what to say. I guess I should
say merry Christmas.
I just hope today hasn't been too hard,
and I'm sorry it's late.
If you want to talk,
I'm still awake xx."*

Today's been an emotional roller-coaster, but when I read this, it hits me again. I miss him. Not what we could've been, but I miss my friend. I finish making the tea's, take Ethan's to him, then take mine up to my room, where I lie down and call Dan.

"Hiya," he says, "you alright?"

"Yeah, I am now today's over, but don't worry. Can you just talk to me?"

"Sure."

I love how he can talk about anything and everything on cue. It's a skill, and I could listen to him for hours.

"It's been crazy, here today," he says, "Andy's whole family have been over."

Andy is Dan's new step-dad. "There're literally loads of them. You know, I've got eight step-cousins now. The oldest is only thirteen, so, as you can imagine, it was crazy."

"Sounds wild."

"Yeah, it was. Mum was bouncing Andy's baby niece, she held her up and wound up with a face full of sick! It was hilarious."

"Oh no, your mum's a total clean freak."

"I know," he laughs, "after she screamed, I couldn't tell if she was gonna cry or throw up herself."

I drink some of my tea, then just lie back and listen. Eventually, the subject moves along to Tuesday.

"I'm travelling up to Dad's in the morning. So, I'll spend tomorrow with him, then come to yours, first thing on Tuesday?"

"Yeah, that's great. What do you wanna do?"

"D'ya wanna carry on our Christmas tradition?"

"A Lord of the Rings marathon? Do I ever! I didn't think you'd have twelve hours to spare."

"Sure I do, but we have to order pizza for after Two Towers."

"Obviously. Will you bring sweets?"

"Sure," he says, "I can't wait to see you."

I can't wait to see him too, but there's something I need to tell him first.

"Me too. Listen, do you remember that boy, Eden, that I mentioned from college?"

"The one who kept getting his friend to ask you out for him, like a ten-year-old?"

"Um yeah." I know I shouldn't feel apprehensive, after all it's Dan. But I feel like I need his permission. "Yeah, he… asked me himself, and we had a date. Is that ok? I don't want to hurt you."

"Are you together?"

"Yeah."

For a few seconds there's silence. "Dan?…talk to me."

"An," he says gently, "if I'd have had the guts to tell you how I felt sooner, then I dare say I'd still be in Teesside, and we'd be together. I didn't, I moved away and I've got to live with that. Listen, you're my best friend, and I love you, but I don't expect you to stay single."

"Thank you, Dan…but why didn't you have the guts to tell me?"

"Doesn't matter."

I only asked out of intrigue, but that response was short, too short. Now I need to know.

"It does to me, did I do something? Say something?"

He sighs, then the line goes quiet. I can't take this.

"Dan? What did I do?"

"An, it really doesn't matter."

"It clearly does. When you moved away, you said you'd wanted to tell me for ages. I can tell by your voice, Dan. I've obviously made some mistake, and if I'm really your best friend, then you'll tell me, so I don't make the same mistake again."

"Ok, I was going to tell you at school, but you weren't there…"

"When?"

"Just after your mum and dad died, but I didn't know that at the time. I just thought you couldn't face school because of the rumours."

"What rumours?"

"An, I don't want to hurt you…"

"Please, Dan."

"I heard," he sighs, "I heard you'd had sex with Alex Murray, and I couldn't believe it. You hate him as much as I do, but he was showing everyone a picture of you, and I… look I'm sorry."

"What picture?" This is a nightmare, I should've known he'd take a picture.

"You and him on a sofa, you were wasted. He was telling everyone that he was so good, you had to sleep it off. I'm so sorry."

My throat closes, so much so, that my voice is no more than a distressed squeak. "So, that's why you didn't? Because you were angry with me?"

"I wasn't angry with you," he says, "well, maybe a bit, but you were pissed. I was fuming with him, he was talking shit. That's why I lost my lunchtime pass…he was bragging, and I punched him in the face…I just had to shut him up.."

"Wow! Thank you, but you still let it stop you?"

"An, he told everyone you were easy, that he didn't have to try. Now, remember all this happened before I knew about the accident. So, I could've asked you out, but what would you have said?"

"I'd have said yes."

"I know, and I didn't want to make things worse for you. I planned to wait for it all to die down, till I got back from my holiday. Then, I heard about the accident and bottled it. I knew you needed a friend."

I'm a mess. Tears roll down my face, as I try to catch my breath. I have to tell him, I just have to.

"Dan…"

"Please don't cry." He interrupts.

"Dan, listen. I didn't fall asleep after."

"I don't think that matters." He says kindly.

"It does. Listen to me…I didn't fall asleep after."

"What do you mean?"

"I was easy, because I was unconscious. I didn't even know it had happened till the next morning, and I didn't know much until we heard him and Chloe."

"Whoa, back up a bit. Who's we and which Chloe? What did you hear?"

"Ok, I knew something wasn't right, because I'd never sleep with him, no matter how drunk I was. But I didn't know what had happened, until me and Becca heard him freaking out to Chloe Griffiths. She'd put something in my drink, to knock me out."

"Fucking hell, Anna! That's rape!"

"I know."

"So, what're you gonna do? Have you been to the police?"

"No, it was like, two months later when we heard him and Chloe, and I was a mess. I couldn't face all that."

"Could you go now?"

"Not really, it's my word against his. Plus, I could get Rich into trouble if I did."

"Why?"

"I asked him to give Alex a warning…like a trip to hospital, kind of warning."

"Too right." He says. "Are you ok?"

"Yeah, I never have to see him now."

"So, at the prom?…"

"Dan?" I interrupt, "can we talk about something else?"

"Sorry, yeah, course we can."

We talk for a while about college, music, movies and everything in-between. In fact, the conversation flows so easily, that I hadn't heard Tommy come home. I only realise, when he pops his head around my door.

"Sorry," he says, noticing that I'm on the phone. I ask Dan to hold on.

"It's ok," I say to Tommy, "how was work?"

"Alright. Listen, I'm gonna take Ethan home now, d'ya want to come and say bye?"

"Yeah, give me two minutes."

Tommy nods and closes my door.

"Sorry." I tell Dan. "I've got to go."

"I should be going to bed anyway. So, I'll be at yours on Tuesday morning, ok?"

"Yes, get here early."

"I will. See ya later."

I then hurry downstairs, just as they are getting ready to go.

"Thanks for staying." I tell Ethan, as I rush to give him a hug.

"I wasn't gonna leave you on your own."

Once they've gone, I go back upstairs, change into my pyjamas then crawl into Tommy's bed. Just as I sink my head into the pillows, Eden texts me. It's a screen full of heart emojis, so I reply with a screen full of smiley faces. After discussing Alex with Dan, and learning that he knew all along, makes me realise what Alex has taken from me. I can't let him ruin anymore of my life, I want to keep Eden fresh. He's beautiful, and I love how he makes me feel, so if I can keep him from ever knowing about Alex, then I'll be happy. That will be the true fresh start.

I don't have to wait long for Tommy to get back. I hear him lock the door, then come straight upstairs. He's exhausted, usually if I'm in bed first, he'll get changed in the bathroom, instead he just kicks off his jeans, wriggles out of his shirt and falls into bed.

"Are you alright?" I ask.

"I am now today's done. Have you been ok?"

"Yeah…" I tell him about my conversation with Dan, what was said about Alex and our movie plan for Tuesday. "Are you gonna watch with us?"

"I'll watch a bit," he laughs, "but I don't think I can face twelve hours of hobbits. Listen," he rolls onto his side and strokes my cheek, "I don't want to upset you, but I'm worried. It wasn't easy, pulling you out of that hallucination…and, I'm sorry that Ethan had to see."

"It's ok." I whisper.

The truth is that I'm sick of talking about these. I know Tommy needs me to, it helps him deal with it. That's how his mind works, if he can find a pattern of triggers, or if they're are any differences in the things I see, then he'll try to conjure a formula, a way of fixing me. That's why he was so happy when Julie gave me the steps, and for a long time they worked. If I could name something around me for each of my senses, I'd keep my mind in 'the real.' I tried to do that today. I tried so hard, but I couldn't concentrate because of all the screaming, and John was so loud. His voice was like the base note, and Sarah and Liv filled in the rest, there was no room for anything else.

"Annie," he says softly, re-grabbing my attention, "what did you see?"

I shake my head. "I didn't see anything." And that's true. "It was pitch black. I heard John balling at Liv, then his voice kind of melded into a deafening roar. I heard waves, and on top of that there was a constant high-pitched squeal."

"So, that was why you wouldn't let go of your ears?"

"Probably. I think I just need to face it, I'm not getting better."

"Yes you are, don't say that."

"I don't know, maybe I'm just tired. Do you mind if I play with your hair?"

"Not at all." He says, as he shares my pillow and cuddles me in. After only a few minutes of me gliding my fingers through his curls, I hear his breathing deepen, so I kiss his head.

"I love you, Tom. Sleep well."

December 26, 2016 Monday 10am.
Anna:

The weather's certainly reflecting my mood today. It's cold, but the sky's blue, and as I practically skip through the allotments my phone rings.

"Emilia." I sing, as I follow the path into Normanby.

"You sound happy," she laughs, "what you up to?"

"I'm only meeting Eden!"

"It's true?" She squeals, "he wasn't lying."

"Yes! We're together."

"So, what changed your mind? What did he do?"

"He asked me himself, obviously…and he was so sweet."

"You see, Anna. I told you he was nice."

"You did, so what're you doing today?"

"Probably start the next unit for college, but I called to ask where you're going for your placement. If we have to arrange our own, we may as well go together."

"Yeah. I was thinking of James Cook Hospital, then if Tommy's working, I'll only have to get one bus. Is that ok?"

"Yeah totally," she says, "it's only one bus for me too."

"Great. It'll be good working with you."

I reach the crossing, and see Eden at the bus-stop, on the other side. He hasn't noticed me yet, so I say bye to Emilia, before hurrying over the road. I'm not sure what takes over me, but when our eyes meet in the distance, I forget all the strangers around me, run and charge straight to him. There's no time for 'hello,' he just picks me up, and plants his lips on mine. For a fraction of a second, I pull back so only our noses are touching, but I want more. So, stroking the back of his neck, I pull him in for a proper kiss, like our first.

"Hiya." He says, softly kissing me again. He's stunning. He smiles, as I trace my fingertips down his nose, over his cheeks and along his jaw. He's masculine but soft, and those

275

lips…I love them. I fling my arms around his neck and hug him tight.

"I'm so glad you came."

"So am I," he says, putting me down. "I'm sorry about yesterday."

I look away and shake my head. The truth is, I'd cry if he stayed away because he thought I was ignoring him.

"So, which way is it?" He asks.

"That's the quickest," I tell him, pointing to the way I just came, "or we could go the long way around?"

"Sure." He takes my hand, and I lead him away from the village, past Tommy's pub, then up some concrete steps to the old railway lines. It's just a stony path now, shielded by high trees and bushes either side, but apparently, it was once used to shunt iron-ore from the old mines.

"So?" He says, "how long does it take you to get to college? I felt like I was on the bus forever."

"About an hour and a half. But I usually get a lift, so twenty minutes or so."

He then stops and sits down on a bench, 'here,' he says, pulling me to stand between his legs.

"Obviously, it's good for me, but why did you pick a college so far away?"

"My dad. As soon as I said I wanted to be a nurse, he got all involved. He said Stockton was the best, so I applied. See, no-one argued with my dad."

"Well, I'm glad he said that." He holds onto my hips, teasing me even closer as he slides his hands over my bum. This is all new to me, but it feels so natural. "Kiss me." He whispers. I lean in, then take a sharp inhale, as he slides his freezing cold hand up the back of my coat and under my clothes. Shuddering, I accidentally bite his bottom lip. He doesn't seem to mind, in fact I actually think he likes it, because he just smiles and holds me tighter.

"Don't do that." I giggle.

"Do what?" He asks innocently.

"You know, don't put those cold hands on me."

"What?" He laughs, "these cold hands." He then presses both of his icy palms, flat to my back. I squeal. I leap back and run, he sets chase and soon catches me. We're both stumbling and laughing, as we trip over each others feet.

"You said you were a fast runner?" He says, taking hold of me, so we don't fall.

"I am," I whisper, tiptoeing up to kiss him. "I wanted you to catch me."

About an hour has passed when we get home. Funny really, a walk through the lines usually only takes fifteen minutes. Eden follows me in, and I show him where to put his shoes.

"Aren't you cold?" I ask, as he takes off his coat. How he can leave the house in just a T-shirt and coat in December is beyond me.

"Nah, I'm alright. So where is he?"

"Tommy? He's still in bed, he was working last night. But, you didn't come to see Tommy," I smile, giving him a hug, "you came to see me."

He smiles, as he loosely rests his hands on my shoulders. But, he's lost the fun, excited feel from earlier.

"Are you ok? Have I done something?"

"Oh no, course not, I…"

"Come on." Taking his hand, I lead him into the lounge. Hopefully, if we cuddle up on the sofa, he'll relax. As he sits back, I lean in for a kiss and slide my arm around his waist, so he's cradling me.

"Anna, lift up…what if he comes down?"

"You're really nervous, aren't you?"

He nods, so I sit up and tuck my feet under his thigh. "Don't be. Tommy's lovely."

"He is to you, babe…but Adrian said something."

"What?"

"My family are like, proper nosy. They wanted to know all about you, what your parents did, where you're from. I had to tell them, so they don't embarrass or upset you. Mum said she wanted to hug you, then Adrian said your brother's essentially your dad now. So yeah, I'm shitting it."

"Trust me." I tell him. "My brother is nothing like my dad." I find it odd that people think of Tommy like that. To be honest, I couldn't imagine him sitting Eden down, acting all fatherly, with a list of cringe questions. That's not him.

"Alright," he nods, "but what was he like with your past boyfriends?"

"You're my first."

"Shut up! There's no way you've never had a boyfriend."

I feel weird now, almost ashamed, even though that doesn't make sense. I whisper that it's true, but I can't look him in the eyes, so I just give him a fleeting smile and fiddle with the charms on my bracelet.

"So?" He asks, gently touching my hand, "does that mean you're a virgin?"

I've talked myself into a corner, how can I possibly keep my past from him now? I was a fool to think I could.

"I…I've only done it once, but I really can't talk about it." My eyes are burning, but I manage to stop myself from crying.

He takes hold of my hand and says, "You don't have to tell me, and I won't rush you."

"Thanks, it's just that…when we do it, I want it to be perfect."

"It will be, I promise." He kisses me softly, so tender.

After a few minutes, my phone beeps with a text from Tommy.

"Coffee please x."

"2 minutes x."

"I just need to make Tommy a coffee, d'ya want one? Or a tea? I'm having tea."

"Can I have a tea?" He asks, "with two sugars."

"Sure, come with."

After I've made the drinks, Eden takes ours to the lounge, while I head upstairs with Tommy's.

"You look happy." He says, as he props himself up and makes room for me to sit down.

"That's because I am."

"Is he here yet?" He asks, as I give him the mug.

"Yeah, but he's really nervous about meeting you. So be nice…please."

"I am nice!"

"You're lovely, I just mean don't tease him."

Tommy shoots me a mischievous smile, from over the rim of his mug.

"What?" I ask.

He shakes his head.

"Tommy, what?"

"So, asking if he's planning on nobbing my little sister's out of the question?"

"You can't ask him that! But…it's not out of the question."

He loses the smile, and stands his mug on the bedside table. "Do you think you're ready for that?"

"I think so, I do like him."

"It has to be your choice, but don't rush. If he really likes you, he'll wait."

"Did you and Leanne wait?…Sorry, I know you don't like talking to me about all that."

"No, it's ok. I'm not like that anymore, you can ask me anything."

"Can I?"

"Sure."

"What was it like?"

"A lot of fumbling under the covers, to begin with," he laughs, "we were both virgins you see, and she was really nervous."

"So, how long did you wait?" I ask again.

"About a month."

"I don't think I want to wait that long."

279

"Fair enough, but only do what you're comfortable doing. I would like you to get some contraception from the doctor, but in the meantime there're plenty of condoms in here." He says, tapping his bedside drawer. "Take what you need."

"Thank you." I give him a quick hug, then move to the door. "Remember, Tom, no teasing."

"Trust me, will you?"

"I do."

I hurry back down to Eden, and find him sitting on the sofa, holding both of our drinks.

"I didn't know where to put them," he says, "you don't have any coasters in here."

"Oh, we just put them on the TV stand," I say, taking hold of mine, "it's glass, so it's fine."

"Ok," he nods and puts his drink down to cool, "um, did he say anything about me being here this early."

"Relax, he's not an ogre." I take a small sip of tea, put my mug down and lower myself   onto Eden's lap.

"Anna…" he says, as I move to kiss him again.

"It's ok. Tommy'll drink his coffee, then he'll have a shower. You've got time to kiss me."

At last, the boy from earlier has returned. He seems to loosen up; even caresses my thigh, as I kiss him softly. Then we here the creak of floor boards, above us, as Tommy crosses the landing. Eden pulls away.

It's funny, but I want Tommy to hurry up then, when Eden meets him, he'll realise that he's been worrying for nothing.

December 31, 2016 New Years Eve.
Saturday 6pm. Eden's Birthday.
Anna:

Eden was worried about meeting my brother, and he's just one person. Tommy was great, all he did was mention football, then I couldn't shut them up. They got along so well. It was really nice actually, but I've got to meet his friends, his family, and the one I'm worried about, Neve. She's already made her mind up about me, and I don't like it.

There're five or six cars parked on and around Eden's driveway. Tommy turns his car around and pulls over on the opposite side of the cul-de-sac. Even from here, I can see loads of people all drinking and laughing inside. I'm nervous.

"You're being brave, you know." Tommy says as I un-clip my seatbelt.

"Why?"

"Going in there on you're own."

"I'm not that brave, I've just texted him to come out for me."

"Ah well," he laughs, "you're nearly there. Here he is." He nods, as Eden steps outside. "Right, you, I'm already late, so give us a hug before I go."

"I guess I'll see you next year." I say quietly in his ear.

"You will. Go on, have a good night, and I'll be back around one."

Eden nods to Tommy, and when I get out of the car, he gives me a hug, but waits until Tommy's drove away before kissing me. He's so cute.

"I've got you something." I say, handing him his present and card. After I heard that he liked Red Dwarf, I just had to buy him Rimmer's penguin puppet. He tears off the paper and grins.

"It's Mr. Flibble!" He slides his hand straight into it and playfully pecks my nose. "Mr. Flibble's very cross."

"Get off." I giggle. He kisses me again, before taking me inside. A vibrant hum of laughter and conversations seep into the hallway. The moment I nudge his arm, to say 'don't leave me,' a homely looking woman steps out of the lounge.

"Love," she says, making Eden blush, "aren't you going to introduce me?"

"Mum this is Anna, Anna…my mum, Jane."

I see where he inherited his bright blue eyes from. She uses hers to size me up, and I can only look at her for a moment, before I start blushing myself.

"Hello." I smile briefly, and look up to Eden.

"Hello, pet. Come on, you must meet the rest of us."

"Mum," Eden says, "she's just got here, leave her alone." Opening a cloak cupboard behind him, he holds out his hand for my coat, "you can put your shoes in here too."

"Sorry," his mum says, "I don't mean to embarrass the poor girl."

Behind her, next to the cupboard, are the stairs. Eden places our shoes in the cupboard, nudges his mum aside and heads up.

"Eden?" I squeak awkwardly.

Jolting his head, he says, "Come with."

I smile again to his mum, who moves to let me by.

"Just because it's your birthday," she calls, "don't think you can stay in that room all night."

"We won't." He groans.

Then as I follow him upstairs, he tells me that Emilia's coming later. This is great, I know I'm super happy to be here with him, but having another person who I know is a bonus.

No sooner have I stepped into his room, he's closing the door behind me and pushing me hard up against it. Squeezing my wrists, he holds my arms high above my head.

"Get off me." I shout, as he forcefully kisses my neck. He instantly lets go and jumps back.

"Oh, Anna. I'm sorry." He looks mortified, and I just stand there, rubbing my wrists. "I am so sorry," he says, "I just wanted to kiss you, I…I thought you'd like it."

"No, I'm sorry." Why can't I just be normal? "Can we sit…please?"

"Yeah, course." He sits next to me on the edge of his bed, and holds my hands. "I'm sorry," he says again. "Did I hurt you?"

I shake my head. I mean he did, but I have to explain. I don't want to, in case he thinks I'm crazy, but if I don't say anything, then he's going to think I'm crazy anyway. I need to be brave, so I hesitantly pull back the sleeves of my jumper, revealing the angry scars on my wrists. Yes, the bracelet has helped me not to scratch during the day, but most mornings, I still wake up with fresh grazes.

"Shit," he gasps, "I…"

"It's not your fault, and I didn't mean to freak out. You must think I'm stupid."

"No, I don't, I think you're gorgeous…I didn't mean to hurt you. Can I cuddle you?"

"Please."

As we lie down together, I find myself apologising again. Partly for freaking out, and partly for not giving him the truth.

"It's ok. Your wrists look really sore, and I did hold you pretty hard."

"It's not just that, you kinda scared me, see, I…I'm claustrophobic."

"That's ok, I know all about that."

"You do?"

"Yeah, our Ellie's claustrophobic."

In an instant, I feel one hundred times better. If I'm honest, I don't know how I expected him to react. I always seem to fear the worst, like him going cold on me, mocking me, but he didn't. He's sweet, kind and forgiving, and as we lie here, he whispers between kisses that he'll never push me like that again. We lay for ages, holding each other. I touch his face, stroke his cheek and I want to touch his hair, but it's so perfect that I daren't. I feel like I should tell him that I love him, but I can't, I don't love him yet. I know I feel something strong, but I hardly know him, and we've only been together a week. I do know this, he's beautiful and, he makes me want to do things that I've hardly ever thought about before.

"Eden," I say nervously, "I'm guessing you've done it before?"

"Done what?"

"You know…"

"Oh," he nods, hugging me tighter, "I have, yeah."

"Do you want to do it with me? I think I might be ready."

"Are you serious?"

"Yes." I slide my hand under his T-shirt and run my fingertips over his back. "I do." I kiss him and realise that, I've kind of committed to it, so now, the next step is to ask him when.

"Oh, Anna." He takes my hand, moving it to the firm bulge in his jeans, "feel that, babe? I can't wait to do it with you, but there're way too many people here, and I want to relax and make it special."

I'm frozen, I'm holding his thing. Yeah, it's through jeans, but I'm actually holding his thing.

"Ok, so what do you suggest?" I ask.

"Day after tomorrow, everyone will be out. If you still want to, we'll do it then…and I'll make it perfect. Is that ok?"

"Yes."

Kissing me hard, he rubs the back of my thigh, and an intense throbbing accelerates between my legs. His hand moves higher, eventually resting on my bum. I want something now, this isn't like me, but I'm running with it. I let go of his thing, roll onto my back and hold open the waist of my leggings. "Touch me." I whisper. He doesn't hesitate, he gently slides his hand down and into my knickers, and starts to slowly move his fingers. He's definitely done this before, because he seems to know exactly, how much pressure to apply. My heart races, as he pushes them deep inside me, moving them like he's beckoning me. He kisses my neck again, he tries to kiss my lips, and I want to kiss him back but I cant. I'm dizzy and breathless. I never thought I could feel like this, the tingling through my body, the rush of adrenalin. It's perfect and I don't want him to stop, but stop he must, and far to suddenly, as somebody knocks on his door.

"Denny?"

Quickly removing his hand, Eden whispers. "It's Ellie! And I wish she wouldn't call me that. What do you want?" He calls back, as I straighten myself up.

"Dad said you have to be sociable, and Emilia's here… can I come in?"

"No! We'll be down in a minute."

"But I wanna meet your girlfriend."

"I said, we'll be down in a minute!"

"Ok." She says. Then we hear her scurry away, and Eden turns and hugs me.

"Are you ok?" He asks.

"I am, that was so nice, thank you. Can I kiss you?"

He smiles as he leans in, and as his lips touch mine, he apologises for his sister.

"It's ok," I giggle, "we've got Monday to look forward to."

"We have."

"So, why don't you like being called Denny?" I ask, as we move for the door.

"Aww, don't."

"It's nice, my brother calls me Annie."

"Yeah, I heard him say that. But please, don't ever call me Denny."

"I won't…you know, I hate my name too."

He looks confused. "What? Anna's a nice name."

"No, Anna's short for Annalee." I tell him. "But please, don't ever call me it."

"I won't."

January 04, 2017 Wednesday 1.50pm.
Medical Centre Waiting Room.
Anna:

My first therapy session in almost three weeks, and I'm
eager to get inside. I need to explain, I have to tell her that
I've failed. Julie gave me steps to follow, a fail-safe. For
months I've followed them, but at Christmas, I didn't. It's
not just the hallucinations. I've grown up in these past few
weeks, but there's something else, something holding me
back. I'm confused, but I can't just blurt it out. What will
she think?

When Julie calls me in, Tommy gives me a hug, then
makes his way out, to wait for me in the car.

"Happy new year, Anna." Julie says, as I follow her into
our usual room. I return the sentiment, head straight for the
refreshments table and offer to make her a coffee.

"Thank you, that would be lovely."

For a while now, I've asked her to sit beside me rather
than opposite. It's less like an interrogation. I finish making
the drinks, and we sit on the sofa that faces the courtyard.

"I've, um had a set back." I mumble, as I sip my tea, "I
saw my mum, but it wasn't like before," I add quickly,
before she has a chance to answer. "She was happy. I had
another one too, and that was like the others, but this one
wasn't. It was like she was forgiving me, she told me she
loved me."

Julie listens intently, as I go into more detail. It's still a
bit difficult, but I explain how I felt. I explain how it
affected Tommy, and sparked his own regrets. After some
time, Julie nods.

"I wouldn't see it as a set back." She says, as she kicks
off her shoes and tucks her feet up. "There're many stages to
grief. When you've lived with a person who's treated you
negatively, and in turn you've reciprocated that negativity, it
becomes very difficult to see the positives. I feel you've
moved out of the unhealthy cycle that you were living in

286

regarding your mum. As you've told me recently, positive memories that were once buried, are beginning to surface. As a result, you seek reconciliation, this is normal. What's also normal, is to picture or imagine that reconciliation…"

Imagine? She had my undivided attention until she said that. I did not imagine it. She was there, Mum was there. Her voice was real, I know it sounds ridiculous, and it probably is, but I heard her. She misses us and she loves us. That's what she said, and nobody's going to take that away from me. But if she thinks I imagined it, because it's what I want, then she's suggesting I wanted to see all the other horrors too. Does she think I want to see them drown over and over? Or does she think I want to drag myself along a pitch black cliff face, naked and covered in blood, with an umbilical cord hanging between my legs? No, I most certainly don't.

"…I definitely feel that would help."

Not again. I've missed half of what she's saying.

"Sorry," I say, "what would help?"

"Did you drift off again?" She smiles.

"Sorry, I did yeah."

"As you know, I'm primarily a bereavement therapist. Although I'm trained to deal with relational issues, and panic attacks and such, I'm not a mental health specialist. I do feel, very strongly, that we should request a referral from your GP. Obviously this won't affect our sessions…"

This is a nightmare. I can't see a mental health specialist, I'd be admitting defeat. Along with a load of mixed up words, I hear Julie mention the possibility of medication, or at least I think I do. Well, no-one's going to make me take anything, that's for sure.

"I…I don't know," I interrupt, "I'd need to think about it."

I feel cold, like all my defences are stripped away. I can't sit here, so I stand, move to the window and stare out to the courtyard. I need to figure everything out, I need to regain control of this session. So, I drum my fingers on the glass, turn and change the subject.

"You know," I say cheerily, "something awesome happened over Christmas."

She smiles and nods for me to continue.

"Well, I've started seeing this boy from college, he's called Eden and he's so cute. On our first date we went bowling, and he deliberately lost every game. After, we walked and walked, we weren't really heading anywhere, we just wandered around the retail park, talking. I didn't think I could feel so easy, with someone who I didn't really know, but he's lovely and so funny."

This is better, I can easily fill the session with talk of Eden, and with a leap of excitement, I rush back to the sofa, sit so I'm facing her, and eagerly tell her everything.

"It's like he wants to be with me all the time, I love it. His sister, Neve thinks he's too clingy. That's why I was scared of meeting her, but she was quite nice actually, I think she's just jealous." I talk for ages, telling Julie all of Eden's little nuances; like the way he raises one eyebrow when he smiles, and that he'll let me touch any part of him, except his hair. Well, he'll let me run my fingers over the shaved back and sides, but the quiff's off limits. I don't mind, I think it's cute. I go on and on about how affectionate he is, how he always wants to cuddle me, and how he's got wandering hands. That leads me on to the night at his birthday party, obviously I leave out the part where I freaked out. I don't want her to think he's forceful, because he's totally not.

"That was the night we decided to do it," I tell her, "but we chose to wait till Monday, because his house would be empty. The first time was awkward, I was so nervous, but he was really nice about it, didn't rush me at all. The second time was better. Then, by the afternoon, it felt like we'd always been doing it. He loves that he can throw me around…not aggressively. I mean, I'm little, so he can pick

288

me up and put me in different positions. He said I'm really good."

Julie's never heard me talk about sex before, I bet she can't believe her ears, I can hardly believe it myself.

"He sounds very exciting," she says, with a cautious smile, "but, I wouldn't be doing my job if I didn't ask, are you using protection?"

"Yeah, we are." Ok, Anna, this is the best chance I'll have to tell her. "I dreamt about him last night…we were in my room, and it was the summer. It was a hot day, and we'd been doing it for ages. We were both pouring with sweat, it was running in my eyes. So, I closed them for a second, but when I opened them, it wasn't Eden on top of me…it was Tommy."

I don't know what I expect her to say, I know it was only a dream, but still, I dreamt about sex with my brother. It's so wrong. I pause for a second and look to her, silently pleading for a proper response, I really can't deal with another gesture for me to continue. Luckily, she speaks.

"I understand that it's confusing," she says calmly, "it sounds like this boy has awakened you sexually. With that comes a lot of different emotions, and when we sleep our mind reorders thoughts, feelings and so on. In your case, there's some entanglement between the boy who excites you, and the brother who you love. Remember that we can't control our dreams, and I don't think you need to worry."

She's unfazed, completely unfazed. Not that I want her to, but she'd soon lose her composure if she knew that I liked it. I didn't want to like it, I couldn't get back to sleep so I just laid there. I tried to get it out of my head, but instead I found myself imagining it happening for real. I felt awful, and guilty, so I cuddled into him. Naturally he held me, he always holds me when I cuddle in, but this time it was different.

Chapter 6

I love Fridays. It's the only day that both, me and Anna have a two hour lunch. I was going to take her back to mine and make her some food, as an 'early birthday' treat. I thought, we could maybe have a bit of fun after, but Emilia's decided to tag along. Great. We'll still go to mine, but I'm not cooking for both of them, so on the way there, we grab a sandwich to take back. Obviously, I buy Anna's.

"Here," Emilia grins, plonking a meat feast baguette on the counter, as I'm about to pay, "you owe me that, for the cake I got you last week."

Looks like I've got no choice, because before I know it, she's ran off to wait with Anna outside. I know Em's my friend, actually she's one of my best friends, but she's taking the piss. All I wanted was a couple of hours alone with my girlfriend, no chance of that now.

When I join them, Anna lifts her arms around my neck and pulls me in for a kiss, then as Emilia steps aside, she says.

"Thank you, I couldn't say no when she asked to come with us."

"It's ok, babe. I just had something special planned, that's all."

"I'm sorry."

"Don't be daft." I kiss her again, then give her a cuddle. It's not easy to be annoyed with Anna, after all, it's not her fault that she's too nice.

12.40pm Home.
Tommy:

Now to wait. I've spent the past hour, re-writing my CV and sending it to practically every store with a make-up counter, between Middlesbrough and Newcastle. Hopefully, with my retail experience and portfolio, I may catch a break. I close the laptop, and see Stu opening the garden gate. I should probably make sure I've still got some of that apple tea left, otherwise there'll be hell to pay.

"Afternoon." He says, as I open the cupboard. Cool, there's a few left.

"Hey, you wanna tea?"

"Please. I won't stop too long though, I just popped by to pass this on, for the little lady." He says, handing me a perfectly wrapped box, with a little pink bow.

"You didn't have to buy her anything."

"I know, but I saw it and just had to. See, it's a gorgeous silver, daisy necklace, and I thought, a flower for a flower."

"You're soft as shit, you are."

"No more than you, Tom Tom. No more than you."

I can't argue, so I just laugh and finish making the drinks.

"You know," I say, as we move to the lounge, "I'm picking Anna up at half four, why don't you come with and give her the gift yourself? She'd love to see you."

"I would, but Dylan's taking me away for the weekend, and we're leaving at three."

"Fair enough."

We sit down, and my phone beeps with a text from Annie.

"Eden wants me to stay over at
his tomorrow night. And his mum
won't let us share a room.
Tom, I haven't slept without you
for 9 months!
What do I do?

He's right next to me,
so text, don't call."

"Sorry, Stu." I say, "I just need to answer this."
"Of course, is everything alright?" He asks.
"Yeah," I sigh, "I'm just sorting something out for Anna."

Personally, I think Eden's asking too much. It's the night before her birthday, obviously she's going to want to be here, at home. It takes me a few minutes to figure out what to reply, and I feel Stu watching me as I deliberate.

"Does Eden know about your nightmares?"

"He knows a bit,
not much, though."

"Ok, you've got 2 options.
1, Tell him no,
2, See if he wants to stay here.
You wouldn't be alone,
and I'll only be across the landing."

"Option 1's out of the question.
But if he stays,
and I have a bad one??"

"Like I said,
I'll only be in my room.
But you might not have one.
So don't worry."

"Ok, I'll ask him. Thank you."

"No worries."

"You sure, you're alright?" Stu asks, as I massage my temples.

"Yeah, Anna's seeing a lad from college, and if I'm honest, I just can't read him."

"How so?"

"I just don't trust him, you know. I'm probably being over protective because he adores her, but he seems to have a weird hold over her too. Like if he wants something, she feels like she can't say no."

"Sexually?"

"No. She's enjoying that side of things. She's assured me it's on her terms, and I believe her…"

"Because she can't tell a lie to save herself?"

"Exactly. But this lad, it's weird, Stu, I can't put my finger on it. It's loads of little things and if I point them out individually, I'd look petty. For example, if they go to the cinema, it's always his choice, and it's not like she wants him to watch chick-flicks, because she hates them. Then some evenings, she just wants to chill with me, yet she has to give him a reason why. And when they do spend time together, he always wants her to go to his. And she'll give in. Listen, this is a text she sent me on Monday."

"I miss you.
Please come and get me.
There's nothing wrong,
I just want to come home.
Love you."

"Bless her heart," he says, "you guys melt me. Was she supposed to be staying over?"

"No, they haven't done that yet, that's what she was just texting about."

Behind the flamboyant facade, Stu's one of the wisest people I know. He's accepting, and I've never known him to be judgemental. With that in mind, I show him the texts.

"The thing is, Stu, since the accident, Anna doesn't sleep well. She has a lot of nightmares, so I've been letting her sleep in with me."

"Ok, it's not conventional but it's understandable. Would you like to know what I think?"

"Sure, go on."

"You say he always wants her to chill at his?"

I nod.

"I think he might be threatened by you."

"Possibly, but he doesn't know where she sleeps, and I've always been welcoming."

"Doesn't matter." He says, shaking his head. "Think about it. This is just my opinion, but they're romantically involved. If you and Anna are as close with each other, in front of him, as you are in front of me, then he'll be threatened. I know I would be."

I guess he's got a point.

Eden's House.
Anna:

Jane, Eden's mum, is even more house proud than my mum was. She's at work now, but that doesn't stop Eden from being terrified to let us eat in the lounge. Me and Emilia smiled discretely, while he laid out place-mats and coasters on the dining table.

"So will you stay?" Eden asks, handing me a drink.

On the way here, he asked me to stay over tomorrow night. I don't have a clue what to say, so I asked my brother. I mean yeah, I've told Eden some of my issues, but he'd never understand why I need to sleep in with Tommy. As I wash a mouthful of panini down with tea, Tommy replies.

"Anna?" Eden asks again.

"Two minutes." I tell him. I don't want to keep him waiting or let him down, but I can't stay here.

"You're wasting your time," Emilia says, as I text Tommy back, "Anna doesn't sleep out, do you?"

294

I shake my head.

"Please, babe. I said I'd take the sofa, you can have my bed."

There's no way I can say no, it will break his heart. I finish texting with Tommy, close my phone and lay my hand on Eden's thigh.

"Why don't you stay at mine, my bed's tiny so we won't have much room, but we could make it work."

Both him and Emilia put down their sandwiches, and stare at me like I've just said something outrageous.

"What?" They ask in unison.

"We can sleep together?" Eden says. "Would Tommy be alright with that?"

"Yeah, he's just said so. What's wrong? Don't you want to?"

"Yeah. Course I do but..."

"But what?" Turning him to face me, I stare into those stunningly piercing eyes, until he tells me what's bothering him.

"If we share a bed, he'll know we're doing it."

"Is this what it's meant to be like? Hiding, like it's a dirty secret?"

He shrugs.

"He already knows." I say softly. "Eden, he's my best friend, we talk. Who do you think gave me all the condoms?"

As my eyes dart between the two of them, I realise, not just how easy going Tommy is, but how Mum was too. I remember her letting Leanne stay in Tommy's room, as soon as he'd turned sixteen. So long as Dad wasn't home.

"So…" I ask, "are you staying?"

"And get to spend a full night with you?" He says. "I'm already there!"

February 04, 2017 Saturday 10.30pm. Home.
Anna:

Tommy's been silently teasing me for most of the evening. He was smirking, because I can't keep my eyes open. Now it's his turn, we were all watching a movie, and Tommy's fallen asleep along the other side of the sofa. I should just relax and take a nap myself, but I'm staying awake for Eden. The last time he was here, I fell asleep, and he wasn't overly pleased. I tried to explain that I was just tired, but he was upset. He thought I was bored with him. I wasn't, and I don't want him to feel like that again, so if I can force myself to stay awake then I will. Although, I do hope he appreciates the struggle, I mean he's cuddling me, I'm laid against his chest, naturally the next step is to fall asleep.

"Anna." He says, nudging me.

I push myself upright and smile, "I'm awake."

"It's ok. Do you mind if I have a shower? I need to wash my hair."

"Sure, come on, I'll get you some fresh towels."

He follows me upstairs, to the box room. It's pretty much a dumping room, aside from a built in cupboard, where we keep all the towels and spare bedding. The rest of the room is still piled up with boxes, from Mum and Dad's.

"You know?" He grins, as I hand him a couple of towels, "when I've finished in the shower, do you think you could try that thing I asked for?"

"I…um," I don't want to say no, because he's asked so nicely, and now he's giving me puppy dog eyes.

"Please," he whispers, leaning in for a kiss, "I'll return the favour, I know you want me to, because you always keep it smooth."

I definitely don't want him to do that. I only keep it smooth, because it looks ugly with hair. Besides, I wouldn't know what to do with my hands. I'd be so embarrassed, his face down there, and what if he tries to kiss me after? No,

296

I'm not ready for that. I don't even think I'd like it anyway. I suppose I could do what he wants, after all, he'll have just had a shower. I mean he's always squeaky clean, but...

"You don't want to," he says, interrupting my mental ramblings, "it's ok."

"No, Eden...I want to, but I don't want you to go down there on me."

"You sure? It's ok, you know."

"I'm sure."

He kisses me again, then cheerily dances across the landing. I hurry back to the lounge, where I promptly wake Tommy. He groans and blinks a few times, then closes his eyes again.

"Tom, please wake up." I kneel down and shake his arm, "I need to know how to give a blow job!"

He's now very awake. Stunned and eyes wide.

"Fuckin' hell! You can't ask me that."

"You said I could ask you anything." I exclaim through an anxious whisper.

"I did but...Annie."

"Please, Tom. He's just asked me, and I need to do it right."

"Hold on, you told me that sex was on your terms?"

"It is. I want to do it, but I have to do it right. I can't be that girl."

"What girl?" He asks.

"The type of girl that Rich takes the piss out of, for being crap. I know you do too, I've heard you. I cannot be that girl."

"Alright, alright." He sighs. "Ok, right um, well...first of all, shit, you know how to make a man feel uncomfortable."

"Tommy, get over yourself. We talk about sex now. Please, I need your help."

"Ok." He nods. "You're right. Ok, right. Firstly don't try and take it all straight away, you'll just gag. I'm assuming it's gonna be foreplay?"

I nod.

"In that case, you don't want to go too fast, and you need to get it quite wet. Trust me, the wetter the better. Just keep a nice easy rhythm," sighing, he scratches and shakes his head, "get yourself comfortable, you'll need to use your wrist a little," he says, miming the action, "and then you should be able to keep going for a while."

"And he won't...you know, in my mouth?"

"Shouldn't do, it takes a while when you do it like that. Besides, one way to tell if he's nearly there, he'll tense up."

"Thank you so much. Can I have a hug?"

"Course."

"If I sleep ok tonight, without any nightmares," I mumble into his shoulder, "will you want me to go back to sleeping in my room?"

"Not unless you want to."

"I don't."

"Then stay with me."

That's a weight off my mind, and I'm feeling confident. So, after saying goodnight to Tommy, I kiss his cheek and head up to my room. I pass the bathroom and close my door behind me.

Despite being anxious about sleeping in here, I'm super excited. So much so, that Emilia met me in Middlesbrough today, to help me buy something pretty for tonight. I've bought silky pyjamas to sleep in, they're little red shorts with a matching lacy camisole. For now, I've got on something like what Mum used to wear, black lace, French knickers with matching bra. I quickly get undressed, replacing my usual plain underwear, with these pretty things. The knickers aren't all that comfortable, but I guess I'll get used to them. As I hear Eden turn off the shower, I pull my hair out of the high, messy ponytail and dance in front of my mirror. After a couple of minutes, he opens my door, wearing only a towel, tied loosely around his waist.

"What'cha doing?" He grins, sliding his hands over my hips.

He's so sexy. He looks different with his freshly washed hair, falling over his face.

"I was getting ready for you. You like?"

He nods down to the towel. "Have a look and see for yourself."

I slide my fingers over the top of the towel, and gently tease it, until it falls to the floor.

"Wow! You do like." I'm a bit nervous but, the excitement soon takes over. Taking hold of it, I give it a little squeeze, and nudge him back towards my bed. "Sit down and lie back." I whisper, kneeling down between his legs. Tommy said to start slow, so I begin by stroking it while softly kissing his inner thighs. Then, gradually move up and wrap my lips over his end. As I massage the head with my tongue, I find it's not as scary as I thought, it's actually really nice. I'm not sure how wet it's meant to get, but as I take it a little deeper, some saliva dribbles down him and over my fingers.

"Whoa, babe," he moans, "you're a natural."

Yes. I'm doing it right. I close my eyes, and he begs me not to stop.

February 05, 2017 Sunday 3am. Home.
Anna's birthday.
Anna:

My first night with Eden was going well. After we did it, we cuddled and talked, then I managed to get to sleep.

Now, only a few hours later, I'm snatched from my dreams as he rips off my shorts, forces my legs apart and rams himself inside. I don't want it like this. He's not even giving me chance to warm up, I'm dry, and he's tearing my skin. I need him to stop, I'm begging, but I can't make a sound. Surely, if he sees my face then he'll know to stop. But, I can't even look him in the eyes, because he's squeezing my wrists above my head, and pressing his face into my neck. I hate it. With each thrust, he's pushing his entire body weight down harder on my chest. In a desperate plea for it to end, I let out a yelp, but it's more like a cough, and it's in this moment that he lifts his head. It's not Eden, it's Alex. His laugh is like a sickening roar that I can't escape, and there's no sign of Eden. I have to get away, I try to scream, but nothing, nothing comes out. Then, in an instant my mattress is saturated, as a gigantic wave surges through my bedroom door. I'm going to drown. If he doesn't stop now, I'm going to drown. I thrash and scream but again, I'm paralysed. He's not giving in, he wants me to suffer, he's going to kill me. As he slides a pillow over my face, icy water creeps around my neck. Somehow, I manage to raise my legs and kick myself free. He falls back into the water, and as I shield my face from the spray, my room returns to normal. There're no waves, no Alex, I look for Tommy, but find Eden, sleeping beside me.

"I'm so sorry." I whisper, as I wipe my eyes and hurry out of the room.

Eden:

I asked Anna if she was ok, when she got out of bed, but she didn't answer. I guess she didn't hear me, but then, my mouth is dryer than a bucket of sand. When she comes back, I'll tell her to get me a drink. Five or six minutes pass. It could be more, I can't be sure. I might have fallen back to sleep, but if I did, I don't know how long for, and she's still not here.

"She's probably fell asleep on the loo," I laugh, flinging back the covers, "looks like I'm getting my own drink."

The bathroom door's not fully closed, so when I pass, I say her name, but there's no response. Ok, she was probably thirsty too. I creep downstairs, quietly enough so I can scare her, not a nasty scare, just a little one. That's weird, the whole downstairs is in darkness. I hope she hasn't came down to sleep on the sofa, I mean yeah, there's not much room in her bed, but the plan was to cuddle up.

"That's good," I mutter, as I look in the lounge, "she hasn't."

So where is she? She must've been in the bathroom, and just didn't hear me. Oh well, I grab myself a drink and head back up.

At the top of the stairs, I hear voices coming from Tommy's room. It's Anna. Why's she in there? It's the middle of the night, and she's still wearing sexy undies. I know I shouldn't, but I stand behind the door and listen. Shit, she's crying, why's she crying? I don't think I did anything wrong.

"Annie," he says, "it was just a dream, come on you're ok now, tell me what happened, please."

"It was Alex. He had me pinned, he was going to kill me, Tom."

"Oh, Annie," he says, "I've got you, and he won't hurt you again. He wouldn't dare, not after Rich's warning."

"I want to stay with you."

What the actual...?

"I know, sweetheart," he says, "but if Eden realises you've gone, he'll want to know why, so stay, if you're prepared to tell him."

"I can't. You know I can't. I…just hold me a minute then I'll go back."

I really don't know what to make of this. I think I hear movement, so I go back to bed. I slam my head down on the pillow and turn to face the wall. I've heard of Rich, but I've never met him. But Alex? Who the fuck is Alex? And what did he do to my girlfriend?

After a few moments, I feel Anna get back into bed and slide her arm over my waist, but I wait a few more minutes, before asking where she went.

"I had a nightmare." She says.

I'm confused and a bit annoyed, but I'm no bastard, so I roll over to face her.

"I'm sorry," she says, "I…"

"Do you want a cuddle?" I interrupt.

"Please."

Later That Day.
3pm. Eden:

When we woke up this morning, I made the decision to put what happened in the night behind us. Easier said than done, but it's Anna's birthday, so I have to try. She's been super clingy all day, even when her family were here. Apart from that, she's acting like nothing's happened. I wish I could do the same, but I can't get passed the weird feelings. I want to go back to normal, but how can I? Anna went into her brother's room, which in itself is kind of ok, but she wanted to stay there. She wanted him to hold her rather than me. I mean, I could've cuddled her after a nightmare, I could've told her she was ok. I have to make her tell me why, it'll drive me crazy if I just leave it. She's relaxed now, and we're alone in her room, so this is the best chance I'm going to get.

"Can I ask you something?"

"Yeah," she yawns, lifting her head off my chest.

"Come on, Anna, I wanna talk. Tell me you're not falling asleep."

"I'm sorry."

"Anna, I…" before I can say anymore, her brother knocks on her bedroom door. Marvellous.

"An, can you come downstairs?" He calls.

"Two minutes," she says, then turns back to me, "what's wrong?"

"Nothing," I sigh. "Go on, you should go."

She nods and pushes herself up. "Will you come too?"

Great. If I say no now she'll think I'm a dick.

"Please?" She asks again, this time taking my hand.

"Alright."

Downstairs, Tommy's stood by the front door, with a very rough looking fella who hugs Anna, the moment we step into the hallway.

302

"Happy birthday, kidda," he says, "you'll want to put your shoes on."

"Ok." She grins, but when she grabs hers, she hands me mine too. "come with," she says.

I can't refuse when she looks at me like that, all bright eyed and innocent. I just wish last night hadn't happened, because I really do love her. I follow them all out of the front door, to the road, where Tommy unlocks a sixty six plate, red and black Ds3.

"Happy birthday." He says.

"You're not serious!" She squeals. "Is this for me?"

"Sure is." He laughs, catching her as she leaps into his arms.

I get that she's happy, who wouldn't be? But this hug goes on way too long, and I don't like the whispering in each others ears either. When he eventually puts her down, she asks him why.

"A car, I mean. I can't even drive."

"You will soon," he says, taking her hands, "I've booked you on an intensive course, over half term…and besides, Dad bought me a car for my seventeenth."

"Yours was a rust bucket," she says, peering through the window, "this is brand new."

"Go on," he smiles, "get in, have a proper look."

Before I know it, they're both in the car, and Tommy's mate's walking back to the house, well I may as well go inside too, there's no point standing out here like a muppet. When I knock on the window to tell her, she opens the door and smiles.

"I won't be long," she says sweetly. Oh man up, Eden. It's her first birthday without her parents, and Tommy's only doing what they would've done.

"Take your time, babe. I'll wait inside."

"Thank you."

In the house, Tommy's mate is boiling the kettle.

"Alright, kid." He says. "D'ya wanna drink?"

"Um, tea two sugars...I...I'm Eden." I'm stuttering like an idiot, but this guy's huge and he looks like a cage fighter.

"Rich." He nods, as he pours the boiling water.

Rich? This must be who Anna and Tommy were on about. I have so many questions about last night, who's Alex for one, and what kind of warning did he give him?

"There y'are," he says, handing me my tea, "so, I hear you're at college with Anna. You doing nursing too?"

I shake my head. "Creative media."

"You wanna make video games?"

"Not really my thing, I'm into web design."

"Cool."

Neither of us sit down. We're locked in an amicable stand-off, while he slurps his drink. I hate silence.

"So," I ask, "have you known Anna long?"

"Could say that," he laughs, "I'm practically family."

This is suicide; and I'm not even sure why I'm contemplating it, but I have to know. In a bid to mask my nerves, I casually stand my mug on the dining table and slide my hands in my pockets. "D...do you know Alex?" I ask.

Silence. It's just a few seconds but it feels like an age.

"Our paths have crossed, why?"

"Nothing, she just said his name in her sleep."

"You've got nowt to worry about," he says, shaking his head, "Anna's with you, you should trust her."

Ok, that went well. Not exactly what I wanted to hear, what I need to know is why she's having nightmares about him.

"I do trust her, and I...I'll never hurt her."

Another drawn out silence. He glares at me, until Anna and Tommy burst through the front door, then all he says is a firm 'glad to hear it.'

"Glad to hear what?" Anna grins, as she throws their shoes on the pile.

"Nothing, kidda. Eden and I were just having a little chat, weren't we?"

"Yeah."

"Aww, Rich," she laughs, slapping his arm, "don't wind him up."

As soon as she says that, things go from bad to worse. She stands between us, pressing her back against me. Then she grabs my arms, pulling them around her. This is so awkward, to keep them around her waist I've got to lean over her like a creep, and if I don't then I'm stood holding her tits. I wouldn't normally care, she's got perfect little boobs, but I can't be touching them in front of these two bodyguards.

"Anna," I say, pulling away.

"Are you ok?" She asks, as those two glance to each other, then to the floor.

"I'm fine, can we just go back upstairs?"

For a second, she hesitates and looks at Tommy. He shrugs, and she whispers sorry to them both, before leading me up to her room. When I close the door, she hugs me.

"Don't worry about Rich," she says, "he looks scary, but he's a teddy bear."

She tiptoes up to kiss me, but I stop her. If I let her kiss me then we'll lie down, and we'll end up having sex, and as nice as that is, I won't get any answers.

"Eden?" She whispers, "what have I done?"

I want to say 'nothing' and forget the whole thing, instead I just mutter 'where do I start,' under my breath.

"Where do you start?" She says, trying not to cry, "am I that bad?"

Eden? I ask myself, what're you doing? "Oh come here." I pull her in for a cuddle and ask her softly, where she went last night.

Hiding her face in my chest, she mumbles something.

"Anna, just tell me the truth. You're the one who constantly goes on about being honest, and I've never lied to you."

"Tommy's room." She whispers.

"But why?" I ask, pushing her off me. "So what? You were in there, cuddling him like you cuddle me!…You know what? I knew where you were, I just wanted you to tell me. What I do want to know, is why you wanted to stay there, rather than wake me?"

"I, I just…"

"And not only that, I wanna know who Alex is, and what kind of warning did that Rich give him?"

"Please don't."

"Tell me, Anna, I need to know that, that 'teddy bear' isn't about to warn me, if I put a foot wrong."

"It's not like that."

"Well, what is it like?"

"Eden, I promise! I'll never get Rich to hurt you, but please…don't ask about Alex."

"Just fucking tell me. We can't go on if you keep secrets. I'm your boyfriend, I love you! I have a right to know."

Anna shakes her head. "I can't." She cries, reaching for the door.

"Don't you run away! Since we got together, you've made a huge deal about how you despise lying, all seems a bit hypocritical doesn't it."

"I haven't lied! Don't you see? I just want to put all that behind me."

"How can I see?" I yell, "you haven't told me anything."

Usually, her crying would be enough to calm me down, but this has been bugging me all day. The fact that she's hiding this, makes me question every word she says. I can't let it go, and I'm not letting her run downstairs that's for sure. So, as she grabs the handle, I jump in front of her, pressing my back against the door.

"Let me out." She cries.

I hate myself for locking her in when she's claustrophobic, but what choice do I have? She tries to barge me aside, then in hysterics she backs away and unloads.

"Fine! Alex raped me, ok! He raped me and got me pregnant, happy now?! And, as for me being close to Tommy! Why don't you ask him how he felt, fishing me out of a bath of blood, when I lost it!"

Raped? Anna's been raped? I wish I'd never asked. In the next few seconds, thousands of questions speed through my head, but I'm not going to say any of them out loud. I want to cuddle her and make her feel safe, but she won't let me.

"Come on then," she snaps, "anymore questions? I suppose you want to know how he did it!"

"Anna, I…babe?"

I should've left it alone, she told me where she was, that should've been the end of it. Now she's crying her eyes out, and I can do fuck all to stop her.

"I hate him, Eden. I hate him, he didn't stop there, he's made my life hell." She then looks past me and shakes her head. She looks terrified, so I try to grab her hand, but she pulls away.

"Leave me alone!" She screeches. She's frantic, even falls back on the bed, as she tries to get away. "Get off me!"

"Babe, I'm not gonna hurt you."

"I can't, I can't!" She repeats over and over. What's going on? It's like she can't even see me, and it's more than crying now. She's growling from the pit of her stomach.

"Anna, please, I am so sorry…let me hold you." I'm begging, but she just contorts herself like she's trying to scream. She's shaking, and I can't make it stop. I need help, so I rush to the top of the stairs.

"Tommy!" I call. "There's something wrong with Anna."

Almost instantly, he rushes upstairs, pushes past me and darts into Anna's room.

"I'm here, Annie." He says, as he drops on the bed, beside her. He doesn't even care that she's kicking out, he just takes it. He moves closer, and she whacks him one, right across his face. That's got to sting, but he's not bothered.

"It's me," he says, holding her face, "look at me."

This is freaking me out; she won't stop shaking, or open her eyes. I can't really hear what Tommy's saying to her, but he's not stopping, and I know I should keep my mouth shut, but I can't.

"What's wrong with her? Is she gonna be ok?"

He nods, but keeps talking, resting his chin on her head.

"Please be ok." I whisper. I'm useless, absolutely useless. I've seen panic attacks before, our Ellie has them, but I've never seen anything like this.

Eventually, she stops fighting. She doesn't even look at me, just cuddles into Tommy and sobs.

"He was here," she tells him, "Alex was here."

"No, Annie. It wasn't real."

Tommy slides to the floor, so Anna can get comfortable. As he pulls a pillow under her head, he tells me to get her some paracetamol, from the kitchen.

"Rich'll show you where they are."

I nod and step outside, but I wait behind the door, for a second.

"He knows I woke you," she tells him, "and he asked about Alex…and I, I got angry then I saw him. Alex, I saw Alex."

"Shh, it's ok. You're ok now, just rest."

I don't know what I expected to hear, but I've still got a lot to figure out.

Once I've got the painkillers from Rich, I grab her a drink and rush back up, but from outside her door, I hear her say.

"I need you to tell him, Tom. Just tell him."

I don't think I want to know anymore, it's bad enough that I can't un-hear what I just heard. Oh, suck it up, I tell myself as I go in.

"Here, babe." I say softly. She props herself up to take the tablets, then gives me the glass, before lying back down.

She must have been petrified, when he did that to her. No wonder she was so nervous when we first did it, I remember thinking that she was actually a virgin, that she'd lied when she'd told me she'd done it once before. It was the way she hid under the covers. We'd awkwardly done it twice, before she let me see it. And now I know why. I want to be alone with her to say this, but Tommy's not budging, so I kneel down by her bed, between them.

"I'm sorry, Anna."

"It's ok," she whispers, "you do have a right to know... Tom? Please, tell him."

"What's she already told you?" He asks, but I can't bring myself to say it out loud. I just sit there looking dumb.

"He knows," Anna says, "what Alex did, he knows about the baby, and what happened in the hotel."

"So, what more do you want me to tell him?"

She squeezes his hand and says. "Everything, Tom. He needs to know how he did it, and about me."

"Right," he sighs, lowering his head, "there was a..."

"Stop." I interrupt. "Babe, I know you wouldn't lie, but you don't have to tell me this."

She lets go of Tommy's hand and grabs mine. I don't even care that he's right next to us, I throw myself forward and cuddle her tight.

"I'm so sorry," I say again. "If you can't tell me yourself, babe, then I don't want to know."

February 14, 2017 Tuesday 4pm. Valentines Day.
Home.
Anna:

Tommy wasn't exaggerating, when he said my driving course would be intensive. I have to drive for five hours, every day this week, and I'm only allowed a few short breaks. Tommy's currently flat out on the sofa, with just the glow of the TV illuminating the room. I grab the fleecy blanket and make myself cosy on the other side. As I sink my head into the cushions, my phone beeps, it's a text from Emilia.

*"What're you and Eden
doing tonight?
Or don't I wanna know?"*

*"Hiya, probably get a takeaway
and watch a movie."*

The truth is, I don't know what we're doing. Things aren't going well with us now. He rarely smiles, we hardly kiss, he still lets me hug him, but they're brief. And as for sex, yeah we still do it, but not as often, and it's like he's completely detached. I don't think I've ever felt so empty. Since my birthday, it's like I'm damaged goods, or he thinks that I'm crazy. Honestly, I don't know which would be worse.

I don't want to think wrong of him, it's not like he's mentioned Alex or the hallucination, but something's not right. After a minute or so, Emilia replies.

*"Is that all you're doing,
a movie?"*

*"I don't know, Em.
He's coming over later,
and Tommy's working,
so we've got the house
to ourselves."*

*"Well I'll know
not to text later then."*

She then sends me a screen full of hearts and aubergines. I wish I could tell her that it's all going wrong, but if I did, she'd ask why. She'd ask Eden what his problem is, then he might tell her what happened. I can't risk that, so I send her a smiley face.

I asked Eden to stay again tonight. I hoped that if I could just spend one full night, without freaking out, then we could go back to how things were. Of course Tommy was wary, but it made no difference, Eden declined. He didn't give me a reason, I suppose if he'd said anything other than the obvious, it would've been a lie, so I get why he didn't. Anyway, I'm wasting valuable nap time chewing over this, so I switch my phone to silent and close my eyes.

5.20pm. Eden:

"Alright." Tommy says, stepping back to let me in. "Anna's asleep in the lounge, d'ya want to wake her up, while I make a cuppa?"

"Has she had another one of those…things?" I ask.

"No, she's just tired."

"Ok, that's good."

I've never known anyone, who sleeps during the day as much as these two. I'd have no chance in our house, if Mum's busy, we can't even chill on the sofa, without her thrusting a duster in our hands. Me and Neve are quick to spot when she's on the warpath, Ellie's less so. It does annoy me that Anna falls asleep so easily, but when I see her there, all tucked up with a blanket, I can't help but smile. I've still got a lot to figure out, but for now, I'm just going to sit on the floor and look at her. She's gorgeous.

I am regretting saying no to staying tonight, and for stopping Tommy when he was about to explain it all. She would've let him tell me everything, and they would've probably answered any questions. That's the thing; they would've told me, not Anna, they. It's stupid, but it feels like Anna and Tommy are the couple, and I'm just an extra. But I do love her.

"Doesn't she want to wake up?" Tommy asks, as he brings in our drinks.

"I haven't tried yet. I tell him, as he stands them on the TV unit. "She just looks so comfy."

"Yeah," he tilts his head and smiles, "she does. Listen, I'm going for a quick shower, do you need the bathroom first?"

"Nah, I'm alright."

Once he's gone, I move back and give her a nudge.

"Eden," she yawns, "hiya." She moves to cuddle me, but I pretend not to notice, and stand up to get the teas.

"Here, Tommy's made you a drink."

"Thanks," she says quietly, "are you ok?"

"Yeah, why wouldn't I be?" I hate being cold with her. I'm crazy about her, but I can't get my head around it all. Anna's so small and nice, it kills me that she was raped, and I want to help her but I can't handle it.

"Can we talk?" She asks, taking my hand, "about what happened on my birthday?"

"Forget it," I shrug, "it's fine."

"I can't."

The atmosphere's thick. She leans forward to look me in the eyes, a move I try to avoid. It's like she sees my thoughts when she looks me in the eyes, there's nowhere to hide. So, after a brief glance, I look at the floor.

"Like I said, Anna. Forget it."

For a minute or so, I drum my fingers against my mug and stare into my tea.

"Eden?" She says, but her voice is tight, and when I look up, I see tears in her eyes. I look away, but softly tell her not to cry.

"You think I'm dirty, don't you?"

"What? No way." I down the rest of my drink and tell her not to be silly.

"I'm not being silly! You can't even look at me, it's as though you're repulsed. You've gone off sex, and when we do, it's like you're somewhere else!"

"No, I'm not repulsed. It's just a lot to take in, that's all."

"Please, Eden. I need you."

"Oh, babe, I'm sorry. Come here." I wipe her tears away, and as I slide my fingers through her hair, I gently kiss her.

She's hesitant at first, but relaxes as I run my fingers down the back of her neck.

"I want to feel close to you." She whispers. "Later, could we have a bath together?"

"If that's what you want?"

"It is."

February 18, 2017 Saturday 11am. Home.
Anna:

In a week, I've gone from never sitting behind the wheel of a car, to passing my theory test and completing my driving lessons. Maybe that's why I feel so skittish, because I've got too much time on my hands. I'm nervous for Monday; I've got my practical test, first thing, then I've got to go straight to my placement. My thoughts bounce between all of that, college, and Eden. Valentines day ended up being nice, but I haven't seen him since. We've spoken and texted, but he's gone cold again, so I've decided to push myself. I've agreed to let him take me to a football match. He's been asking me to go since we got together, but I've always said no. Hopefully, if I survive, then we'll go back to normal for good.

"What time do you need to be in town?" Tommy asks, as he sets a plate of toast on the table.

I take one of the golden slices. "Half one," I tell him, "kick off's not till three, but Eden said to get there early."

"You gonna be ok?" He asks, scraping butter over a cremated slice.

"Yeah…well, I hope so."

"You know the drill, baby girl. Call if you need me."

Baby girl? He's never called me that. Ever.

Riverside Stadium. Half-Time.
Eden:

Two nil up, as the half-time whistle blows. That was awesome. As usual, everyone begins shuffling out. Everyone except me and Anna, she's just sat watching the crowd.

"Babe?" I ask, taking hold of her hand, "are you ok?"

"Yeah I'm good, it's good." She gives my hand a squeeze, and her voice carries a nervous laugh, "I didn't expect it to be so loud when they scored."

"We, when we scored."

"Yeah, that's what I meant."

"Do you want me to get you a drink or anything?" I ask, but she just shakes her head. So, I stroke her cheek, brushing my thumb over her lips. "I'm so happy you're here. I know it's scary, with all these people. You know I love you, don't you?"

I want her to say it back, but instead she says, 'yes, I do,' smiles and leans in for a kiss. I love how soft her lips are, and that they always taste like cherries.

"Sorry," I say, after a few minutes, "but, I'm gonna have to leave you on your own. I need the loo."

"I'll go with you."

"Ya what?" I laugh, "you can't go in the men's."

"I know, I'll wait outside."

I don't think she realises how crowded it'll be out there, but if I make her wait here, she'll think I'm being a dick.

"Ok." I take her hand, and she squeezes it tight as I lead her through the fans. I leave her near the wall, not too far from the queue's.

"Eden?" She calls, as I head to the loo, "don't be long."

"Relax, babe," I call back, "I'll piss as fast as I can."

When I step into the men's, I'm met with a queue from here to Mexico. Marvellous. 'Hurry up, people,' I mutter, willing them all to piss quicker.

314

A few minutes later, when I've finished, I rinse my hands and head back to rescue her. She's not there. I scan the crowd, but I can't see her. She's probably realised that it's quieter at our seats, and headed back, so I grab a drink then go back too. But when I get there, I see our seats are empty. Ok, now I'm worried, Anna doesn't know her way around. She could be anywhere. Ok, let's work this out logically, she might've gone to the toilet. I rush back out, while I call her phone, but it goes straight to voicemail.

"Come on," I say, as I pace outside the ladies, "answer your phone." Just then, three girls, leaving the toilets smile at me.

"Hey," I say to them, "I've um, lost my girlfriend."

"That was careless." Giggles a pretty red-head.

"Yeah, hilarious. Look, I can't go in there," I say, nodding to the ladies, "can one of ya just have a look? Her name's Anna." I show them the picture from my phone, and the red-head agrees. I try calling Anna again to no avail. After a few moments, the girl comes back.

"She's not in there." She says.

"Ok, thanks."

"Here," one of the other girls says, handing me a scrap of paper with a number on it. "If she's left ya, call me."

They all giggle and head back to the stand. Almost everyone's gone back now, so I throw the number in the bin and head to the exit. I ask the steward there, if he's seen her leave.

"She's small," I tell him. "Blonde and she's wearing a pink hoody."

"Ah, yes. There was a girl, she was talking on the phone. Looked a bit upset if you ask me, and in quite a hurry."

"Thanks, mate." I rush outside, turn towards the car park and see her pacing, a few metres away.

"Babe!" I call out. She turns, runs and throws her arms around me. "I tried to call you, why didn't you stay where I left you?"

She's trembling. "I couldn't stay," she cries, "there were too many people, Eden. All pushing and shoving, I got knocked down, then when I tried to get up, I tripped and fell back over. It was so embarrassing! I couldn't breathe."

"Aww, it's ok." The noise from the stadium signals that the second half's starting, so I take her hand. "Come on, babe, let's go back inside."

"I can't go back."

"Well, you can't stay in the car park."

Suddenly a look of guilt flashes over her face, and I realise why her phone went to voicemail, she must've been talking to someone. She's called Tommy, and of course he's coming for her.

"What the hell, Anna? A few people bump into you, and you freak out. Why did you call your brother and not me?"

"I don't know, ok!...I panicked, I knew he was only round the corner, at Rich's. I didn't know what else to do."

"You should've called me." I repeat. "Me. I'm your boyfriend, Anna, but you always run back to him. Whenever there's anything wrong with you, you run to him. I wanna look after you, but you never fucking let me."

"That's not true."

"Yes it is!" I snap, quickly turning my back on her. I just want a second to calm down, so I don't say something I'll regret.

"Eden?"

"Anna," I sigh, "I've never met anyone like you. On one hand, you're so honest that I can believe every word you say, but on the other hand, you're so tight with your emotions. You never let me in, not properly. What's going on with you, babe?"

"Now? You want to do this now? Tommy was going to tell you everything. But I know that's not how you wanted to find out. So, on valentines I asked to talk to you, I was going to tell you everything myself, but you didn't want to know." She stops for breath and wipes her tears. "Eden, apart from the odd time, you've been as cold as ice with me since my birthday. I don't know where I am with you. Just tell me what you want from me, because I don't have a clue!"

"Anna," I say, taking her tear stained face in my hands, "I want you to love me. I want you to trust me like you trust him. I want to be a proper couple. I get that you're close to Tommy, but if we're gonna work, I need to be number one."

Sobbing, she presses her face to my chest. She says my name, and I lower my head, hoping to hear 'I do love you,' but instead I hear a different four words.

She says, "I can't promise that."

I immediately break the cuddle. "What's the point then?" What does she mean? That she can't put me before him, or that she can't ever love me?

"Please, don't say that." She cries, and tries again to hug me, but I can't. "Eden, you know what you mean to me…" She stops pleading for a second, when we see her brother pull into the far end of the car park.

"Anna, just tell him you're ok, and come back in with me, please."

"I can't. What am I gonna say? 'Oh yeah, you've dropped everything to come for me, but I don't need you now, so run along.'"

She's got a point, but I can't let her leave. She has to choose me. My heart's thumping.

"If you," I say, voice shaking, "get in that car, then…then we're finished."

Anna's screams at me. She's hysterical, but I can't make any of it out. I'm just stood, asking myself, what the hell have I just done? But through her outburst, one question is clear. She grabs my arm, squeezes tight and says,

"You love me? If that was true, you wouldn't make me choose!"

I want to take it back, but I can't speak. I just stare at her, as she stands torn between me and her brother. She looks away, and I whisper her name. Tommy's waiting only a couple of metres away.

Anna turns back to me. "How did we come to this?" She asks, but I don't know how to reply. I guess I'm still clinging onto the faint hope that she'll stay. "Eden," she says, "I could've loved you…in time. I'm so sorry." She lightly strokes my face and tiptoes up to kiss me. "I really am sorry." She says as our lips touch. Then that's it, she walks away, and I'm left wondering why I didn't just hold onto her. Now, I've lost her.

February 20, 2017 Monday 1pm. James Cook University Hospital.
Anna:

Mine and Emilia's placements are on different wards, but they're not far from each other. So, right now, I'm waiting by the stairs for her, then we'll head down to the coffee shop for lunch. I had my driving test this morning, and this is the first time we've seen each other, today.

"Well?" She asks eagerly, as we step inside the stairwell, "did you pass?"

"Sure did."

"Awesome! So you can drive me home?"

"I came straight here. I haven't even driven my car yet." At the bottom, we head down the corridor. "But, I can take you home tomorrow."

"Yey!" She grins, grabbing my arm, "when we finish here on Friday, do you wanna go on a road trip? Find somewhere for food."

"Sure, sounds good."

We join the queue for the coffee shop, where she pulls out her bobble and shakes out her fiery mane. "That's better," she sighs, "I hate tying my hair back. My feet are killing me," she says, as we wait, "and I think I've seen more wee today, than in my entire life."

"Ah, have you been emptying bed pans too? I've been working with a HCA called Sue. She kept saying, 'you need a strong stomach to work here.'"

318

"Mine's like that," she huffs, "talks down to you."

"Yeah, she did until I made the mistake of mentioning that my dad was a surgeon."

"Then what did she say?"

"She said 'was? Why did he stop being a surgeon?' So, I said, 'because he died.'"

"Whoa, what did she say to that?"

"I don't think she knew what to say...I didn't mean to be harsh, but it's like she thinks I'm stupid, just because I'm young. So, what panini do you want?" I ask, as we move forward to the end of the counter.

"Oh, are you buying?"

"Yeah."

She grabs a sandwich, and when we pass them over to be put on the grill, I see a familiar face behind the counter. It's Dylan.

"Hello," he says cheerily, "are you alright?"

"Yeah, I'm here on placement. Did you have a nice holiday?"

"We did. Stu's sulking because he wants to go back. Well, we both do really. Anyway, what drinks would you like?"

"Two medium hot chocolates, please."

"Cream and marshmallows?"

"Yes, please."

As I try to give him the money, he shakes his head. "I'll get these, you go and sit down, I'll bring them over."

"Aww, thank you."

When we've found a table, I take off my hoody and Emilia gasps.

"What's wrong with your wrists?"

Emilia's seen the state of my wrists before. I usually just cover them with my sleeves and rub in antiseptic cream, but the HCA insisted on covering them with dressings and bandages.

"It was Sue," I tell her, "she said open wounds need to be covered."

"Yeah, but they're just scratches?"

"I know."

I really hope that I'm working with someone else tomorrow, and I'll wear a long sleeved top. These bandages make them super itchy.

"Anyway," Emilia grins, "no more ward talk, we're on a break. So, what did Eden say when you told him about your test?"

"I haven't told him."

"Why not?" She asks.

"Because we broke up, on Saturday."

Her jaw drops and it hits me; her and Eden have been friends for years, and I'm the outsider. She's going to take his side. For a few seconds, she just stares at me, I feel my pulse speeding up and a sickly feeling growing in my gut. If that's how it's going to be then I can deal, I've been alone before and I can do it again. I don't want to though, I really like being friends with Emilia, and as a cry works its way up my throat, I look down to the table and swallow hard.

"Anna," she says sympathetically, "don't cry. What happened?"

I can't be seen as the bitch in this. So, I give her the facts as they happened, and explain everything from the moment the half-time whistle blew.

"I should've just waited in my seat, then it wouldn't have happened. I wouldn't have had a stupid panic attack."

"But Eden's good at dealing with all that," she says, "Ellie gets them."

I don't want to contradict her, but all Eden's dealt with, is his sister hyperventilating and needing to breathe into a paper bag. He's proved that he can't handle my issues.

"The panic attack wasn't the problem," I tell her, "that was the trigger, Eden couldn't handle the fact I'd called Tommy, instead of trying to find him." I go on, telling her everything from him finding me outside, to when I kissed him goodbye. I pause for a moment, and thank Dylan as he brings over our lunch. Then, when he walks away, Emilia scoops a spoonful of cream from her hot chocolate and asks.

"Would Tommy have been ok if you'd stayed?"

"Yes, if he thought I was ok. But he could see just by looking at me, that I wasn't. You know, I begged Eden to come with me, I was an absolute mess. I was crying and pleading, but he just stood there, and I knew he was serious. So, I kissed him and said I was sorry."

"Anna, you're killing me. This is so sad. So, what did Tommy say, when you got in the car?"

"He didn't say anything. He drove us out of the car park, and once we'd got round the corner, he pulled over. Neither of us said a word. We just un-clipped our seatbelts, then he hugged me, and I cried. Obviously, I told him everything, but that wasn't until we got home. Then, he said not to call Eden, or text him."

"Why not?"

"Because he ended it, and I'll look desperate if I chase him. Tommy didn't say to block him or anything, he means if Eden contacts me, then yeah, I can reply. But he's got to make the first move."

"Do you want me to talk to him?" She asks.

"No, if he contacts me, I want it to be because he wants to. And don't worry about college, I won't make it awkward for you, if he hangs with us at break. I'd still like to salvage some kind of friendship with him."

"Thanks. I still can't believe it, you guys were so cute together."

I guess we were on the surface, and for the most part we were really happy. I don't know if I should feel guilty because, even though it hurts to lose him, I also feel relieved. I don't have to worry about saying the wrong thing, I can nap without upsetting anyone, and I don't have to re-live a nightmare, by explaining Alex. I think in some way I did love Eden, and I know I didn't say it, but I thought I'd shown it. Clearly, that wasn't enough.

Chapter 7

One Month Later.
March 25, 2017 Saturday 12pm.
Guisborough Woods.
Anna:

It's the first day of the Easter holidays, and Tommy's brought me to the woods. It's just what I need, college has been so tense since my break up with Eden. I mean, it's been a month, but him and his mates seem to hang with us, far more than they did before we got together. We're not nasty to each other, in fact he's really polite. Well, it's a forced politeness, that I know he wouldn't give me if Emilia wasn't stuck in the middle. Maybe him sticking around, is his way of punishing me for not choosing him, I don't know. I just wish he'd find a new girlfriend soon and move on.

From the car park, Tommy and I head up the muddy steps to the main walkway. It's a wide, stony path that leads to the trails. There's a little cafe there, and I wait outside while Tommy pops in for a bottle of juice. We always share one at the start, and another on our way back. When he returns, we walk a few more metres, then veer off to the right and climb over a stile, that leads up through the trees.

"When do you start your new job?" I ask.

Tommy's been offered part-time work selling cosmetics, at a department store near my college. It's not his dream job, that would've been a permanent position at the theatre, but he's realised that there's not much chance of that happening.

"In around two weeks." He says, ushering me in front.

The path's all but disappeared, bare mud where the grass has been worn away, and raised tree roots form the narrow trail up the bank. "I need to give notice at the pub." He says.

"Officially, it's two weeks, but Tracey said I only have to work one, because she owes me holidays."

"So, you've got a week off?"

"Ah ha."

This is awesome. As my mind spins through all the possible things we can do, I lose concentration, and catch my foot under a root. The other foot slides back in the mud, and as I throw my hands out to stop me falling, I accidentally send my rear end crashing into his front.

"Whoa," he laughs, catching me by the hips, "I got ya."

This is so embarrassing. My cheeks are on fire, and all I can say is sorry.

"It's fine, An. Good job I was there, or you would've gone flying."

"Yeah." I mumble, and press on up the hill. There's no logical reason why I should be embarrassed. Tommy's seen me at my worst, so surely a little stumble wouldn't bother him. We reach a ledge where the ground levels, we pause there for a minute, and he smiles. He's not bothered at all, he just lays his arm over my shoulder and looks down towards the fields below.

"What do you always say," he asks, "when we reach this point?"

"That I don't feel so small."

"And do you feel small?"

"Actually yeah, I still kinda do."

"Right then," he jolts his head to the trail above, "we need to go higher."

I'm not sure that going higher will make much difference, but through an almighty yawn, I agree.

"You up to this? We can take the easier route?"

"No, I'm fine."

We continue on, and this time Tommy walks in front while I follow. I do love it up here, especially at this time of year, when there's hardly anyone around, it's so quiet. A little further up, and the trail widens, Tommy moves beside me.

"Can I ask you something?" He says.

"Yeah."

"Look, I don't want you to feel like we're going around in circles, but I know you're still having nightmares."

"Have I woke you?"

"Yeah, and you've stopped talking to me about them." We move further up, using the tree roots as stairs. "I'm still here, Annie. Even if they're the same as before, you can always talk to me."

I was hoping he wouldn't bring this up. I don't want to keep secrets, but there are some things that I really can't tell him.

"I know I can but, it's not the nightmares at the minute," I sigh, "I'm kinda used to them. Now I'm getting these strange dreams, and some can be really confusing. Sorry, I don't mean to disturb you."

"I want you to disturb me." He touches my arm to make me stop, "and, what do you mean, confusing?"

"Nothing, it's ok."

"It must be something, An, if it's keeping you awake. Please talk to me, don't shut me out."

I need a minute to figure this out, so I pull my hoody down over my bum, and sit down on a grassy mound. Tommy crouches beside me, he looks me square in the eyes and asks again. I have to tell him. He's my brother, and I hate hiding things from him.

"I'm sorry. I haven't told you, because some of them are about you."

"How so?"

I can't say it aloud, but after an awkward thirty seconds, of me cringing and hiding my face, he gets the picture.

"Oh hey, it's ok." He stands to stretch his legs, and holds out his hand. "Come on, they're just dreams."

As I take his hand, he pulls me to my feet and gives me a huge bear hug. "If you could control dreams, then you would've put an end to your nightmares months ago."

I guess he's right, so for now, I'm just going to enjoy this walk with him, and push those dreams out of my head.

5.30pm. Home.
Anna:

As soon as we got home from the woods, Tommy had a call from our uncle, John. Sarah wants to go through the family photographs, so they're on their way over now. I don't think I'm ready to open them yet, but as I push another box, from the spare room to the landing, I tell myself that we aren't the only ones grieving.

It's strange, but the smell of dust from these boxes, is a stale reminder of just how long Mum and Dad have been gone.

"That's the last, Tom." I call down.

While he carries them to the lounge, I give myself a minute, and open the window, but the moment's short lived. As soon as I rest my arms on the windowsill, I see John's car pull up outside.

"Ok," I sigh, "let's do this," but I wait until I hear Tommy open the front door, before going down. After the usual pleasantries, Tommy makes some drinks, then we all go into the lounge. John sits on the sofa, with Sarah kneeling awkwardly at his feet. I sit beside my brother, amongst the boxes on the floor. I feel uncomfortable. It's the atmosphere, like there's an unstable serenity that's keeping me on edge.

"Thanks for doing this," Sarah says, "I…it's probably best if we explain." She looks to John, to take over.

"What your aunt wants to say, is this past year has been awful."

Sarah bows her head and nods.

"Despite what you think of us," he adds, "we're not insensitive, we know it's been difficult for you two. Now, Sarah's been seeing a therapist, and she's the main reason why we're here. She thinks it would be a good idea, if we made a memory album of your mum."

They both seem different today, like they're waving a white flag on a fight that they can't win. Relatable. Sarah's clearly wounded, but she's not biting at me like she usually does.

"Right then," Tommy says, sliding her a box, "do you two want to go through that one, and we'll start with this?"

It's not that Tommy's uninterested; it's complicated, but he does feel for Sarah, and he knows her. What John just said, is probably all she's wanting to tell us.

Tom hands me a pile of loose photographs. As I begin flicking through, I see that many are varying stages of Mum's flower displays. We both smile, as I show him a picture of our old back garden, where Mum's carefully cropped out our messy mud pit at the far end. For a while, the only sounds in the room, are that sucking sound you get when opening pages covered in cellophane. And the flicking of photos, like a dealer shuffling a deck of cards. Then Sarah nudges John.

"Remember that?" She says, showing him a picture.

"What is it?" I ask.

"It's the first holiday that we went on together. John looks so young there." She smiles and turns the page. "We were only courting then. You know, that was a lovely holiday. Austin rented a villa overlooking Lake Como."

"It was a good holiday," John adds, "but your Ellen wasn't impressed."

"It wasn't like that, love. She just preferred France."
John nods.

After an hour or so, of reminiscing past holidays, Christmases and birthdays, I find a picture of me and Dad. We're both asleep on the sofa, and I'm cuddled into his chest. This is weird, sure I recall hugging him, but I don't ever remember sleeping on him.

"How old was I there?" I whisper, discretely showing Tommy the picture.

"Three or four, I guess."

"Was I close to him?" I ask quietly, while John and Sarah are having their own conversation.

"Yeah, well until the night…you know."

"That he hurt you?" I whisper.

Tommy nods and continues flicking through an album. I stare down to the picture, it suggests a completely different story to the one I've lived. I must've loved him, he was my dad. I can hardly remember what we were like before that night, other than bits and pieces. But in this snapshot, he loved me and I loved him. He was holding my head, protecting me. I remember the rage in his eyes, when he slammed that belt against my brother's back, I remember feeling desperate, and I remember hating him. The fire in that hate eventually dwindled, to the point where my feelings towards him were indifferent at best. I wish that night hadn't happened, then I could miss my dad without feeling guilty about it. As I sit here dwelling, the sadness hits me like a thud to my chest, and I feel Tommy's arm around me. We just look at each other, neither of us speaking. That is until I notice Sarah, watching me.

"I'm ok, Tom," I say, giving him the picture, "I just need a minute."

The sun's going down, so on my way out to the kitchen, I flick the lounge light on. After a few minutes of leaning against the patio door, breathing in the cool night air, I feel Tommy behind me.

"You ok?" He asks.

"I'm sorry, but I think I miss him."

"Don't be sorry, he was our dad."

"I hate this feeling, Tom. All these years, I've been angry with him for what he did to us, and I always thought that if I forgave him, then I'd be betraying you…"

"You wouldn't." He interrupts.

"That's how I felt, though. And you still blame him for the accident."

"Yes." He sighs, "I do, but he was still my dad…I dunno, An. You could say that I love him and hate him at the same time, but don't feel like you can't grieve."

"Would you understand, if I said I wanted him to hug me?"

"Course I would."

Some quiet moments pass, Tommy slides his hands in his pockets, and we both stare out to the garden. What am I doing? I'm stood here, beating myself up over a past that I can't change, wanting a hug from someone who was never there, when my brother's right here.

"Will you hug me?" I ask.

"Always."

Later, back in the lounge, Sarah neatens her healthy pile of photo's.

"You know," she says, "this is all I have of Ellen's…I was wondering if you still had some of her clothes and things?"

"I…I'm sorry," I say hesitantly, "I bagged most of them up, for the charity shop."

"You did what?!" She snaps. "Didn't you keep anything? She was your mum!"

Tommy's quick to defend me.

"Hold on, Sarah," he says, "I told you when we'd be clearing the house. I said you could go and take anything you wanted. It's not Anna's fault that you didn't."

"Yes. I should've taken some of her things, but I couldn't face stepping into her bedroom, it was too much…but that little madam, she obviously thought nothing of just throwing her things away." She then directs her twisted glare at me. "You, sweetheart. You got your wish…"

"Sarah, that's enough!" John demands. Usually, I'd stay quiet and let Tommy speak for me, not this time.

"I never wanted this," I start shakily. "I love Mum, it tears me apart that she's gone, that I never got to square things with her. I made a massive mistake by throwing her clothes away, and I'm sorry. But you weren't there, and it was my decision to make, anyway I didn't throw everything. We still have her jewellery and some of her silk scarves." I look to my brother for permission, before saying that she can have some of those.

"Thank you." She says, as Tommy stands to go and get them.

We hear him rummaging around in his bedroom above us, but Sarah doesn't speak. She just flicks through the pictures that she's set aside. John reaches over and squeezes my hand.

"Sorry," he nods, "it's ok."

I think back to Mum and Dad's memorial, and the things Sarah said to me afterwards. She was so cruel, and I ran away in tears. That's not me anymore, I've made my peace with Mum now, and I don't need my aunts forgiveness. I don't even care what she thinks of me now, I've told her how I feel, and that's all I can do.

A little while later, Tommy comes down with Mum's jewellery box and some other bits and pieces.

"Here," he says, handing them over, "I've kept a ring and some necklaces for Anna, but you can have the rest."

"Thanks, love." She says.

He sits back down beside me, and opens the last box. Sitting in the top, is a slightly smaller box marked *'Thomas Henry and Annalee Elizabeth.'*

"Can I have that one?" I ask him.

"Sure." He slides it over, and I lift out two baby albums. One's pink and one's blue, with the title *'Baby's First Year.'* I set mine aside and open Tommy's. The first picture is him sat on someone's lap, I think it's Dad's, but his head's been cropped out of frame. Tommy's got bright red cheeks, huge brown eyes and a massive smile. I guess he looks around eight months old, but I can't be sure, I'm no good with ageing babies. I'm taking my time with this album. On each and every page he's smiling, he looks like the easiest baby ever, and Mum looks perfect. She, and everything else in the photo's are immaculate and coordinated. That is until the last page; judging by the balloons and party food, it's clearly his first birthday. He's been stripped down to a nappy, a few brown curls sit softly against his forehead, and he's completely covered in chocolate cake, I mean completely from head to foot. I can't help but smile, Mum hated mess, and this would've had her flapping. I can see it now, she'll have said to Dad, *'darling, darling, hurry up and take the picture! This boy needs a wash.'* Hearing her voice in my head, like that, really makes me miss her.

I have another rummage through the box, and check the dates on the other albums.

"Tom?" I say, "are these the only baby pictures?"

"Think so, why?"

"I can't find your newborn ones."

"Of course you won't," Sarah huffs, "Ellen wasn't given any."

"What?" I look at Tommy, then we both look at Sarah. "What do you mean?"

She closes the album and sighs.

"There're no newborn pictures, because he was six months old when they got him."

The room appears to shake around me, and Tommy grabs my hand. He's talking to Sarah, but I'm numb, and all I can hear is my pulse. Tommy's adopted? This can't be. I can feel the panic swelling inside. My grounding technique, I need to use my grounding technique, but I can't even remember what I'm meant to focus on, let alone name it five times, or whatever it is that I have to do. Instead, I force out Tommy's name.

"Can you hear me, An?" He asks.

I nod.

"Course she can bloody hear you." John booms, and I'm suddenly snapped back into the conversation. Tommy doesn't answer him.

"How? Why?" I ask?

"Annie," he says, "they thought we knew."

"Right," Sarah says, "your mum and dad asked us never to mention it, we'd assumed that was so Thomas wouldn't feel different. But, Tom, they must've at least told you. Think about it, you need a birth or adoption certificate, when you apply for a passport or a driving licence."

"They didn't." He says. "I've never needed my certificate, Dad applied for my first passport and my provisional. You don't need the birth certificate to renew."

My world's crashing down, and John thinks it's a good time to go and make a cup of tea.

"Does..." I can barely get the words out, "does this mean, he's not my brother?"

Tommy, still holding my hand, is quick to say it means nothing of the sort, but at the same time Sarah says, 'not by blood, no.'

"Yes I am!" Tommy snaps.

I don't know what to do, so I just cling tightly to his arm and cry.

"This isn't true," I say, "it can't be, he's my brother, you're my brother, Tom."

He wraps his arms around me, and holds me tight, too tight. There's a riot in my head. Of all the questions I could ask, I find myself pulling away and saying, 'who was his mother?' But there's no time to get an answer, because more and more questions spill out.

"Did they know her? Did you know her? Why did they adopt? Why not just have a baby?"

"Annalee." Sarah says firmly. "Settle down. No, they didn't know her, and it's not that simple. Not everyone can just have a baby…for goodness sake, your dad was infertile."

Whatever I say now is going to be wrong, so I keep my mouth shut and hold onto my brother. No-one else speaks either, this is agony. Everything we thought we knew has been torn apart, and she's just sat there, clinging to her pictures of Mum.

John comes back, carrying in a tray of steaming mugs, and Sarah breaks the silence.

"Don't think you weren't wanted, Thomas. You were adored."

My brother pulls out his bobble and lowers his head, so his curls fall over his face.

"Dad was infertile?" He mutters, then John's eyes look accusingly at Sarah.

That's when it hits me. "So, am I adopted too?" I say it aloud, but I can't be. I've seen pictures of me and Mum in the hospital. Tommy shakes his head.

"Look, I've said enough," Sarah says, gathering her things, "we should go."

"No." John orders her to stay put. "We are not going anywhere. You started this, woman, and these two need answers."

"Please," Tommy adds, "we need to know."

"I'm so sorry, Ellen." Sarah sighs, pressing her face into her palms. "Ok, I'll tell you, but let me explain, because things are never black and white."

"Go on." Tommy says.

"You need to know, that Ellen loved your dad. When he got the job in London, he asked her to go with him. She didn't want to, London's big and busy, and I know you think your mum was confident, but she wasn't. She'd lived here her whole life, and uprooting wasn't an option. She wanted to stay near her friends, near me. Austin wasn't happy, but my sister was stubborn, and he couldn't change her mind.

After a year or so, Ellen suspected that he'd been messing around, behind her back. It crushed her but she never said a word to him. Months went by and she tried to push it out of her head, and she thought a good way to do that would be to take an evening class. That's where she met Steven."

"Steven?" I ask.

"Yes. Now, that's all I know about him. She only told me what'd happened, when she found out she was pregnant.

And she only told me then, because that's when she ended it. Ellen came clean to your dad. He insisted that he'd never cheated, and she began to doubt everything. Anyway, long story short, they managed to work it all out, but it was a huge strain on their marriage."

I don't want to hear any more, Sarah tries to justify it all to us, but I'm done. Our lounge is a sea of memories that feel like they're from someone else's life. When I pick up a picture of Mum and Dad, and run my fingertips over their faces, I realise that I never actually knew them. I only know Tommy, but now we've lost the blood that binds us together.

"If my dad wasn't my dad, and my brother's not my brother, what happens now?" I say as I stare at the floor and cry. Tommy grabs my hands.

"Annie, look at me." He says, holding them up to his face. "You are my sister. You hear me? You are my sister. This doesn't change a damn thing. I love you, and I'll always love you. I need you to know that." His voice is strained, and he can hardly look at John or Sarah, but he stares at me with desperate eyes.

"I do, Tommy!" I sob, throwing my arms around him. Neither of us can hold it in any more, and as we break down, John tells Sarah to pick up her things.

"Come on," he says, "now, it's time to leave."

"We're sorry, kids." Sarah adds. "We'll lock the door behind us."

We hear the clunk of the keys, landing on the door-mat, but neither of us move. I can't let go, I can't not be close to him. It's clear that he feels the same, because when he shuffles back to cross his legs, he keeps hold of me and pulls me onto his lap.

"It's ok," he says, "everything's gonna be ok."

He's right, of course he is. I mean, we still have each other, and we'll go on living as we are now, but there're so many questions. Why didn't they tell Tommy? What's so shameful about adopting a baby? Was it that their perfect family image would be tainted? Some perfect family. Then another question comes to mind, and I'm almost afraid of the answer, but I have to ask.

"Do you?…" I don't know how to say this, so twisting my fingers into his hair, I press my face against his shoulder. "Tom, do you think you'll want to find your real mother?"

"No. Do you want to find this Steven?"

I shake my head. "No way." Even if I did want to, I wouldn't know where to start. Mum kept him a secret, and if Sarah's telling the truth, then she doesn't even know his last name. Then there's the fact that he probably doesn't even know about me. No, I don't want to go there.

After a while, Tommy nudges me to move, but keeps a tight grip of my hand. "Sorry, An, my legs have gone dead."

We clamber over the boxes and photo's to the sofa.

"You know," he says, "in some ways it makes sense."

"Does it?"

"Yeah, think about it…I'm not like them am I? Looks or personality."

It's true, he doesn't look anything like them. Mum was just like me, and Dad was tall. He was broad, but not fat. Mum used to say he had a strong gait, whatever that means. He was blonde too, but not as light as me or Mum. Despite shaving his face every day, he always had a course layer of stubble, like the prickly side of Velcro. It's funny how I've never noticed my brother's lack of resemblance, to me he's always just been Tommy.

"Are you ok?" I ask.

"Yeah, I think so." He then nods to the floor. "We should really pack all these away."

"Ok."

"Are you alright?" He asks.

"Yeah. I kinda felt like, after seeing that picture of me and Dad, that I'd got him back. Well, a memory anyway, something I could hold onto. Now that's gone."

"Not being blood doesn't stop him being your dad, An. Neither of them were my blood, but they were still my mum and dad."

"I guess you're right…and you're still my brother."

"I am." He says softly.

"Are you hungry?" I ask. "Because I am, but I don't know if I can stomach anything."

"Yeah," he sighs, checking the time, "it's half eight, listen should I just make us some porridge and a fresh cuppa, then we'll get rid of these?"

"Yeah, that sounds good."

10.30pm. Anna:

Once the last box is packed and stacked neatly back in the spare room, Tommy closes the door, and we both just crash on his bed.

"What a fucking day." He groans, as he lays flat on his front, shoving his face into the pillows.

I lie down too, resting my head in the small of his back. My mind's so noisy right now; so, I just stare up to the ceiling. Mum had another man's baby. That must've been agony for Dad, and every time they looked at me, they'll have been reminded. No wonder they argued so much.

"Tom, I've just had a thought."

"Go on."

"Maybe you weren't the reason Mum and Dad were always fighting back then. Maybe it was me…well what Mum did?"

"It's possible, baby girl, but we'll never know. Listen, I know you, and I don't want you blaming yourself for any of this. You're a good person."

"Thank you, but no wonder Mum didn't bond with me, and Dad gave up when I pushed him away, I was the product of an affair."

"The product, Annie," he sighs, "not the cause. She made her choices, you can't blame yourself."

"Thanks, Tom…you're my favourite person, you know?"

"Ditto."

We're not even ready for bed yet. The only light shining, is the one from the landing. I soon find my eyes closing, then after a few minutes, I sink into a dream where I'm still semi-conscious.

"Dreaming of being with you doesn't seem so wrong now." I mumble, then jolt myself awake as I suddenly realise what I've said. Throwing myself to the edge of the bed, I hide my face in my hands.

"I'm so sorry," I tell him, "I shouldn't have said that."

I'm so stupid. Adopted or not, he's still my brother. I'm wrong, very, very wrong. I soon feel his hand on my back.

"Lie down, Annie." He says gently. "It's ok, go to sleep."

But I can't. So, I turn around, and in the dim light, I look at his face.

"I'm sorry." I say again, "I shouldn't be thinking about you like that, there's something wrong with me…I'm so messed up."

"No, no, don't say that. I've thought about you, I didn't want to…"

"What? You have?"

"Yes." He says shamefully. "I've been fighting feelings like that for months."

I'm confused, he's never given any indication that he felt like that. Initially, I wonder if he's saying it to make me feel better. But then the past few months speed through my head, and I begin to see. He has looked at me differently. All the times I've turned and caught him smiling at me, or looking at my lips, like Eden used to do, when he wanted to kiss me. And calling me 'baby girl.'

As I sit here, he lifts his hand and gently tucks my hair behind my ear. "Annie, I love you, and having those thoughts isn't wrong…not now we know the truth. See, we're free to do whatever the hell we want."

"What are you suggesting, Tom?…That we actually do it?"

"I'm not suggesting sex," he says, "well I am, but not just sex. I'm suggesting us."

He's serious too. But, if I were to say yes, and we do it, what would happen if I'm not good enough? Or if things get weird, and we lose what we already have? Or even worse, that we fall out and I lose him altogether. That's a thought I can't bear.

"No. I need my brother. I can't do that with you."

"I know," he sighs, "I'm sorry, I just love you. More than I could ever love anyone, we're both messed up An, but I just feel we should be as close as we can."

"I get that, and I love you too, but…I need to think, just let me think." I tell him, as I stand and rush to the door.

"Where're you going?"

"For a bath, I need to clear my head."

Moving quickly over the bed, he grabs my hand, "I'm so sorry, sweetheart. Look, we're just in shock and, and our emotions are everywhere, I…"

"I know, Tom. It's ok, I'm coming back."

Tommy:

Tommy you fool. You're supposed to be her guardian. We need to talk and now, yes she's in the bathroom but she has to know that I'm sorry, that she's safe. What am I thinking? I can't just go charging across the landing and burst in on her. She needs space, and I need to calm the hell down. Ok, ok, she said she was coming back. I'll just wait then explain that I was wrong, she'll cuddle in, we'll get some sleep, and put all this craziness behind us.

A good ten minutes pass, and I'm beginning to think that waiting isn't the best idea. So, I go to the bathroom and knock on the door.

"Tommy?" She calls.

"Yeah, are you ok?"

"I am, but could you come in?…I wanna talk."

"You sure? You're in the bath."

"Just come in, please."

I hesitantly push the door open and look inside, but I can't see anything. She's leant forward with her arms folded over the rim. So, I turn around and sit in front of her, with my back rested against the bath.

"I am sorry, Annie. I promise you, nothing needs to change."

"You're my world, Tom. Seriously, I'm nothing without you." She presses her forehead on my arm. "See, I don't just love you. It's so much more, and I'm petrified that I could lose you."

"You'll never lose me, no-matter what. But please, just forget what I said, you're my sister." I take a quick glance to the inscription under my bracelet, 'brother and friend.' That's what she needs.

"Um," she whispers, "there's something I need to know."

"Go on."

She doesn't go on. She's silent. So, I spin around but she hides her face.

"Look at me, An."

For a moment she doesn't move. I ask again, then she turns her head and looks right through me.

"Have you ever kissed me?" She asks, "I need to know if it was real."

She was awake? It would be so easy now, to say that she'd dreamt it, but I can't lie to her, especially not tonight.

"Once, and I am so, so sorry."

"Was it on my prom day?"

I nod. "I only meant to kiss your cheek, you looked so peaceful and I…"

"Come here." She interrupts. I move closer and she delicately touches my face, then very hesitantly, leans in and kisses me. She's so tender and gentle, but she pulls back a fraction to look me in the eyes. "I needed to know the truth," she whispers, "and that I'll never lose you."

Fixing her eyes on mine, she moves her body back from the rim. She shows me her glistening skin, as the foamy water glides down, over her firm and perfect body. With the instinct of a teenager, I hold my hand out to touch her, and as I cup her breast, she lays her hand over mine.

"I love you, Tom," she smiles, "and I am yours."

Anna:

Tommy's speechless, but he takes me by the hands; and as I stand, his eyes dance over every part of me. He doesn't care about getting wet, he just wraps his arms around me, and I wrap mine around him. And when I trace my fingers over the back of his neck and into his hair, he touches his face to mine.

"I adore you." He whispers. "You ready?"

My entire body's yearning for him, all I can do is catch my breath and nod. He lifts me from the bath, and I hook my legs around his waist. I genuinely can't tell if it's his heart racing, mine or both, but before he moves, I ask him to kiss me properly. Then, he carries me back to his room.

This should feel wrong, but wrong is a world away from what this is. He sits me on the edge of the bed, and as he peels off his damp T-shirt a hint of nerves escape me. He smiles and brushes his thumb against my cheek, then begins unfastening his jeans.

"Can I do it?" I ask, placing my fingertips on the button. "Yes!"

My hands tremble, as each button pops open revealing his thing, bulging under his shorts. He quickly kicks off his jeans. This is it, this is really it, I'm about to do it with my brother. With Eden it was just fun, I mean yeah I liked him, but this is different, it's so much more. It's not just my body that I'm giving him, but my soul. That very thought, and everything I feel for him pangs through my chest, so, closing my eyes I lean forward, hold his hips and softly kiss his belly. Then I feel him slide his hands over mine, tucking my fingers under the band of his shorts.

"You definitely sure?" He whispers.

"Yes, Tom. I am."

Together, we slide his shorts down and instinctively, I take hold of his thing, kiss the end and guide it into my mouth. After a minute or so, of massaging it with my tongue, I take it deeper and faster until he takes a sharp inhale.

"Slow down, Annie," he gasps, "it's been a while."

"I…I'm sorry."

"N…n…no," he says, bending down to kiss me, "it's just, wow! You're really good at that. Will you lie back for me?"

I move further up the bed, then as I sink my head back in the pillows, he crawls over me. His dark curls fall over my face, his body's shielding mine, and in that lingering second, we look deep into each others eyes. It's like I can see his heart.

Beginning with that super sensitive area of my neck, just above my collarbone, he covers me in kisses. No part of me goes untouched. Those beautiful soft, full lips brush over each of my breasts, then down to my navel and I tremble again. He's going down there. He slides his hands under my bum, pulling me to his face. I don't know what to do with myself, so, I grip the duvet and squeeze. I've never felt anything like this, so warm, so gentle, yet exhilarating, heart-stopping, intense. He's not stopping, and the feeling builds and builds and builds until my heart feels like it's exploding. I'd beg for him to stop, but I don't want him to, I want him to go on and on forever, I want to scream with pleasure, but I manage to hold it in.

"Are you still taking your pill?" He whispers, as he moves back up to kiss me.

"Yes." I pant. He kisses me again, and I taste myself on his lips. I honestly didn't think I'd like the taste, but as he positions his thing and pushes it inside me, I realise that on him I do. On him it's sensual, *he's sensual* and he's mine.

An hour or so later.
Tommy:

I can't remember much after making love to Annie, I must've fallen straight to sleep. I rub my eyes into focus, and see that she's wide awake, sat up and staring into the light of her phone. It's strange seeing her sat there naked, not strange as in wrong, but strange in that I still feel the need to wrap her up, to protect her. Which is odd in itself, as I'm still naked too.

"Hey," I say, as I brush my fingers against her arm.

"Oh, sorry. I didn't mean to wake you."

"It's fine. Was I asleep long?"

"About an hour," she sighs, laying her phone on the bedside table. "I didn't want to go to sleep."

"You alright? You're not having regrets are you?"

"No." She then turns, lays her hand on my cheek and looks right through me. "How I feel about you, is the only thing I'm sure of…but I do need to talk."

"Sure, but will you lie down? It's chilly."

"No, if I lie down I'll fall asleep. I've already said, I don't wanna go to sleep."

"Fair enough. If you're not gonna lie down then I'll just have to sit up." I open my arms for a hug, and she cuddles in.

"Are you still my brother?" She asks, "I just don't know what we are now, I mean, what I should call you. I love what we did, and I want it again. I just don't want to lose my brother either, is that wrong?"

"No, Annie, I don't think it is. Lift up a minute, I want to show you something."

She leans forward while I reach into my bedside drawer, then cuddles back in, as I hand her the note she wrote for my birthday.

"You know, when they said I'd been adopted, I thought I'd lost everything. But now, I don't feel like that at all. You see here?" I say, pointing to the part where she's written that

341

I'm her rock and best friend. "I've never actually told you this, but you're my best friend too, you have been for a long time."

"I thought that was Rich?"

"He's my best mate, but no-one knows me like you do… no-one. What I'm trying to say is I'll always be your brother, you're my sister, my best friend, my partner and everything in-between."

"We've survived a lot of shit, me and you, haven't we?" She says.

"We really have. Listen, baby girl, I want you to know that we're equals. I need you as much as you need me."

Annie folds up the note, and stretches over my lap, giving me a perfect view as she puts it back in the drawer. Fuck me, she's got a tight ass. It's like a sexy, round peach. I can't help it, but I have to give it a squeeze.

"Tommy." She giggles, as she pushes the drawer closed. "Can I kiss you again?"

"Do what you want, I'm yours."

She kisses me, but only for a second, then runs her fingertip over my lips.

"There's something else." She says. "You know when I sucked your thing?"

"My thing? You can call it a cock, you know!"

But she just laughs and shakes her head. "Anyway, you said it'd been a while. You don't have to tell me if you don't want to, but exactly how long is a while?"

"What? You wanna know when I'd last had sex?"

She nods. I didn't want this conversation. I still want to protect her, but I'll never hide anything from her again, not even my past.

"It was the night before the accident."

"When I was at Becca's party?" She asks.

"Yeah, when you said you wouldn't be staying over, I went out and picked up a girl."

"That was a year ago?"

"It was. Why do you want to know?"

342

"Just do," she shrugs, "I don't know. I know you used to do it a lot, I guess I'm just scared that we'll run into one of those girls. She'll tell me something awful, something you did together...I just think, I'd rather hear that kind of thing from you."

"Ok. I've had a fair bit and yeah, it was fun at the time, but it wasn't fulfilling, and I certainly wasn't into anything weird. Listen, if you're worried that I'll miss all that, then don't. Look at me. I will never hurt you. You're everything to me, and I meant it when I said I adore you."

She hugs me tight and softly kisses my chest.

"Thank you, I just needed to hear that. Tom?...I don't want to sleep because I'm scared I'll have a nightmare. I don't want anything ruining this."

"I know, I had a feeling that was the reason."

Usually when Annie cuddles in, she'll jabber on about nothing to stop herself falling asleep, then eventually she'll give in. Not tonight. Tonight she tilts her head to look me in the eye. She lifts her thigh over mine, pushing herself against me and stroking my chest.

"I want to do it again." She grins.

"Absolutely."

April 08, 2017 Saturday 1pm. Home.
Anna:

Despite the rain bouncing outside, we still have the patio door open. I could sit here all day, breathing it in. I love the smell of rain, not cold, dirty winter rain, but spring rain, the kind that freshens everything up, ready for summer.

Tommy's singing and dancing while he makes our lunch. He's so funny. This time last week, I was struggling with disturbing thoughts about him, that feels like so long ago now.

Since then we've done it every day, sometimes twice and I love it. Tommy calls it making love, I think that sounds old fashioned, but he's right, that's exactly what we do.

343

This morning, before we got up, I just looked at him lying there and knew that I wanted to please him from start to finish. All I cared about was how I was making him feel. While I was riding him, he held my hips, and not taking his eyes off mine, he smiled. But, it was more than a smile, it was a promise that this is us, forever. I was so overwhelmed that I couldn't even speak, I felt like my heart wasn't big enough. I could feel tears in my eyes, but I didn't want him to see, he obviously did see because afterwards, when I was about to move, he pulled me close and hugged me so tight. We didn't let go of each other, and as his thing softened inside me, we fell back to sleep.

"Hey," he says, turning up the music, "come and dance with me."

I can't help but giggle as he spins around, wiggling his hips.

"You'll have to put that knife down." I laugh, as he grabs hold of my waist, pulling me so hard that I crash into his chest. He loses his balance, stumbles back against the fridge, and as he tosses the butter-knife to the work surface, it clatters and crashes to the floor. Tommy can't stop laughing, it's not even that funny but his mood's infectious. I haven't seen him this happy for so long, it's like he's weightless. I burst into hysterics too, then leap into his arms, squeezing my legs tight around his waist.

"I love you." I tell him through a breathless laugh, right before planting my lips on his. What starts as just a little kiss, quickly grows. He could take me now, right here against the kitchen cupboards. I'd love it if he did, if he…

"Oh my goodness!" We hear from the patio. Tommy drops me, and we turn to find Stu standing there, stunned.

"Stu…I, um," Tommy stutters, as he helps me up. "I wasn't expecting you…look I, listen I can explain."

"I was just passing, so I thought I'd pop in to tell you my good news…but it looks like you're busy, I should go."

Not knowing what to do next, I shrink behind Tommy and turn the music off.

"Don't go, Stu," he pleads, "let me explain."

This is the first time that I've seen Stu genuinely flustered, and I can tell he's torn. Eventually, he agrees to stay.

"Thanks, mate. Thank you." Tommy hands him a tea-towel, to dry the rain from his face.

"You know, Tom," he sighs, taking off his shoes and coat. "I don't have a judgemental bone in my body, but this is dangerous. You're brother and sister."

I should leave this to Tommy, after all Stu's his friend. But as my brother hesitates, I find myself saying, 'we're not!'

They both suddenly stare at me. Tommy looks wounded. "I mean we are," I add, "but we're not blood, we found out last week."

We all stand silent for a moment, then Tommy offers to make Stu an apple tea.

"Yes, I'll have a drink."

"So, what's your good news?" Tommy asks him, as he fills the kettle.

"Well, I asked Dylan if we could buy our own place, and he said yes!"

"Aww, that's great." I say. I want to give him a hug, but instead, I just kind of stand there, awkward.

Stu's just found out our secret, and Tommy's trying to act like nothing's happened. He just flicks the kettle on, then turns and gives him a hug.

"That's awesome, mate," he says, "that's awesome."

After making us all a drink, Tommy tries to explain again.

"Listen, Stu. Like Annie said, we found out I was adopted."

He must be nervous because his voice is shaking, and he always refers to me as Anna, Annie's what he says when he's talking to me directly.

"And we…" he says, but Stu stops him. Shaking his head, he lays a friendly hand on Tommy's shoulder and beckons me to them.

"You two are the closest pair I've ever known. I've always felt the love between you, and after hearing news like that…Oh, my friends, I do understand. You don't need to explain any further, and your secret's safe with me."

"Thanks, mate." Tommy says. "Obviously, you can tell Dylan, otherwise it'll be awkward when we're all together, but don't let him breathe a word."

"You don't need to worry, Tom."

April 10, 2017 Monday 2.30pm. Home.
Anna:

Dan travelled up to his dad's yesterday, for the last week of the Easter holidays. As usual he's coming over to see me, in fact, he's just texted to say that he's on his way.

To say I'm anxious is an understatement. Today's the first day of Tommy's week off, before starting his new job. So, as he's home we figured we had two choices; we either act normal, like regular brother and sister. Or we tell Dan the truth. Both are tricky, I mean if we don't tell him and accidentally slip up, what will he think? He knows we've always been close, but we're different now. It's all over me, like everything in my heart is written on my skin. I could hide it for a little while, but Dan's staying till late. And usually, when he comes over, we chill in my old room. Tommy trusts me, but for his sake, I wouldn't feel comfortable doing that now.

Tommy came to the conclusion that the only real choice is to tell him. After all, once Stu knew the truth about us, he understood. I've already told Dan that my brother was adopted, he even knows that I wasn't Dad's, but I'm still on edge. This is serious, if he doesn't understand, I could lose my oldest and very dear friend.

346

While Tommy flicks through Netflix, I pace the lounge floor.

"Here, Annie." He taps his legs, and tosses the TV controls on the sofa. "I'm worried too," he says, as I sit on his lap, "but you need to calm down, or you could make yourself ill."

He's right, I was lucky to keep my head in 'the real' when Sarah let the truth out, and that was the first time since my birthday, that I've felt it slipping. Something like that would be far from helpful right now, but I don't think I'm anywhere near there today.

"I'm ok, Tom. I just want him to understand why I love you, you know…like this."

"I know."

Neither of us say anything else, because there isn't really anything else to say. All we can do is wait. So, while I fiddle with the charms on my bracelet, he holds me tight. I press my cheek against his head and try to relax.

Around ten or fifteen minutes pass, then we hear Dan's cheery knock on the front door.

"Do you want me to stay, while you tell him?" Tommy asks.

"I don't know…I do, but I think it will be better if you're in another room."

"Go on then." He nods, patting my thigh, "you best let him in."

I jump to my feet, but suddenly feel the need for him to stay. "Don't go straight upstairs," I say, "just like, be normal."

"Annie, chill. I'll say hi, then if you want me to leave, just ask me to find your necklace."

"My necklace?"

"It's code, sweetheart…for bugger off."

"Oh, I don't want you to bugger off."

"I know, daft arse." He laughs, as I go and open the front door.

As usual, Dan's pristine; smart black jeans and a pale blue shirt. He's got his jacket hooked on his thumb, flicked back over his shoulder.

"Hiya," he smiles, then gives me a hug as he steps inside. "I've missed you."

"I've missed you too."

And I have. The last time I saw him was Christmas, when we commandeered the lounge, laid out a sea of snacks and cushions on the floor, and spent an entire day watching Lord of the Rings. That was fun.

While I make some drinks, Dan pops in the lounge for a quick chat with Tommy, then joins me in the kitchen.

"So, what's new with you?" He asks.

I might not need Tommy to go upstairs, this could be my chance to tell him, but before I can engage my brain, I'm already asking sarcastically, 'what? Since yesterday?' But he just laughs and shakes his head.

Me and Dan still call each other most days, and that's not counting the text conversations.

"There is something," I say, taking the milk out of the fridge, "but you first, what's new with you?"

"Well, you know that girl I told you about?"

Dan went to a party with some friends from college, at the weekend. He hooked up with a girl called Maddie.

"The party girl?"

"Yeah, you know I said that we had loads in common, music, movies, books, everything?"

"You're together, aren't you?"

"Yeah. I wanted to tell you in person, and I know it's a bit soon, but we both feel the same…she's pretty awesome. Here…"

Aww, his hands shake, as he opens his phone to show me a picture of them. They're in a packed lounge, cuddling up on the sofa, both laughing so hard. She's beautiful, long ginger hair, she looks similar to my friend Emilia. Only Maddie's cheeks aren't as rounded, and her hair is silky and tamed.

"Dan, she's stunning. I'm super happy for you."

"Thanks." He says, as I turn and hand him his tea.

"Wait here, I'll just take this to Tommy."

I give Tom his coffee, along with a quick kiss. "I'm gonna tell him now."

"Ok, I'll stay here."

I kiss him again, then go straight back to the kitchen.

"Now I know how you felt at Christmas," Dan says, "I was so nervous about telling you."

"Don't be…I um…I'm with someone too."

"Are you? Like actually with someone? You didn't even tell me that you liked anyone."

"Sorry, I didn't say anything, because you kind of know him."

"How? Did he go to our school?"

"He did, but he wasn't in our year…he's older."

Come on, Anna, I tell myself. I can't even look at him, and my face is on fire. I get why he's confused, we usually tell each other stuff like this. He'd told me about spending the night with Maddie. So, it was no surprise when he just said that they're together. It was no surprise at Christmas either, when I told him I was with Eden, because he already knew about him. But regarding Tommy, I haven't said anything, other than talk about the adoption.

"An? What's wrong?"

"I haven't lied to you or anything. I just didn't know how to tell you, or what you'd think of me if I did. Or if you'd even want to stay friends."

"What do you mean?" He asks, as I lean against the patio door and look outside.

"I didn't tell you that I liked someone, because we didn't get together like that…it was a huge decision, and there was so much to think about. See, we're not sure how people will react, but I…I love him."

"Are you telling me what I think you're telling me?"

"What do you think I'm telling you?" I wish this wasn't so difficult. I hear every word as they leave my lips, and it

349

sounds like I'm playing a guessing game. "I'm sorry, Dan. I know I can trust you, but this is a big deal."

He moves closer, so he's standing right over me, and lowers his voice.

"An…I don't want to say what I think you're saying," he nods back towards the lounge, "only in case I'm wrong."

"You're not wrong." I whisper.

"And…I'm not surprised."

"What?" How can he not be surprised? I've pretty much admitted that I'm in a relationship with my brother. I know Dan's chill, I mean super easy going, but to not even be surprised? I don't have a clue what to say now. Obviously, I was apprehensive, but I had a plan on how to explain. Now I don't need to, but I feel like I do. I want to.

"Can I tell you something?" He asks, as he steps out to the garden and sits at the patio table, "without upsetting you?"

I nod and follow him.

"You remember when I told you that I was moving away?"

"Yeah, it was in the summer holidays."

"And it was then," he says, "that I told you how I felt."

I'm not sure where he's going with this, so I just mumble a questioning 'ah ha' and wave my hand for him to go on.

"Ok, now backtrack to before your mum and dad's accident. I knew then that I wanted to be with you, and you know why I didn't say anything."

"I know, we've been through all that. I don't get what it has to do with me and Tommy, and why you're not surprised?"

"Well, once I decided that you just needed a friend, I wasn't going to tell you at all. But I nearly did at the prom. I fell in love with you that night, and the one thing that had been stopping me, kind of evaporated. That was until he picked you up…it hit me then. Obviously, you're closer since losing your mum and dad. But you two love each other

350

so much. It's overwhelming, and there's no way I could've competed with that."

"We've only been like this since we found out." I tell him defensively.

"I know, I know. That's not what I'm saying. What I'm saying is that, I know if I'd have stayed, we would've got together, because I couldn't stay and not be with you. But it wouldn't have worked, then I'd have lost you completely, and I couldn't deal with that. You see, An, it doesn't matter who's in your life, he's always been your number one. So, when you told me that you two weren't blood, I just knew it would only be a matter of time."

"Wow, ok. So, what happens now?" I ask.

"What do you mean?"

"Are you still my friend?" I ask hesitantly, as I trace my fingers over the scars on my wrist.

"Yeah," he laughs, playfully nudging my foot. "I'm happy for you. You're with the one person who can love you more than me."

"I'm so grateful for you, Dan. Maddie's a lucky girl."

"Nah, I'm a lucky boy."

I've done it, I've told him. I'm almost floating in the freedom of that door being closed, but in doing so, another one's opened. Another issue that me and Tommy will have to face, that anyone who knows us may come to the same conclusion. We're not blood, so it's only a matter of time. This would make keeping us/our relationship a secret difficult. So, we have to be super careful. We need to figure out who else we want to tell, and after that, it's best if we keep the adoption a secret too.

April 19, 2017 Wednesday 2.30pm. College. Anna:

My files land in the car boot with a thud. I hate being late, but I'd totally forgot that I have a counselling appointment, in thirty minutes. Luckily, my tutor didn't mind me leaving college early. I jump in the car, and as soon as I set off, I switch my Bluetooth on, and call Tommy.

"Hey, you're out early." He says.

"Yeah, are you busy?"

"No, I've just got in from work, why?"

"I only forgot about my session with Julie! It starts at three. Can you meet me there?"

"Sure, I'll be in the car park."

"Thank you. So how was work?"

"Yeah, it's ok. Quieter than I thought it'd be."

"Can you teach me how to put make-up on? I don't mean a full face, I'll still let you do that, I just mean something to make me look natural but fresh, you know?"

"Course I will."

"Great, love you."

"Love you," he says, "drive safe."

Later, at the medical centre, Tommy and I are sat waiting for Julie to call me in. This is my first session since before Easter, before our relationship changed. The time's gone three, and as I look across the square, waiting for her to appear, all the usual nerves decide to kick in.

"Tom?" I say, anxiously tapping his arm.

"What if I let it slip? You know she has a way of making me say things."

Thankfully, we're the only ones in the waiting room, because he looks frightened; stern but frightened.

"Please don't." He pleads, under his breath. "She cannot find out."

"Ok, I won't."

"I mean it, Annie. You're old enough to give consent, but until your eighteenth, I'm still your guardian. You're technically a minor, so she'd be in her rights to contact social services…"

"And split us up?" I interrupt.

"If she thinks I've hurt you, then yes, she could."

"You hurt me?" I shake my head, letting out a sarcastic huff, "you're the last person who'd hurt me."

"We know that." He says, as Julie trots over the square. "Anyway, just relax and remember I'm only outside." He gives me a typical brotherly hug, then makes his way to the exit, and I follow Julie into our usual room.

Everything in my mind is overshadowed by this dense cloud. All me and Tommy want is to be as close as we can. If I slip up now, all of that would be stripped away. What would happen to him? I've read stories, where teachers and students have been in love. As soon as their cover's blown, she's suddenly a child, a victim, and he's a sex offender. Tommy's twenty-two, that's old enough to be a teacher, and I'm seventeen, a minor. What am I doing? I think, as I stand at the window and stare out to the courtyard, I can't compare our relationship to that of a teacher and student. Our love's so much more, it's deep, it's pure. We've grown up together, there're no barriers between us, nowhere to hide. I mean yeah, the sex is awesome, but it's not just about that. Without him I'm only half a person. I can't and won't let anyone, no matter how good their intentions, take him away from me. I need to keep my wits about me, I'm not going to drink the 'truth inducing' tea. Today, I'm going to smile, and see if I can convince her that I don't need these sessions anymore.

"It's beautiful today, isn't it?" Julie chirps, suddenly appearing at my side, "here, I've made you a cup of tea."

I stare into the golden liquid, as a cluster of bubbles float on the surface. I feel like a patient in an asylum, and Julie's the nurse who's disguised my meds.

I don't want her to think I'm rude, so I take the cup and pretend to sip.

"I've been sleeping better," I tell her, as I move to the sofa and place the cup on the coffee table. "I'm not getting as many nightmares."

Julie joins me on the sofa, and kicks off her shoes.

"I am pleased to hear that. And the visions?"

Proudly, I announce that I haven't had one since my birthday. "And that was February."

353

This is going well, I almost say aloud, as I instinctively reach for the cup of tea. Obviously, I stop myself at the last second.

Julie smiles. "So, the grounding technique is helping?"

"Yeah. I mean I don't really use it anymore, but I don't think I need to."

"You've certainly came a long way," she sings, "a far cry from the shy girl, who first shuffled in here."

"Um, thanks."

Everyone likes a compliment, but hers just reminds me of the old, frightened, naive mess that I used to be. I want to move on.

I turn the conversation around to college, and for some time, I go through as many different aspects of my course as I can.

I've been coming to these sessions for nearly a year, and I'm fairly sure that Julie can see when a secret's being masked by a cloud of irrelevant talking. But this is my plan, and to not arouse suspicion, I keep the conversation flowing. I speak enthusiastically about everything, from how I'd eventually like to work on a trauma ward, to ways of preventing bed sores on immobile patients. Sometimes, I imagine calling Dad and telling him everything I've learned. That's an odd feeling really, I haven't called Dad for years. He, like everyone in the family, would call me. He'd want to know why Mum wasn't answering her phone, or sometimes, he'd ask me to fax him documents from his study. As I explain this to Julie, I feel the words 'he wasn't my real dad' falling out of my mouth.

"My aunt told me." I add, and for the briefest of seconds, I fear our cover's blown, but with a swift exhale, I compose myself. She's not going to figure it out just from that, so long as she doesn't find out where Tommy came from, then we're fine.

"Could you tell me how receiving that news made you feel?" She asks, as I spin some of the charms on my bracelet.

"It's hard to say really. You know we had issues, but he never actually told me that I wasn't his. You could say he ticked most of the 'dad' boxes; he provided for me, he took an interest in my school work, and when I was little, we were close. I am grateful for that, I mean he didn't treat me any different to Tommy."

"Yes, but how did you feel?"

How can I answer that? I was already devastated when I got the news, the fact I wasn't Dad's wasn't my main focus.

"I don't feel anything. I guess I'm still numb." My answer is the closest to the truth that I can give her, but it still feels like a lie. I am numb, but I do feel something. I feel regret, I shouldn't have shut Dad out. I look back to the day after that night, with older eyes. Dad tried to apologise. While I slurped the milk from my cereal, he came down to the kitchen. He tried to hug me first, he kissed the top of my head, but I shrank away like a little hedgehog sticking its prickles out. So, he moved to Tommy, I watched as he laid his hand on my brother's back, but he pulled away too.

"For crying out loud, Children!" He said. "I'm not going to hurt you."

Then, as he left and closed himself in the study, Tommy whispered, 'Too late.'

"Anna?" Julie says, bringing my head back to the session. "You must have been miles away. I was just saying that there's no need to worry, it can take a while for these things to sink in. It's quite normal."

"Is it normal to look at your phone, hoping to see, 'Dad calling?'"

"Absolutely. You've grown beautifully since losing your parents, it's only natural to crave that contact. The next step would be to acknowledge that, accept where you are within your family right now, and continue to grow into the strongest version of yourself. There will be times where you feel deep sadness, don't bury those feelings, let them out. Give them space, give them room, but don't be weighed down."

I guess she's right. But all I meant, was that I want him to call, to make sure I'm finishing my homework, or something.

My mouth's so dry. I've never gone through an entire session without a drink, and as there are only five minutes left, that cup of tea is beginning to look tempting. After all, what could I possibly say in five minutes? While Julie gives me some positive advice, I reach for the cup and take a sip, but it's gone cold.

As the last few minutes tick by, she says that she wants to see me again. Great, I'd love to tell her that I've had enough of these sessions, but I'm not that brave.

I store my next appointment in my phone, then hurry out to the car park. While I've been inside, Tommy's moved his car next to mine. Seeing me, he rolls his window down.

"Hey," I say, leaning down against the door. "That was hard…"

"You didn't tell her?"

"Of course I didn't. I'm not stupid."

Discreetly running his index finger over my hand, he smiles, "I know you're not. D'ya wanna get your car, and we'll talk at home?"

"I don't know, Tom. I'm chewed. These sessions are supposed to make me feel better, but I just feel tense. I talked about Dad, and how he was with me; how I always had to work hard. I'm sick of being good. You know, I don't know what's going on with me. It's like I'm sick of it all; nightmare's, hallucinations, having zero confidence and generally just being scared of everything. I guess that's why I've spent all my life trying not to piss people off. Mum, Dad, Sarah, Becca, Eden, even Julie…you know, there're times I want to scream at her. I want to tell her she's asking irrelevant questions, and I've got this unrelenting itch inside me to just do something wrong."

"What're you saying to me, sweetheart?"

"I don't know."

As I rest against his car, he tries to hold my hand, but I just rub my temples and growl. I feel like I need a run, I don't know where, I just want to run and scream. I'd push myself so hard that it would hurt, then I'd push some more. But I don't know if even that would suffice, I need something more, something daring. I look into Tommy's beautiful brown eyes, and see the answer right behind him.

"I need a release, Tom. I want to drive somewhere, where no one will find us, bend over in the back and just do it. I want it rough."

He's stunned, he just sits there, eyes wide. Realising what that must sound like, I quickly back down.

"I'm sorry. I'll just get my car and we'll go home. I'm sorry, please don't think bad of me."

"Of course I don't think bad of you. I was just shocked, because that's not how we do it, I like to look at you. We make love, but you're essentially asking me to fuck you."

"Don't say it like that. Anyway, I like to look at you too. I love how we do it, but I…it's ok, just forget it."

"Annie," he smiles, "it's cool. If that's what you need… listen, get your car and follow me home."

"Why home?"

"Because, daft arse. If we're gonna do it like that, then I doubt you'd want to drive back on your own."

"Ok."

Once I've followed him to the house, I lock my car and jump in his. But when I do, he opens the door to get out.

"Where're you going?" I ask.

"Just getting some condoms."

"Why? We don't use them."

"Annie, we're gonna do it in the car, where there're no bathrooms…trust me." He taps my leg, then heads inside.

This isn't exactly what I had in mind. I just wanted to follow him somewhere, jump in the back and do it. Now, I can't help but feel like we're losing the spontaneity, and I'm half tempted to go inside too.

I shouldn't have asked him. This is the kind of thing that he would do with girls that he didn't even know. He told me, on the night that we first got close, he wasn't fulfilled by that. 'That's it.' I tell myself, as I shove my car keys into my hoody pocket, 'I'm going inside,' but the moment I open the door, Tommy comes running back to the car. With a huge excited grin, he taps the bonnet and jumps back in the driver's seat.

"You ready?" He says, starting the engine. "Should we go have some fun?"

"Yes, I'm ready."

Ok, so it's not as spontaneous as I wanted, but that doesn't matter. After all, he's right, I don't think I would like to drive back on my own. This is still daring, we're going to do it in broad daylight, and just seeing that flash of naughtiness in his eyes, has sent my excitement flooding back. As he drives away from our road, I lean over, press my chin against his shoulder and hug his arm.

"So, where're we going?" I giggle.

"To the Moors, there'll be loads of quiet places up there."

The North Yorkshire Moors are so pretty and full of little hideaways, we're lucky to have them practically on our doorstep. So long as you can find your way, away from the main roads, you can lose yourself in no time.

Tommy soon finds us the perfect place; a little cubby hole, shielded by a horseshoe of forest, with only fields as far as the eye can see. The moment he turns off the engine, I un-clip my seatbelt and slip between the front seats, to the back. Tommy then jumps out, flips his seat forward and climbs in the back with me.

"You slinky little thing." He grins. As he pulls the door closed, I slide a hand under his shirt and pull him in for a kiss.

Even though we're as hidden from view as we can be, the danger aspect of what we're about to do hits me. My heart's racing, and I can't stop smiling. Tommy pulls the condom from his pocket, and kneeling on the seat, he drops his jeans and shorts. While he rolls it on, I wriggle my leggings and knickers down, bend over and hold onto the panel, under the window. He hasn't got much head-room, so getting into a good position is fidgety, but we manage. He pushes his thing in, gently at first, but quickly builds up his rhythm.

This is everything I wanted; hot, sweaty, hard, fast, exhilarating. If anyone's walking through the forest now, they'll see us, but that just adds to the thrill.

After barely two minutes, we both finish together, then slump back against the seat, in a breathless euphoric heap. No more than a minute passes, when another car ambles along the road, between us and the fields.

"Good thing we finished when we did." I laugh, frantically pulling my leggings back up.

Tommy nods and smiles, as he wraps up the condom with some tissues. He re-fastens his jeans, before pulling me in for a cuddle.

"I love you." I say, as I shuffle around and lie back against his chest.

"I love you too, baby girl."

Tommy's always given me pet names. I sometimes wonder if he thinks about it first, and what it must feel like as the words roll off his tongue. I can only imagine it feeling weird.

"Tom?"

"Yeah?"

"Do you want me to call you anything?"

"What like?"

"You know," I smile and play with the hairs on his arm, "you call me loads of things, and I only ever call you Tom."

"I don't mind. Is there anything you'd like to call me?"

It would be nice to have that special name that no-one else uses, but the only thing I can think of is so cringe, that I can't even say it aloud without laughing.

"What's so funny?" He smiles, tickling my waist, "come on, little Annie. Tell me."

"Ok, ok stop tickling…I was gonna call you my teddy bear."

Obviously there's no way I would actually use this in a serious conversation, I just thought it was funny.

"Ha ha, teddy bear? Oh dear me." He squeezes me tighter, and for a while, we sit here, testing out other ridiculously stupid names, that we'll most definitely never use.

Chapter 8

Four Months Later.
August 14, 2017 Monday 5.30pm.
Home.
Tommy:

The perfect end to a busy day at work, begins with an ice cold beer, straight from the back of the fridge. I snap the cap from the bottle, peel off my socks and sit out in the garden. I do enjoy my job, showing women how to apply cosmetics properly, and actually having my advice taken seriously. But, on a day as hot as today, I'd have rather been out here, than being stuck inside a busy department store. As I unfasten the top buttons on my shirt, I feel Annie behind me. She hugs me and kisses my cheek.

"I thought I heard you come in." She says softly.

"Hey you," I sigh, then take a swig, "it's been a long day."

"Are you ok?" She asks.

"Yeah, just tired. Are you alright?"

"I guess...I um, didn't think you'd want to cook so, I've ordered a Chinese."

"Good call."

"I'm gonna lie down on the sofa for a bit, you should too, if you're tired?" She then briefly hugs me tighter, but before she lets go, I take her hand and kiss her wrist.

"I'll be through in a minute."

"Ok."

It's been over four months since Annie and I became a couple. To be honest, I didn't truly know what to expect. I think I assumed that aside from making love, nothing much would change, and Annie would continue to need me. I'm not suggesting that she doesn't need me anymore, but our dynamic, despite neither of us wanting to admit it, was almost fatherly. Obviously, she still looks to me for guidance, but now I can rely on her too. We're a partnership, she has a clear plan for her future and a growing medical knowledge, that Dad would have been proud of. Sometimes, I watch her as she sits in the glow of her lap-top, working on her assignments, she's so driven and focussed.

"She puts me to shame, that's for sure." I mutter, as the sun beats down on my face, while I sip on my beer. Judging by the smell from up the road, one of the neighbours must be having a barbecue. I didn't realise how hungry I was until now, but Annie made a good choice, I bloody love Chinese.

I finish my drink, then join her in the lounge. She's curled herself up, facing the back of the sofa. I've got to say, just lying there like that, she's sexy; tiny denim shorts clinging to that compact little ass. She stretches out her legs and moves further on, for me to lie down behind her. I know I'm tired, but sleep's the last thing on my mind. I softly kiss her shoulder, her neck, I run my fingertips along her thigh, and although she smiles, I get the feeling something's wrong. She shuffles around and kisses me, but there are tears in her eyes.

"What's wrong?"

"I'm sorry. I'm really, really sorry."

"Hey," I sweep her hair behind her ear, "what've you got to be sorry for?"

"You have to know, that I've taken my pill every day, every day, Tommy. I have."

I've seen that look in her eyes before, I know exactly where this is going. Strangely, I'm not surprised, and even as I stare at her now, and she whispers those words, I'm not shocked. I probably should be, but I'm not. We're going to have a baby.

"There's nothing to be sorry for." I tell her, but she just looks at me and sobs. "Don't cry," I say, stroking the tears from her cheeks, "it's ok."

"Ok? I thought you were going to shout at me…"

"No, no, no. Please don't say that, and don't be sad. You're having my baby."

"But, Tom, what if I lose it? I can't go through that again…and what about college and everything?"

"Shh. You won't. I know the signs now, and there's no way I'd let you go on like that again. I promise, Annie, first sign of pain or anything, I'll get you checked out."

"I'm scared, Tom. I'm not ready."

"I know, but we'll be fine."

"Will we?"

"Of course we will. I promise."

I only get to hold her for a second, before we're interrupted by a firm knock on the front door.

"That'll be the food," she says, drying her eyes, "should we eat it outside?"

"Yeah, I'll get it, and you grab some plates."

Later, when we've munched our way through the sticky chicken and noodles, Annie pushes her plate away and nibbles on a spring roll.

"What're we gonna tell people?" She asks, "I mean Sarah for one, she'll want to know who the father is."

Of all the things for her to think about, and her head goes to Sarah. But it's not just Sarah, although my sister's right. Our aunt doesn't need much of a reason to give Annie the third degree. An unplanned pregnancy with no apparent father on the scene, would be just the feast she'd like to get her teeth into. She'd love it. I'm not about to let that happen, it may seem like a coincidence, but since we became a couple, I've been toying with an idea. Now that Annie's pregnant, it actually makes a lot more sense.

"Tom? Did you hear me?"

"I heard you, I was just thinking…how would you feel about moving away?"

"Do you mean like run away? Where would we go?"

"Doesn't matter where, An. I just mean a fresh start."

"A fresh start does sound good…I guess if no-one knows us, we could be a normal couple." She sighs for a second and shakes her head. "But we'd still have to answer questions, what would we tell John and Sarah?"

That woman has way too much of a hold over Annie, and I hate it. But it's true. We could lie to them, we could say that the father was some boy from college, but we'd still have to decide what to tell the child. Even if we do move away, they would want to visit, and I'd hate it if my child couldn't call me Daddy. We would have to tell them. Right now, the only people who know about us, are Stu, Dan and Ethan. Ethan took it really well, but as it turns out, he and Olivia already knew about my adoption, and were also sworn to secrecy. Annie and I trust Ethan completely, so if the time comes to tell his mum and dad, we know he'd be in our corner.

"Listen, An. What do you think of this? I know you were going to apply to Teesside uni, but how about you apply somewhere else? You'll have to squeeze in your last few units of college-work, to get finished before the baby comes, so it'll be a bit stressful, but I'll help you. Then next summer, we'll move?"

"I didn't think uni was an option now…"

"Course it is," I interrupt, "your life's not over."

"Yeah, but who's going to look after the baby if I'm at uni?"

"Me, daft arse. I'll go back to bar work, I'll only need a few nights a week, so it would work out fine."

"Ok, let's say we do this, I mean, it does sound like a good plan, but what do I tell people in the meantime?"

"If anyone asks who's it is, just say you don't want to talk about it."

"Ok," she nods, "it's a shame we can't just go now. I hate keeping us a secret."

"Me too."

A little while later, as I pick at the prawn crackers, Annie stands and starts stacking up the dirty dishes.

"Leave them," I tell her, "I'll sort them out."

"It's ok, I'm going in to get my hoody anyway, so I may as well. D'ya want another beer?"

"Please."

She clatters around in the kitchen for a few minutes. When she comes back out, she stands the bottle on the table and sits on my lap.

"Are you sure we'll be alright?" She asks, as she pulls out my bobble and runs her fingers through my hair.

"I think so," I nod, and hold her tight, "we're always alright."

Three Weeks Later.
September 04, 2017 Monday 10.30am.
Stockton.
Tommy:

Rich resents the title of 'personal trainer.' He's a strength coach, and has been since we left college. Usually, if we're training together, then we'll use his gym in Middlesbrough. But since starting my new job, I figured it would save me time, if after work, I trained in a gym nearer there. That's where we're headed now.

"I can't believe I'm letting you drag me to a girly fitness gym." He laughs, as I pull into the car park.

"Calm your tits, man. You're going as a guest, it's not like you're getting a membership."

"Too fuckin' right, I'm not."

"Ha ha, get over yourself."

Inside, a young lad on reception, gives Rich a brief questionnaire to fill in. Once that's out of the way, we dump our bags in the lockers, then pass the cardio machines, over to the free weights. We need to warm up, so we grab some lighter plates off the rack, and he notices a couple of girls in the room next to us, stretching on the yoga mats.

"I suppose this place has its perks." He grins.

"Ever the optimist aren't ya."

He stacks the bar and lies back on the bench, I stand by his head, while he begins his first set.

After fifteen reps he winks. "How's life behind a make-up counter?"

"Fuck off." I laugh. I'm not ashamed of my work, far from it, but it's not exactly a manly topic to discuss at the gym. We switch places, and I knock out my set. Truth is, my mind's not really here.

"Work's alright." I tell him, as we switch again.

It is frustrating when a customer has been using the wrong shade for half their life, and they refuse to change. While he begins his second set, I remember something that Annie said this morning. She agrees my plan to move makes sense, but she doesn't want to wait. She wants to go now, to pick up her second year in a different college, where no-one knows us. I can see her point, I hate skulking too. After all, we're not blood, so we really have nothing to be ashamed of, and I dare say that our relationship is a lot healthier than some other couples.

"Anyway," I mutter, "I won't be working there much longer."

"Why?" He grunts, "I thought it was permanent."

"We're um…moving…I've decided to go with Anna, when she goes to uni."

"Shit, Tom." He sighs, lifting the bar back on the rack. "You gotta let her go. I know you wanna protect her, but she'll never experience life if you're always there."

I shake my head. Annie and I have been together almost six months, but Rich doesn't know yet, and keeping it a secret from him has been hard. The thing is, our baby and the commitment I made to her, are the only reasons that she's going away to uni anyway. If I was still just her brother, she'd have only applied to Teesside.

"Tommy." He says again. "Did ya hear me?"

"I heard you…listen, you know I'm adopted, right?"

"Ah ha," he says, lying down to finish his set.

366

"That whole thing's a massive deal, and…" shit, my palms are sweating, "well, I…we, we've had to question it all, and how it changes things/us." I take a deep breath, while I figure out the best way to say this. I knew telling Rich would be difficult, that's why I've put it off for so long. "Anyway," I sigh, "we've decided that we need each other."

"Course, mate." He heaves. "I know how close you are, but you're not gonna lose her…and she has to stand on her own two feet."

"I don't think you're hearing me. Rich…I mean, we're together."

"Dude! Don't be fucking daft." He says. "You can't, she's your sister. That's incest!"

"Keep ya voice down, and no, it isn't. We're not blood."

"You think that matters?! Blood or not, she's your sister. You really need to think about this before…"

"It's too late." I interrupt. Again, he stops what he's doing and shoots me a questioning glare. "Rich, we're a couple and…"

"And?"

I can't look him in the eyes, so, I stare off to the side. "She's having my baby."

I turn around, and he's stood right in front of me, with his clenched fist hurtling towards my face. In one move, he knocks me on my arse. The sickly taste of blood quickly fills my mouth, as the girls through the doorway, and everyone around us, stop and stare. Humiliated and furious, I scramble to my feet.

"What the fuck, Tom! Pregnant? You're twenty-three and she's seven-fucking-teen!"

"Right." I say bitterly, spitting blood into my hand, "like age has never bothered you before."

"Not Anna!" He backs away and snarls. "I could never look at her like that." As he storms out, one of the yoga girls rushes over to me.

"Are you ok?" She asks.

"Yes." I say shortly, then pick up my towel from the bench, but when I turn, she's still stood there staring at me. I don't know what this girl wants me to say, but I'm in no mood for conversation.

"Excuse me." I say, moving her aside. I then march through into the changing rooms, grab my bag, but on my way to the door, I catch my reflection in the mirror. I look terrible so, I take a minute or so, to wash my face. It was stupid to tell him here. I knew it in my gut, he still sees Annie as a kid. She's not a kid, she's mature, far more than he was at seven-fucking-teen.

Once I've calmed down, I head out to the car, where Rich is waiting. He's stood fast, glaring at me, by the drivers side door.

"You can beat me up all you want," I call out, "it's not gonna change anything!"

That's true, but I know if he takes me up on it, I'll stand no chance. We haven't had a proper fight since school, and back then, the odds were more balanced.

"I just want my keys," he says, nodding to my car, "that's all."

I've known Rich for years, I know what that look means. Sure, he's angry, but he's detached too. If I let him go now, then that's it. He'll wash his hands of me.

"Sure," I nod, and unlock the door, "but, Rich…let me give you a lift."

He grabs his keys and sighs.

"Please?" I ask again.

"Alright."

The atmosphere in the car is dense. I had so many explanations, but as I pull out of the car park, they all disappear.

"I get why you're pissed," I tell him, "I do…"

"You broke the rules." He interrupts, "you know the rules. We never touch a mates ex, or a mates sister."

"And I haven't."

"No!" He snaps. "You're fucking your own sister!"

"Come on, man. We're not blood. Yes, we were raised as brother and sister, but we're not. And I'm not fucking her, I love her, and she loves me."

For a little while, he just stares out of the window, knocking his knuckles against the glass.

"Call it what you want," he eventually sighs, "but if you're having sex, then you're fucking her."

"I said it's not like that. We're not related, and Anna's not some little piece of ass. You know exactly what she means to me."

Great, another awkward fucking silence. Only now, it lasts until we're almost at his house. As I pull up outside, he rubs his eyes and groans.

"I know you love her, Tommy…but answer me this. Who's idea was it?"

"What?"

"Was it your idea?"

"Sort of, why?"

"Shit, Tom. Don't you get it? That girl worships you, she'll do anything you say."

Now I know what he's getting at, and he's got no fucking right. "I didn't force her! Do you even know me?"

"I'm not saying you forced her…"

"Well, what are ya saying?"

"I know you." he says. "You've got a way with words."

"You're not saying I forced her?!" I snap, as he opens the car door. "So what? I manipulated her? I'm telling you, it wasn't a decision we made lightly. I fucking love her!"

I doubt he gives a shit what I say, because he just grunts, "See ya, Tom." and gets out of the car.

4.20pm. Home.
Anna:

Because of my previous miscarriage, the doctor sent me for an early scan. We went this morning, before college. They told us that I'm nine weeks gone, and that everything

369

looks fine. But, I don't feel fine, yes the baby is healthy, and I'm not bleeding, but the sickness has been relentless. I Googled some remedies, and apparently, I should eat little and often. So, I'm keeping small packets of ginger biscuits in my bag. They do take the edge off, but that's about it. Anyway, I'm glad to be home now, and after kicking off my shoes, I peel off my jeans and lie down along the sofa.

I love the smell of Tommy's aftershave on the cushions. I close my eyes and rub my cheek against the fabric, but the second I feel myself dropping off, I'm pulled back. I feel Tommy hugging me. Opening one eye, I see he's sat on the floor beside me, resting his face against our baby.

"Hiya." I whisper, and run my fingers through his hair. "You ok?"

"I am now." He sighs.

"Do you want to talk about it?"

"In a minute," he says, "how was college?"

"Tiring…I had to keep leaving the room so I could be sick, and my tutor was going to send me home. I didn't want to tell her, but I've been sick every day, and I didn't want her…"

"Hey." He interrupts, "slow down."

I didn't realise how fast I was speaking, but we'd agreed not to tell anyone at college yet.

"Relax, it's ok." He says, as he kisses my belly, "you won't be able to hide this for long anyway."

"Thank you, so, do you wanna talk about your day yet?"

"Annie?" He sounds deflated.

"Tom, look at me."

He shakes is head, and after a few seconds, he lets out a long tired groan. "Annie, did I pressure you into this?"

"Into what? Tom, what're you talking about?"

Another sigh, then he slowly lifts his head and looks me in the eyes.

"What happened to your face?" His bottom lip is bright red and swollen.

"Rich," he huffs, "I told him about us, and about this." He adds, laying his hand on my belly.

"So, what? He hit you!?"

He nods. "Yep, he thinks I manipulated you into this."

"You didn't. This was as much my idea as it was yours, I'm with you because I want to be."

"Yes, but when I first asked you, you said no."

"I thought you only wanted sex, and I couldn't be just another notch in your belt."

"Come on, An. You know I'd never treat you like that."

"I know, but I wasn't thinking straight. Once I was sure of what you were really asking, I knew it was what I wanted."

"Good," he nods, "because I couldn't handle it, if you thought I'd taken advantage."

"Don't be silly. So, what else did Rich say? Did you explain?"

"I tried, but he wasn't having…"

We both jump, as someone repeatedly bangs on our front door. Tommy leaps to his feet, to look out of the window.

"He's here!"

I'm not sure exactly what Tommy's feeling right now, but I'm scared. I'm vulnerable. I'm laid here in only a hoody and a pair of knickers. Rich is banging on the door, and Tommy's just staring at me.

"What're you going to do?" I ask.

"I have to answer it." He then quickly picks up my jeans, "put them on."

"I can't, they hurt my belly."

"Ok." He helps me up, and wraps the blanket from the back of the sofa, around me. "You go get some leggings on, and I'll let him in."

"Ok, do you want me out of the way?"

"No. I need you by my side."

He waits until I reach the stairs, before answering the door. My heart's racing, but I rush around to my old room, throw on some leggings, then take a second to catch my breath, before going back downstairs. I don't have a clue

371

what I'm going to say to Rich, or if anything I do say will make a difference anyway. Tommy said he tried to explain, and he ended up with a punch in the face. I suddenly feel ill again.

When I get downstairs, I see they're both stood in the kitchen. They're super tense, and it looks like anything could happen. Then Rich says, "Look, man, sorry about your face."

Tommy just shrugs and shakes his head.

Rich hasn't seen me yet, but Tommy has. He silently pleads with me to stand with him, but I'm kind of hovering feebly by the dining table. I want to move, but my feet are glued to the floor. I've never been afraid of Rich before now.

"Annie, please." Tommy says.

My heart's breaking through my rib-cage but I move, and in grabbing Tommy's hand, I find my strength.

"You shouldn't have hit him." Even as I say this to Rich, I can't look at him. Which annoys me, because that'll just make him think I'm ashamed, I'm not. So, I lift my eyes from the floor, and tell him confidently, that I don't care if he doesn't approve, I love Tommy, and nothing is going to change that.

Rich hardens his face and folds his arms. "Your love isn't in question, kidda." He says. "The problem is, that you're sleeping with your brother."

"Look." Tommy intervenes. "You made your feelings perfectly clear earlier, if you've just come to have a go at Anna too, then you know where the door is."

I'm confused, in an instant Rich's entire demeanour softens, and he shakes his head.

"That's not why I'm here...you two are like family, more so than my actual family. I just wanna know something."

"What?" We both ask together.

"Tommy, you said that it wasn't a light decision...just tell me, how long exactly, did you leave it before jumping into bed together?"

Tommy just turns around and fills the kettle. It shouldn't matter how long we waited, it was our decision, ours and no-one else's. But, if we're going to get past this, then we have to at least explain why.

"It was the same day." I say, my voice is shaking and as Tommy turns and looks at me, I feel my throat closing.

"The same day!" Rich snaps. "So, yeah, you really took time to think it over."

"I told you," Tommy repeats, "it wasn't a decision we made lightly."

Rich directs his attention back on me.

"So, Anna? You find out you're not blood, he suggests sex, and straight away you climb into his bed? Didn't it feel even a bit weird?"

"It wasn't like that!" I persist, "we talked for ages, there were things we needed to work out first, but don't you see? We need to be together, we thought we were blood, we had a bond that no-one could break, then in an instant it was gone." I don't want to cry, I don't want to give Rich that satisfaction, but as I get more and more worked up, there's no holding back. "We need this," I say, looking to my brother, "we need to be as close as we can. And getting in his bed wasn't weird at all, because I've been sleeping in there since the accident anyway." I've said too much, so I touch Tommy's hand to apologise, but he just shakes his head and lays his arm around me.

"This is fucked up." Rich sighs, "you've been sharing a bed for a year and a half. Guys, you can't sleep next to someone every night, without it having some effect on you."

We watch him pace the kitchen floor, while he figures it all out.

"I knew you were close before, but shit…"

"We did what was necessary," Tommy interrupts, "there was a lot going on back then. Annie needed me. Now, we need each other."

I'm tired, and it's clear, as Tommy leans back against the work surface and stares at the floor, that he's had enough.

"I can't ever agree with this," Rich says, "but like I said, you're my family, and I'm not prepared to walk away. This is your life, and now you've made it fucking complicated, I just hope you know what you're doing." Shaking his head, he takes a moment to look each of us in the eye. "And I'll just have to deal with that."

Four Weeks Later.
September 27, 2017 Wednesday 4.30pm.
Medical Centre.
Julie:

"I'm ok. You see, now we've got this baby to look after, there's not a lot of room in my head for anything else. So, thank you for everything, but both me and Tommy agree, that dredging up the past, isn't right for me anymore." Anna trips over her words with feigned confidence, as she hurries for the door.

I'm perplexed. Despite seeming a little preoccupied, when she broke the news of her pregnancy, Anna has had a fairly productive session. She spoke of her parents, and although Anna still carries pain and sadness, she has an understanding now, that only comes with maturity. She appreciates that they were, 'regular human beings, just doing their best to survive.' She also spoke excitedly, of her plans for university, and how she feels ready for a fresh start. So, I struggle to understand why she would want to end her sessions now, and in such a sudden way.

At this moment, there is nothing more that I can do. My only option is to leave her for a few days, then give her a call.

What strikes me, I ponder, as I pack away my appointment diary and make myself a fresh coffee, is that the manner in which she left seemed unnatural, as though it wasn't her choice. Of course that is presumptuous, but as I stroll around the room, I replay the session.

One thing I did find peculiar to hear, was that her brother is 'happy' she is expecting. Now, seventeen is young to fall pregnant, but it is certainly not uncommon, but for him to be happy about it? I find that quite alarming. What is also alarming, is their plan to raise the child together.

Which brings me back to my earlier concerns, regarding her 'hallucinations.' Anna came to me, convinced that her only escape from them, was through her brother. I think in some ways, her reliance on him is more of a hindrance than a help, especially if their situation were to change. If he were to meet someone special, for example, then Anna may well find herself alone. She's in a vulnerable position, and given the opportunity, I would have strongly advised against her ending our sessions.

"I'm not sure." I sigh.

Ideally, I would've liked to take matters further with their social worker, but other than a gut feeling, there is not an awful lot that I could complain about. There are no indications of violence, excessive consumption of alcohol, neglect, or sexual abuse. From an outsiders perspective, he is a responsible, caring and loving older brother, a father figure. Personally, I worry that he feeds Anna's insecurities, perhaps he feels that he alone can fix her, and by agreeing to help raise the child, he has sealed her need of him.

September 29 2017 Friday 4.30pm.
College.
Emilia:

Anna told me a secret today. I was a bit surprised, considering she's not seeing anyone, but I guess it makes sense. I mean, it's not natural to throw up twenty times a day, and go on eating. I only wish she could've stuck around after lunch, because I had like so many questions, but she had to go. She did answer one though, that she's not with the dad. Well, she kinda answered, actually, she just looked sad when I asked her who he was. Whoever he is, he's a dick. Poor girl's been through enough.

Eden said that he'd come to mine, after college. So, at the end of class, I push my way down the stairs, to wait outside, but on the way, he creeps up behind me.

"Hey, scruff." He laughs, ruffling my hair, "I didn't think I was good enough for you, now Anna drives you home every night."

"She doesn't take me home every night."

"Whatever, where's she gone anyway? I saw her leaving earlier."

"Dunno. She just said Tommy's planned a surprise, so she had to go."

"Hmm." He grunts, as we leave the car park and walk down towards the foot-bridge, that stretches over the river, into town. "So, Tommy clicks his fingers, and she goes running?"

"He's just being nice, I think it's sweet."

"Sweet?" He laughs.

I'm not getting into this right now. Yeah, Eden's nice to her face, but as soon as she's gone, he starts. He does nothing but bitch about her, and I hate it. He's changed.

"What is your problem, Eden! You and Anna broke up ages ago."

"Wasn't my fault."

I can't believe what I'm hearing. "Yes it was!" I insist. "You made her choose between you and her brother, what was she supposed to do?"

"Hang on, what's she been saying?" He asks, jumping in front of me to make me stop.

"She told me what happened, at the time! You know, she felt awful about freaking out. Yeah, she called Tommy, but she needed you. She's claustrophobic, you of all people should know how that is."

"Sure I do, but I was with her."

"You were with her? You made her choose, she was desperate and she begged you to go with her, but you just stood there. In one breath you told her you loved her, then in the next, you left her for some stupid game."

"Now, hold on a minute! I laid it all down, I told her exactly how I felt, and she walked away. Look, I know she was crying so, she might have asked me to stay, I can't remember. But Anna walked away, not me."

"Not before kissing you! After begging you to go with her, she kissed you, one last time. You should've got in that car too."

"What? With him! No way. Listen, you only know half the story, but if you can't see how controlling her brother is, then you must be blind. Anyway, Em, what's your point? All this was months ago."

"My point is, she's never insulted you, never…but you can't help yourself."

"She never insults me?" He huffs. "What, ever?"

"Honestly," I sigh, "so, can you spare me the bitching?"

"Sure, if that's what you want."

3.50pm. Home.
Anna:

I wouldn't say that I'm someone who hates surprises, but I don't exactly love them either. Tommy's been super secretive these past few days, and no-matter how hard I've tried, my attempts to make him tell me have failed.

"Ah well." I say to myself, as I lock my car and head to the house, "moment of truth."

In the hallway are two small suitcases, packed and ready. So, we're going somewhere for the night, but where? Ok, maybe I am a bit excited.

"Annie?" Tommy calls from the bedroom.

"Yeah?"

"Come here a minute."

I drop my books on the table, before rushing upstairs. In the bedroom, Tommy's stood, staring at himself in the mirrored door of his wardrobe. He's wearing dark blue jeans and a beautiful deep red, tight fitting top with long sleeves and a granddad collar.

"Wow," I gasp, "you look nice." I genuinely can't remember the last time he wore colours, but the burgundy makes those dark eyes look even deeper.

"You think?" He asks, smoothing his hair back into a bobble, "I'm not sure."

"Are they new?"

"Yeah, I went shopping with Stu…and I let him talk me into trying colours."

"Well, I love them." I smile, sliding my arms around his waist. "So…our suitcases are in the hall? Where are we going?"

He gives me a cute half smile and moves my arms up to his neck. "We, little Annie, are going for a romantic weekend, in a luxury hotel."

"Serious?"

"I'm serious." He picks me up, and as I hook my legs around his waist, he hugs me so tight that I could cry. "You'll love it," he says in my ear, "it's a huge country manor house. I've bought you some dresses, in case you feel like dining in the restaurant, or we can order room service… whatever you want. The grounds are stunning too, and there're loads of walks we can do. You see, no one knows us, we can be a proper couple."

"I love you so much." I whisper, then kiss him softly. "You're the best brother ever."

He hasn't put me down, but we both kind of freeze, and in that split second, share a look. I don't think either of us know if I should've said that or not. I quickly apologise and tap his shoulder, for him to put me down, but he doesn't.

"It's ok," he says, touching his face to mine. "I am still your brother, we haven't lost that. And I love you. See this weekend as a taste of things to come."

"I will."

The love I have for this man is insurmountable. I'd never understood until we got together, why people say, *'it hurts*

378

to love you.' I always thought it was just some cheesy line, but when it hits you, like truly cuts through your heart, it's overwhelming. It can happen at the most unexpected times, sometimes, I have to take a sharp inhale and stop what I'm doing, just so I won't cry.

"Do I have time to get changed?" I ask.

"Sure." He puts me down, and crawling over the bed, reaches for a bag. "Here, I bought you these too."

They're dark blue, denim leggings.

"Seen as your regular jeans are uncomfortable now, I thought you'd like these, they're nice and stretchy."

"Awesome, I'll feel a bit more like me again."

"I'm glad you like them, because I've packed you a couple of pairs, light and dark. But I wasn't sure, so your black leggings are in there too."

"Thank you."

**6pm. On the road to the Ainslie Hall Hotel.
Anna:**

Growing a human is exhausting. That, coupled with a two hour car journey, would've ordinarily been enough to send me to sleep. Not today. Today we've sang ridiculously loud, and terribly out of tune. We've laughed, reminisced about the past and imagined the kind of life we have to come. Obviously, when we move we'll have to leave the world of social media behind us, but that's no big deal. I still have to decide what to do about Emilia, I really want to stay in touch, to tell her the truth. I had the chance to do just that this morning, I'm so comfortable around her, and it's like we just click, but she's too close to Eden. Even if I could explain and make her understand, what's stopping her from letting it slip to him? There'd be no way I could make him understand, it would be ugly. We'd end up arguing, and I've never won an argument with him, not without it resulting in an hallucination. I shouldn't be chewing over this now, this weekend is for me and Tommy, and I plan to enjoy every minute.

Tommy turns off the main road; onto a long gravel drive, that winds through expansive, beautifully tendered grounds. The hotel itself, looks quite similar to where I had my prom; old, Gothic and grand.

"Wow." I gasp as Tommy parks the car, "it's huge."

"Did I do alright?"

I un-clip my seat belt, lean over and lay my hand on his lap. "Yes!" I slide my other around the back of his neck and pull him in for a kiss. "I want you."

"Well, lets get inside, and you can have me." He looks at me wantingly, and kissing me back, his hand wanders over my thigh. I'm feeling impatient, so I kiss him harder, then pull away and open the car door. As I move to jump out, he adjusts the bulge in his jeans.

"You see the effect you have on me." He laughs. I just give him a sultry grin, and he grabs the cases from the boot, and we head inside.

Once Tommy's checked us in, a porter leads us up through a maze of winding stairs and corridors, into a magnificent suite. The bed is the first thing I see, dark wood, four poster with black velvet drapes, sitting proud in the centre of the room. It must be one of the honeymoon suites, because it's huge. The window alone is impressive, with its romantic lattice leadwork and its sheer size. It reaches the ceiling, from the decorative window seat below. Even that, with all its cushions, it looks more like a sofa. Tommy has modern taste, I never imagined that he'd pick somewhere like this, but I love it. While he has a word with the porter, I quickly pop to the loo. The luxury doesn't stop in the bedroom, the bathroom's bigger than our kitchen. The huge roll-top bath could easily fit both of us. This is going to be an awesome weekend.

When I go back in the room, the porter's left, and Tommy's locking the door. There's no question on what's about to happen, everything today, has been building up to this. We instantly collide. It's funny, we're feeling all sexy, but it's not easy keeping a kiss going while you're fumbling, trying to take each others clothes off. Mine are easy for him, elasticated waist, my cashmere jumper, and he can undo my bra with a flick of his fingers. But his…my fingers aren't working today and I just can't get that belt undone.

"Hey, I'll do it." He says, before quickly ripping it off. While he kicks the rest of his things away, I let my knickers drop to the floor, then guide him back towards the window seat.

"Oh," he grins, "I like it."

He likes it even more in a second, when I push his back against the cold glass. As he sits down, I drop to my knees. First I kiss his thighs, slowly moving to his thing, but I take my time. So, when my lips reach the end, he's practically begging for more.

"Please, Annie, come on." He groans, but I just flash him a smile and start again.

"You know what happens, if you rush me."

"Oh, baby girl, you're awesome." He pushes his hands into my hair and lets his head fall back. "Just do whatever you like."

I can't leave him wanting for long. I need him, and as I push it deep in my mouth, he whispers a breathless 'thank you.' I love doing this for him, to me, it's the most intimate act we can do. Knowing each others bodies, and the exact touches needed to bring us to the brink, it's exhilarating.

After a few minutes, I sense his belly tensing, so I move back, and he lifts me up to straddle him. I don't want this to end, so, we take a few moments kissing, before I position his thing and sink myself down upon it.

"I love you." I whisper, as I close my eyes and wrap my arms around his shoulders. He brings me in so close, so tight, but not too tight, that I can't still rock my hips. This is my absolute favourite position, his face against my breasts. His breath is hot, and my pulse's racing, so fast that my heart could burst from my chest.

I push faster and faster and faster, and as my hair clings to my glistening face, I half open my eyes. There're people strolling the grounds outside, all it would take is one of them to look up, and we'd be caught. Part of me thinks of moving to the bed, but naughty Anna takes over and I grind even harder. Tommy's close now, I can feel it. All his muscles close in around me, I squeeze my thighs tight, we're almost there. His breaths are short and fast, and every part of my body floods with adrenalin. Like running those last few metres on the track, I push myself harder to get us to the finish line, where we both let out cries of relief.

He slides his face up to my neck, and I melt into his.

"That was awesome." He says, as we cling onto one another. "You…are awesome."

"So are you."

We should really move to the bed, but neither of us want to let go. We're glued to this seat, glued to each other, in full view of anyone who might be looking. It wouldn't matter to me, all anyone would see is two people making love, they don't know who we are.

We do eventually move, and I rush into the bathroom to freshen up, while Tommy lies down on the bed. I quickly sort myself out and go back to lie with him, but when I step out of the bathroom, he hands me my phone.

"You've got a message from Eden."

Eden hasn't text me since the morning that we broke up. "Seriously?"

"Yeah," he says, "he wants to buy you a hot chocolate."

"I don't understand," I say, as I lie down and cuddle in, "why now?"

"Dunno."

"Neither do I, I want to tell him to do one."

"Do it."

"I can't, Tom. You know he still hangs with us, it wouldn't be fair on Emilia if I made things difficult."

"Ok, why don't you ask why he wants to meet."

I nod and send Eden the question. He replies straight away.

"I just want to see you.
Like, away from college.
I get why you might not want to,
so I'll just say it…
I miss you. Xx"

"What do I say to that?" I ask, after reading out the message. We spend a few minutes deliberating and eventually, we make our decision. I send Eden a reply.

"I don't want to hurt you,
but I don't think you'll feel the same,
when I tell you that I'm pregnant."

"Wow! Who's is it?"

"Right, Annie." Tommy props himself up a bit and rubs his eyes. "Type this, word for word."
I nod and do as he says.

"It doesn't matter anymore,
that arsehole is long gone.
The last thing I need right now
is a relationship.
All that matters is my baby."

"Whoa, ok. I understand.
How far are you?"

"13 weeks."

"Ok, I hope it goes well.
I guess I'll just see you at college."

I lay the phone on the bedside table, then press my face to Tommy's chest. "I hate lying about you like that."

"I know, sweetheart, but it'll stop him asking anymore questions."

September 30, 2017 Saturday 9am.
Ainslie Hall Hotel.
Anna:

Eggs, bacon, sausage, tomatoes, mushrooms, black pudding and plenty of toast. I couldn't finish it all, but Tommy demolished his without a hitch, he loves a cooked breakfast. A couple of fluffy pancakes, with maple syrup and crispy bacon would've been enough for me, but they weren't on the menu. I'm not complaining though, what I had was delicious.

"Can we take a walk, after this?" I ask, as Tommy downs the last of his coffee.

"Sure," he says, looking around the restaurant, "are you ok?"

"Yeah, I'm good." And I am. But last night I felt out of place, or at least that's how it seemed when we came down for dinner. A restaurant full of well-to-do couples, and then there was us, trying to blend in. I didn't want to feel anxious, because Tommy had put so much effort into planning this weekend, so I stayed quiet. As soon as we were seated, I could feel everyone's eyes staring at me, burning the back of my neck. Yes, Tommy had made me up, and my dress was elegant, but I didn't belong here. I knew it, and they all knew it. I started to scratch. Tommy's seat had its back against the wall, whereas I was exposed, everyone could see me. People were brushing past me, as lots of conversations blended into one middle-class hum. Then in only a few moments, my fears subsided. Tommy stood up and offered me his hand. At

384

first it made it worse, we'd only just sat down, and now we were getting up again. But as I stood, he gave me a brief, but warm and gentle hug before discretely guiding me to take his seat.

Breakfast isn't quite as formal. I'm super happy, but I'm full and I'm itching to move, so we finish off, then pop back up to the room for our hoodies, before heading out to the gardens. The weather isn't as sunny as it was yesterday, but it's certainly not cold. We stroll down the semi-circular stone steps from the main entrance, and head towards the green.

"Two minutes." Tommy says, as he stops to shake a stone from his shoe.

Once he's pulled his shoe back on, we follow the path to the right and weave our way through tapered hedges, to an ivy covered archway. Yesterday, from our room, I saw many couples strolling out here, admiring the scenery, but today there's hardly anyone. As Tommy leads me to an ornate bench in amongst the flower beds, I giggle and squeeze his hand.

"What're you smiling at?" He asks.

"Look up," I nod up to our window, "there were loads of people out here, when we did it."

"We probably gave them quite a show," he smiles, as we sit down, "well you did, I didn't really do anything."

"You did later. I love it when you…you know."

"You mean when I…"

"Shh."

"You're funny. You're like a different person when we're doing it, you're all confident…"

I just blush and smile, so putting his arm around me, he pulls me in and chuckles, "there's nothing to be ashamed of. I love it when you go down on me too."

It makes no sense that it embarrasses me, it shouldn't because it's awesome.

"I do love you." He laughs. "My little daft arse."

"I love you too."

"Listen, An. There's something I've been meaning to ask you."

"Yeah?"

"Have I ever mentioned that Stu wants to open his own salon?"

"You haven't," I say, "but he told me that he wanted to, ages ago. You know, when he took us to the hospital, after you sliced your hand."

"Oh right?…What was he saying?"

"Not much, it was more of a, 'one day I'll do it' kind of thing."

"Ok, cool. Well, he's actually doing it now…"

"Serious?"

"Ah ha." He pulls his arm back and turns to face me. "This is where we come in, I um…I wanna help him out. He's got himself a business loan and secured a premises, but setting up is expensive, would you mind if we lend him like ten grand or so, to help him get started?"

"Sure, I think we should help him." It feels strange when Tommy asks my opinion on financial things, I know it's all part and parcel of us being equals, but it's still odd. Actually, there's been something on my mind for a while. So, I guess now we're on the subject, it's probably a good time to ask him.

"Thanks," he says, "I was hoping you'd say that."

I just smile and fidget with my bracelet, while I figure it out. This is crazy, I shouldn't be worried, it's Tommy.

"You don't have to give him any from your share." He says.

"No, I want to…I just want to talk to you about something."

He sweeps my hair aside, leans in and kisses me softly. "What is it?"

"I need to know more about your plan, and I don't like all this 'your money/my money.' I just want to have it all in one place…"

"You want a joint account?" He asks, stroking my cheek.

386

"If that's ok? I mean, it's not like we're ever gonna leave each other is it?"

"Course it isn't. Sure, a joint account makes sense, I'll make an appointment at the bank."

"Thank you…so, your plan? When are we going to look at houses?"

Tommy smiles and shakes his head. "We don't even know what uni you'll be at yet. Once we know that, we'll find somewhere to rent, then we'll take our time and look for the right place for us." He gently kisses me again and tells me not to worry. "We don't wanna rush when buying a house."

"But, together? We'll look for a house, together?"

"Obviously," he laughs, "I'm not gonna do this without you."

"Thanks, and what about our house…and Mum and Dad's?"

"There's already a family in the big house, and we'll probably rent ours out too. Rich said he'll oversee any maintenance. You see, An, everything's going to be fine. I promise."

"Is it though, Tom?" Everything he's telling me makes perfect sense, and the last thing I want to do is dampen his enthusiasm, but it all seems just a bit too easy.

"What do you mean?" He asks softly, "is there something wrong?"

"Not wrong exactly, but Mum and Dad went on holiday, expecting it to be the same as it always was…and they never came home. How do we know that it's not going to go wrong, what if something happens?"

"Don't be daft, come here." He taps his thigh, and I move over to sit on his lap. "Annie," he says, laying his hand on my belly, "nothing is going to happen, I'm with you, and this is us till we're old and grey."

Two Months Later.
November 24, 2017 Friday 2.30pm.
James Cook University Hospital.
Anna:

'Don't hold it in.' That's what my midwife always tells me. She said that holding in urine when you're pregnant, can cause all kinds of issues. So, it's ironic that they expect you to have a full bladder when going for a scan. That's what I'm waiting for now, my second, and so long as there's nothing wrong with our baby, my last scan. I understand that a full bladder gives them a clearer view, but the clinic is running forty minutes behind, and it's starting to hurt. Tommy's irritated too, he's not usually an impatient person, but I can see he's tense. With one hand, he's rubbing my back, and the other is squeezed into a fist, pressed against his thigh, as he tries to stop his leg from bouncing.

Another five or so minutes pass, and he snaps. "I'm not having this." He says. "You can't be expected to wait this long." Just as he stands to complain to the woman on reception, a nurse calls my name.

"Help me up, Tom." I say anxiously, as she calls my name a second time.

"She's coming!" Tommy takes my hand, and I hold his arm as we follow her along a corridor, into a dimly lit room.

"Ok," she says, "can I just confirm, I've got Annalee Anderson, date of birth, fifth of February, two thousand?"

"Yeah, that's right."

"Great, lie down there, will you please?" She flicks her hand to the examination bed, then takes a quick glance at my notes. Tommy pulls a chair over beside me, and she sits on a swivel chair, next to a monitor.

"Right." The nurse says, as she holds out the scanner and a tube of jelly, "should we have a look at this baby?"

I roll my leggings down a touch and brace myself, because that jelly is always cold. The room turns deathly quiet, as she seems to take an eternity, moving that scanner around. She must be looking at it from every possible angle. I can't hear anything, besides her fingers click-clicking on her keyboard. Eventually, she speaks.

"Baby looks fine," she sings, but I can sense a 'but.'

"Although," she continues, "it's measuring a little small for twenty-one weeks."

"Small? She's barely five foot herself." Tommy adds defensively.

She nods to him briefly, then looks to me. "How tall are you exactly?"

"Four foot, eleven." I say quietly. It's embarrassing, I don't like being this small, I mean, I'm only a few inches short of being a dwarf.

"Ok, well I'll chat to the doctor, and he might want regular scans, just to keep an eye on things…but try not to worry. Would you like to know the sex?"

We hadn't really spoke about that. Since we found out I was pregnant, it's just been 'the baby.' Me and Tommy look to each other and smile. I nod to the nurse. She turns the monitor so we can see, and Tommy leans in closer.

"There you are," she says, placing her finger on the screen, "those are his little boy bits."

I'm having a little boy. Tears fill Tommy's eyes, he squeezes my hand, and as his head falls against my side, it hits me. We are actually going to be parents. I know that sounds ridiculous for it to only dawn on me now, but I hadn't really clicked. I guess I've just been going through the motions and hoping I don't lose it.

Later, when the scan is over, and I've been for a long over-due toilet trip, we head along to the coffee shop.

"You go sit down, An." Tommy says, as we notice the lengthy queue.

"Ok." I quickly find a table, tucked away in the corner, and stare at my scan picture. It's so clear. Our baby and he's inside me. My instinct to protect him is now stronger than ever. My earlier miscarriage was difficult, and I didn't feel any emotional connection to it. If I were to lose Tommy's baby, I'd be devastated. I need to stop doing this, I'm torturing myself when there's no reason to, the nurse said he's healthy so I just need to calm down and focus on that.

Tommy soon brings the tray over, quickly followed by Dylan.

"Let's have a look then." Dylan says eagerly.

I hand him the picture, and he tilts his head and smiles. "Congratulations, both of you." He shakes Tommy's hand, then bends down to give me a hug. "Aww Stuey's going to be so jealous that I've seen it first."

Tommy winks and holds out his hand, taking back the picture. "I'm not one to cause a domestic," he laughs, as he takes a photo of it with his phone, and sends it to Stu. "There you go, now you've both seen it."

"Ha ha, well, I still saw it first." He loosely hugs us both again, then hurries back to work.

"Can I keep the picture?" I ask, as Tommy slices the cakes in half.

"Of course, An, it's yours. Are you alright?"

"I guess…it's just what she said, about him being small."

"Don't worry. You're tiny, and I'm not exactly the tallest." He says, nudging his foot against mine, "that's our perfect little boy in there, please don't worry."

He's got a point. I think I just need to let myself get excited.

"How would you feel, if I put it on Instagram?" I feel weird asking this, because I hardly ever post anything anymore, but he's so precious to us, and I just want to share that.

He sips his coffee and nods. "If that's what you want, sweetheart."

"I don't know. I do, but I'd want to tag you."

"Tag me as Uncle Tommy, but if you're doing that, then you should probably tag our friends as well."

"Thank you, I um…I wish…"

"Annie, it's fine, honestly."

It shouldn't be like this. Tommy should be able to shout about our baby too, this is his only blood, and it's not fair.

"Tom, can we go soon? I'm tired and I need a cuddle."

"Sure," he says tenderly, "sure, we can."

7pm. Isabelle's House.
Becca:

We've been playing 'Cards Against Humanity,' for like an hour. Alex keeps giving us stupid answers, but he's convinced that we're cheating. We're not, I just know how Issy thinks, and she knows how I think, call it 'women's intuition.'

While I shuffle the cards for the next round, he grabs a pillow and lays on her bedroom floor. I still feel a bit weird around him, but they do proper love each other, and the past is in the past.

"Why do you have to stay here tonight, Bec?" He laughs.

"Mam's away. You know what she's like."

I had one party ages ago, and she won't let me forget it. I mean yeah, the house got destroyed, but I'm not like that anymore. I thought she'd chill now I'm nearly eighteen, but no, she was going to send me to our James's. Him and Emma go to bed at like half nine, and if I stay up any later, I'd have to be super quiet, so I don't wake baby Penny. Fuck that. I love Penny, but it's Friday night.

Just as I'm about to deal, Issy slams her hand into her pillow and thrusts her phone in my face.

"Tell me that's not real!" She says hysterically, so hysterically that when I take the phone, she knocks the back button and I lose it.

"What?" I ask, but she just growls and snatches it back.

"I can't find it now, but I could've sworn I saw a scan picture."

"Who's?" I ask.

Alex zones out. He just lies back and folds his arms over his eyes. He's not interested when we get our gossip on.

"Anna's."

I seriously doubt that. I know me and Anna aren't best friends anymore, but we have sent the odd text. I think she'd have told me if she was pregnant. But I have to know for sure, so I lay the cards down, grab my phone and have a look.

"I don't believe it," I gasp, "she's pregnant! And didn't fucking tell me!"

"Who's pregnant?" Alex groans.

"Anna." Issy says.

"What? Crazy Anna?"

"Yeah." I tell them. "Listen, she's put '*My baby boy, due April 6th 2018. Mummy and Uncle Tommy can't wait to meet you.*' As if she didn't tell me. That's pissed me off, that has."

"Has she put anything else?" Issy asks. "and why Uncle Tommy? What about it's dad?"

"Dunno, hold on, she's tagged loads of people. *Tommy Anderson, Ethan Naylor, Daniel Armstrong, Stu Wilson and Emilia Cook.* Well, Ethan's her cousin, so we can write him off, and Stu's gay, so…"

"It better not be Daniel's!" Issy snaps, then goes silent, as Alex lifts his arm and shoots her a jealous glare.

"It won't be, if it was, she'd have tagged him as Daddy."

"Have fun playing detectives," Alex huffs and covers his eyes again, "I'm going to sleep."

There are loads of comments, so we roll onto our fronts and painstakingly go through each and every one.

"Look, Issy. That boy she was seeing has said she'll make a good mum."

Issy just grunts, but I think it's nice, even if she was a fool to let him go. I mean, if I had a boy that pretty, he'd be chained to me.

After a while, Issy decides she's had enough. "I'm bored, Bec." She pushes her face into the duvet. "It doesn't matter who's it is, anyway. The fact is, she's too young. I think she should've got rid of it."

"No! If there's one thing I can't stand, it's abortions. You wouldn't murder a newborn baby, and the only difference is that it's inside her belly. It's a life, and she can't just kill it… that's what I told her last time, and that's what I'd tell her now."

Alex instantly sits up. "Back up, Bec." He says. "What do you mean, last time?"

Oh shit, me and my stupid big mouth.

"Nothing, I was just saying that I don't agree with abortions."

"No, you said last time. Issy, babe? Didn't she say last time?"

"Yeah you did, Bec."

"Ok, ok." I snap. "Before Anna had the miscarriage, she told me she didn't want it…"

"Wait." Issy interrupts. "Anna's had a miscarriage?"

"Yes." I tell her, then turn back to Alex. "She asked Tommy to take her for an abortion, but it doesn't matter anyway, because she lost it when they went to France."

"You sure she went to France?" He asks sarcastically, "and not to a clinic?"

"No, I know she didn't. Anna doesn't lie and besides, she knew how I felt about it."

"You're dumb if you believe that," he huffs, "it's all a bit convenient, don't you think? I mean, we both know she hated me…"

"You?" Issy interrupts, "what's all this got to do with you?"

"Because, it was my fucking baby."

"Anna Anderson was having your baby!?" She screams, bursting into tears. Marvellous. And Alex just sits there, staring through the carpet, he doesn't even move.

"I knew you did it with her," she cries, "but I didn't know that."

"Come on, babe…it was one time, we were pissed."

"Save it!" She yells, right before storming out and slamming her door behind her.

I have to go after her. If I don't, then he will, and I just can't be stuck in the middle of an argument.

"I'll go." I tell him, as I throw my phone on the bed.

"Fine."

Home. Anna:

Me and Tommy have been falling in and out of sleep, for the past hour or so. We had planned on coming straight home, after leaving the hospital, but he took me to his work instead. I didn't think it was possible to feel every single emotion all at once, but that's precisely what happened. He introduced me to the girls he works with, as his partner. For so long I've felt tight with secrecy, and when he said it, my insides crumbled. The store's in Stockton, anyone who knows me from college could've been there. I didn't let it show, until we left to look around the baby department.

"What if they go online?" I whispered anxiously, "they'd see who I am to you."

"They won't." He said. "Both my Facebook and Instagram are private, and I haven't accepted any new requests since we got together. Remember, we were already together, when I got this job."

He said that I shouldn't overthink it, and he's right. After all, this is what we want.

Anyway, in the baby department, Tommy said I could buy whatever I wanted. But there was too much to choose from. In the end, I left with a soft blue blanket and a sleep-suit, covered in tiny cars and trains.

I'm starving, but if I stay here much longer I'll fall asleep again.

"Tommy?" I whisper, tickling his side. "Tommyyyy, I need you to feed me."

He just groans and squeezes my hand. I try to pull away, but I can't. Keeping his eyes closed, he grins and holds me tight, then in a second, he slips his other hand under my arm, and tickles my ribs so hard.

"Don't start a tickle fight," he laughs, opening his eyes wide, "that you know you can't win."

Through a fuse of cries and laughter, I try to break free, but he's too strong so, I give in and beg him to kiss me instead.

"Oh, is that a surrender?"

"Yes! You win, you win. Please, Tom…please, let me go."

"Let you go?" He says softly, loosening his grip, "I'll never let you go." He rolls onto his side, sandwiching me, between him and the back of the sofa. He smiles and kisses me so gently, that his soft dark curls fall against my face. "Annie, I adore you."

I kiss him back, this time running my fingers through his hair. It's like I'm fighting with hunger and wanting to stay here with him, but we do need to move. Tommy's going to Rich's tonight, so he'll have to cook something quick. We decide on bacon sandwiches and a nice mug of tea.

Later, after we've eaten, Tommy helps me clear away the dishes, before grabbing his shoes from the pile.

"Do you wanna come with me?" He asks, as he sits down to put them on.

"I would, but I'm tired. I think I'm just going to have a bath, and get into my
pyjamas."

"Fair enough, just call if you need me, ok?"

"Ok," I tell him as he throws on his coat, "I love you."

He grabs his keys, then gives me a hug. "Love you too," he says, "lock the door."

"Ok. See you later."

"See ya."

The past few times that I've taken a bath, I've felt the baby move. It's weird but strangely addictive. I mean, they're not like full on kicks yet, more like bubbles popping, but I still love it.

After turning on the taps, I peel off my clothes, step in and let the water rise around me. It's not long before I feel 'little legs' wriggling. I close my eyes and hold my little bump, it's crazy to imagine him, all tucked up in there. I wonder what he's going to look like, or what we're going to call him. We haven't discussed that yet, but I quite like Chester, or Henry. Tommy's middle name is Henry, so he might not go for that, but I guess we'll see.

As soon as I've turned the taps off and lied back down, my text tone starts beeping. At least three or four messages all come through together. So, I reach for a towel and dry my hands, It's Becca.

"An, I have to talk to you."

"It's SUPER important."

"Please come to mine."

"Anna please!"

"You there?"

She must have seen my scan picture. She'll be so pissed that I didn't tell her first, I feel awful now.

"I'm here.
And I'm sorry, I should've
told you about the baby.
I shouldn't have let you
find out like that."

"Yeah, that was a bit shit,
but there's something else.
It's urgent.
Please, just come to mine.
Like now, if you can. I have to see you."

"Ok, but I'm just in the bath.

I quickly get out of the bath, scrub myself dry and throw on some clothes. I try calling her, as I rush downstairs, but it just goes straight to voicemail. So, on my way to the car, I call Tommy.

"Hey," he says, "you alright?"

"Yeah, I'm just in the car…hold on." I tell him, as I turn the key, it takes a second for my Bluetooth to connect.

"Where're you going?"

"To Becca's. She said she has to see me. Apparently it's urgent."

"Tell her to do one."

"I can't, I've said I'll go."

"What the hell, An? She hasn't bothered with you in months."

"I'm sorry, alright. I shouldn't have said yes, but I did. Please don't have a go."

"Oh, sweetheart," he sighs, "I'm not having a go at you. I just know how tired you are, and running around after her is the last thing you need right now."

"I know, listen I'll just get there, find out what's wrong, then come straight home."

"Ok. Just be careful."

"I will, Tom."

We keep talking until I reach Becca's house, then say goodbye, as I pull onto the drive.

It's absolutely freezing, and I'm strongly regretting not putting a coat on, or drying my hair, but then I did leave in a hurry.

I knock on the front door, shivering like crazy, while I wait. Where is she? I knock again but she's not answering, I step back onto the garden and look upstairs. There's light bleeding through the curtains, so, I knock a third time and try the door, but it's locked.

"Oh, come on, Bec," I mutter to myself, as I dance on the doorstep, "answer the door."

I knock one last time before remembering that Ruth, Becca's mum always keeps a back door key, under a plant pot in the garden. I rush along the drive, but when I close the creaky garden gate behind me, I notice that the door's slightly open, and light spills out from the kitchen. I've got to admit this is odd, but I'm here now, so I may as well see what's going on. Although, Ruth might be a bit shocked if I just walk in, in this state. So, I just push the door open a little more.

"Becca?" I call, but there's no answer. What am I thinking? It's not the first time I've let myself in, and Ruth wouldn't have me standing outside, in the freezing cold with soaking wet hair. So, I gingerly step inside and walk through the dining room, into the lounge. There's no-one here, but I can hear music coming from upstairs. So, I look up there too. I check her room, Ruth's room and the bathroom, but there's no sign. If this is all a prank, then I'm not amused, I'm tired, cold and pregnant. I don't have time for silly games. I'm going home.

When I hurry back down, I hear the sound of the kettle boiling.

"Becca! What's going on?" I shout from the dining room, but she doesn't answer me. It's only when I turn the corner, that my heart stops. Becca's not here, but Alex is, and he's casually making himself a drink.

"Hello, my girl," he smirks, "and what're you doing here?"

For a moment, I just stand there frozen, questioning whether or not this is real. It feels real, but it doesn't make sense.

"I asked you a question," he says, snapping me back into focus. "Why are you here?"

"Becca told me to come. Why are you here?"

"Did she now? Doubt that, you're not even friends anymore."

"I…I know, but she did. Where is she? Hold on, how do you know if we speak or not?"

He doesn't even answer me, just chuckles under his breath, as he squeezes the tea-bag. So, I just stand here, in this surreal scene, of Alex pottering around Becca's kitchen. I haven't stood in this room in over a year. Now, I'm here, watching the boy who raped me, clean up splashes of tea and sugar from the work surface. All the more strange, is that I'm not frightened anymore, he's just a boy.

"So where is she?" I ask again.

"You know what amuses me about you?" He grins, then picks up his mug, moves to the back door and locks it.

"What're you doing?" I ask, but he just slides the key into his pocket, and brushes past me, into the dining room.

"As I was saying." He says, as he sits and lounges back on the little sofa. "Do you want to know why I'm amused?"

"Enlighten me?"

"You and Becca, ok? You were best friends since year seven. Then, as soon as she starts hanging with Issy, you get jealous…"

"I'm not jealous!"

"Yes you are, and you fell out. You've gone for months without speaking. So, tell me, why do you think Becca would call you out, on a freezing cold night?"

"I don't know, that's what I want to find out."

"Wake up, Anna." He laughs. "Becca doesn't even know you're here. She doesn't know I'm here, she thinks I've gone to get us all some food."

"What?" This can't be happening. If she doesn't know I'm here, then she can't have sent those messages, and if she's been with Alex then…I take a few seconds to try and work it all out, but if she's friends with him? If that's the truth? No, I can't believe that, she knew what he did to me, she knew.

"I sent you those texts," he says, "I hoped that you'd come, but I'm surprised at how quickly you dropped everything. Look at you, you're not even dry from your bath. You could call it loyalty," he laughs, "I just think it's pathetic."

This is too much. My pulse is thumping through my head, and as I stare at the floor, I find myself asking why.

"Why?" He repeats, raising a devilish smile, "because, I should be congratulating you. I hear you're having a baby boy."

"What?" I can't believe that he's seen it. I was sure that my Instagram was private. "You lured me here just to congratulate me? I don't believe that for a second. Look, quit playing games, either tell me the truth, or give me the key."

"Truth? Ha ha. Alright then, girl who never lies. You tell me, what happened to our baby?"

"Our baby! You know what happened, I lost it."

"Bollocks! Becca said you wanted rid. Now, I think you knew you'd lose her, so you made up a bullshit story. You'd get rid of my baby and keep your best friend."

"I swear I didn't! No, I admit, I didn't want your baby. I felt sick that part of you was left inside me. And I promise you, if I hadn't have lost it, I would've had that abortion."

"You're lying, Anna! And answer me this…who's the dad now?"

"What?" Alex has a knack of playing his way into my head, I'll happily tell him that I would've got rid of his baby. But this has thrown me off guard. "Why does that matter?" I ask. "He's long gone."

"Long gone?" He scoffs. "If that's the case, why not get rid of it?"

"Because I don't hate him."

"Oh, really? A dude knocks you up and leaves, and you don't hate him?"

I don't know what he wants me to say. I'm shit at lying, and I just want to go home. So, I hold out my hand and snap. "I've told you what you wanted to know. Now give me the key and let me out."

"Not yet, you haven't answered my question."

"No! Ok, I don't hate him, now give me the bloody key!"

"Yeah, but you're still young. You should get rid. You said yourself, you're not against abortions…and without the dad, you're all alone?"

I know his game. He's done it so many times before. He wants me to bite, to fall apart and cry, but he's not going to bring me down today. I think back to this afternoon, when we saw our baby on that screen, and the tears in Tommy's eyes. In that moment, I stop feeling angry, Alex is just an idiot, and all that matters is my baby. So, I rub my bump and smile.

"I'm not alone," I say fondly, "We've got Tommy."

For the first time tonight, it seems like he doesn't have an answer. He just takes a huge slurp of his tea and starts scrolling through his phone.

"Alex! Please, give me the key."

"You know," he sniggers, turning his phone around, to show me my post from earlier. "There was something in your voice just then…ha, it wouldn't surprise me if 'Uncle Tommy' was the daddy."

I can't speak, if I do I'll choke. Am I that transparent? All I did was touch our baby and smile. How could he figure it out, just from that? Surely he'd know that Tommy would stand by me, he's always stood by me. Even Alex knows that. As the seconds tick by, I just stand here, and I feel my feet turn to lead. My tongue is dryer than stone.

"I…um…no." I sound pathetic, but I have to say something, before it's too late. Then my face betrays me. In a mix of shock and morbid satisfaction, he sits bolt upright.

"You're joking me!" He howls with laughter, "he fucking is! Oh, this is gold. The perfect Anna Anderson's getting smashed by her brother…"

"He's not my real brother!!"

"Yeah righto." He laughs, waving his phone, "just wait till everyone finds out."

"Please, Alex, don't!"

Despite my pleas, he just sits there, crying with laughter. I beg and beg, until he looks me straight in the eyes, and his mouth slips into the slyest of grins.

"What's it worth?"

"What?"

"Come on, Anna," he taps the sofa, "you just bend over here and let me fuck you, and my lips are sealed…go on, for old times sake."

"No chance! You raped me once, you're never touching me again.

"Rape? I didn't fucking rape ya."

"Yes you did!" I shout, as he stands and takes the key from his pocket. "I know I never wanted it. And you were freaked out when I said I remembered, you ran straight to Chloe…I heard you talking about it." I'm furious. I can't believe he's smiling, like raping someone is just one big joke.

"Chloe," he grins, "sure, that bitch was crazy, but what she did after watching us was legendary."

"Excuse me? You mean, she saw it?" I can hardly get my words out, but I'm determined not to cry.

"Saw it? The whole thing was her idea, she wanted to watch me fuck someone else, and I chose you."

His words are like an almighty blow to my gut. The way he's tormented me since was bad enough, but Chloe? She watched it? They've hurt me so bad, and have been mocking me ever since.

"I…I was a virgin. Why would you do that to me?"

He just shakes his head and moves to push past me, but I can't let him leave it there.

"Tell me, Alex!" I yell, grabbing his arm. He shakes free. Desperately, I thump him in the back, and in that split second, he's turned and grabbed me by the shoulders.

"Get off me, you crazy bitch!" He angrily digs his fingers in, and pushes me away. I break free, but as I do, my feet slip on the carpet. He trips too, following me down and hard onto the edge of the dining table. I feel an agonising crack through my back, as I bounce off the table and crash to the floor. Pain sears through me, I try to focus but everything's gone blurry, except for flashes of white.

"You really are a crazy bitch, Anna." I hear Alex snap, as he gets to his feet.

Unable to breathe, I panic. "Help me...my back!"

"Quit being dramatic. You're just winded, you'll be fine. Anyway, let yourself out when you're done."

I hear the door close, then everything goes dark.

When I come to, Alex has gone. I need to get out of here, but I cant even sit, let alone stand and each breath is agony. So, I try to take in as little air as possible, but I'm dizzy, like really, sickly dizzy, and my mouth and hands are tingling. This is bad, this is really bad, I can't breathe, I can't, I...I know I shouldn't panic, but my baby! He's inside me, and if I don't get help soon, he's going to die. I'm so cold. I need my baby to be ok, just be ok.

The pain's getting worse, it's searing through my lungs, and the pressure on my chest is immense. I need help. I feel around for my hoody pocket, slide out my phone and press call, but I can't even hold it to my ear. So, I knock it onto speaker and let it slip to the floor, beside my head.

"Hey," Tommy says, "I'm on my way home. So, what was Becca's big emergency?"

"Tom." I gasp. "Help."

"What's wrong?"

"I'm...at...Becca's..." I pray he can hear me, because every word is torturous, no more than rasps of air. "It...wasn't...her...he...pushed...me...am...ambulance...can't...breathe."

"What the hell, Annie?"

"Please...ambulance."

"I'll call now. Stay on the line!"

The line goes quiet, then seconds or minutes later, I hear him say.

"Annie, you there?"

I gasp another yes.

"Annie, who pushed you? What's happened?"

"I…my…rib's…broke…he…he…"

"Who?"

"I…can't…breathe."

"Don't talk. Just stay on the line, I'm going to keep talking to you, but don't try to answer me. Stay calm. You're ok, you're tough. Remember when we were kids, and we climbed those trees by the beck? You always tried to get higher than me."

"I'm…scared…Tom."

I need to save every breath, but I need, I don't know what I need. My chest's being crushed.

"I…I'm…dying."

"No, you're not! I'm coming for you. Just hold on." He talks and talks about anything and everything, pausing only, to shout for other drivers to get out of the way. After a while, his voice shakes.

"I love you, Annie. Everything's going to be ok, the ambulance is on it's way. You're going to be ok, I'm coming for you." He keeps repeating himself, but as the time passes, I struggle to make out what he's saying, and his voice fades away.

Tommy:

There's no time to park. So, I dump the car on the roadside and sprint down Becca's drive.

"Annie!" I call, as I burst through the kitchen. "Annie, I'm here," I drop to the floor beside her and frantically brush the hair from her face. "Come on, wake up!" I scoop her up in my arms, but her body's limp and heavy, there's no way I can stand without dropping her. "Come on, baby girl." I plead. "We need to go home." She's not responding, and I don't know what to do. I was meant to protect her. I have to fix her. "Annie, please wake up." I haven't even managed to get off the floor, I'm just knelt here, like a desperate fool, holding her close to me. I even try laying my face against hers. "Please!" I cry out. "Speak, Annie! Just say something, sweetheart, it's me. Won't you open your eyes?"

There's nothing, but I'm not letting go. If I can just hold her here, she'll feel me. I push her hand up into my hair, hoping she'll just get the strength to move her fingers, then she'll be ok. She'll be ok, she will. But she's not, she's not breathing, and before I know what's happening, I'm being ushered aside by a team of paramedics. They swarm around her, and I stumble, falling back against the floor. I'm useless, all I can do is watch.

Some of them work on her, while another hands me her phone, "This yours?" He says. I just take it and nod. He's talking to me, his lips are moving, but it's like he's behind a soundproof screen. Then, they all look to each other in turn. They know it, I know it, she's gone. My hands are shaking, and all my insides seem to twist. I open Annie's phone, and Becca's messages fill the screen. *'Come now.'* she said. I have to call her.

"Heeyy, Anna," she sings, "congrats on the baby, ha, nice of you to tell me!"

She sounds drunk, and there's music blasting in the background.

"Where are you!"

"Tommy? Is that you?…Issy, turn the music off."

"Yes, it's me. Where the fuck are you?"

"Well, I don't think that's any of your business," she giggles, "unless you wanna come and see me."

"Becca! Quit playing your stupid games, and tell me where you are."

"Ok, ok. I'm at Issy's."

"Why are you there? You told Anna you'd be here."

"I'm sorry, Tommy," she laughs, "but I don't know what you're talking about."

I don't have time for this, the paramedics are wanting to talk to me. I pull myself off the floor, and while I try to focus on what the paramedic is saying, I send Becca a screen shot of their conversation. Then move to the garden, for some air. She suddenly loses the laughter.

"That wasn't me." She insists. "I didn't send those texts, I've been at Issy's all day."

"Well, who did? Think, Becca, who else had access to your phone."

"There's only me, Issy and…" the line goes silent.

"Who?!"

"I'm sorry." She says.

"Sorry?! Tell me, Becca."

"Alright, alright. He could've used it, but we only left the room a minute…"

"Who!"

"Alex."

"Why the fuck are you hanging with that little shit?!"

"He's with Issy and…"

"Save it, Becca. Just tell me where he is."

"He went out to get us some food, now he's gone home."

"I need his address."

"I can't tell you that," she cries, "please, what's going on? You're scaring me."

"You have to tell me, he's…"

She's not listening. "He's Issy's boyfriend!" She cries.

In the background, I hear her friend pleading. I need to cut above the noise.

"You have to." I yell. "He's killed Anna!"

She bursts into hysterics, through incoherent pleas, and cries from both of them, I hear Becca scream. "I have to! He's fucking killed her!"

She gives me his address. "His car's like your old one, your old Corsa," she sobs, "but it's red."

I punch the address into my phone, then sprint down the drive. A paramedic calls me back to wait for the police, but there's no time.

I speed off, but his house is only two streets away. There's no sign of his car so, I pull over, a few houses down. I knock off the engine and lights, then wait. Minutes drag, and in the perpetual silence, I begin to question what I'm doing. Why am I here, when my Annie's dead?

"Annie's dead." I can barely wrap my head around it. She died alone, I wasn't there to save her, and now I've left her. I've done the one thing that I promised I'd never do. I can't handle this, how the fuck am I meant to go on? How does a man live when his soul's been ripped out? I'm going back. I have to, but in the exact moment I move to turn on the engine, a car matching Becca's description, pulls in front of the house. That's him alright, the door opens, and the cocky little shit gets out. Clutching a bag of fast food, he checks his phone and looks around.

Just seeing him and imagining what he did to her, sends my adrenalin soaring. There are no barriers between the gardens, only sporadic hedging. So, keeping out of sight, I leave my car and creep through. I'm almost there, when I catch the edge of my shoe and almost trip, on what I can now see is a rockery. Luckily, I hardly make a sound. I crouch down, but I can't stay here, it's do or die. Making my move, I leap up behind him, raise my right arm and take a huge swing at the back of his head. In an instant he crumples to the ground, and as I lift my hand, I stare in horror at the bloodied lump of rock in my grasp. What the fuck am I doing? I toss it away and retch.

A few seconds pass, and neither of us have moved. So, I hook my foot under his shoulder and flip him over.

"What did you do to her!" I yell, dropping down over him. No response. I must've knocked him out, I grab his collar and shake.

"Answer me, you little shit!" I drive my clenched fist into his face, "answer me!" I hit him again, but nothing. I've lost all control now, I can't stop. Over and over, I hammer my fists down, his blood sprays in my eyes as his head bounces off the concrete, until my arms are too heavy to lift. Like the shooter in a video game, I look down. All I've left of him is a mangled mess, and anyone could've seen me. I need to get out of here.

I scurry back to my car and grab the handle, but my hand slips from the blood. I try again, then slump into my seat. There's no running from this. Flashes of what I've done, thunder through my head, breaking me down. I'm paralysed. I picture our baby and Annie's angelic face, and in agonising grief, I fight my body's relentless urge to gag.

"She's gone." I bark, choking on my own wretched tears.

I don't know how much time has passed when my phone rings, and I only answer because it's Rich.

"Tommy?" He says, "Tom, you there?"

"Yeah."

"Tom, that twat's outed you and Anna as a couple. It's on Facebook! We have to deal with this, now."

"It's too late."

"What's too late? Tom? You alright?…Talk to me, man."

"It's too late." I say, as flashes of blue surround my car. "Annie's dead."

About the Author

Second child of Margaret and Keith Saunders, Victoria was born in 1981, in her home town of Middlesbrough. Along with her sister, Clare, she was raised in a small council estate, at the foot of the Eston Hills. She has always had a somewhat vivid imagination, a day dreamer, so to speak. And during her school and college days, would regularly write short stories and poetry.

Victoria met David Collingwood at Redcar and Cleveland college in 1998, and they married in 2006. The pair have three children; Charlotte (Lotti), Eli and Toby. For some years, Victoria worked as a Nursery Nurse before making the decision to become a full-time mum.

After undergoing spinal decompression surgery in 2016, her hectic lifestyle with the children took an abrupt halt. Her days were filled reading, and it was then that her imagination re-awakened. Early 2017 Victoria toyed with idea of writing her first novel, and thus 'Annalee' was born.

Printed in Great Britain
by Amazon